Psalm 23

Colleen Reeves

ASSIGNMENT CODE

123

Heaven On Earth Series

Colleen Reimer

Scripture taken from the Holy Bible, NEW INTERNATIONAL VERSION®. Copyright © 1973, 1978, 1984, 2011 by Biblica, Inc. All rights reserved worldwide. Used by permission. NEW INTERNATIONAL VERSION® and NIV® are registered trademarks of Biblica, Inc. Use of either trademark for the offering of goods or services requires the prior written consent of Biblica US, Inc.

ISBN: 978-1-4834-3917-4 (sc)
ISBN: 978-1-4834-3916-7 (e)

Lulu Publishing Services rev. date: 11/12/2015

Dedication

To my husband, Jerrie, who has supported, encouraged and believed in me.

ACKNOWLEDGEMENT

I first of all thank God for giving me the gift of writing. He is the most creative writer and has wonderful ideas.

I'm grateful for my husband and for his tremendous encouragement along the way. Thanks also to my children, Jeremy, Matthew, Felisha and Ashley. They have read my books and have given me their opinions and ideas. It is a great blessing to have family to bounce ideas off of.

I had a few family and friends proofread Assignment Code 123 for me. Linda Rayner was the first to read my book and she slogged through the first draft. I have to admit it required a great deal of work! She gave many great suggestions and made corrections where necessary. Thanks for all your help!

Although all of my children read my book, my daughter, Felisha, took time to make corrections and noted them for me. Thanks Felisha for all your hard work. Thanks also to my sister, Laurel Moser, and my friend, Jenn Kononoff, who also proofread Assignment Code 123 and made changes. I also want to thank Hannah Rayner who also read my manuscript and noted corrections.

Thanks also to all who will read this book and the books that will follow.

PREFACE

This book started with my great aunt, Susie Dueck, sharing her story with me. She lived in Conteniusfeld, a Dutch settlement on the Crimean Steppe in Russia. She spent her childhood there and when she was a young teen the fear of World War II advancing into Russia gripped the whole settlement. As the German army advanced close to her home, everyone she knew and loved was affected by the war. The miraculous deliverance that she witnessed on numerous occasions astounded her. She was very aware of the saving power of her God.

Tears came to her eyes as she expressed great gratitude to God for showing her such kindness in sparing her life and allowing her the privilege to eventually move to Canada. Since sharing her story with me, she has gone on to her Heavenly home. I'm so grateful that I had the opportunity to sit down with her and hear her story before she graduated to Heaven.

My great aunt's story is only a small part of the book's contents. I used literary freedom and changed her name and the names of her family members as well as the dynamics of her family to add interest to the story.

I added fictional characters from numerous countries to give a more complete telling of what took place during those horrific years of war. There are those who whole heartedly supported the war and there are those who opposed it. Those within Germany who opposed Hitler opened themselves up to great risk and danger. Jews were at a great disadvantage in many countries and were targeted for extinction. It was a time of great danger and necessary courage for the Jewish people.

Including the supernatural in the book; Heaven's perspective on the war and angels sent on missions, provides an alternate view of what took place behind the scenes. Knowing that Heaven was completely aware of what was coming and what would be required during this time, provides a viewpoint not often seen. God is never surprised by any terrifying situation we face on earth. He already knew what would transpire during World War II before it happened and Heaven was busy preparing for all that it would entail.

Assignment Code 123 begins the story of Hitler's rise to power and how the characters in this book are affected. Each one makes choices that affect their future. For many of them, the option of their future is made for them. The choice of eternal destiny is left to each individual.

Without the consideration of God or Heaven, World War II would only be a dark spot on this planet's history. With eternity in view, we must remember that nothing happens here without God's involvement. He is intimately connected with each happening and each historical account. It is, after all, His Story.

Psalm 123

¹ I lift up my eyes to you,
   to you who sit enthroned in heaven.
² As the eyes of slaves look to the hand of their master,
   as the eyes of a female slave look to the hand of her mistress,
   so our eyes look to the Lord our God,
   till he shows us his mercy.
³ Have mercy on us, Lord, have mercy on us,
   for we have endured no end of contempt.
⁴ We have endured no end
   of ridicule from the arrogant,
   of contempt from the proud.

ASSIGNMENT CODE 123
CHARACTER LIST

(Main Characters are in **Bold** Lettering)

<u>Berlin, Germany:</u>
1. Helmuth and Unna Schluter – German Family
   * Two Daughters:
      * **Beata Schluter**
      * Ilse Schluter
2. Meshulam and Marni Israeli – Jewish Family
   * Two Sons:
      * Fayvel Israeli
      * Doron Israeli
   * One Daughter:
      * Faye Israeli
3. Mrs. Grossman – Midwife
   * Her daughter – Frederika
4. Bastian Haff – Local Bishop
5. Roth and Alda Puttkam – Friends of the Schluters'
   * Two Sons:
      * Adreas Puttkam – Shoemaker
      * Lamar Puttkam – Fine Carpenter
         * Wife: Serilda
6. **Hahn Brauer** – German Soldier
7. German Soldiers – Horst, Gerard, Dieter and Heller
8. German Officer: Dagobert Schenker

1. **David Kohn**: Jewish Rabbi
   * Wife: Devora Kohn
   * Two Sons:
      * Benesh Kohn
         * Wife: Jaffe
         * Children: Lazer, Aliza and Efraim
      * Itamar Kohn
         * Wife: Rachel
         * Children: Three sons and one daughter (Ruth)
   * One Daughter:
      * Sulia
         * Husband: Menashe Yonson
         * Children: Leeba, Ber and Hirsh

2. **Binyamin Levin** – Jewish Doctor
   * Wife: Init Levin
   * Three sons:
      * Hershel Levin
         * Wife: Faiga
         * Children: Jonathon and Baila
      * Joseph Levin
         * Wife: Sonia
         * Children: Simon, Minich, Aliyah and Deborah
      * **Aaron Levin**
         * Wife: **Anka**
         * Children: Amos, Matis and Lola
   * One Daughter:
      * Chava
         * Husband: Dobry Waglewski – Polish Man
         * Children: One son, Two daughters

3. Yankel and Gittel Greenstein (Gittel and Init Levin are sisters) – Jewish Family
   * Two Sons
      * Solomon Greenstein
         * Wife: Heni

- * Daniel Greenstein
  - * Wife: Elisheva
- * Three Daughters:
  - * Chesed
  - * Basya
  - * Ayelet
4. Jaromil and Ewa Trafas – Polish Family
  - * One Son: Jarek
  - * One Daughter: **Anka**
    - * Husband: **Aaron Levin** – Jewish Man
    - * Children: Amos, Matis and Lola

Crimean Steppe, Russia:

1. Baldur and Frieda Brenner – Dutch Family settled on the Crimean Steppe
  - * One Son:
    - * Herman Brenner
  - * Two Daughters:
    - * **Esther Brenner**
    - * Anna Brenner
2. Rose Voth – Esther Brenner's friend
  - * Her mother: Agnes Voth
3. Jenell Schlosser – Herman's Girlfriend
4. Helga Unrah – Frieda Brenner's Sister
5. Gilbert Schultz and Peter Burg – Boys Esther knows from school
6. Samuel and Berta Goldberg
  - * One Daughter: Beatrix Goldberg
  - * One Son: Saul Goldberg

German Leaders:

1. **Adolf Hitler**
2. Joseph Goebbels – Head of Propaganda Ministry
3. Albert Speer – In charge of producing military equipment
4. Ernst Rohm – Commander of the SA Brownshirts

5. Joachim von Ribbentrop – Foreign Minister
6. Herman Goring – In charge of Germany's war planes
7. Rudolph Hess – Served as Adolf Hitler's First Aid
8. Martin Bormann – Replaced Rudolph Hess as Hitler's First Aid
9. Rudolph Hoss – Commandant of the Auschwitz Camp
10. Heinrich Himmler – In charge of the SS forces and killing centers
11. Reinhard Heydrich – Head of the Security Service, the SD
    * In charge of selecting the men to be part of the SS troops
    * Organized them into four Einsatzgruppen (task forces)
    * From there he further split them into Sonderkommandos and Einsatskommandos (special units/killer units)
12. Adolf Eichmann – Head of Reich Central Security Office's Section IV B4 for Jewish Affairs

CHAPTER 1

Poland, 1920

David Kohn shuddered in the cool breeze as he fumbled with the buttons on his coat with one hand. His other hand grasped two large travel bags containing some of their treasured possessions. A tremor took root in his middle, his faith undone as he encouraged his three children to hurry down the center of the road. He looked to his right, to his wife, Devora, who turned worried eyes to him, fear shining from her soul.

"What will become of us?" she asked.

"Don't worry," David replied, "God will take care of us." But he wasn't so sure.

Devora's expression heralded her doubt. Their three children, Benesh, Sulia and Itamar, clung to Devora, grasping her coat, her hand, anything that kept them close to their cherished mother. The frightened Kohn family moved along with the throng of people now filling the street as they looked at the men herding them away from their home.

"Hurry up, hurry up!" They looked like monsters, dressed all in black, each one wielding a weapon. Some carried guns armed with bayonets, others held ram rods and waved them threateningly, while still others held clubs; the hatred in their eyes sending quivers of alarm rushing through David.

Benesh gazed at his father pathetically. "Why did they make us leave our house?"

"I don't know, son."

Sulia spoke softly so as not to attract the black clothed men's attention. "Will they let us go back home again?"

"I don't know," answered her mother.

"This is heavy." Itamar, the youngest, carried one of the large bags containing some of the household items they were allowed to bring along.

David Kohn walked over to his young son and took the bag from him, adding it to the load he already carried.

A shot rang out ahead and screams of terror followed. They all looked up in shock as a voice carried back to them. "I said move! Move faster!" The people ahead of them began to pick up the pace and soon the unfortunate body of the slow mover came into view, his crumpled form lying on the left side of the road. It was an elderly man, a clear gun shot wound to his temple, his cane lying still and useless beside him. Blood streamed down his forehead, the ground eagerly soaking it up. David shielded his youngest son the best he could by providing a partition with the bags he carried. Once past and away from the horrifying sight he turned to Devora.

"I need to find my parents."

Devora's voice shook as she said, "Their house is coming up but maybe they're already walking with the group."

"I have to check." David handed one of his bags to his wife. It would lighten his load during his search.

"Please don't leave us," Sulia pleaded.

David leaned down slightly to his young teenage daughter. "I promise I'll come back as soon as I can."

Sulia started to cry then as David walked ahead. He heard one black clad monster shout, "Stop crying or you'll suffer, girl!"

Pinpricks of fear raced up his spine as he turned back to see Devora grabbing hold of Sulia roughly. "Stop crying. Be brave for me and your father."

Sulia stopped crying then but she looked undone by the threat of harm, her head bent and eyes studying the ground before her as she shuffled along.

David turned and moved through the crowd as quickly as he could. The terror he sensed in the throng of people milling around him was tangible as he scanned ahead for any sign of his parents. It didn't take long before he saw them. They were struggling to keep up to the pace set by the monsters.

Walking up beside them, he said, "Mom, Dad!"

His mother and father turned to him, relief on their faces at his presence.

"Devora and the kids are back in the crowd a ways," he told them.

His mother said, "We're losing ground."

"It's hard to walk as fast as they want us to," David's father admitted.

"I'll stay with you, help you." David already knew it was a pointless promise. All he could hope to do was encourage some increased momentum.

His parents were elderly and both struggled with stiff joints. His father had a bad back and his mother suffered with weak knees. Both used canes and the strenuous and steady pace set by the monsters was extremely difficult for them. The slow gate of his parents worried him. People all around them were passing on either side, eager to please the black clad men who waved their weapons threateningly.

It wasn't long till David began to hear his wife and children's voices behind him. They were gaining on them quickly. Within minutes Devora and the children appeared beside them. His fear spiked dramatically.

"David, thank God you're here!" Devora let go of Sulia, took hold of David's mother and helped her along, while David assisted his father the best he could.

The end of the crowd gained on them quickly and David could feel panic's long fingers reaching for him. Soon they were hugging the edge of the massive throng and the black clad monsters weren't happy about their progress.

"Move it!" One of the evil looking men stepped toward them, raised a club above his head and brought it down hard on David's father's head. "Move, you old man!" The elder Kohn buckled under the impact and fell to his knees.

Anger replaced David's fear. He turned to the man and yelled, "Don't hit him!"

The black apparition of a man sneered. "All right, I won't." Retrieving a pistol from his hip holster, he pointed at it at Mr. Kohn's head and shot. The elderly man was dead instantly.

"No!" David sank to the ground beside his father, while horror gripped him in deep, gut wrenching waves.

Another shot rang out and David jumped to his feet as he saw his mother fall to the ground beside him, a bullet to the back of her neck, cutting off her life in an instant. He spun around to look at the loathing staring back at him.

"Now you can move without any hindrance." The dark veiled man laughed unmercifully, pointed his revolver in David's direction while his family sobbed silently beside him. "Now go! All of you move faster! Hurry!"

David looked at his dead parents once more and then hurried his family along as they rushed to catch up with the others. Everything became a blur after that. The scenery grew distorted and heaviness settled down on his chest making it hard to breathe. It felt suffocating.

David awoke with a start, fear a close companion and sweat pouring from his body as he threw off the covers. Breathing in deep gulps of the crisp, night air, his eyes darted around, taking in the familiar objects of the bedroom. The dresser was opposite him, where it always stood. The door beside it was slightly ajar. The walls held paintings, which normally brightened the room with color. Now the darkness of night caused shadows to creep across the room from the window above the bed, the moon shining dimly through the sheer curtains. He glanced at his wife sleeping peacefully beside him. He swung his legs out of bed, slid his feet into slippers and left the room, wiping perspiration from his brow.

Although he felt relief that it was only a dream, his insides shook as he paced the floor and his body temperature slowly cooled. He wandered to the front window, parted the curtains and looked out at the night. The moon was shining brightly in the sky, washing the view in a soft glow. There were a few clouds in the sky with stars sparkling between them. Everything looked normal and peaceful, as it should in the middle of the night. The houses across the street were dark and at rest except for a soft tint of the moon's glow on each roof. The street lay like a golden ribbon reflecting the moonlight. The road weaved its way past the many houses, the synagogue and the businesses beyond. The trees stood like sentinels, serious and unmoving as they guarded the neighborhood. Not even the sound of a dog's bark was heard in the sleeping vicinity. Everything appeared in order and at rest but it did nothing to shake off the horror wrapped around David's heart.

The dream didn't make any sense. His children were grown, married and some had young children of their own now. That he would dream of his three children being so much younger was confusing. They had seemed so innocent, needy and afraid. They had appeared completely dependent on him and the realization was terrifying. Were they still dependent on him? Was there something he needed to do for them? And why would his parents be shot down in cold blood? He couldn't comprehend the meaning. It was just too horrific!

David rubbed his long beard, exposing his nervousness, and walked to his study desk. Opening a cabinet next to his desk, he saw his prayer shawl folded neatly on the second shelf. Lifting it from its place, he shook it open, lifted it and placed it around his shoulders. He took to pacing again, the tassels of the shawl swaying with his movement, and began to recite the prayers he thought might help but none of them quieted his agitated spirit. It was useless so he finally wandered to the couch, fell to his knees before it, clasped his hands and cried out his fear.

"God of Abraham, Isaac and Jacob, hear my cry for mercy. If there is any reason for this dream then please make it plain to me. I don't understand. What does it mean? It's filled me with dread and complete terror! I can't bear it! Please remove the fear from my heart. My parents, my dear, dear parents! I can't lose them like that! Please, God, have mercy on them!" David gave his anguish full vent as he began to sob at the horror he had envisioned in his sleep.

CHAPTER 2

Resilient and Bold, two mighty warrior angels, met on the lush grass opposite the great gathering hall they had just exited. The angel choir could still be heard singing out songs of adoration to the King of kings and Lord of lords. The voices floated in perfect harmony from the open windows and openings in the roof of the grand hall. It helped to lift the heaviness of the meeting's agenda. The grounds of the angel quarters shone with a holy glow, defying the immensity of the news they'd just heard. Each building glowed from the rich material used in its construction.

"What did you think of the speech Knowledge gave?" asked Resilient. He stood approximately ten feet in height, with broad shoulders, square jaw, intense brown eyes, dark hair and signs on his face of many battles fought and won.

"It was very informative," Bold said. He was slightly shorter in height but no less impressive. His long brown hair fell around his wide shoulders. His eyes shone a brilliant blue with an intensity that would be sure to set his enemies on edge. "I wonder when the forces will be sent out. Something's steadily building on earth and we'll be needed."

"It's surprising."

Bold said, "To a point, yes. We've already sensed the tension and been aware of the enemy's growing boldness."

"That's true."

"Many angels, returning from earth missions, have expressed concern over the events they've seen unfolding."

Resilient nodded. "And yet many, having returned from an assignment, remained ignorant of the things we heard this afternoon, depending on where on earth they were stationed. I'm thankful for Knowledge. He explained and described what is coming in very clear terms."

"And from what he said, this coming conflict will be centered mostly on the European countries."

"It's quite horrifying, even with all we've been through. I wonder why things have to work themselves out this way."

Bold said, "There's always a reason. I only hope that many will be protected and the enemy's plans thwarted in carrying out his all-encompassing scheme.

"The joy and peace surrounding Knowledge, even with the information he gave, was encouraging."

Bold nodded in agreement. "Even in battle, Heaven's peace sustains us."

"But I also feel such seriousness; a growing foreboding; an intense sorrow. It's hard to ignore. God Almighty is grieved over what is about to happen and His sorrow permeates the air." Resilient looked contemplative.

"It makes me wonder." Bold looked off into the distance, across a field of flowers waving in the soft wind. "Maybe we've only heard a small part of what's coming."

"Maybe it's all we can handle at the moment."

"I'm sure that's true."

"I know I'll miss this place," said Resilient. "And to know we're heading into such a vicious battle. It nearly gives me cold feet, so to speak."

Bold grinned at that. "It sounds absurd to say such a thing!"

Resilient chuckled. "I do know this, when the time comes, we will be more than ready to leave here and enter the war."

"And your feet will be hot with the fire of God's will."

"My feet are warming even as you speak." Resilient smiled brightly, knowing it was true.

In a grove of trees only a short distance away, four guardian angels gathered, Courageous, Wisdom, Lovely and Light Bearer. The fruit trees surrounding them filled the vicinity with a sweet fragrance.

The four guardians were also at the Great Gathering Hall but the words they heard were slightly different. They were also warned of the coming danger but their assignment had come to them clearly. Holy Spirit's doing, no doubt. They were to depart immediately and they all felt the weight of their coming assignment.

Courageous was the first to break the silence. "The time has come. We're being sent to serve one with great understanding and spiritual discernment."

Wisdom said, "We'll be serving one who will inherit salvation."

"Yes," replied Courageous. "She will soon be conceived and we will go and stay with her till the end of her life."

Lovely broke in. "I wonder what she will become. I sense that she'll accomplish much in her life."

"And face great conflict and danger," added Light Bearer.

Courageous nodded. "And to think that we're being sent out to serve someone like this is a great honor."

They fell silent, each one lost in their own thoughts. There was no sorrow over leaving, although Heaven was grander and more peaceful that what earth could ever produce. A resolute longing and desire to serve one from earth filled each guardian with a deep yearning to depart as soon as possible. This was what they were created for, what gave them the greatest pleasure. Without discussion, Courageous led the way to where the horse and carriage team would be waiting to take them to earth. The others followed willingly, eagerness and determination filling the air around them. An angel choir accompanied them from above, floating along from on high and encouraging them with songs of victory. It bathed the four in peace.

Germany

Helmuth Schluter walked toward Mrs. Grossman, the midwife, shook her hand and thanked her profusely. Her daughter, Frederika, stood at the kitchen sink smiling. They'd all been through quite an ordeal. Mrs. Grossman and Frederika busied themselves cleaning up. The two would leave soon. They had been at the Schluter home for nearly two days straight. Helmuth didn't wait to see them out.

He walked quickly to the bedroom, opened the door and a mixture of relief and joy stole over him at the sight. His wife, Unna, rested against the damp sheets, her eyes closed in exhaustion. Helmuth leaned over and kissed her gingerly on the forehead, stroking her sweat soaked hair with his hand. The small bundle beside her was wrapped tightly in a white, flannel blanket, one of the many that Unna had carefully sewn and prepared for her first child. Only the baby's face peeked out, her eyes shut and her lips moving slightly.

"Hi, little girl! Welcome to our world."

Unna opened her tired eyes slowly and gazed up at him. Helmuth turned and looked at his wife. The exhaustion from her struggle played around her eyes.

"She's beautiful, …isn't she?" Unna struggled as she smiled weakly.

"Yes, she's a striking baby, but you are the most beautiful to me, Unna. I'm so thankful I didn't lose either one of you." Tears formed in Helmuth's eyes as he struggled not to cry. "I prayed and prayed all night long for you and the baby."

"Oh, my strong, wonderful Helmuth! How could I die when I have so much to live for?" She smiled slightly and closed her eyes in exhaustion.

"Go to sleep. We'll have time to talk later." Helmuth adjusted the blanket around Unna to cover her from the cool January draft in the room and then gazed at his small daughter and spoke quietly. "I think we'll name you Beata. You were born on a cold, January morning but you're coming has warmed my heart like a heavenly breeze. I know you have a special purpose, little Beata Schluter. I feel it in my bones."

Unna opened her eyes once more. "Did you say something?"

"No. Go back to sleep." Helmuth then walked to the door, stopping there to turn back once more to look at his wife and daughter.

Courageous, Wisdom, Lovely and Light Bearer stood around Unna's bed, angels sent as guardians of this new arrival. Unna's four guardians also stood around mother and child in a protective stance. Helmuth didn't see any of them and Unna was completely unaware of the angel company, which surrounded the bed, her tired eyes closed to the world.

Turning his gaze to the ceiling, Helmuth thanked God once more for a safe delivery, for sparing him sorrow upon sorrow. He left the room then, leaving the door open so that the warmth from the wood stove could transfer some heat

CHAPTER 3

Krakow, Poland

Anka wandered past the bakery, shoe store, leather tanner shop, book store and the small restaurant on the corner. She stopped there looking down the familiar street leading to her parent's home. She nervously fingered the fresh loaf she carried as an offering. A vehicle honked loudly and she jumped. To her right, a large delivery truck slowed to a crawl and honked again, warning people who were casually crossing the road ahead of it. A mother and her two children hurried their step toward the sidewalk and the truck drove on.

Anka looked around longingly at the neighborhood she knew so well. There was the Laundromat across the street with its large faded sign where she had spent many a Saturday afternoon helping her mother with the weekly laundry. Beside it was a bakery with a small restaurant, a rival to the bakery and restaurant across the street. On the other side of the Laundromat was a second hand clothing store, well visited and still in business.

Anka gazed down the street, longing filling her, a faraway sadness creeping slowly over her features. Everything had changed for her months ago, the day she chose to marry Aaron Levin, the fine Jewish man she had grown to love. She'd met him when he worked at the large library down town. She loved to read and visited the library often. It was only a matter of time till they met and after numerous visits to the library, their love grew and their future was sealed.

She sighed heavily in resignation. Just maybe her visit today could shift things in a different direction. She sure hoped so. Perhaps her father had softened toward her and toward Aaron. It had been months since she'd seen either of her parents and she missed them. She hoped they missed her equally.

Anka crossed the street avoiding the restaurant to her right and its owner. Donat Kotas had always insisted that Anka and his son, Wiktor, were perfect for each other. He had even had the gall to visit her after her engagement to Aaron and convince her of the fact that Wiktor was the one for her. Part of her father's doing, no doubt. She knew then as she knew now that she loved Aaron and no other would do.

Anka wandered down the street toward her parents' home. Large trees lined both sides of the street, the leaves turning shades of red, orange and yellow. The warm, fall breeze blew Anka's shoulder length, brown hair in wisps around her face. Her hands shook as she approached her childhood home and clung to the loaf tightly, a gift for her father, as if afraid it might drop. She knocked lightly at the door and it opened shortly.

Ewa Trafas stepped forward, her eyes shining brightly in welcome as she held out her arms and squealed in unconcealed delight. "My Anka, come in, come in!"

Anka walked nervously into the house still holding tightly to the loaf and looked around, her eyes darting from place to place, looking for a sign of her father, Jaromil Trafas.

Ewa wrapped her arms around Anka, while Anka placed a kiss on her mother's cheek. It felt so wonderful to have her mother's arms around her, so safe and protected. She could stay here in her mother's arms forever. How she had missed this the past months. Many tears had been shed since her wedding day. Anka held tightly, longer than usual, but her mother didn't seem to mind and returned the hug with equal enthusiasm. Anka only hoped her father would be as delighted at seeing her.

Germany

Adolf Hitler spoke long and loud, rousing the crowd of the German Worker's Party, into spontaneous cheers and affirmations. Although the party had at one point consisted of only a handful of men, the growing political party now boasted of crowds of over two thousand and steadily mounting. The appearance of the young German spokesman was nothing special; in fact he looked rather thin and plain, wearing a cheap shirt, black tie and simply made trousers. His black shoes, when one looked closely enough, showed signs of much wear, the toes scuffed and heels worn. His overcoat rested over the back of a chair on the stage and it looked quite worse for wear. This didn't stop the crowd from listening intently to the strong and convincing speech he gave. He had a way of alluring the crowd, gaining their trust and attention, drawing them into agreement with him in a most inexplicable way.

"Germany is a land of proud people, strong and ingenious, capable and able. Other countries have tried to bury us under unreasonable demands, taking away the best of our resources, humbling us unrestrainedly, taxing our patience and mounting within us a great resentment of such outlandish disciplinary actions it thought to carry through. The present government sits mildly by and allows us, the citizens of this great country, to be stripped bare by the vicious countries surrounding it. The present government is weak and useless to lift the heavy burden infringed upon us and is completely incapable of restoring any sense of national pride in its people. We must unite together and fight this great evil done to it. It is only through a combined, strong effort that this country can once more become the great, strong nation it has always been destined to be. We, the citizens of Germany, need to unite under one Reich, which is devoted to the establishment of new colonies abroad and the creation of a strong people's army. We demand that the Versailles Treaty be revoked." The young orator raised his fists in emphasis.

The crowd erupted with loud cheers, whistles and thunderous clapping. The German orator waited till the voices calmed once more.

"Too much responsibility was placed in our lap for the results of the war. This party promises to do everything in our power to restore national pride, greater living space and to resist the Treaty by building up the army, not only for our own national protection but for our people's pride and economic stability. We need to fight against the evil communist agenda in this country. There also needs to be a ruthless battle fought against criminals to insure law and order. Above all, I believe that no country can dictate another country's national security."

Another round of applause and cheers echoed through the group assembled. The young promoter of the new political party continued on and on, pleasing the crowd as they listened enraptured and enthralled by the ideals and vitality this young leader offered.

"Hear me, citizens of Germany, our greatest enemy is not communism or the countries that imposed on us the Versailles Treaty, economic slumps or lack of food. No, our greatest enemy is the Jewish people! The Jews are enemies of the German people. Jews need to be treated as aliens, without the right to hold any public office. They should be deported. They eat the best food of our land. They hoard it for themselves. Can you feed your families like you wish?"

"No!" The crowd thundered its response.

"If the German people are starving and suffering, blame the Jews. I insist the aliens must depart from here and we must see that they are encouraged by any means possible."

Many in the crowd cheered while a few heckled Hitler's statements. Quickly some police officers, supportive of the new, thriving party, rushed to the disruptive persons and forcefully ushered them out the door.

Adolf Hitler continued on his views and vision for a future Germany as the crowd continued to applaud and esteem him. He smiled in pleasure as his speech reached a climactic end and the crowd stood and clapped enthusiastically in agreement as he exited the platform.

The speaker hurried to a back room and met his trusted assistant. "I want you to gather my closest friends of the Party and my superiors and have them meet me at precisely two o'clock this afternoon."

"Yes sir."

That afternoon, Adolf entered the small meeting room and noticed the presence of the men he had requested. Adolf Hitler took a seat, folded his hands on top of the table and smiled in pure delight at his new found position of the National Worker's Party. When the conversation in the room quieted he began the meeting.

"Gentlemen, we are part of a new and emerging political force and I think it would do us well to have a symbol, a sign of our party, that would represent who and what we are. It would elicit more pride in the members and draw us together in a greater unity than what we have so far enjoyed. If the unity and the success we have experienced gives us cause to rejoice, then think of what a party symbol will do for the grounds of accord and increasing membership. Every time a German sees our symbol it will remind him of the growing power of this political group and we will gain greater recognition and more German's will be drawn to join our ranks."

A few of Hitler's military superiors were in the room and one of them, Omar Borg, was the first to reply. "I like the idea, Hitler. Why don't we send out a bulletin, requesting those faithful to the party to come up with ideas for the Party symbol? We'll negotiate over the ones submitted and then make our final decision. We could place it on our political flag and then our party will have even more exposure to the general public."

Strom Reiter, another of Adolf's military superiors, spoke next. "That's sounds good but I also feel we need another platform to advance our cause. We need a newspaper to let the German people know more widely about our political agenda and to make the nation aware of the option of this party."

Hitler nodded and said, "Great idea. Yes, let's start on that immediately." He considered for a moment and then asked, "Did you have a particular newspaper in mind?"

"I've done some research and it seems that the People's Observer is the newspaper of choice. I've already approached them and they seem willing to sell as long as they can continue to work for us and publish our paper."

"Are they agreeable to our Party agenda?" Adolf Hitler looked interested but concerned.

"Yes, the paper is well known for its anti-Semitic and anti-communist editorial policy."

"Wonderful!"

Omar Borg faced Strom. "Why don't you go ahead with that plan then?"

Strom Reiter nodded.

"About the name of the party, shouldn't we shorten it slightly? It seems rather long and laborious." Kiefer Schulman gazed at Adolf and the other men as he waited for the reply.

"We could come up with an abbreviated form, something catchy and unique." Omar wondered aloud as he gazed at the wall across the room.

Mr. Reiter cleared his throat. "We have plenty of time for that. We have some new ideas to work on for now and with the way things are shaping up, the increased membership and the growing interest in this party will consume our time as we continue to deliver speeches and gain the public trust. The agenda of our party is truly catching the interest of the German people and I believe our political goals are ringing true for the majority of our listeners. Allowing Adolf to be our spokesperson has been a tremendous boost for the entire party."

Omar added to the praise. "You have a way with words, Adolf, and a way to get and hold people's attention. They rally around you in a way I haven't seen in a very, very long time, if ever, I might add. Keep up the good work. I can tell you this, Adolf; your work has only begun."

"It is my joy to serve my country in this way. The things I speak of are my passion, my life." Adolf emphasized it with clenched fists and moved in terse movements with deep emotion. "I'm honored to serve this party."

CHAPTER 4

Krakow, Poland

Rabbi David Kohn exited the synagogue and released a satisfied sigh as he looked out on the grassy yard filled with the members from his synagogue. The meeting had gone well, his message had been well prepared and he felt pleased. God was surely smiling on him this day. The bright blue sky testified to it and the warmth of the sun gave witness. He noticed Devora visiting with some family members close to the street. Their two oldest, Benesh and Sulia were both married with children of their own. Benesh and Jaffe had two children. Sulia and her husband, Menashe, had a one year old little girl.

David's youngest child, Itamar, was still living at home at the age of twenty. He had his sights on a young lady named Rachel. It wouldn't be long till he and Devora had the house to themselves. It was a sobering thought. Where was time going? He smiled as he watched his two oldest grandchildren running around the legs of their father. He sighed in pleasure. Children and grandchildren were such a blessing.

His smile quickly faded as his dream filled his mind. It still made no sense to him but he couldn't seem to wipe it from his memory. He refused to think on it another minute. It was only a dream and it was too beautiful a day to allow his mind to wander there. Everyone seemed to be enjoying visiting under the sun, shining in a clear, blue sky.

More members exited the doors and stopped to shake David's hand. He spoke a few words of farewell and they proceeded down the steps and onto the green grass. David's eyes noticed some young women to the left.

Chava Levin stood beneath the big oak in the center of the yard with her cousins gathered around her. She was a pretty nineteen-year-old, dressed in a knee length dress in a shade of light blue, ankle socks and black Sabbath shoes. Her dark, curly hair was a replica of her mothers, except for the gray strands, and her curls bounced on her shoulders as she talked. Her cousins, Chesed and Basya, sisters, looked in awe as they studied Chava's new ring. David could almost see the diamond sparkle from here. He had heard it was quite large.

Chava's father, Binyamin Levin, had stopped by last night with the news. Binyamin had been clearly upset. Chava was engaged to a Polish man, Dobry Waglewski, and her father was not happy. He was afraid for his daughter, understandably. It was no secret the hatred most Poles held for Jews. That a Pole would even consider marrying a Jewish girl, no matter how pretty, was nearly unheard of. David felt concerned as well but he had to impart some measure of faith, after all, he was the Rabbi. It was his job.

He scanned the crowd and saw him. Binyamin Levin was in deep conversation with his brother-in-law, Yankel Greenstein. Their wives were sisters. Init and Gittel were also part of the conversation. Yankel and Gittel's two daughters were the girls admiring Chava's new ring.

David was deeply curious so he headed that way. His long robes swished in the slight breeze as he walked, with his long white beard framing his face and falling majestically across his chest, ending in a thin point near his waist. He overheard the conversation as he neared.

"You better watch your daughters, Yankel. My daughter is sure to have a bad influence on them. Not only is Chava engaged to a Pole but he's a rich Pole at that and those are the most dangerous kind. I don't know what I've done wrong in raising my children. First it was Aaron who married a Pole and now Chava's heading in the same direction. I should never have allowed Aaron to marry Anka. Look where my lenience has led. Chava is only following in her brother's footsteps."

"Aaron and Anka are happy though, are they not?" asked Yankel.

Binyamin said, "I suppose they're happy enough, but the trouble it has started. I don't know if it's worth it. They will undoubtedly have a hard time in life. Mixed marriages like theirs will be filled with misunderstandings and harsh treatment. I don't understand why my children can't see further into the future and see the hardships awaiting them. It's very disconcerting."

"Perhaps it won't be as bad as you anticipate. You have accepted Anka haven't you?"

"Yes."

"And she seems very happy to be Aaron's wife. They look like they love each other." Both men looked over at the group of young couples standing beside the synagogue doors. Anka and Aaron stood close, Aaron gazing into his wife's eyes at times with Anka responding with a pleasant smile. "And besides that, Init seems to treat Anka like a true daughter-in-law. It doesn't appear to bother Init too much having a Polish daughter-in-law." Yankel looked at Init. She had turned from her sister to look at him as she heard her name discussed.

"Would you mind not talking about me behind my back while I'm standing right here?"

Yankel only grinned.

"I truly do love Anka as my daughter and I try to alleviate her distress."

"What distress?" asked David, joining in the conversation.

"Oh, Hello Rabbi," said Init. "It's about Anka's parents. Actually it's her father who has basically disowned her. She misses her parents and brother a lot and longs to see them. It has become an impossible dream. She wants her life with Aaron but she also desires a relationship with her parents and brother."

Binyamin continued, "It's a difficult choice she's made. Now we're all the family Anka has. I feel sorry for her but what did she expect? This is the way things are. It is better if the Poles marry Poles and us Jews stay with Jews. Do you see now, Yankel, why you must forbid your children to marry Poles? It is nothing but trouble and heartache for them."

"You make me thankful that Solomon is already married and to a good Jewish girl. They're expecting their first child, did you know that?"

"No! Well congratulations, Yankel! You'll be a grandfather!" Binyamin slapped his brother-in-law on the back.

"It's wonderful news," agreed David. This was the first he'd heard of it.

"I know it. I feel much too young to be a grandfather." Yankel's once dark beard now showed flecks of white, defying his statement.

"We're not that young anymore. Our children are marrying and having children. My, my, where has the time gone?" said Binyamin.

"I don't know. It's a sobering thought."

Gittel shook her head is disbelief. "Yankel, you're forty five and I'm forty three. We're not that young anymore."

"Speak for yourself, Gittel. I feel young and I'm not ready for grandchildren yet."

"Well, I'm ready. I haven't held a baby for so long. Ayelet, my baby, is already fifteen and growing into a young lady. I'm so excited for Solomon and Heni. Heni's already beginning to show and she's only three months along. I can't wait to hold their baby, my grandbaby!"

Yankel turned from his wife and looked at Binyamin. "So when is Chava getting married?"

"They haven't set a date but Dobry did come by two nights ago to ask permission for Chava's hand in marriage." Binyamin's forehead creased in concern.

"So was that the first time you've seen Dobry?" Yankel asked.

"No. I've picked Chava up from the factory and I've seen him those times. I should have known from the beginning. What boss stands outside with his employee and visits with them after work? I did warn Chava to keep her distance from him but what chance did she have? She worked for his father and so he had every opportunity to make advances. I should have forced her to quit there the moment I noticed Dobry's attention. It's entirely my fault."

Gittel reached for Binyamin's arm. "Now, now, brother-in-law, don't blame yourself. Although forcing her to quit might have been the best thing. His infatuation with Chava obviously began well before you noticed it and even if she would have been forced to quit, Dobry might have still continued his advances. Chava's a smart girl, with a good head on her shoulders. She feels Dobry's a good man so we must trust her judgment. God has a way of working things out to His own ends."

Binyamin snorted. "I don't believe this was God. This was a young man who noticed an exceptionally pretty, young Jewish girl and he couldn't resist. I only hope Chava won't get hurt too much in the process. She deserves a good man and to marry into a family that will treat her right. I'm afraid for her."

"I'm afraid too. She's my only daughter and I want the best for her." Init Levin's face twisted in fear.

Gittel placed an arm around Init's shoulders. "Don't worry, sister. We must put our trust in God. He will take care of Chava. We are Jews, God's people, and God has always taken care of us."

David felt required to agree, "That's right, Init. God will take care of Chava."

"If God has always taken care of us then where is our home and where is our land, Gittel?" asked Yankel. "We are like foreigners in another people's country"

"We have a home. It's just down the street," declared Gittel, staring at her husband in confusion.

"You know what I mean. We belong in the land of Israel. God has forsaken us."

"God has not forsaken us. I'm ashamed of you, Yankel! Remember who you are," reprimanded Gittel.

"Oh I remember just fine. I'm a Jew living in Poland, surrounded by angry Poles who hate Jews. How's that for remembering."

David was surprised at the outburst. Of course they all felt similar but to hear Yankel say it so openly was surprising.

Binyamin smiled before joining in. "This is the only home any of us knows. We were all born here so this is just as much our home as it is to the Poles."

Yankel looked angry as he answered and pointed his finger. "This will never be our home as long as we're surrounded by Poles who refuse to accept us. Haven't our children always been harassed by neighboring children, called dirty names, been afraid to walk to school, terrified of being beaten? Why? I'll tell you why! It's because our children are Jewish and the other children are not. Even for us adults, it's best if we have our own communities and stay to ourselves. At least that way we don't have to face the constant hostility from our neighbors."

Binyamin said, "They do business with us though, sell to us and don't seem to mind the services we provide."

Yankel rubbed his thumb and finger together, "It's all about money."

David felt compelled to say something. "Is there some dissatisfaction in this life we enjoy? We have to remember that God has abundantly blessed us here, given us wonderful families, businesses, a certain amount of religious freedom and so, compared to the life we could be living, it's important to always give thanks to God. He is the one who has given us all things to enjoy."

Yankel spoke, "I don't argue with that, Rabbi, but I do complain about God not taking up our case and giving our land back. The land of Israel belongs to us so why has it been nearly two thousand years since we've lived there."

"Well to be entirely correct, many Jews do choose to travel to Palestine and settle there, even as we speak." Rabbi Kohn gazed intently into Yankel's eyes. "Is this what you want to do? Resettle in Palestine."

"That's a loaded question especially the age I'm at. My children are grown, getting married and having children. It's not that easy to pack up and leave anymore. I should have considered this when Gittel and I were first married."

Rabbi Kohn said, "And so, you chose to stay. God's doing no doubt. He decides the exact places we are to live so that we will seek Him. Stop struggling with your place in life, Yankel, and accept God's will." There was an indistinct twitching in his eyes. David hoped the nervous habit wasn't too visible. It had started the night of his horrible dream and the dreams that followed had only added to the problem. He couldn't seem to shake them.

"It's an easy thing to say, Rabbi. It's not so easy to do."

"I know it, but what other choice do we have. I also have a wife, children and grandchildren. I know what you're feeling, but this is our home and where we belong for now. When the time is right, God will again grant us our land." David Kohn faced Binyamin and Init Levin. "And as for Chava, we must trust in God. He has her in His hands. We must believe that. Aaron and Anka seem very happy together and she seems to fit in well with our Jewish beliefs and traditions."

Init said, "Yes, she is trying hard."

"Does Chava's fiancée respect her beliefs?"

"I don't know. I hope Chava doesn't forget her beliefs or that she's a Jew once she marries," Init said fearfully. "Right now she's in love so the future seems bright and sunny in her eyes. I only hope it remains this way for her."

"That's a bunch of wishful thinking! Chava's in for a world of hurt!" Binyamin's serious, stony face brought the conversation to a halt. The group stared at him.

David Kohn cleared his throat. "Let's all pray that Chava's future will be covered under God's loving care." He then excused himself and wandered to speak with others gathered before the synagogue.

CHAPTER 5

Germany, 1921

Adolf Hitler's legs shook slightly and perspiration formed on his forehead but no one noticed as he forcefully made his demands known.

"I make this request not as a power hungry man but through my concern for the National Socialist German Workers' Party. It is only through iron leadership that this party will become what it was meant to become, not a pitiful western association. That is why I ask to be made first party chairman and that you endue me with dictatorial powers. With these endowments I vow to bring this party under control, stop the wild outburst of those who have no respect for authority and bring unity and one purpose to our party. It is my concern for our continued success and my deep fervor to right the wrongs in Germany that I make this request."

There was hushed whispering in the room. Adolf's one time superiors discussed his request, wondering about its wisdom while at the same time realizing its necessity.

After a few moments Strom Reiter stood and cleared his throat. "I can see the need to bring this party more fully under control. There are too many voices and too many opinions and those who branch out on their own bring fragmentation to our purpose. From the example of the government now in power, the leaders' inability to bring some much needed reforms in this country is obvious. Unemployment is running rampant and more beggars fill our streets daily. It is quite clear to me that drastic change is needed and it may as well begin with our party. If anyone is able to revolutionize the destiny of Germany, it is this party, so yes; I give my assent to your requests."

The other men also, one by one, gave their approval. Hitler smiled in relieved gratitude and pleasure.

From that day on the party ceased to observe democratic procedures. Adolf Hitler became the absolute leader and began to expect from his followers, complete obedience.

Germany, summer 1923

A light streaked through the air as a large angel landed on the roof of a tall building in Munich. Deliverer waited as another flash of light landed beside him, Peace, his comrade in the mission.

The tall structure overlooked much of the city but stood in a location not pivotal for the main evil activity that roamed the down town streets at night. Thankfully no evil presence lurked on this critical spot and his arrival had gone undetected, with the streak of light most likely thought to be a falling star. It was vital that he fulfill his mission and if it was only to delay the inevitable then so be it but it must be delayed.

Deliverer looked to the skies and waved his hand in encouragement. Tens of angels at a time began to descend to the roof, then another group floated down and then another until there was a detachment of over two thousand angels assembled together. Deliverer and Peace were in charge of sending the messenger angels out two by two to rouse the saints to prayer.

The angels on the outer edges lifted their wings and flapped them slightly; creating a misty, fog surrounding the whole group, shielding them from early detection by the horde of darkness in the city. Deliverer retrieved their marching orders from the fold of his robe, entrusted to him in the Great Throne Room, and straightened out the papers in his hand. Angels, previously assigned together, approached the two in charge and Deliverer gave them their instructions, directions and assigned saints.

Soon duos of angels could be seen ducking through alleys, weaving down streets or flying mid air being careful to avoid being seen as they made their way into the designated homes, apartments and buildings.

People awoke for no apparent reason, feeling burdened beyond measure to pray. Babies cried out and children wandered to their parent's bedrooms as the initial wake up call resounded in many homes. Parents were forced to deal with the unwelcome disturbance. Some people, upon wakening, wandered to the kitchen for something to eat and drink and then hurried back to bed. There were a few who headed the call to pray but the angels worked steadily, determinedly, sometimes waking up people multiple times during the night and the many nights that followed.

A fly buzzed over their heads in constant determination, landing here and then there, only to be waved on by an irritated hand. After a few minutes of this constant annoyance, Helmuth Schluter finally got out of bed, switched on the lamp and began to stalk the marked fly. He first glanced at the clock on his nightstand and noticed the time, one twenty-three. He let a frustrated sigh escape as he wiped the sleep from his eyes.

"There you are," he said quietly, not willing to wake Unna. He picked up a single slipper from the floor, a useful tool to swat the fly.

The fly was sitting quietly, for the time being, on a chair by the bedroom door. Helmuth swatted the fly, only to miss as he watched the bug circle above him in frightened, irregular movements back and forth through the room. Helmuth focused on the peace-disturbing insect as it finally slowed its frantic flight and came to rest once more on the bed. This time Helmuth didn't miss as his slipper came down hard on the doomed creature.

"There, I got you!" In his excitement, he forgot to keep his voice down.

Unna sat up groggily, trying to see through her sleepy eyes. "What are you doing, Helmuth? You frightened me! Did you pounce on the bed?"

"I killed a fly with my slipper. It was at me for a good half hour. I couldn't stand it any more, but now it's taken care of." A crooked smiled twisted his lips.

"Oh, that's all it was. You sure know how to give a person a fright."

"I'm sorry, Unna. Go back to sleep."

Helmuth placed his slipper back on the floor and curled up under the warm covers. He tossed and turned for a few minutes and then turned toward Unna, her back facing him. He placed a hand on her back gently as if afraid to disturb her again.

"Unna?" Nothing. "Unna?"

"What?" Irritation filled her voice.

"I'm sorry to bother you again, knowing how tired you always are these days, but I feel such heaviness in the room. Do you feel it too?"

"I feel tired, Helmuth. That is what I feel."

"Okay, go back to sleep. I'm sorry for bothering you."

Helmuth lay awake, struggling to relax. To him it seemed like hours passed as he lay there, the darkness filled with warning. He tried to brush it away like a bad dream, forcing his mind to think of comforting things, like his feathery soft pillow, his down filled blanket, the alarm that would shout its decree at six in the morning. He was just about to doze off when the baby cried out. Helmuth lay completely still in hopes that would make her fall back to sleep. Unna moaned in protest beside him. As the cries continued to increase in intensity Unna finally moved.

"Why this night? I'm so terribly tired and Ilse insists on eating at what time?" Unna looked at the clock and it showed three twenty-one. "Why is she awake so soon?"

Unna left the room and soon returned carrying three-month-old Ilse in her arms. Climbing back into bed, she held Ilse to her breast to nurse as she rested her head back against a pillow. Helmuth watched his wife as her eyes closed and her head rolled to the side. With a jerking motion, she snapped back awake and straightened, but it didn't take long till her eyes closed again, nearly falling asleep in the process.

Footsteps echoed from the hall and Helmuth glanced that way to see Beata enter the room. Unna looked up too and noticed their daughter in the doorway. Beata stood there, holding her blanket and rubbing her eyes, her nightgown reaching to the floor and her feet covered by warm stockings.

Three year old Beata cried out, "I'm scared, Mommy!"

Unna slapped Helmuth beside her. "Get up. Someone needs you!"

"No."

"Oh yes, Helmuth. I can't nurse Ilse and take care of Beata too."

Helmuth slowly got out of bed and wandered to take Beata by the hand. Together they walked back to Beata's room. Helmuth was about to lift her into her bed but she resisted violently.

"No, no Daddy. I don't want to go back to bed. It's scary in there!" She began to cry, big tears flowing down her cheeks and her whole body shaking with fright.

"What is it, Beata?"

"Something scared me, Daddy."

Helmuth held his daughter tightly as he sat down on her bed. Beata snuggled in close and Helmuth wrapped his arms around her.

"Should I pray for you?"

"Yes Daddy. I would like that."

Helmuth began to pray quietly at first, not quite confident of how to pray but then there seemed to be a force behind his words as he continued with greater authority and determination. When he ended, the heaviness in the home was lifted and the fear gone. Beata snuggled even further into Helmuth's arms and he sang a German lullaby. She relaxed quickly after that. After another softly sung lullaby, Beata was fully asleep and Helmuth placed her back into her bed, covered her, kissed her forehead and left the room.

Unna was finished feeding Ilse and passed Helmuth in the hall on his way to bed, Ilse in her arms. Unna returned, hurried under the covers and snuggled close to Helmuth to warm her cool feet and soon both were sound asleep.

CHAPTER 6

Fall, 1923

The opportunity seemed perfect, divinely arranged so that the planned putsch was sure to be a success. The three leaders of the Bavarian government were planning to hold a large patriotic rally in one of Munich's expansive beer halls. They felt intimidated and menaced by Hitler's rising popularity in the region and they believed holding a political rally to explain their own political goals would bolster their own status and just maybe dampen the rising enthusiasm for the Nazi party.

"What do you think of it?" Hitler pointed to the map lying on the table, pinpointing the street where the beer hall was situated and then following it to the other beer hall in another area of the city.

Captain Hermann Goring nodded approvingly. "Yes, there's no better time than now."

Rudolf Hess said, "Yes, just remember what Mussolini was able to accomplish in Italy. Nothing is impossible to us."

Hitler smiled in pleasure at the memory. "I'll never forget what he told the representative I sent to him last year."

The other men in the room prepared to listen once more to the repeated conversation they'd heard numerous times. They didn't dare show impatience or boredom over the matter.

Hitler sighed contentedly and then continued. "I sent my representative to ask Mussolini if his army of Blackshirts would resort to force if the Italian government refused its demands. His answer will be forever engraved in my mind. He said, 'We shall be the government, because it is our will!' What an answer! And on October 28, 1922, Benito Mussolini and his Blackshirts entered Rome without a fight. He now controls Italy and this was accomplished by his party's will and courage and so we must be strong and know that much can be accomplished through our sheer resolve and unyielding will."

Hitler looked down at the map once more and then back to his faithful followers and leaders of his military. "Now this is how our putsch will play out." Hitler then proceeded to explain the strategy of the takeover.

～ぱ～

November 8, 1923

Hitler made his way to the beer hall shortly after eight o'clock where the scheduled Bavarian political rally was well under way. He strode with a strong gait although his appearance was nothing spectacular. On his back was his familiar tattered trench coat, his shoes looked well worn and not necessarily stylish and he carried a slouch hat in his hands. He came in unobtrusively, looked around the bar and wandered to the counter. After ordering a beer, he sauntered to stand quietly by a pillar in the crowded hall. His unusual, shortened moustache tweaked slightly as he focused on the men on the platform. They were the three main leaders of Bavaria; Gustav von Kahr, General Otto von Lossow and Colonel Hans von Seisser.

Gustav von Kahr, the conservative civilian commissioner, stood at the podium, speaking of the virtues of his government, the many so-called reforms undertaken by his aggressive cabinet and the constant and progressive changes yet ahead. The two other leaders sat quietly on stage waiting their turn to speak; General Otto von Lossow, commander of the army and Colonel Hans von Seisser, chief of the secret police. General Otto von Lossow noticed Hitler's presence first and threw open, nervous glances in his direction. General Lossow leaned over and whispered to Colonel Seisser who immediately looked in Adolf's direction, a severe frown forming on the Colonel's face. Hitler refused to acknowledge the leaders' awareness of his presence, but focused his attention on the commissioner's speech, his thoughts on the activities to follow. Hitler's eyes darted to the doorway often, in anticipation of his troop's arrival.

Outside, vehicles filled with Nazi storm troopers arrived and the men quickly surrounded the building. Nazi troopers were stationed at every entrance, and they quickly surrounded the Bavarian police on duty. Obviously outnumbered, the confused police did nothing but stand in shocked inaction.

Shortly after eight-thirty, Captain Hermann Goring, the SA bodyguard unit for the Nazi Party, and Rudolf Hess entered the beer hall. Hitler smiled as he saw them. He removed his pistol from its holster and joined his men.

The bodyguards moved around Hitler, brandishing their weapons visibly and shouting "Heil Hitler!" The crowd was thrown into confusion as Hitler and his group advanced toward the stage. Cries of shock and disbelief filled the hall. Eventually the crowd became impassable and Adolf Hitler and his men came to a standstill well before the envied platform. The crowd was in an uproar, some shouting one thing and other's hailing Hitler as the new leader of Bavaria. The crowd was definitely out of control and it was then that Hitler stood on a chair, waiving his pistol in mid air.

"Quiet!" Hitler's command went unheeded and the uproar continued. Hitler then released the safety and fired a round into the ceiling. The uproar quieted abruptly as the crowd hushed in complete shock. "The national revolution has broken out! The hall is surrounded!" Hitler then hopped down from the chair and the crowd made way for him. He walked toward the stage unhindered.

Hitler ascended the steps and faced the three men standing together in stony resolve.

Gustav von Kahr was the first to speak. "What are you doing here? This is a personal party rally and you have no right to barge in and take over! You are breaking the law. I demand you and your men leave immediately!"

"I'll call my men in and you'll be sorry!" Colonel Seisser, chief of police stared menacingly at Adolf.

"We will not leave nor will your police do any such thing. They won't respond. They are surrounded by my SA troops. I think it would be in your best interest to hear what I have to say. Why don't we discuss my proposal in a separate room?" Hitler pointed to the stage door leading to the offices beyond. Hitler led the way with the three Bavarian leaders following grudgingly.

Hitler placed his pistol on the table in the office, looked at the three men before him and began. "I love Germany as you do. I have committed my life to serve this great nation. I do not wish you any ill will or harm. My only wish is to unite Germany under my new party. I believe the Nazi party will offer new hope and will bring our people together to fight against the evils inflicted upon it. My only goal is to save Germany from two evils; republicanism and Communism. These two monsters have crippled our country and caused more poverty than any other thing. My desire is to set this nation free. I believe the Nazi party is able to bring this to pass. We have a wide support of members who believe in us. I can promise you, right here and now, that you will all be given important positions in the new national government I will form. Germany is ready for change and I'm inviting you to join me in bringing that change to this great nation."

Gustav von Kahr responded immediately. "No! I have no interest in joining the Nazi party. Germany already has a government and we are part of it."

Hitler looked at the other two men.

Colonel Seisser shook his head, anger flashing from his eyes. "I will not submit to your heavy handed method. You barge in at gunpoint and abduct us and now you want us to join you? This is preposterous!"

General Lossow stood, with a grim expression. "This discussion is over. I will not be part of your ludicrous party. I see now that it's made up of a bunch of criminals, worthy of jail time!"

There was a knock at the door and Hitler lifted his gun as the door opened. "Oh good, it's only you. Come in General Ludendorff. I was expecting you." Hitler pointed the gun in General Lossow's direction. "I'll ask you to take your seat, General.

Otto van Lossow's eyebrows drew together in deep anger but he begrudgingly sat down.

"As you can see, gentlemen, General Ludendorff is fully supportive of this revolution and a man as highly esteemed as he, one of Germany's top military leaders, should have good insight as to what is best for Germany." Hitler moved his hand toward General Ludendorff, making way for him to speak.

He spoke of his confidence in Adolf Hitler and his ability to bring great reforms and improvements for all of Germany. It took some time but he finally persuaded the two military leaders to accept Hitler's plan and finally Commissioner Gustav von Kahr also gave his approval.

Hitler stood quickly, returned to the waiting crowd to deliver the news. The crowd responded with cheers and rambunctious applause. After a short speech, Hitler hurried to discuss his next course of action with his faithful followers.

Hitler faced General Ludendorff and said, "I need to contact Captain Rohm. Where is a telephone I could use?"

"There's one just around the corner."

Hitler hurried and relayed the good news to his faithful follower located at another beer hall, where he was addressing two thousand SA supporters. "Rohm, I want you to proceed with your men to the army's headquarters in Munich and take over the building. Let me know when you have successfully completed this."

"Yes, Fuhrer. I'll get right on that."

Hitler returned to the beer hall, where his troops were celebrating their victory. He joined them, his face beaming with pleasure at the seemingly easy takeover and eventual agreement of the Bavarian leaders. The Bavarian leaders sat at a table alone, drinking beer, looking grim and speaking quietly. Hitler strode toward them smiling brightly.

"You will see, men, that this course of action was necessary and that Bavaria, along with the rest of Germany will greatly benefit from this revolution and any ill effects you feel tonight will quickly disappear in the gratefulness you will have toward our new national government."

"You seem very confident," said Commissioner Kahr.

"Yes, I am absolutely confident of a strong united Germany. A Germany we can all be proud of."

Commander Lossow said, "Perhaps our pride is not what is most important here."

Hitler looked incredulous as he faced the army commander. "You, of all men, should know what humility can do to a man. Did you not command a post in the war?"

"Yes I did."

"Then you know what a sound defeat has done to the German people, never mind to one who was commanding and leading other men to defeat. I am surprised that you would not care to lift the German people from their debased humility and restore pride back to their spirits. This is what I plan to do and having your approval is vital to my success."

"It is a grandiose plan, Adolf. One man cannot possibly bring about so much change for a defeated country."

"This only proves, Commander, that your vision is too small. I believe that someone like myself, someone with extensive plans for this country, can bring about the changes necessary to instill pride in our people once more."

"You may have vision but bringing it about in such a forceful manner is not an acceptable practice, neither to us nor to the people of Munich."

"Colonel Seisser, I did not force you to accept my plan, did I?"

"No, we did agree to it." The Colonel's eyes darted downward.

"That is exactly as I see it. I simply explained my plan and you eventually saw the benefit and ultimate virtue, not only for Munich but for all of Germany. It is good to have unity and oneness in a country." Hitler smiled brightly. "Have a drink, men, and enjoy the victory of the Nazi party. I can assure you that I will." With that Hitler wandered off to join General Ludendorff at a table surrounded by Nazi supporters.

Deliverer and Peace looked out from their post over the military barracks. A truck approached and drove through the gate, skidding over the stones to an abrupt stop by the main mess hall. Four large angels slid from the top of the truck and landed on the ground, looking up to see Deliverer and Peace watching from the tower in the center of the yard. Soldiers exited the truck and strode with determined steps through the door of the mess hall. The angels followed close behind. One man ran toward the living quarters. Deliverer and Peace kept their post, high above the military grounds and watched for any trouble.

A group of soldiers were relaxing for the evening, drinking, laughing, playing pool or card games and listening to a popular singer, the music flowing from the record player in the corner.

The largest of the soldiers from the truck, a lieutenant, walked toward the relaxed soldiers, beside a pool table and slammed his fist down hard, drawing the attention of everyone in the room. All became silent and hushed as all eyes focused on him.

"We just came from the political rally at the beer hall. The Nazi's charged us and took over the meeting. Adolf Hitler is proceeding with a putsch and with his revolution is planning to take over our government here and eventually the rest of Germany. He took our leaders at gunpoint and forced them to accept his terms."

A few cheers rang out, those faithful to the Nazi cause. Other voices were raised in anger and shock.

"I say he needs to be stopped," continued the lieutenant. "He will destroy this country of ours with his high-handed ways. All those in favor in putting a stop to this madman, come stand with me." His face was stern and serious as his eyes bore into each of the soldiers.

Suddenly a large group of soldiers, some in casual wear, others partially dressed in their uniforms, dragging their guns and ammunition, entered the mess hall. The first one spoke, "What's going on here. Someone came and told us there's an emergency."

The lieutenant repeated his speech, more impassioned and with greater fervor than before. One by one the soldiers came and stood in support to stop the Nazi cause.

Only a handful of men remained where they were. A few weak demons scrambled around the Nazi supporters, frantically devising a comeback. One soldier finally said, "You don't know what you're doing. If our government and military leaders have agreed to Hitler's demands, if you attack Hitler, then you'll be opposing our own government officials. It can only mean tremendous bloodshed for us all."

No one noticed one young soldier slipping out a side door, a demonic presence leading the way.

The angels rallied around the lieutenant and soldiers supporting him, encouraging and strengthening the men in their resolve. "We will not kill unless absolutely necessary. All I know is that some upstart Hitler will not take over our country through mere force. He has no right to push his party agenda on me or any of the German people. Now either you can join us or we will restrain you here before we put a stop to Hitler's nonsense."

"What can you possibly do against the strength of our leader's decision? And what other soldiers will rally to your cause? Your plan is already doomed to failure and will most likely result in punishment not only for you but for all the soldiers you're commanding."

"You forget your place, young soldier. There are many still loyal to the Bavarian Government, many soldiers who will willingly join me in defending it and I will not for one moment believe that our leaders willingly sold us out to that aggressive nothing, Hitler." The lieutenant faced the men loyal to his cause. "Every man prepare to relieve our state of this vile Nazi regime. Get your uniforms, weapons and meet me in the yard outside this building. I'll call the other military barracks and rouse as many as I can find to stand with us. We will be ready to leave within half an hour."

Men streamed out of the building and the lieutenant left to make the necessary calls.

The lone soldier who had left the building jumped into a military vehicle and made his way to the beer hall in record time. He relayed the news to an SA bodyguard, who in turn informed Adolf Hitler.

It didn't take him long to make arrangements. General Ludendorff was placed in charge of the situation at the beer hall and Adolf left with a few guards for the military barracks.

As the men began to gather on the yard, a truck approached and parked only meters away. Adolf Hitler exited the truck to the shock of the men gathered. They didn't see the entourage that accompanied Hitler, for the company which traveled with him was growing and the myriad of demonic spirits now his constant companions assisted and helped him in every endeavor. The foul creatures danced and gyrated grotesquely as they anticipated dominating and controlling this rabble group.

Adolf Hitler stood before the men in relaxed confidence, placing the men somewhat at ease. A large, manipulating spirit stood over Hitler, with large talons digging sharply into his shoulders and the demon's mesmerizing eyes boring into each soldier's soul as it demanded to control the situation.

"Men, I can see your devotion to your country and to your leaders. I commend you for this. What an asset you will be to the new National Government I plan to institute. Each one of you has shown his undying loyalty and constant commitment even to the end. I am thrilled to inform you of the success of the revolution and your leader's glad acceptance of a strong force to bring radical change and renewed pride to the people of Germany, which is exactly what I plan to do for the citizens of this great land." He took a breath and gazed purposely at each man.

"My will is to bring great improvements to the common people, to give each of you a place of importance in protecting this great country of ours and to rule to bring pride back to each of us. I'm sure you can all see the value of the agenda I bring with a national government. I seek to bring unity and oneness to the German population. I promise you, it will be a great improvement on every front and I commit myself to you as your servant to bring about necessary change. Can I count on your support?"

The lieutenant seemed flustered and confused as Hitler's eyes bore into him. He seemingly forgot his resolve only a few minutes before. "I, I…"

A soldier beside the lieutenant spoke, "I for one am in support of change. If our leaders approve of it then I see no reason why we shouldn't stand behind them. If they believe change is necessary then so do I."

A few more soldiers voiced their approval while the ones most opposed to Hitler's takeover were overcome with speechlessness, confusion pasting their features with stupidity. Demons shipped in with the Fuhrer, roamed around the undecided soldiers, whispering, conniving and speedily convincing them of the so-called truth of Adolf's words. A feeling of apathy flowed freely now through the ranks, rendering the previous resolve of the soldiers useless. Even the outspoken lieutenant was rendered powerless by the strong force of the large demon's influence.

The angels opened their wings and joined Deliverer and Peace on the high point of the tower as they watched the remainder of the proceedings from there.

"Have we failed? All our work seems to have been in vain." The largest of the four angels looked at Deliverer with discouragement.

"No, you haven't failed. Hitler is exactly where he was drawn out to be. You'll see in time." Deliverer nodded in encouragement and the four angels sent out on assignment breathed a sigh of relief as they watched Adolf Hitler return to the truck, with his guards and large entourage of demons and watched as the truck left the military grounds.

Deliverer turned to his left and spoke. "I want the two of you to head to the army headquarters in Munich. The telephone operator will need courage."

The angels unfurled their wings and disappeared into the night sky.

Hitler waltzed back into the beer hall, a small smile playing around his lips and certain airiness to his step. He noticed General Ludendorff at the bar and headed that way. Adolf slapped Ludendorff on the back in triumph.

"I have succeeded in diffusing the situation and they have come to see the wisdom of this putsch. The military personnel are very consolatory and willing to cooperate. I feel victory in the air and another reason to celebrate!"

"I'm glad your mission was a success. I was truly concerned for your safety and it's wonderful to see you back here." Ludendorff signaled to the bar keeper for another drink for Adolf.

"Is there any other news?" Hitler's attention became distracted as he noticed the table once occupied by the three Bavarian leaders now standing empty.

"No other news as yet, sir."

Hitler spun around and scanned the room carefully.

Ludendorff noticed his leader's unease. "Is anything wrong, Adolf?"

"Where are Kahr, Lossow and Seisser?"

Ludendorff became visibly uptight. "General Lossow asked for permission to go to his office and issue directives about the revolution."

"And the other two…where are they?"

"They also insisted they had to go and make arrangements."

Hitler spun around, with outraged face and glared at the general. "How could you let them go?"

Fear laced General Ludendorff's eyes. "But they gave us their word of support. I am sure they are men of their word. They wouldn't lie to us. I'm sure of it."

Hitler paced back and forth, disillusionment replacing his confidence only moments before. "I'm not so sure. This throws everything into a different light. If only you would have forced them to stay."

Captain Ernst Rohm had full control of the army headquarters in Munich, with a large group of the SA regiment backing him. Hitler had arrived minutes earlier and spent his time pacing, fuming, wondering how the putsch would turn out, his worried face appearing every so often to check with Rohm on any fresh news. Rohm had been made aware of the situation with the Bavarian leaders.

Suddenly Ernst Rohm stood, with a sudden knowing look, and hurried to call some troops and gave them orders. They rushed into the next room, seized the telephone operator and as he protested loudly at the rough treatment, they hauled him into the adjacent room to stand before Captain Rohm.

Two angels followed the operator and watched the encounter from the doorway. They looked pleased with the success of their mission.

The noise of the encounter alerted Hitler and he re-entered the room looking flustered and confused.

"What is this, Rohm?"

"I suspect the telephone operator has been working against us."

Two Nazi guards held the man tightly by the upper arms, in a standing position as Hitler slowly approached him. Rohm spoke first, "Have you been working against us?"

The operator refused to speak. Rohm took the liberty and punched the defenseless man hard in the stomach.

The operator cried out in pain and bent over at the impact. "All right, I'll tell you." He straightened the best he could. He coughed and then began. "I have transmitted all of General Lossow's orders and he is definitely opposing this so-called putsch. All the necessary authorities have been notified and I'm quite sure there is a large number of our population working against you. It would be best for you to surrender."

Ernst Rohm turned a gloomy expression in Hitler's direction and Adolf clenched his fists in frustration. Hitler clearly upset, stalked off to the telephone operator room and slammed the door.

Just before three in the morning a wire message came through and Hitler was the first to see it. He stared at it in disbelief for a moment, all hope draining from his face. It stated in part that the three leaders were repudiating the Nazi putsch and that promises of support extracted at gunpoint were null and void. Hitler grabbed the paper and strode into the next room.

Rohm was still there, sitting with some guards and high ranking SA supporters. The telephone operator sat in a chair, guards sitting beside him with guns resting in their hands.

Hitler waved the paper before the men. "This confirms the operator's testimony. General Lossow has sent a wire and he has repudiated our revolution and is calling it invalid."

"How can he do that when he agreed to it?" one of the men said.

"I will not be discouraged by this. There are still many in this city that support us and will come to our defense. I will not give up hope." With strong conviction shining from his eyes, Hitler left the room.

An hour passed before Hitler re-entered and stood firmly before his faithful followers. "I'm going back to the beer hall to rally my men. I can't stay here another moment. The suspense of the night is agonizing."

The next morning word reached Adolf at the beer hall that Ernst Rohm and his men at the military headquarters were surrounded by the Bavarian army and state police. General Ludendorff and Captain Goring were present when the news came.

Hitler didn't waste time. "We can't allow the Bavarian army and police to stop us now. We're too close to victory. We'll organize a march with our elite troops of the Party, my hundred-man bodyguard and the member's of the SA regiment and we'll converge on the military headquarters. I am quite convinced that the army and police would never shoot on their own people. What do you think, General Ludendorff?"

"I think it's a good idea. It's unthinkable that the Bavarian army would turn against me. They are men I've served with and had charge over. They are sure to be sympathetic to our cause. I say we do it."

"And you, Captain Goring. What do you say?"

"I'm in favor of the march. Let's hope it's as peaceful and uneventful as we anticipate."

"Then prepare your men and have them wear the swastika armband on their left arms, so there's no doubt which men are for our cause. We'll march out at noon."

The march proceeded without incident; some onlookers even joined the ranks as they made their way through Munich's streets toward the military headquarters. At a bridge, leading to the heart of the city, a small force of state police tried to stop them but they were unsuccessful as the large crowd, the forward ones armed with bayonets, pushed their way through.

It wasn't until the two thousand man group turned onto a narrow street that they were stopped by green-uniformed state police. Midst the tussle a shot rang out and a police sergeant fell to the pavement, dead. It wasn't sure who had fired the shot but the police were quick to retaliate and soon shots rang out all over as the police fired on the Nazi supporters. Adolf Hitler's body guard jumped in front of him taking a number of bullets and as he went down he pulled Adolf down with him. Hitler looked at his loyal bodyguard lying still beside him and he was immediately aware that Ulrich Graf was dead.

Soon a few other loyal Nazi members rushed to Hitler's side, protected him and escorted him to a side street and on to where his car was parked, a gift from the Party.

Although Hitler managed to escape, the state authorities caught up with him the following day, where he was staying with trusted friends, the Hanfstaengls', and was immediately transferred to a cell in Landsberg Prison.

His trial began in February 1924, where he was sentenced to five years in Landsberg Prison, with six months off for the six months he'd already spent there.

Deliverer and Peace stood on top of Landsberg Prison as the dejected form of Adolf Hitler was escorted to his cell. The two angels were surrounded by many of their fellow comrades. The grounds and building were teeming with demons and yet none ventured to bother the heavenly detachment. They were too occupied causing fights and strife within the prison and besides, none of them were interested in taking a beating. Deliverer smiled at each angel as they rejoiced in the victory.

"We've accomplished what we came for. Adolf Hitler is contained for now, although I've been told he'll accomplish one of his purposes even during his confinement and he'll eventually ascend from his pit of despair. We have, at best, hindered him for a while. This was our assignment, our second assignment."

They all knew the first assignment, to rouse the saints to prayer, hadn't been as successful as they had hoped.

Deliverer continued, "I and a handful of you, the ones I have already assigned, will stay for a time to ensure details are taken care of. The rest are released to return to Heaven for further instruction and refreshing. We will all meet again soon. Farewell comrades."

With the command given, the majority of the angelic troop unfurled their wings and like bolts of lightening streaked upwards toward the sky. As they departed they left a heavenly glow lingering above the prison. Peace remained behind with a handful of special assignment angels. He would stay with Deliverer till they were both called home again.

Peace finally broke the silence. "Will Adolf Hitler really spend another four and a half years behind bars?"

Deliverer faced his friend. "I regret to say 'no'. There's a demonic army being routed and released as we speak to ensure his early parole. If he spends a year and a half in total, it will be enough."

"Is that our next job and why we need to stay here?"

"Yes." Deliverer then turned his eyes to the sky and began to sing a song of praise to the One who deserved all the glory and honor for the successful mission.

The other angels joined in and soon the guardian angels throughout the city joined in as they sang and rejoiced at the mercy and grace of God Almighty.

Demons slithered away, covering their ears, hiding, until the debilitating praise would end.

The surrounding atmosphere was filled with a heavenly glow as the triumphant song persisted, lifting the angels to a new level of strength, filling them with great joy and surrounding them with Heaven's approval.

CHAPTER 7

Landsberg Prison, 1924

The cell was spacious and sufficiently furnished. An improvement by any standards from Hitler's early years when he suffered as an impoverished painter. Although the place was nothing to brag about, the accommodations gave no reason for complaint. He was even allowed to leave the prison for short periods and return before dinner. He was given permission to receive gifts given by the Nazi party, like a typewriter and all the paper he needed.

Rudolf Hess was in prison with him. Not only was he a faithful supporter but he was proficient at shorthand and notation. So while they licked their wounds, they kept each other company. But the room didn't have the appearance of defeated allies in retreat. Both men looked intent and focused, with a mission in mind. Rudolph busily wrote out Hitler's dictation at the expansive desk located against one wall.

Rudolf wasn't a large man but his firm, square chin and piercing, blue eyes under bushy dark eyebrows made an impressive appearance. He looked ruggedly handsome, his back straight and rigid as he sat patiently waiting for Hitler's words. Above all, his loyalty to the man he considered his leader was unwavering despite the place they both found themselves in.

Adolf sat in an armchair, chin slightly elevated, gazing at a spot on the ceiling, formulating his next thought. His previous depression was indiscernible in the hub of this exciting project. He had never written a book before and he looked liberated as his thoughts materialized with paper and ink.

Rudolf waited patiently for his leader to continue.

A large evil spirit was attached to Hitler's shoulder. It had been there for many years and hardly had to transfer thoughts to his slave anymore. Hitler had readily adopted every train of thought, theology and dictation. He was a ready recipient of Hell's agenda, a pawn in the spirit's hand. The dark entity's red, bulging eyes glared brightly in anticipation, his large talons firmly embedded in Adolf's soul and his black scaly flesh moving and scraping in agitated excitement. He whispered into Hitler's ear, gazed at Rudolf and grinned in wicked delight.

Hitler smiled, mimicking the evil spirit hovering over him, before launching his next thought. "For me this was the time of the greatest spiritual confusion I have ever had to go through. I had ceased from weak-kneed, uncertain waffling on this issue. I had firmly become anti-Semitic. Difficult thoughts once more tore at me, repressive and insidious, but this was the last time. After studying extended periods of human history, I realized that the activity of the Jewish people was wholly focused only on the attainment of this earth. How could the world have been promised to them?" He continued on, dialoguing his theology and belief system for Rudolf to transcribe. "I began to delve deeply into the teachings of Marxism and through this study became completely aware of the answer. Fate itself screamed its decree."

Rudolf wrote furiously to keep up with Adolf's prolonged oracle. He looked up as Hitler slowed and pondered another thought.

"Far be it from the Jew to gain victory over the other races of men. If this should ever happen, their crowning victory would issue in the destruction of the world and all men would vanish from its face." Hitler's face twisted in profound contentment and pleasure. "Therefore I am firmly convinced that by blaming the Jew for the difficulties of this world and fighting against them, I am in direct agreement with the will of God Almighty."

Adolf leaned back in the armchair with his head touching the wall as he studied the ceiling for a moment.

"Is the second chapter complete?"

"Yes it is but I have so many things on my mind, I would prefer continuing immediately with the next so as not to lose my train of thought."

"Yes, that's fine. Let me prepare the next sheet and stretch my hand."

After a few moments, Hitler was speaking fervently of his view on democracy and its evils. "The creation of democracy has showed itself for what it is, a complete disgrace, bringing great weakness to leadership. It allows a leader to place responsibility of decisions on the majority vote, rendering him the ability to hide behind the people he has vowed to lead. This allows him to unburden himself of all accountability at any time, while he begs for their approval on every major decision that is made. It is a repulsive and cowardly form of governing, devoid of all courage and strength of character. A leader of such deplorable character prefers dishonor, unable to rise to a decision with unwavering commitment."

Hitler took a deep breath and then continued on and on about his views and rejection of the present form of government in Austria. An hour later the dictation was done and Adolf stretched and stood. He went to gaze out on the prison yard from the single window in his room. His dream was coming to fruition right before him and he looked pleased. To write down his dreams, vision, plans, political views and ultimate desire for the nation of Germany seemed to energize him.

When Rudolf had time, he'd type up the notes on the typewriter supplied by the faithful supporters of the National Socialist Party.

Rudolf also stood and gathered up the papers he had filled. A frown furrowed his brow. "Fuhrer?"

Adolf turned to face him.

"I have a question. Doesn't it seem a trifle excessive to focus all the world's ills on one nationality of people?" He appeared nervous even as he spoke it.

The dark spirit on Adolf's shoulder hissed and spat immediately, its red eyes filled with rage. Adolf's response was swift and furious. He walked quickly to within a foot of the man, glared at him with deep anger, pointed a finger squarely at his chest and shouted, "If you don't agree with me then get out! I will not have a betrayer of the Nazi party sitting in the same room with me!"

After lowering his finger, he said, "This is the same kind of nonsense the Jewish people are busily promulgating throughout the world, that they are righteous and holy and better than us; the chosen people! The German people are the highest race in the world! We are Aryans and there is no race that even comes close! If the Jewish people have not had the strength to gain back land for themselves in these last thousands of years then just perhaps they don't deserve any land or any right to exist! Do I make myself clear?"

Rudolf was presently squeezed back against the wall, where Adolf had angrily driven him to. Fear oozed from his features as he responded. "Your view is very plain, Adolf, and I do support you. I believe you know what's best for Germany."

"That's right." Adolf straightened, pulled on his shirt collar and visibly reigned in his high strung emotions. "This country is in a mess. Unemployment is sky high, inflation is terrible and the people of Germany are desperately looking for a strong leader to bring reform." He sighed deeply and took a step back.

"Great people always overcome in their struggle against the weak. There are many historical accounts I could point to that bears out this truth." Adolf then gave some examples that supported his ideology.

He continued with, "The animal world also demonstrates this point. Smaller, weaker animals are overcome and destroyed by stronger, more agile animals. It's the way God has created things to be. Is it our fault that we are stronger and more highly developed and that the Jews, for instance, are weaker and unable to defend themselves? No, it is only a matter of fate and I am only a player in this grand game of life." Hitler took a seat in his armchair, folded his hands in his lap and gazed at his friend across the room.

Rudolf stood stiffly, nervous admiration shining from his eyes. "It's about time for dinner. I'll type these out this evening and get them back to you tomorrow."

"Yes, that's good. We'll continue with dictation tomorrow." Adolf looked suddenly tired, the afternoon's work and his outburst of anger having depleted him of all energy.

Across the road from Landsberg Prison, Deliverer and Peace stood with four special assignment angels, Hesi, Reo, Clement and Tario. The four messenger angels had recently arrived and joined the two at their post beside a large oak tree, its spreading branches and large trunk, suitable for camouflage. With the abundance of pine trees crowded around the oak, it made concealment easy.

Reo was the first to step forward. "Deliverer, Peace, I successfully entered the prison warden's office and was able to obtain the information necessary.

"And, what was his assessment?" asked Deliverer.

"His report to the Bavarian Ministry of Justice is very favorable. In it he states that Adolf Hitler has become a much quieter, more mature individual and that his pension toward rebellion against the government has been quelled."

Deliverer looked stern but not surprised. "It's what I expected. Hitler has an uncanny way to mold and twist people to think positively of him. His God-given gift of speech and conviction is being twisted by Hell to accomplish its own agenda and it has turned him into a controlling, manipulating force. It sounds like Adolf is headed for an early parole. Thank you, Reo, for your report."

Reo nodded. Deliverer turned toward two of the other angels.

"Clement, Tario, what did you discover as you made your tour of the saints in Germany?"

Clement stepped forward first. "It is as we suspected. The saints have once again fallen asleep on their watch. They are no longer praying as intensely and their requests are focused on their own needs and concerns. They no longer sense the approaching danger."

Tario spoke next. "Not only does my report match Clements' but I found the saints hearts becoming hard and calloused through the difficult situations they're going through. The testing they are experiencing, the cares of life and the worries of this age, is causing their love to grow cold. Their concern is only for their own welfare and for their relatives well being."

"Thank you Clement and Tario. This is also as I suspected. Many saints were concerned with the aggressive views of Adolf Hitler but now that he's in prison, they believe the danger has passed and that the country has forsaken the Nazi Party as a part of history. Their personal troubles have caused the saints to fall asleep and unless God Almighty commands another awakening, there is little we as heavenly messengers can do."

Tario said, "I also sense that the hardening of the saints will cause them to eventually support Adolf Hitler wholeheartedly." He gazed at Deliverer. "Am I correct?"

"Yes," he said resolutely.

Shock was written on the other angels' faces. Peace appeared stricken at the news.

"God's people, the saints in Germany, supporting an enemy of God's chosen people?" asked Reo.

Deliverer turned a serious gaze in his direction. "It's hard to believe and yet it has happened before. Many people of this world hate God's people, the apple of His eye, and are determined to extinguish them."

"This will never happen!" Clement looked suddenly fierce and protective.

Deliverer said, "Always remember, my fellow comrades, that God Almighty always leaves a remnant."

"Is that all that will remain?" said Reo.

"We don't know everything yet. All we are certain of is Adolf Hitler's supposed intentions and hatred toward them. The rest God will reveal as time progresses."

"May I speak?" Hesi had held back but his face shone with a radiant glow.

"Yes, please do." Deliverer smiled at the smallest of the special assignment angels.

"I was sent to the saints who supposedly might still be awake and watching. I can assure you all that there is a remnant within this country that truly are awake and that still hear and see in the spirit what's taking place. Holy Spirit is still able to warn them, burden them and move them to intercede for the coming events."

"But is it enough to stop what has already started?" Peace asked.

"I don't believe it's enough to stop what we all feel is building and growing all around us." Hesi suddenly looked despondent. "Although if others were to join them and their numbers increased, they could certainly use the authority given them by God to hold back the force of evil. I believe it's possible to rouse the saints, now asleep, back into action. It would take more angelic messengers, of course, but I believe it's possible." His eyes shone with hope.

Deliverer said, "I'm sorry, Hesi. No more angelic messengers are scheduled to be sent. I have heard no new directions from Heaven. Each saint already has their allotted four guardian angels and if they are not able to influence their charges to pray then no more help will be sent. I may be missing something but I'm quite sure things will play out from here."

Peace's eyes lifted to the heavens, his longing to depart strong and poignant.

CHAPTER 8

Berlin, Germany, 1928

The ornately ostentatious church stood in stark contrast to the more plainly decorated buildings surrounding it, with the high belfry and steeple rising majestically into the clear blue sky, the bell chiming out a familiar hymn, calling the faithful to worship. The stained glass windows sparkled in the sunlight, the bright colors dazzling the eye. The stone building spoke permanence, with its heavy structure and huge, supporting columns out front and yet the intricate carved moldings, surrounding the tops of each, gave it an elegant flavor. The brass bell in the tower could be seen for blocks and the sound of its melodious ring could be heard for miles. The land around the church was flat and combined with the low lying houses, the sound of the bell's tune spread across the surrounding area superbly.

Helmuth and Unna Schluter took a seat on one of the long, wooden benches with their two daughters, Beata and Ilse. Beata was eight years old and she recognized many throughout the sanctuary. Their neighbors, Egbert and Gretchen Adler, sat a few rows up. Mrs. Ernestine Grossman, a widow and midwife, and her daughter, Frederika, sat close to the front. Ernestine Grossman's grown children were scattered throughout the sanctuary with their spouses and children. The house of worship was filled with many familiar faces, neighbors, friends, family members and acquaintances. The local baker and his wife, Manfred and Agathe Schwanz, sat across the isle with their five children seated beside them.

In front of them sat Roth and Alda Puttkam. He was the local shoemaker, although his shoes weren't as good in quality as a well known Jewish shoemaker in another part of the city. That's what Beata's mother always told her. Roth Puttkam still made a good living, with many Germans not willing to support a Jewish business owner. Roth had two sons. One, Andreas, was willing to learn his fathers business and who would most likely take over in time. The other son, Lamar, had started his own business as a fine carpenter, making magnificent wood furnishings, and was doing quite well, drawing the attention and interest of the more well to do in the area. Beata had heard her father speak of it.

Many other local business owners filled the pews but toward the back were the many who struggled to make ends meet. They worked in factories and warehouses, earning a minimal wage to feed and support their families and many were unemployed. Beata had heard her parents talk of the crises from time to time and their concern for these families.

The congregation hushed as the bishop stood and held his hands high to signal silence. He spoke a recitation, the congregation following obediently, and then he prayed a written prayer from his prayer book and took a seat.

Outside, unseen by any human but clearly visible in the spirit, a light blazed through the sky, then another, and then four others as they landed before the church and made their way through the doors to stand behind the back pew.

Beata watched as the usual song leader stood and walked to the podium to direct the singing. After a few songs, the song leader took his seat and the bishop stood once more, his majestic, flowing robes swishing around him as he walked toward the podium. Bishop Bastian Haff spoke a blessing over the audience, sprinkled some holy water out toward the congregation and then cleared his throat.

"God is our Father, our Savior and our Lord. We worship Him this day in all reverence and fear. My message today focuses on our reverence, our worship and our honoring Him in all things. It is our duty as His children to revere Him, to honor Him with our daily lives."

Bishop Bastian Haff's voice droned on and on in a monotone hum. It was difficult even for the most devout follower to stay awake and alert through the boring, non-expressive oration. Unna elbowed Helmuth, as he began to nod off beside her. He sat up straight, confused for a moment and then shook his head to wake up more fully. It wasn't long before his head was bobbing back and forth, his eyes heavy until another sharp jab brought him back to present.

Eight-year-old Beata glanced at her father and grinned at the comical display. She couldn't help but yawn through the message too so she didn't blame her father.

The same scene was played over and over again throughout the church pews. Men and women both struggled to focus on the dull sermon as the Bishop spoke, his monotone voice soothing like a mother's lullaby. People yawned excessively and children started to fuss and grow impatient. It was not until the Bishop began to speak of a certain subject that the congregation began to take notice and awake from their induced slumber-like state.

Demons jumped into action, poking, prodding people to listen as the large demon beside the bishop dictated the last part of his sermon. Like an obedient slave, he repeated dutifully every word that entered his ear.

He pounded the podium for emphasis. "God sees our distress and our dismay. Our country is fraught with problems. We are a people embarrassed, humiliated, reprimanded by another country almost beyond repair. It's a shameful end for normally such a proud, resilient people. The nation of Germany deserves better than this. And who is to blame for our bestial state? Is it not the same ones to blame for our precious Lord Jesus' death? I say, yes it is."

Beata stared at the bishop in shock but listened as he continued.

The bishop cleared his throat. "The Jewish people have been nothing but trouble since that time on. They not only crucified their own

Messiah but they are the cause of all the evil and filth in this world. It is to their blame which I lay the whole demise and humiliation of this great country of ours. I advise each one of you to read Adolf Hitler's book entitled, Mien Kampf. In it, he describes his great struggle and I highly recommend it. Within its pages, Adolf outlines his views on the Jews. It is a thought provoking book and gives one cause to stop and think. As Adolf suggests, I encourage you to buy only from Germans and leave the evil Jews to fend for themselves. Do not support them and do not encourage their evil work. This is one way we can honor our Heavenly Father by fighting against the Jew. I charge you one and I charge you all, resist the Jew. Now let us end in prayer."

Beata glanced over at her parents. Helmuth and Unna Schluter's eyes were glued on the Bishop's bowed head as he led the congregation in the usual blessing. They turned to gaze at each other in shock but quickly diverted their eyes downward as they joined the rest in the benediction. Beata couldn't even pretend to pray, not after that. Her stomach turned and she felt like she just might throw up.

Deliverer and Peace stood behind the back pew. They could see the despicable demon hovering around the Bishop during his whole speech. The two angels were well acquainted with his kind. It was a spirit of deception and it danced around the Bishop, grabbing his sleeve at times and whispering excitedly into his ear. Everywhere the Bishop walked, the demon shadowed him like a faithful dog. The Bishop was clueless to the demon's presence but readily repeated everything the spirit spoke. The man of cloth was clearly accepting the counterfeit for the truth.

Deliverer shook his head sadly. He then pointed to where the Schluters' sat. "Do you see their guardian angels? They've shielded them and protected them from the lies. They still see and hear." He pointed to others who also were surrounded by guardians.

The others nodded in understanding. They knew then that the Schluters' and the others surrounded by angels were true children of the Most High.

Deliverer turned suddenly and waved for Peace and the four special assignment angels to follow him. They slipped through the front doors of the church and congregated on the sidewalk. Deliverer faced them with a serious expression.

Hesi was the first to speak. "The service was quite unusual. There weren't the normal amount of angels in the service that are usually present for the amount of people attending."

Reo blurted out, "Yes, and the guardian angels that were present didn't position themselves as they usually do during the song worship or the so called 'preaching'." He shook his head in disgust.

During church services angels would open their wings, float high above the heads of the parishioners, close to the front, above the altar and pulpit, in a circular position and worship the One who sat on the throne. The Lamb was worshiped vigorously and openly by all angels in a service which honored and glorified God and the Lord Jesus Christ.

Peace confirmed it by saying, "There was little done in the service which honored Father God. I'm sure you noticed that the guardians that did attend the service stood in a wounded position. Their strength is being sapped and their ability to move and deliver has been compromised. There was little sense of peace in the service. It's not a good sign."

Deliverer said, "The angels, which surrounded the Schluter family, were the only ones who were not injured."

Clement spoke next. "Did you see some of the guardian angels leave just before the bishop stood to speak?"

Tario responded, "I saw it and I don't blame them. They would have definitely been weakened even further by his speech."

Tario and the others looked across the street, where many of the guardians were gathered holding their own church service as they sang and worshiped. They were being strengthened during the process.

Deliverer pointed to them. "That home belongs to one of the remnant and the angels are welcome there. There is freedom on that land to worship as they desire."

The other angels nodded in understanding.

"Look at that foul creature on the corner." Tario pointed to a demonic being, hanging on to his position of authority on the roof of the church, but clearly affected by the debilitating praise pouring forth from the angelic group so near his territory.

Peace said, "If only there was a way to remove that foul spirit permanently. It is intolerable to see a demonic spirit with authority over a church. A church should be a place of great peace and restoration."

Deliverer sighed and then finally addressed the special assignment group. "This church is only a representation of countless number of churches throughout Germany, Austria, Poland, Czechoslovakia, Russia and many other European countries that preach the exact same message of hatred toward God's chosen people. The poison of this message is growing, like a venomous seed in fertile ground and soon it will produce a harvest of such disproportionate hatred and violence that it will be hard to believe or contain. There is a growing false belief that the Jewish people are the cause of all the wars that have ever been fought and that they are the source of all the heartache, discomfort and economic despair of people everywhere. It is an evil lie from the pit of Hell and yet these," Deliverer waved his hand toward the church followers now exiting the building, "for the most part, believe the lie and will follow it through to its conclusion."

Hesi's face contorted in disbelief. "Do you really mean that Christians will willingly join in with the destruction of the Jewish people?"

Deliverer looked resolute and strong. "It is my understanding that the answer is 'yes'. For some it will be through pure ignorance. They will have no idea what is really taking place. It has happened numerous times throughout history and served Satan well in alienating Christians from the Jewish people."

Reo said, "But earlier you said there would be a remnant. Did you mean that to be true for the Christians as well?"

"Yes Reo, there will be those Christians who will not buy into the ruse. They know God's word better than some and they will know the truth. There are those who love God enough to obey Him above all others. There is always a remnant." Deliverer nodded to his comrades and looked at them one by one. "Peace will be, within a few short years, taken from the earth." He looked at the four angels before him, Hesi,

Reo, Clement and Tario. "Your time of departure is close. But before you leave, there are a few things that still need to be accomplished."

Peace said, "And we stay?"

"Yes. We still have work to do."

CHAPTER 9

Crimean Steppe, Russia, November, 1929

Three-year-old Esther smiled at her baby doll. She laid it down on the home made blanket her mother had made for the toy and wrapped it the best she could. It didn't look right, part of the blanket hung down funny in one corner. Oh well, she didn't know how to fix that.

Four guardian angels, Goodness, Faith, Pieter and Marinus, surrounded her, having been there since her conception. They never strayed far from her side. The largest one, Goodness, was her main guardian and he smiled at her as she played in her childish way.

Esther looked up at her mother, Frieda Brenner, who sat in her rocking chair beside the wood burning stove with a basket of wool on the floor and her knitting needles clicking a steady beat as she finished off the edge of some wool socks. Her mother finally looked down at her and smiled. Esther grinned back and went back to her doll play.

Her eight-year-old brother, Herman, was sitting at the kitchen table, his school books spread wide. Esther didn't know what he was working on but it looked hard. He called it mathematics. Even the word was hard to say. She didn't even try. An exasperated sigh escaped his lips and she turned to look at him.

"I don't know why I have to go to school. I'd much rather stay home and help Dad around here. There's so much to do and school is a complete waste of my time. Can't I stay home and skip school?"

"Absolutely not!"

Esther looked between the two and listened to the interesting conversation.

"But school is dumb and boring!" Herman twirled his pencil around and around as he spoke with great animation and overemphasized each word.

"School is good for you. It will teach you how to read and write and how to figure out math."

"Did you go to school?"

"I took a few years of school."

Esther wondered why Herman was talking so loud. It was hard to take care of her baby doll with him distracting her.

"How many?" Herman looked completely interested in the coming answer. It didn't look like he wanted to do whatever he was doing there by the table.

"It's not important. I took a few years, just enough to teach me a few things."

"I've had a few years of school too. I've learned everything there is to know already and anyway, who wants to learn Russian. We're Dutch. Why can't we learn Dutch or German instead? Please... can I quit?"

"No Herman, now get back to your studies."

"I'll ask Dad when he gets back. He'll probably let me quit. He works too hard and he needs my help."

Something about what Herman said wasn't right because Esther noticed her mother stand in a hurry. Her doll was forgotten in her lap as she watched what would happen.

Mother set her knitting down in determination, walked over to Herman and pulled his ear hard, causing him to yelp in pain. Esther felt sorry for him.

"Don't you try to work behind my back when I've already told you that you can't quit school! You show the proper respect to your mother, boy!" Frieda finally let go. Herman's ear shone bright red.

"That hurt really bad!" Herman rubbed his ear and looked quite deflated.

"That'll remind you about listening to your mother the first time."

Esther watched her mother wipe her hands on her apron, something she always did when she was upset. Esther felt bad for Herman. She placed her hands over her ears and wondered how it would feel to have such a very red ear.

"I fully understand how you feel about learning Russian but that's how our school system is now. When I went to school we had our own teachers and we could pray, read the Bible in school and speak German all we wanted."

Herman sighed and said, "You're going to tell it again, aren't you?"

Mother didn't answer his question but kept talking. "All the Dutch teachers were exiled when the red army, the communists, came into power and they placed Russian teachers in our schools. The government wants us to learn the language and become more like the country we belong too. I know it's difficult for all the children from our Mennonite villages to learn their Russian but you know it quite well, Herman, and you are doing wonderful in school. There's no reason for you to quit now. You're a smart boy and both your Father and I want you to continue."

A cry came from the next room and Frieda hurried off to retrieve the youngest of the Brenner children. Herman's face showed relief at escaping a certain and continued long lecture. Esther felt relief for him and soon turned her attention back to her doll.

Frieda soon returned with one-year-old Anna in her arms and set her down beside Esther.

Anna speedily grabbed Esther's doll and began to crawl away.

How dare she! Esther cried out in outrage, started after her sister and was about to knock her over and take back her prized toy when her mother intervened.

"Now, now Anna, you have your own toys." Frieda picked up Anna once more, tore the doll from her hands and handed it back to Esther.

Esther was glad. Anna cried in protest, but Mother walked resolutely over to a small wooden box in the corner, containing a few simple, home-made toys and found the doll she'd made for her youngest. She set Anna down beside the box, a few feet away from Esther and handed her the doll. Anna seemed satisfied and Esther felt relieved.

Frieda mentioned something about starting supper and disappeared into the kitchen.

A few minutes later, the front door opened and Esther's father, Baldur Brenner, walked through, his brown hair tousled and disheveled as he pulled off his hat and set it on the hook beside the door. Esther stood and walked toward him. She held out her doll for him to see. He smiled and patted her head. He placed his jacket on the same hook and sauntered into the kitchen. He took his place at the table and Herman's grouchy face greeted him from the other end. Esther followed her father and crawled into a chair close to him, dragging her doll to the table to face her.

"How's your homework coming?"

Herman looked at his mother, who gave him a warning look.

Baldur looked from one to the other in confusion. "So, what's going on here?"

"My homework is boring, but I have to do it." He looked at Father dejectedly.

"That's right, Herman. Homework is important. How else will you ever learn to read and write?"

"Do you know how to read and write, Dad?"

"I know how to read a little. But I want more for you. I want you to know how to get along in this world well and that means learning and becoming literate. It's good for you even though you don't like it. You'll thank us someday, son."

"I don't know about that." He held his pencil in one hand and rested his cheek on his open palm, his elbow resting on the table. His enthusiasm was nonexistent.

Esther felt even sorrier for him.

Frieda walked over to the table, her potatoes peeled and set over the stove to heat. "Herman here thinks its time for him to quit school and start working."

Baldur stared at Herman with an amused expression. "How old are you?"

"You don't know how old I am?" Herman looked confused.

"I know, but I want you to tell me. How old are you?"

"I'm eight."

"And how many years have you gone to school?"

"Two."

"And you think that's enough to learn everything?"

"Yes."

Baldur passed a newspaper across the table towards his son. "Then tell me what this article says."

Herman grabbed the paper and stared numbly at it. He fidgeted slightly, his eyes squinted and his mouth twisted in consternation. Esther watched him carefully, wondering what he was doing.

"Well, what does it say, son? Your mother and I are waiting."

Herman finally looked up. "I know the first word."

"And, what is it?"

"It says 'The'."

"And you think you're ready to quit school?"

Herman only shrugged his shoulders in surrender.

"Herman, one day I want you to be able to read this paper so well that you can tell me what it says. I can read only parts of it and I learn from what I hear others say, but I want more for you. I want you to be my ability to read and write."

Herman slouched down in his chair, finally, fully comprehending his destiny and immediate future and realizing that helping his father around the farm, on a constant and consistent basis, was not one of his close future pursuits.

Esther thought he looked awfully unhappy and she felt sorry for him again.

Mother sat down beside Father. "So why did you bring this paper home, Baldur? You hardly ever bring newspapers home."

He reached for the paper Herman had pushed to the center of the table and pointed to the front article. "This explains why the Russian government has decreased our food stamps. Last month there was a U.S. stock market crash and it's affecting many countries around the world. I overheard the men yesterday in Gnadenfeld say that many wealthy people have committed suicide in the United States over their loss of money. Even people in China and throughout Europe are feeling the fallout and people are losing their hope in life and taking their lives. Some people have lost everything they owned. Many people are feeling very desperate." He shook his head in disbelief. "They must be extremely hopeless to kill themselves. I can't imagine that kind of despair."

"Then it's good we don't own much. We don't have much to lose so there's not much to be sad about. But even so, we still have much to live for. We have three beautiful children and we still have food to eat."

"But, this article says that things will get much worse. There is shortage starting everywhere, loss of jobs and the experts are predicting great inflation."

"Inflation? What's that?" Herman piped up.

It sounded like another big word to Esther. The conversation was getting boring. She lifted her doll, causing the blanket to fall away and she patted her dolls cheek.

"That means our money will not buy as much as it has till now. Everything will cost more."

"But we have a farm, a small farm, and it will surely be enough to get us through, won't it?" Frieda's face was positive despite the gloomy news.

"God has always taken care of us before. I don't see why He wouldn't now."

"Yes, we will just trust God." Frieda turned guilty eyes to her husband. "Some meat with our meals would be a wonderful bonus though. I cooked our last meat last night. We have only potatoes and peas tonight. And bread of course."

"We will trust in God. Potatoes and peas will have to do until God blesses us with more. We still have some extra money and maybe I could buy some chickens from the Ukrainian village tomorrow."

"Don't spend our little money on food we could do without, Baldur."

Herman's eyes were glued on his parents, his homework forgotten as he soaked in the information.

Esther thought she should maybe listen again as she noticed the increased interest on Herman's face.

"We have chickens, a pig and a cow. Couldn't we kill one of them for meat?"

Baldur smiled at his young son. "If we kill a chicken, we will have fewer eggs and we need all the eggs our chickens produce. If we kill the cow, we won't have milk and if we kill the young pig now, we'll have meat for a week maybe and then we'll go almost a year without because I don't have enough money to buy another piglet. No, we'll go without now for a time and then when the pig is plump and round in early spring, we'll slaughter it." Baldur looked at his wife. "We have lots of potatoes and lots of canned vegetables. That will last us till the pig is fattened."

"Some meat sure would be good," Herman grumbled as he gazed down at his math homework.

Baldur said, "Herman, you need to be thankful that you don't remember the famine years. It hasn't been that long ago that many, many people died in the Mennonite villages because of great famine. It was after the civil war and there was hardly any food anywhere and if our Mennonite brethren from Canada hadn't intervened and sent help, we would have all died. It was an awful, awful time."

Herman gazed at his father in wonder. "Why wasn't there any food?"

"War does that to an area. Soldiers come in, live with you, eat your food and the fighting keeps farmers from working their fields. Bullets are whizzing back and forth and there's no way farmers would risk a bullet to their heads while planting their fields. So no fields grow, there's no wheat in the fall and no crops to harvest. Whatever garden plants are planted are stolen by roving criminal bands or eaten by the armies that wander through. In the end there's little left for the village people to eat."

Herman's eyes grew wide as he listened intently. "That's awful, Father!"

Esther thought it must be awful because of how everyone was looking.

"Yes, it was awful. But now, we have food and we can feed our children. This is a great blessing, son. Don't ever forget it."

Herman only nodded in reply, Esther's eyes peeled on him, her hero.

Germany, 1930

It was summer and the situation was dire for the entire country. More than three million people were unemployed; beggars began to appear on numerous street corners and the dissatisfaction with the current government was increasing. Germany's president, Paul von Hindenburg, seemed incapable of turning things around. The man who had the true power in Germany, Chancellor Heinrich Bruning, with his conservative economic policy, also could not stop the galloping inflation and unemployment.

As the elections approached for September, Hitler spent tiring hours delivering speeches throughout Germany, drawing huge crowds of people, who were awed at his promises and his charismatic style. When the election results finally came in, the Nazi Party had their largest gains ever, 18.3 percent of the total vote compared to the 2.6 percent they'd gained in the 1928 election.

Hitler was ecstatic and celebrated his great increase in votes with his trusted friends and supporters at a beer hall in Munich. Many men gathered around him, laughing and congratulating him, the victory as much theirs as it was Hitler's. Man after man came up to him, shook his hand, smiled in great excitement and offered their praise and congratulations. Hitler appeared in his element, successful, applauded and much pleased at the day's outcome.

Not only was the election a success but his book, *Mein Kampf,* sold fabulously that year and brought in a large amount in royalties. The extra funds allowed him to live well and also to contribute to the Party's further advancement by establishing a Nazi Party headquarters in Munich. It opened in January 1931.

CHAPTER 10

Poland, 1931

Anka Levin picked the last of the peas from her small garden behind their spacious home and stood to stretch her tired back. She placed a hand on her lower back and rubbed the achy spot. Her stomach protruded well beyond her normal frame, giving away her progressing pregnancy. Her face was flushed with the summer heat while the sun beat down relentlessly from a clear blue sky.

Standing still, four buckets of peas standing at her feet, she clutched her back with one hand as she watched her two boys run back and forth through the yard. They were playing tag or some such sport. She smiled at the sight and chuckled as the youngest son tumbled to the grass and the other tripped over him, sending him sailing head over heels to the other side. Both boys stayed on the grass, looked at each other with elbows resting on the lawn and began to laugh uncontrollably. They rolled back and forth over the green turf, giggles filling the air with sweet childlike abandon.

Anka, after a contented sigh, bent down to grab hold of two of the buckets and slowly made her way toward the house. The bread she'd worked on earlier had risen sufficiently. She slipped it into the oven to bake, shelled a few peas, enough for a soup and stared with dinner.

Later in the afternoon Aaron, Anka's husband, came home and walked into the kitchen. He stopped in the doorway, looked around and visibly inhaled.

"It smells wonderful in here. You've worked hard today." Aaron came toward her then. "You shouldn't work so hard this late in your pregnancy." He wrapped his arms around her round frame and kissed her meaningfully. "I love your cooking, I'm not complaining, but I don't want you to overdo it."

"I do feel tired."

"You picked the peas fresh today?" Aaron turned to the piles of unshelled peas still lying in the sink.

"Yes."

Aaron looked deeply into Anka's eyes. "No wonder you look so tired."

"I don't look that bad, do I?"

"You look beautiful, like always, but you do look tired." He took her by the hand and led her to the table. "Here, turn around."

"What are you doing?" Anka giggled at the attention while he undid her apron and placed it on the table. He turned her around and made her sit.

"I'll serve the supper while you rest." Aaron smiled sweetly as he went to get bowls, plates and cutlery.

Anka felt a rush of gratitude as she allowed Aaron to take over.

He set the table quickly, dished the hearty soup into a large serving bowl and cut the bread. "Where are the boys? I haven't seen them."

"They've been playing outside the whole day. They love being in the yard in such wonderful weather."

"I'll go get them." Aaron left and soon returned with Amos and Matis, their faces, hands and clothes well showing the play of the day. They were covered in mud, grass stains and who knows what other kind of thing. They even had grass sticking from their hair, but through all the grime, their smiles were priceless.

"Oh my, boys! You'd better go wash up." Anka grinned as she watched the two best buddies wander off to the bathroom.

Aaron glanced at her. "They sure are a pair those two."

"They're inseparable."

"I'm glad we had them only two years apart. They are the best of friends."

Anka rubbed her tummy. "This one will be more of a loner."

"That depends if we have more."

"Oh Aaron, I can't keep up now, what would I do with more."

Aaron only smiled.

After supper Amos, six years old, and Matis, four years, ran off to play and their loud sound effects to their cars and trucks could be heard plainly in the kitchen. Aaron cleared the table, washed the dishes and then brought two bowls of unshelled peas, and a garbage container to the table. As the two of them worked together to get the shelling done the silence stretched between them like a comfortable wool blanket, thankful to be together and no words needed to bolster their love. After a length of time Aaron glanced at her, a smile tickling his mouth.

"Have you thought further about a name?"

"Yes."

"And…"

"Well, if it's a girl…" Anka stopped and looked at Aaron uncertainly and then continued, "I think I'd like to name her Lola."

"That's Polish."

"I know. Do you mind?"

"No, I'm okay with that, but why Lola? I mean, is there a special reason?"

Anka's heart twisted with longing and sorrow. "My best friend growing up, the one I did everything with, her name was Lila. I'd like to name my daughter as a reminder of my very dear friend."

Aaron was silent for a moment. "Lila has never come to see you, has she?"

"No."

"Wouldn't naming our daughter after her only remind you of all you've lost?"

"Maybe, but I'm thinking that a daughter named for my once best friend would be a way of replacing what I once held so dear. It would remove the huge loss I've felt for so many years. I've been blessed greatly since leaving my childhood home. I mean, look at our precious boys and I have the most wonderful, loving husband." She smiled then and continued. "But I can't deny that the hurt inflicted by the people I loved and cherished cut me deeply and I've never recovered. Perhaps by naming our daughter Lola, it would heal my heart." She gave him an uncertain look.

Anka was Polish and had married a Jewish man, something not well accepted to most Poles or Jews for that matter. Her father had been livid over her decision and had promptly disowned her. She'd been back once to visit, only months after their marriage, to try to convince her father of Aaron's love for her and his ability to care for her, financially and in every other way.

Jaromil Trafas, her father, had faced her with anger and with unmoving resolve in his decision to hate Aaron. He had told her in no uncertain terms that she had embarrassed and shamed him in marrying a pig Jew and that he would never forgive her. She had never gone back to see her parents since. Her mother was heartbroken at the exchange and begged for Jaromil's understanding but he hadn't budged.

"All right, that's decided then. I actually like the name Lola. It's nice for a Polish name." He smiled in encouragement and Anka finally relaxed and turned her eyes back to the peas in front of her.

"I have a name for a boy if we have a third son."

Anka gave Aaron a curious gaze. "A Jewish name, I'm sure."

"Well those are the names I'm accustomed to but I have another suggestion."

"And…"

"I was thinking of the name Jacek."

"It's almost like my brother's name, Jarek."

"Exactly."

Anka grew lost in thought as her eyes stared off into space, looking at nothing in particular. Deep sorrow and pain once more shot through her but she also felt a growing pleasure. She slowly turned her eyes to her husband and smiled. "I like it. It's a perfect name for a third son."

There was a tentative knock at the door. Anka set the baby down on the couch, removed her bonnet and turned toward the door. She and Aaron and their children had just come home from the Sabbath service at the synagogue. She couldn't fathom who would be at their door. There had been no one out on the street except for other members from the synagogue.

She opened the door and stopped in shock.

"Hello, Anka."

Anka finally found her tongue. "Mother! What are you doing here?"

"I…I came to see you." She looked extremely nervous. She turned back and checked the street before facing Anka once more. "Please, may I come in?"

Anka finally remembered her manners and stepped aside. "Yes, of course." She closed the door after her mother.

"How did you get here? It's a long walk."

"I took my bicycle. I left it by the fence."

"Oh." Anka didn't know what else to say. She still felt shock over her mother's presence in her home. Ewa Trafas had never undertaken to come for a visit before.

Ewa was a fine looking woman for someone in her fifties. Her hair was mostly the auburn color she had always had with only a few streaks of grey showing here and there. Her frame wasn't slim but she kept herself well dressed in the style of the day. Her hat was practical for riding and her shoes were a sturdy brown walking pair.

Anka couldn't restrain the joy that suddenly hit her. She opened her arms and her mother embraced her with tears in her eyes.

"Oh, my baby. I couldn't stay away any longer. How I've longed for this day."

Anka's heart soaked in the words, like an ointment to her wounded soul.

"Oh Mother, Mother, I've also dreamed of you coming!"

"I've missed you so much, my dear Anka." Tears flowed down Ewa Trafas's cheeks as she kissed Anka's face over and over again.

Aaron and the boys stood to the side and watched the unusual display. They had taken off their jackets and hung them on the hook. Their shoes stood at the front door. Usually the boys raced off as soon as they entered the house, more interested in play than adult conversation.

But now they stood stock still, in shock that their mother was embracing a total stranger.

Ewa and Anka finally released each other and Ewa began to take note of her grandchildren, children she'd never met. She first looked at the young boys standing still by Aaron's side.

"What are your names, boys?" She bent down to their level.

Amos, the oldest one and the most outspoken, spoke for both of them. "I'm Amos and I'm six, and this is Matis, and he's four. He's shy so I usually do all the talking. He's very smart though and he's my best friend." Matis stood slightly behind Amos, very willingly allowing his older brother to speak for him.

"It's very nice to meet you both." Ewa looked at Anka. "You have very handsome boys."

"Thank you." Anka's face glowed as if she'd received the greatest gift of all, praise and adoration from her mother, something she'd longed for and desired for so long.

"And who are you?" Amos asked Ewa.

"My name is Mrs. Trafas." Ewa looked at Anka, unsure of how much to tell the boys.

Anka stepped forward and addressed her sons. "This lady is my mother and your grandmother."

"No," said Amos, shaking his head. "We already have a grandmother and her name is Init Levin. She's our grandmother." He crossed his arms in certainty.

Anka tried again. "That's true, Amos. Init Levin is your father's mother and she is your grandmother." Anka pointed to Ewa Trafas. "This is my mother and she is also your grandmother."

"Then how come we've never seen you before? Where have you been?" Amos looked confused.

Ewa laughed. "I've been gone for too long but now I'd like you to get to know me and I'd like to get to know you."

"Does that mean you'll come back again?" Anka asked hopefully.

"I'd like that. All I can do is try."

"Dad doesn't know you're here?"

Ewa looked down to the floor. "No."

Anka's face fell at the news but she shrugged it off quickly, walked to the couch and handed her new bundle into her mother's arms. "Mother, this is our newest addition."

Ewa reached for the baby and held tightly, folding back the pink blanket covering the child's face. "Oh my, she's beautiful!"

"Yes, she is and she's a wonderful and easy baby too." Anka felt delighted at the opportunity to share her joy with her mother.

"What did you name her?"

"Lola."

"It's a beautiful name for a beautiful girl." Ewa gazed at the little face in peaceful sleep.

"Thank you."

Anka then proceeded to prepare lunch. The meal was filled with talk and reminiscing, Anka and Ewa gazed at each other and smiled often; held hands frequently and Anka wishing for the day to never end. The boys were thrilled to have another grandmother and the attention that came with it. Ewa Trafas showered the boys with home made candies and chocolate, and held Amos on her lap while he told her stories. Matis liked Ewa's attention but stood a safe distance away, not trusting the strange lady quite yet.

"Have you seen Jarek lately?" asked Anka.

"No. I haven't seen him since Christmas. He moved to Slonim with his family in January."

"He's married?"

"Yes, he's married and has two children. He got a job in Slonim with the railroad." Ewa's face looked suddenly much older and so sad.

"I'm sorry, Mother."

"I still have you close by." Ewa smiled brightly in spite of her losses.

"Yes that's right." Anka also smiled, hoping that things would be different now. "And Father, how's he doing?"

"He's doing well. His heart has been bothering him though. He's had tests done but they can't find exactly what's wrong. He gets these pains but then they go away again."

Anka only nodded. "Does he ever speak of me?"

"He never speaks of you in good terms." She gazed at her daughter sadly. "I'm sorry."

"It's alright." Anka tried to be brave but the knowledge still cut like a knife.

Ewa suddenly stood as she glanced at the clock. "Oh dear, I've stayed much too long. Jaromil will wonder where I've stayed. It takes me over an hour to get here. Can you imagine that? I have to hurry now." Ewa quickly kissed the boys, the baby and then clung desperately to her daughter, kissing her cheek over and over again. Anka hung on gratefully. Ewa finally let go and turned toward Aaron, who had been silent most of the afternoon.

"You have treated my daughter well, Aaron. Thank you for all you've done for her."

"You're welcome, Mrs. Trafas. It was nice finally meeting you."

"Thank you both for your hospitality. I'll come again. I promise." With that Ewa hurried out the door and with one more wave she cycled down the street and out of view.

Anka watched her mother till she disappeared. How she longed for things to be different. If only they lived in a country where Jews were accepted and respected. She exhaled deeply. "But, Poland is home," she said to no one but herself. She turned and walked into her house.

CHAPTER 11

Germany 1932

Adolf Hitler looked at the faces of his close supporters sitting around the large restaurant table and nodded in satisfaction.

"Well, we're getting closer all the time. I am very encouraged by our progress this last year. Our message is spreading and the German people are recognizing our potential benefit to our great country. The election in March proved a huge jump in popularity for our Party. Although President Hindenburg won the vote, he did not achieve the necessary majority. A second election was imminent and undeniable. Our campaigning, designed by Joseph Goebbels, was rigorous and it was fantastically successful."

The men gathered were aware of this information but hearing it again brought looks of satisfaction all around.

"Airplanes showered leaflets on numerous towns and villages, fifty thousand propaganda disks were mailed to those owning record players and I delivered speeches in all the major cities in Germany. Goebbels and I worked tirelessly to secure the votes we needed. And then, July thirty-first, the second election results came in."

The group gathered shouted at the known outcome and cheered their leader heartily. Hitler appeared in his element at the raucous applause and approval.

"After the second election we, the Nazi Party, now hold 37.4 percent of the seats, which works out to 230 seats, more than any other party holds at present. We have more than a third of the total vote. I feel greatly encouraged and emboldened to make my next move."

Rudolf Hess leaned forward, "What move is that, Adolf?"

"I don't see myself as the president of Germany, although I did campaign for this."

Shock scurried around the table and all stared expectantly at Adolf to explain.

"The real person with power in this country is the Chancellor. The present Chancellor, Papen, is doing nothing to turn the tide of economic crises in this country. There are over six million people now, throughout Germany, who are unemployed and the situation is only worsening. I will demand the president to appoint me Chancellor in Papen's place. This is what I will be. I see myself as such and this is what I will pursue. I will not stop till I achieve it." Adolf stuck out his chest and beat it with a closed hand.

The group cheered again, already quite aware of Hitler's determination and his success at the things he pursued.

Deliverer and Peace stood outside of President Hindenburg's office and waited for the assigned moment. They heard a sound down the hall and watched as General Kurt von Schleicher, one of President Hindenburg's chief advisers, walked toward them and entered the President's office. The two angels followed quietly and without notice. They slipped into the office unseen and stood at attention just inside the door. They watched as General Schleicher approached the President's desk.

President Hindenburg's six foot, five inch frame filled the room with his impressive stature as he stood and shook hands with his advisor. President Paul von Hindenburg had served for an extended time in the German Army, being a field marshal during World War I and although he was eighty four years old he still commanded respect through his size and powerful, deep voice. The President nodded for Schleicher to begin and took a seat behind his desk, in his high backed, black leather chair.

The General took the seat opposite the President, removed his hat, held it in his hands and cleared his throat. "Mr. President, I've been in conference with Adolf Hitler and he has a request of you."

Hindenburg looked somewhat irritated at the mention of the name of his most determined rival. He slowly nodded for Schleicher to continue, while he tapped his pen rhythmically on the desk.

Deliverer got into position behind President Hindenburg, opened his wings to impart strength to the older man and spoke words of courage and wisdom to him.

"Adolf Hitler is asking to be placed as the Chancellor of Germany, in place of Papen. He also requests, well I suppose he demands, because of the economic mess of the country, to be given power to rule by decree. He believes he can straighten out the country's mess and to be completely honest I believe he's the man who can get something done. Look what he accomplished in his election campaign alone. He pursued it relentlessly. Perhaps with his boundless determination he could also bring positive change to Germany. He is…"

Deliverer's own fury transferred quickly to the president and the reaction was immediate.

President Hindenburg responded by pounding his fists on the desk and rising to his full height, drowning out quickly whatever Schleicher was about to say next. His voice boomed in displeasure.

"How dare Hitler demand this of me? He has no experience in governing and can't even control his own unruly SA troops. He knows nothing of running a country. I refuse to give up this governing position to a nobody like Hitler!"

Schleicher, clearly quieted by the powerful and forceful denial, answered meekly, still seeking but with a more humble approach. "What about the position of Vice Chancellor? Would it be possible to appoint Adolf Hitler to that post?"

Deliverer knew, a heavenly knowing, that this was no threat at all. He backed away and let things work themselves out. Peace nodded from his position behind Schleicher.

Hindenburg turned away from the desk and gazed out of the large window overlooking the grounds of the presidential building. After a moment of silence he turned back, his face slowly losing its red temper glow. "I suppose this might be possible. Chancellor Papen would still maintain all real power in Germany and it might make this Hitler fellow back off."

"So, I should offer this position to Adolf?"

"Yes."

Schleicher left the room to deliver the message and Deliverer and Peace followed closely. Schleicher walked down the hall and entered the room where Hitler waited. Hitler jumped up quickly from his chair, his face serious, questioning and expectant.

"So, what has been decided? Did the President agree to my proposition? Will Germany finally get the relief it has been begging for?"

General Schleicher diverted his gaze from the intensity of Hitler's eyes and focused on his hat in his hands. "I'm sorry, Adolf. The President refuses you the position of Chancellor."

Adolf's shoulders slouched visibly at the news.

"But I do have an offer that will surely please you."

Hitler lifted his eyes, a new light of hope showing. "What offer is that?"

"President Hindenburg has offered you the vice Chancellor position. It is open and available to you if you agree to it." He smiled his encouragement.

Hitler's mouth tightened in determination. "I refuse the Vice Chancellor position. The position I want is the Chancellorship! I want nothing else but that!"

"But the Vice Chancellorship is a very important position. I would suggest that you at least consider it. This country needs strong men with strong ideals to cure our ills. Please think about the offer."

"No, I've already considered and I refuse it! It is not what I came here for! I will not consider any other option but Chancellor of Germany." Hitler swooped up his briefcase, walked briskly to the door, opened it and walked down the hall without looking back, leaving General Schleicher staring after him in open mouthed incredulity.

In November, after another election, Chancellor Papen still could not put together a majority government in the Reichstag and finally resigned his post, leaving Germany without a Chancellor. General Schleicher was appointed next as Chancellor of Germany but within a few short months he had succeeded at alienating all of the political parties in Germany and lost the faith of President Hindenburg. Schleicher finally resigned in January 1933, once again leaving Germany without a Chancellor.

Deliverer and Peace stood outside the presidential offices, surrounded by Hesi, Reo, Clement and Tario.

Deliverer was the first to speak. "We can do no more here. God Almighty is calling us back home. We need to prepare for what's coming."

"What will happen here now?" Tario asked.

"The Chancellorship is wide open. There are many industrialists, who have been courted and promised many things by Adolf Hitler. They have already come to his defense and encouraged the President to give the position to him. President Hindenburg refused of course, Peace and I saw to that, but his resolve is weakening. He is growing weary of the process and disillusioned with the men he has chosen. Hindenburg has asked Papen to once more consider the Chancellorship position but he has flatly refused it and to add to the growing confusion, Papen has mentioned to Hindenburg that he is completely convinced that only Adolf Hitler is able to resolve the governmental crises."

"So is that it then? We have failed our assignment and we return to Heaven, our 'tail between our legs' so to say?" Clement looked disgusted with the outcome.

Peace added, "It seems that peace is not part of future plans here. It causes me great sorrow."

Hesi spoke next. "If only President Hindenburg had stood his ground and not given in to that snake."

Deliverer smiled slightly. "He hasn't given in yet but I believe he will bow his will to the advice he's received. I believe Adolf Hitler will soon begin to reign."

Reo stared at Deliverer. "So if we leave now, what will happen to Germany?"

Deliverer hung his head. Sorrow wrapped his frame in a thick, suffocating blanket, with a heavy foreboding that weighed upon his chest; an impending horror too great to think on too long.

Peace felt it too and his shoulders visibly sank at the weightiness of the realization.

Suddenly the surrounding atmosphere lit up as if on fire, enveloping the six angels in a warm cocoon of safety and love. It was intoxicating, uplifting and filled each angel with such encouragement and strength that each bowed in humble worship as they recognized its source.

The Son of Man stood in their midst, shining like the sun in the noonday sky, the rays of His loving warmth surrounding them in a bubble of approval. Slowly, the brightness of His coming dissipated and He signaled the angels to look at Him. Love and acceptance shone from his eyes and it was worth more than a thousand victories over the forces of darkness. Soaking up the great love extended to them, the angels were overcome by joy that began to erupt deep within them.

Jesus smiled at each one, love and favor flowing from Him in great waves of heavenly power. "Your assignment for now is complete. You have done well servants."

His words were like dew falling on the mount of Carmel, sweet and fragrant, like the lilies growing in a valley. They brought peace like a river flowing deep within the spirits of each angel.

"There is nothing more that can be done here. The German population is making decisions and will continue to make decisions that will influence many people. We can do no more for the present. There are many still in this country that know Me, hear Me and listen to My voice. They will continue to serve and obey Me through the worst of times. Those who call themselves by My name but who refuse to listen to Me, will suffer the greatest harm. A great evil is about to be released from this place and it will change and shift things, not only in the heavenlies but also the physical aligning of nations, the world view of nations and a great shift for the nation of Israel."

Deliverer's forehead creased in wonder. "But Master, there is no nation of Israel. Your chosen people are scattered in nearly every nation and among every people."

Jesus' face appeared sorrowful but also stern, unyielding and completely sure of what was to happen. "What has been set in place will happen. My heart yearns and cries for My people. If only they would allow Me to gather them under My wings, like a hen covers her chicks, but they are not willing." Jesus' sorrow suddenly vanished as He gazed at each angel, one by one, great hope shining like a beacon from His eyes. "God won't allow his people to be oppressed forever. No, there is great hope for my chosen people. Anyone who curses them will certainly fall under a curse, but those who bless them will themselves be blessed."

Jesus' words caused the angels hearts to swell in renewed hope and filled them with an enduring peace.

"You are relieved from your duties here and are free to return to Heaven for a time. Most of you will be needed here again in the great battle that is coming but for now you may return to Heaven to rest and prepare." With that, Jesus' presence slowly dematerialized and He vanished from sight, while His glory-filled presence lingered in the atmosphere surrounding them.

A moment later two magnificent horses pulling a fiery carriage stopped a stone's throw away. The majestic pure-white creatures neighed and pawed the ground in eagerness, ready to leap into action as soon as the cargo was ready. The precious stones embedded into the carriage and harness pieces sparkled and shot out colorful prisms of light in every direction as the fire engulfing the team danced around them.

Deliverer, Peace and the other four angels watched as the horses slowly calmed to wait patiently. Deliverer turned to the others and said, "This is our ride. I feel torn between the two worlds. I feel I should stay and help somehow and yet, due to the Master's words, I know we need to leave. His way is always the best way."

Deliverer turned and was the first to enter the carriage. Peace followed next and then the rest. The horses waited for the command.

"Go!" shouted Deliverer.

With that, the team rose immediately into the air, a flow of fire streaming behind, with gold like dust lingering in the atmosphere, the gems and precious stones causing a glittering display as the team rose high and quickly disappeared from sight.

Two demonic beings, with dark scales covering their forms and bulging red eyes, saw the horse and carriage team arrive and then leave as they hid behind a building for protection, afraid of detection and possible punishment.

One of them wheezed his assessment, "Aha, the great warrior, Deliverer, and his cohort, Peace, have left. How proud the dark master will be of me when he learns from my lips that they're finally out of the way."

"You're not the only one who saw them leave. I'll tell our dark master first!"

The first demon swiped at the second in pure hatred with his sharp talons cutting the other demon deeply across his leathery cheek, bringing on a scream of pain. Green vapor floated from the cut and surrounded the creatures face.

"You will not tell our dark master, you imbecile! I will tell him! Such news will gain me much respect from our lord and their departure will gain me much needed space to accomplish my work." He puffed out his chest trying to gain the upper hand. He already stood a foot taller than his companion and it was clear he wanted to ensure his stature over the smaller demon. "You will take your place, you inferior, weak one! You will show me the respect I deserve!"

The wounded, smaller demon lunged at the other demon's gnarled legs and sunk his fangs deep into his knee, drawing out a putrid stream of sulfuric vapor. The larger demon screamed out his anguish, extended the talons on his twisted hands further and dug deep into the biting demons back in revenge, bringing on a cry of pain from his companion in darkness. The first demon kept his talons deeply buried in his companions back and began to laugh haughtily as he realized his superior position, with his companion kneeling in pain before him.

"You agree with me now that I will tell our lord first?"

The smaller demon wheezed and coughed in utter agony. "All right, all right, you foul friend! Release me and you can tell our dark lord the prized news."

The large demon finally released his tenacious grip and when he did, green vapor poured from the second demon's wounds, filling the air with the vile, sulfuric smell. The bigger demon hurried off, lopping off on all fours with his comrade slinking slowly behind him, clearly in pain and suffering from his efforts in opposing his comrade.

CHAPTER 12

Germany-January 30, 1933

Beata Schluter filled the pail with potatoes and set it on the floor of the shed. She then picked up the heavy blanket and draped it over the remaining few potatoes at the bottom of the insulated, large bin. The winters in Berlin were never too cold and this insulated box was sufficient in keeping the potatoes from freezing through the winter months. There was a light dusting of snow on the ground and it would probably stay for a few days with the telltale, icy wind blowing through the city. Beata closed the shed door firmly behind her, held her winter coat tightly around her chin while her other hand held the pail of potatoes as she hurried toward the back door of the house. She stopped at the door to remove her winter boots.

Her guardian angels, Courageous, Wisdom, Lovely and Light Bearer, surrounded her. Wisdom whispered into her ear, "Look at the sky."

She turned her eyes heavenward and concern filled her at the sight. Dark, beckoning clouds seemed to be funneling toward the earth. She gazed in wonder for a few moments, then finally tore her eyes away and walked into the house.

She walked into the kitchen and set the pail of potatoes on the counter.

"Is that all that were left?" asked Unna.

"No, we have a few more potatoes. We didn't get many this year did we?"

"It's troubling. Usually we harvest enough to last us at least till nearly planting season. If our neighbors don't have some to share we'll have to start buying vegetables and I don't know if we can afford that."

"Don't worry, Mother. We always get by." Beata gazed at her and smiled.

"I don't know. Food isn't as plentiful as it used to be and things are hard at the plant."

She looked at her mother in concern. "Daddy won't lose his job, will he?"

"No. I don't believe so but there are always rumors of people being laid off and many people are without work. Egbert Adler, who lives down the street, hasn't had a steady income for many months now. His wife, Gretchen, is looking so thin and his children look shabbily dressed. Gretchen has resorted to selling her baked goods but I don't know how that can possibly support them all. We help them out as we can but things are very bad for them right now." Unna Schluter had deep lines of worry across her forehead as she gazed out the kitchen window.

"I thought I heard Daddy say that the government is trying its best to improve the situation."

Unna gazed at Beata with a slight smile. "Your ears are too big for you. I'll have to remind your father to hush about important adult matters when you girls are around."

Beata gazed intently at her mother. "I'm not that young anymore. I'm already thirteen and I want to know what's happening in my country."

Unna wiped her hands on a towel and faced her daughter. "All right, yes, I suppose you're getting older. It so happens that our government is all talk but little action. Our situation has been difficult ever since the war and things are getting worse. There are millions of German people without work and many starving, needy people everywhere. I'm sure you've seen the beggars on nearly every street corner."

"Yes, I have noticed that. That won't happen to us will it?"

"I certainly hope not. We need a leader that can put things back in order. Everyone is losing hope." Unna looked off into space, fear crowding her eyes. "I couldn't bear standing on a street corner to beg."

"That would be terrible!"

"Well, Beata, your father has a good job," she placed a hand on Beata'a cheek, "but things have slowed down for his company and many men have already lost their jobs."

"That won't happen to us!" She knew it like she knew her name. How she knew, she wasn't sure, but she knew it had to be true. She was thirteen and was aware that she couldn't possibly understand all that her mother said or the fear she saw in her eyes, but God would be with them and take care of them. There was a deep assurance within her.

Beata's four guardian angels surrounded her, hovered close to her as Holy Spirit imparted the confidence of His loving care.

"Ah, to be a teenager again, with no worries and such an idealistic view of life." Unna smiled in longing.

Unna turned back to her work and Beata wandered to the back door and gazed through the glass window at the sky once more. She knew it wasn't her age that gave her the confidence. She felt peace down in her middle, the place where her God dwelt. There was positive unsettledness too. Something about the sky didn't seem quite right.

"Mother, have you noticed the sky?"

"No." Unna lifted her eyes and looked out the window, scanned her white, snow covered yard and then lifted her eyes to the mostly blue sky.

Beata frowned. "It looks different, darker somehow. I don't know. It looks unusual to me."

"It looks fine to me. There's hardly a cloud in the sky."

"But you haven't looked up. It seems like the grey clouds are rolling downwards like a funnel right on top of us. It's the strangest thing. It seems like an eerie omen."

"You have too great an imagination. You'd better use it for beneficial things like helping me cut and prepare the potatoes for supper."

"Something's not right. I can feel it." Her mother didn't answer so Beata slowly tore her eyes from the ominous clouds and shrugged her shoulders in resignation as she sauntered to her mother's side.

The front door opened and closed with a bang, followed by hurried footsteps down the hall to the kitchen. "Mother, Mother, look what I found." Ilse, Beata's nine-year-old sister, almost ten, bobbed into the room, her eyes showing great concern and in her hands a fluttering, wounded robin. "I found it lying beneath our apple tree in the front yard. What would a robin be doing around here in the winter? What could be wrong with it, Mother?" Ilse stood, winter boots coated with snow, dripping a steady stream of melting snow on Mrs. Schluter's clean floor.

"Ilse, how many times must I tell you to leave your boots by the door?" Just as suddenly, Unna's eyes filled with concern as she focused on the wounded creature in her daughter's hand. "Let me see that poor thing."

Beata stared at the injured bird and her eyes widened in fear. "It's an omen. Remember the dark clouds I saw? Something's very wrong!"

Unna Schluter turned toward Beata in frustration. "Stop with your superstitious talk! There's nothing wrong with the sky and this bird was probably caught off guard by a stalking, starving cat or some such thing. Let's just take a look at this creature and stop jumping to conclusions, all right?"

Beata looked down at the floor in embarrassment. "I'll get the bandages." She hurried down the hall and returned momentarily.

Unna held the injured fowl in her right hand as Ilse placed a soft towel on the kitchen counter. After setting the robin on the towel, Unna examined it carefully. Her nursing tendency was evident as she skillfully, but gently pinpointed the source of damage. "It's a broken wing. We'll need a splint. Is there any splint in our nursing supplies, Ilse?"

Ilse rummaged through the home made emergency kit. "I don't see anything like that." She stared at her mother anxiously.

Beata offered, "I'll go get a stick from outside."

"Yes, please do."

Beata grabbed her winter coat and boots and hurried through the back door and to the towering trees that lined their back yard. After some digging, she found some twigs, gathered a few to ensure getting the right size and hurried back to the house.

Unna selected one and proceeded to bandage the wounded animal. After standing back to examine her handiwork, she turned toward her two girls. "Will you two find one of those weaved airy covers from the garden shed that we use to cover garden plants?"

The girls hurried outside together and soon returned holding the large coned cover before their mother. Unna took it from them, and placed it on the floor.

"Yes, this will be perfect to contain the robin while it heals." After settling the robin in its new home Unna turned to face her girls once more. "Now I need some juicy worms to keep this bird alive. Even some dried cherries from our tree would help. I don't know if there'll be any left. The birds probably finished them off by now. The worms might be a problem. The ground is hard and I'm not at all sure you'll find any. I don't have a lot of time to nurse this bird back to health so I'll need your help. I still have my house cleaning job so I don't have much time for nursing. I expect you girls to find out what the bird will eat and feeding it will be your responsibility."

A gusty wind began to howl through the slight cracks around the back, kitchen door and Unna hurried to the door to see what the commotion was. Large flakes of snow had begun to fall in abundance, nearly blinding the eye from any further than the edge of their yard. The sudden appearance of the wind blew the new snow in blinding waves, first one way and then the other. The temperature was noticeably dropping as the wind forced its way into the kitchen through the cracks of the door.

"Where did this storm come from? The sky was clear and blue only a few minutes ago!" Unna looked dumbfounded as she grabbed some towels from a drawer and placed them on the floor, below the door, scrunching them tight to the cracks to keep out the cold breeze. She then turned and looked at Beata, who was intensely watching her mother. "I suppose you were right. There was a storm descending on us and I was oblivious to it."

"I think it means more than just a storm, Mother. It's an omen."

"Let's not go quite that far now. It's a sudden storm, that's all."

"But what about the bird I found outside at the same time?" asked Ilse.

Beata smiled at her. Ilse would usually come to her aid in defense and she proved it once more.

Unna crossed her arms and stared seriously at her daughters. "So you both think these things are omens?"

Beata shrugged her shoulders. "They could be." She placed her index finger on her middle. "I feel it in here."

"I suppose time will tell. Now, I need to tend to my work and I want you girls to find food for an injured robin."

The girls searched but found nothing that would do. When their father, Helmuth Schluter, came home he agreed to give them one of his prized sunflowers, drying in the basement. Beata and Ilse were overjoyed with his agreement and the robin seemed just as happy. Over time the bird slowly grew stronger and its wing healed.

Resilient landed beside a large grove of fruit trees, the scent flowing over him in sweet waves of heady aroma. He folded his wings away, close to his body. He grabbed a ripe fruit from the tree closest to him, smiled and bit into it, the juice spilling down his chin and onto his warriors uniform. He glanced down to see the juice disappearing and evaporating as soon as it touched his pure, elaborate clothes. He stood impressive in height, at least ten feet and easily reached some of the tallest branches of the tree beside him. His sword was strapped to his side, carefully enclosed in its sheath, but his other ammunition and protection was being carefully stored until the designated time of departure. His long, blond hair blew in the slight breeze of Heaven, his square jaw set firmly as he gazed intently at the heavenly scene before him.

Water cascaded down a twenty foot drop and landed in a plume of excited spray as it dived into the small lake that formed its base. The water then scurried on past the grove of trees and gurgled and splashed its way over rich stones and gems as it made its way toward the Great City. The water sang and rejoiced in its elation of carrying the very life of God Almighty and spreading it everywhere, bringing refreshing and joy to each one that happened to pass by or enter its life giving flow.

Resilient chose to watch the water's lively flow instead of wander into its refreshing, powerful current. He gazed in peaceful contentment at the life that grew profusely everywhere. Lush growth filled the landscape and was especially thick and full close to the river's edge. Purity and beauty surrounded Resilient as he basked in Heaven's glory and perfection. He finished the last bite of the lush triangular shaped fruit and threw the center core on the ground, which immediately vaporized and vanished from sight. He sighed contentedly as he searched for the one who had summoned him here. He noticed movement above him and looked to the top of the waterfall as an angel hollered from the edge of the falling, bubbling water.

"Yahoo!" With that the angel pushed off and fell head-first into the lake below, water splashing up in a spectacular color display. The many gems and precious stones lining the small lake and river bed caused the flume of water to dance with rainbow like shafts of light.

Momentarily, the diving angel appeared and swam toward shore, smiling broadly at the exhilarating sensation. He stood in the shallow water at the rivers edge and as soon as the air of Heaven touched him, he was immediately dry. He walked toward Resilient with outstretched hand in welcome.

"It's good to see you, my long time friend!" Resilient took Deliverer's hand in his and grasped his arm with his other. Deliverer did the same.

"It's been a long time hasn't it?"

Resilient asked, "Where have you been so long? I haven't seen you for at least twenty earth years."

"And you've been here that whole time?" Deliverer grinned widely.

"No. I've been back and forth frequently on a number of missions."

"Yes, that's always the way it is. I have to admit, I've been busy for the Master too."

"Where have you been?"

"I was serving in many locations, but mostly in Europe."

Resilient nodded. "I've heard there's a lot going on there. So, why were you sent back to Heaven? Is your work done?"

"No, not nearly. God Almighty thought it best to send me back here for a while. I feel that some refreshing was most likely necessary before the next mission. There is an evil looming and growing stronger and if something isn't done to stop it, it will soon engulf that whole region."

Resilient heart filled with concern. "Can you tell me any specifics?"

"Only that there is a deep darkness growing, an intensity of evil power gaining momentum and only God our Father knows the extent of it and the influence this mounting dark power will exert over Europe. There seems to be nothing containing the rising cloud of evil and nothing holding it back. The possibilities are staggering."

"Why would God allow this evil to grow without hindrance?"

"Oh, it's not without hindrance but the volume of support for the evil is greater than those who oppose it. Peace was with me and our main mission was to rally prayer support from God's people and to hold this tide back for a time. We went into dangerous places filled with our enemy's forces to urge people to pray. But I'm sad to say that not many took our warning seriously. There are too few who are truly praying against this evil. Without prayer support there is little we can do to stop events from playing out."

"The Jews will suffer greatly," Resilient said knowingly. He'd heard reports.

"Yes, but so will many others. The unchecked malevolence that will be released will cause much suffering and pain."

"So it will become all encompassing?"

"It will become all encompassing for Europe, yes and perhaps it will extend beyond that. I haven't been told the whole scope of its influence but I know that it will continue to grow."

Resilient said, "I'm sure we'll be informed as we need…"

A lightning bolt flashed beside the two angels, stopping Resilient's flow of conversation. The bright light slowly ebbed. Bold's form appeared as the light faded and he grinned in mischief. "I like to make a grand entrance. It tends to shock my enemy into flight and fear. Did I frighten you?"

Another angel descended after him, Wrath, but he chose a more humble entrance, floating down beside his comrade speedily but without fanfare.

"Your tactics are becoming quite tiresome, Bold." Resilient gazed in piqued apathy. "Over thousands of years and you still haven't changed."

"You mean my entrance didn't impress you two?"

Deliverer spoke, "When your strength defeats our foes unequivocally, then I might be slightly impressed. Here in Heaven, your antics only show your immaturity."

Bold laughed raucously. "I suppose I'll have to prove myself on the battle field then, won't I?"

"The only one you should be interested in impressing is God. We are little awed with your power or your might." Deliverer smiled.

"Yes of course, of course, but I thought my entrance would bring some amusement and wake you two out of your stupor."

Resilient said, "It wasn't stupor at all but an intense discussion of the evil advance on earth and our upcoming departure." With a serious expression, he faced Deliverer. "Do you know when we'll be sent out?"

"I've only barely arrived and you speak of departure?" He gave his friend a peculiar look. "I have a sense that it'll be soon but maybe you'll be sent more quickly than I. I don't know. God will summon you when the time in right."

"I'm ready right now. I can feel the urgency growing every day and I'm itching to go and join the fight." Bold's hand cradled the handle of his sword while his face showed extreme determination and desire.

"To inflict wrath on the enemy already burns within me." Wrath's jutting square chin and intense face bore the signs of his comment.

Deliverer informed Bold and Wrath of the news he had shared with Resilient. "It won't be much longer now. Many angels, warriors and special messengers have already returned from their missions on earth and are being refreshed and restored before being sent out again. They have done what they could and the initial assignment has been completed."

"You're referring to rousing God's people to prayer?" asked Bold.

"Yes" said Deliverer.

All four already knew it hadn't been as successful as Heaven had anticipated. Movement on the grassy turf drew their eyes. They immediately fell to their knees and bowed their heads at His coming presence.

Jesus walked toward them, Abraham flanking his side. Abraham wore a severe and pained expression. They stopped before the angels and waited till the angels lifted their eyes.

"I see you've returned, Deliverer," said Jesus with a smile.

"Yes, Master."

"Please stand. I have some things to tell you."

Resilient and the other three angels slowly stood to their feet, their eyes averted in reverence.

"I need to warn you that the future assignment you will undertake will be full of intense danger and resistance. Great wickedness is being released and an evil cloud is forming over many areas. Some sense the approaching danger but many are numb and blind to its growing force. Although you don't know the full outcome of what will take place on earth, there is much for the people of earth to mourn about and they will mourn when it overtakes them."

"So you're saying that there's no way to turn back the tide of evil?" asked Resilient, lifting his eyes to the Lord of lords.

"No. If God's people wake up and begin to intercede, perhaps some things could be changed."

The four angels and even Abraham himself stared at the Master, longing for some good news, knowing that He already knew all things.

"Will they change?" Deliverer finally asked.

Jesus closed his eyes, a tortured but determined look on his face. He opened his eyes and said, "No, nothing will change. The seeds that have been sown will bring forth fruit. Whatever has been planted will be harvested. I can tell you this; the harvest won't be welcomed or pretty."

All four angels bowed their heads at the heaviness of the words.

Abraham finally spoke, "It's too much to bear, Lord! My descendants, I feel for my offspring!"

Jesus reached over and placed a hand on Abraham's shoulder. "Remember, that mercy triumphs over judgment. Although judgment will be released, my mercy will flow like a river. Some will only receive my mercy through judgment."

"Lord?" asked Abraham, his eyes still shining with anguish.

"Some will not receive me unless faced with death. My house will be filled. God Almighty would have preferred a different way, a more willing acceptance. Always remember that the greatest battle is not in the physical."

Knowing crossed Abraham's face, "For our struggle is not against flesh and blood, but against the rulers, against the authorities, against the powers of this dark world and against the spiritual forces of evil in the heavenly realms."

The four angels nodded in agreement.

Jesus said, "Yes, that's accurate. Although the world will hate the physical harvest it receives, Heaven will rejoice in the abundant harvest of souls."

Deliverer smiled then. "I have a strong sense that we will have a battle like no other. Although the danger will be great, it will be an adventure like no other."

"It sounds like we'll have our hands full. I can't wait to show my great boldness in defeating the forces of darkness." Bold began to shine in desire and a heavenly glow surrounded him.

Jesus chuckled. "Yes, there certainly won't be a lack of adventure or danger. I'm eager to show you what is taking place in Heaven, even as we speak, but that can wait." His face took on a serious tone. "I want you to know that many things will be changed as people call on my Name, even during the worst of times. I am well able to deliver and protect. Those who know Me will call on My Name. Some who don't know will call on Me and I will answer."

The words fell like healing balm on those who heard.

He turned to Abraham and gave him way to speak.

Abraham sighed heavily and a yet a resigned peace had settled on his features, a knowing of God's hand and wisdom in all things. "I have been informed that my people will suffer greatly. It wounds me to know it, but I also know that I will have the privilege of their presence soon. So I am grieved but also anticipate their salvation. I have been placed in charge of the battle strategy from Heaven's war room. You will all need to attend a meeting planned in a week's time. I will lay out the battle plan then and weapons and ammunition will be allotted. We will meet early morning and the meeting should extend for the length of the day."

The four angels nodded and bowed at the waist in respect to the great father of faith. They never worshiped a child of God but he was deserving of great honor.

Abraham grew silent and turned to Jesus.

Jesus said, "That's all for now, my servants. Know that Holy Spirit will be with you in every mission you accomplish. I will never leave you or forsake you, no matter how dark and wicked things become."

A warm, electrical flow moved from Lord to servants so that they were surrounded by Heaven's force, in a cocoon of love and safety. To experience His presence lifting them, encouraging, filling them with His love was the epitaph of Heaven's glory. The angels fell to their knees, their strength ebbing in the flow of his power. They bowed low before Him, their faces to the ground at His feet.

Jesus bent down, touching each angelic servant on the head. Power pulsed through them at the touch, rendering them incapable of rising. They lay immobile, glorifying the King of kings and Lord of lords, praise erupting from their lips.

An angel choir, flying high above, joined their anthem of praise, filling the air with a tangible quaking.

Jesus looked to the sky and smiled. He looked back at the bowed angels and said, "I declare blessing over you. May you be blessed as you serve God Almighty!" He walked away then and slowly the power surge ebbed. Abraham followed Jesus, eager to stay in His company.

After a while, Resilient and the other three angels slowly stood and found greater strength filling them than they had known in a long time. Being in His presence always accomplished much. All four felt energized and ready for whatever lay ahead.

CHAPTER 13

Adolf Hitler made a slight bow before President Hindenburg as he received the coveted appointment. The date was January 30, 1933 and the many Nazi supporters attending the official ceremony looked thrilled. Hitler couldn't keep the smile from his lips as he was sworn into the office of Chancellor of Germany. He appeared pleased as his long awaited dream was fulfilled before his eyes. The ceremony flew by in a blur of excitement and relief.

After the formal procedure, Adolf met with some of his main supporters and they all congratulated him exuberantly. Joseph Goebbels, a twinkle of excitement in his eye, approached Hitler, shook his hand and smiled.

"Congratulations, my Fuhrer! What a victory for the Nazis! I insist we celebrate with a parade through the streets of Berlin. I'll organize it and plan it for tonight but I will need your permission of course."

After a moment of thought, Adolf said, "Yes, it's a splendid idea. What better way to announce my victory. Plan the parade for this evening and have the SA and the SS troops be a part of it. It must be impressive. The troops must carry numerous Nazi flags and the parade should be announced by radio so that as many people can come out to join and see it as possible."

Goebbels said, "Yes, those are excellent ideas. We should also arrange, since the parade will take place after sunset, to have the troops carry lighted torches. It will certainly declare that a great light has appeared in the land and is about to light up all of Germany."

"That's a wonderful idea! Implement that as well." Hitler smiled broadly and nodded in approval.

That evening, the troops and close supporters thronged through Berlin's streets, thousands strong with torches blazing in the evening darkness. Looking from above, it appeared like a flow of fire, moving through the streets like a snakelike apparition, stretching for miles as it approached the presidential building and then on to the Chancellery, the place where Adolf Hitler and the Nazi Party now held power. The large group was escorted by bands playing martial music, the sound of drums and the constant flowing fiery show a mere foretaste of what was to come. As the large group passed the Chancellery and Hitler appeared in a window high above, the crowd erupted in cheers.

"Heil Hitler! Heil Hitler! Heil Hitler!"

The sound was deafening as it echoed over and over through the streets, showering the district with its allegiance, its devotion and praise, declaring approval and paving the way for a new era of hope. To those who viewed it with a high degree of skepticism, the river of blazing fire parading past them appeared ominous and threatening, especially to those clearly targeted by Adolf Hitler's aggressive views in his book, *Mein Kampf.* Communist politicians gazed on in anxious trepidation, clearly knowing Hitler's strong stance against all communists and his clear articulation of them as a great enemy.

The Jewish people of Berlin and throughout Germany listened fearfully to their radios as the broadcasters reported the parades proceedings to the minutest details. Their fate in Hitler's popular book was clearly laid out and his pure hatred of the Jewish people gave them no reason to celebrate. They shivered to think what Hitler's rise to power might mean for their future and they mourned the day as others rejoiced.

April 1933

The shop was located in the Jewish neighborhood, in the large city of Berlin, surrounded by similar Jewish stores. It was well cared for with the freshly painted sign hung perpendicular to the store, held in place by a swinging frame. The sign swayed slightly with the afternoon breeze, its words in dark brown over a painted picture of a shoe in shades of blue. The front sidewalk was swept and cleared of all debris, the front glass windows shone with a recent cleaning and the outside of the shop was constructed of brick, reinforced glass and well maintained, freshly painted frames.

The owners, Meshulam and Marni Israeli, a husband and wife team, worked together, both just as gifted as the other as they repaired shoes for their many customers. Not only did they diligently do repair work but they were expert craftspeople, designing and crafting many useful shoes, not only for their trusted Jewish patrons but for many Germans who relied on their supply and quality. Their shoes were well known and their reputation traveled far beyond their Jewish community.

Beata followed her mother, Unna Schluter, into the well lit store. Unna smiled at Meshulam Israeli who stood behind the counter. He nodded in greeting with a slight look of unease. Unna began to browse through the rows of shoes lining the shelves and Beata kept close to her.

Unna made the long walk from her neighborhood every year, bringing shoes in need of repair and scanning the shelves for the latest and most practical foot wear for her family for the coming year. It wasn't often that Beata joined her on this trip but she enjoyed it tremendously each time she'd come.

"How are you doing today, Mrs. Schluter?"

Unna turned to face Meshulam. "I'm doing well, Mr. Israeli. How is the shoe business?"

"It's doing very well in spite of what's taking place out there." Meshulam's face was grave and serious as he pointed out his front window. "I'm surprised to see you here at all. Aren't you afraid of the government's decree?"

"I pay no attention to such foolishness! No matter how popular the Nazi Party is in this country, they cannot control our every move. Just because they have boycotted Jewish businesses does not mean I will stop shopping here. As far as I'm concerned, you're the most talented shoe maker in all of Berlin and nothing will prevent me from buying from you."

Beata felt extremely proud of her mother at this moment. She couldn't remember her mother being this brave and forceful before and it caused her heart to swell in agreement.

A small smile appeared on Meshulam's face. "I'm glad to hear it from you, Unna. If only the majority of Berlin's people felt as you do then perhaps I would feel more comforted."

At that moment Marni Israeli entered from a doorway behind the counter and she hurried to greet them. "Why, Unna Schluter! It is wonderful to see you here."

"It's good to see you too, Marni. How is business so far? The boycott hasn't hurt you has it?"

Marni looked painfully toward her husband and then answered. "Not too much. Most people have ignored it, though others, like some SA men, placed a poster on our shop. Meshulam removed it shortly after the SA men left. We hope we won't be targeted because of our outright rebellion of the government's decree. To be honest, we are angered by the new Chancellor's policies and his moves against us."

Unna gave both of them a look of empathy and concern. "I don't blame you. It's repugnant and distasteful what this new Chancellor is willing to implement. One can only hope that his motives will stop with this one act."

Meshulam looked away as he spoke. "I believe it's wishful thinking to long for this, even though I also hope for the same. I'm thankful that there are faithful customers like you, Unna, who see our dilemma and refuse to be influenced."

"So the boycott has not hurt you so far?"

Marni said, "No. It's been ineffective with our customers. They just ignore it."

Just then a shout was heard outside and something hit the storefront window with a large smack. Meshulam rushed to the window and looked out at a ripe tomato, smeared against the glass and watched it slowly slide down and land in a mashed mass on the walkway outside. A group of teenagers laughed and screamed insults as they passed by. Meshulam watched as one of the boys reached for an item in the bag he carried and handed something to the boy beside him. The boy wound up, as if ready to throw a baseball, and hurled the item against the window of the next Jewish business, a bakery across the street. The sickening smack could be heard clearly but the offending vegetable didn't penetrate the thick glass. The trouble makers only managed to dirty and deface the bakery establishment.

"Stupid kids!" Meshulam turned back, his face showing his disgust as he looked at Unna, Beata and Marni. "They're only kids out to play pranks."

Marni gazed at her husband, her eyes intense and filled with anger. "They are German teenagers, filled with Nazi propaganda and they are attacking Jewish businesses! They are not only playing pranks, they are displaying their parents' views and feelings toward us. It frightens me!"

He walked toward his wife and spoke quietly but loud enough that Unna and Beata couldn't help overhearing. "It's nothing. Don't worry so. Besides, we have a fine German lady here who would like to shop. Let's leave our concerns for another time." Meshulam stared at his wife in warning and then turned toward Unna. "I'm sorry about that, Mrs. Schluter. Please forgive us for displaying such inappropriate behavior in our usually well structured shop."

Unna ignored Meshulam's uncomfortable rambling and moved a step closer to both of them. "I'm the one who should apologize. The way the German government is treating you is deplorable and many people are treating the Jew without regard of God and without consideration of judgment. I want you to know that I do not agree with the government's decision and I absolutely oppose it; my presence in your shop today shows that I do. I'm sorry to say, that many, who call themselves the children of God, in this city, agree with Adolf Hitler. I want you to know that I do not agree with his ideas or plans. I am vehemently opposed to his views in his book, so please, if there's anything I can ever do for you, let me know. All right?"

Beata felt doubly proud of her now. She stayed a step behind her mother but applauded her in quiet support.

Marni's eyes misted as she listened and wiped at them in embarrassment. "Thank you, Unna. You don't know what that means to us."

Meshulam held out his hand and shook Unna's in gratitude. "I also offer you my thanks, Mrs. Schluter."

Unna smiled at the response. "My husband also shares my opinions and we were not the only ones who shook in fear when we learned of Hitler's appointment as Chancellor. He's an evil man and we're convinced he'll do this country harm."

Meshulam smiled, "You have extraordinary vision."

"I believe my daughter has even better vision." She turned to point at Beata.

Beata smiled shyly and shrugged.

"She sees things and understands things far beyond her years. Beata has a real gift for knowing things, sensing things and I believe I would do well to believe her the first time she shares her premonitions. She knew the day of the Chancellor appointment that something ominous was on the way and I thought she was imagining things. She saw dark clouds gathering over Berlin. She knew something was wrong before we ever realized Hitler was taking the Chancellorship."

Meshulam and Marni stared at Beata now and she squirmed uncomfortably. They looked confused and unsure of what her mother was saying. Questions blanketed their faces.

Unna smiled nervously. "I'm sorry to take so much of your time. I'll get back to shopping and let you continue with your work."

Meshulam nodded and returned to mending a pair of shoes behind the counter. Beata felt relieved. Marni followed Unna and pointed out the latest designs and trends. Beata followed behind the two. Marni lifted a pair of women's shoes from the shelf and held them out for Unna to see.

"These are made from the finest leather anywhere and are a practical walking shoe for nearly all seasons and are useful for casual wear or for something dressier. Wouldn't you agree?"

Unna gazed longingly at the dark, brown pair, well aware that her own well worn shoes were direly in need of replacement. "I do agree that they are beautiful and if I had all the money I wanted, I would certainly consider them." She reached for the shoes and stared at them from every angle, longing filling her eyes. "I must consider the immediate needs of our family and not focus on my desires." She handed the shoes back. "Could you show me some practical shoes for a thirteen-year-old girl?" She pointed to Beata. "She needs some new shoes. Her present ones are entirely too small for her."

"Yes, of course, follow me." Marni led Unna to a rack on the side wall.

Beata tried some on and soon decided on the appropriate pair. After picking out another pair of shoes, work boots for her husband, Helmuth, Unna took her purchases to the counter. Marni added up the total and Unna paid. At that moment, a young teenage boy walked into the store from the doorway behind the counter, carrying a single shoe.

"Father, what do you think? Did I do it right this time?"

"Bring it here and let me have a look." Meshulam took it from the lad and examined it. "You see here, Doron, the lacing is too loose at the toe and the heel is not securely attached. This shoe will last maybe two weeks out there." Meshulam pointed outside. "You have watched me work and I expect better quality than this. I know you can produce a quality shoe. Practice, practice and more practice is what is needed."

Doron's shoulder's drooped slightly at the reprimand. "I've tried so many times and I still can't get it right. What am I doing wrong?"

"All right, I'm about to sew this shoe together." Meshulam held up the one he was working on, a light, beige woman's walking shoe. "Watch me carefully this time."

Doron was completely transfixed and focused as he gazed over his Father's shoulder.

Unna had stopped in mid stride and stood staring at the teenage son of the shoe makers. Marni Israeli cleared her throat and brought Unna out of her reverie.

"I'm sorry; I didn't know you had children."

Marni smiled shyly. "We have three wonderful children. Doron here is our second. He's fourteen. He's eager to learn the shoe making trade, a thrill for Meshulam to be sure. Our oldest, a son, Fayvel, is twenty and is in his first year of university here in Berlin. He wants to be a doctor. He's a smart boy."

As if on cue, a tall, handsome young man entered through the same door Doron had entered only moments earlier. He held a ledger in his hands with a pen placed behind one ear. Beata couldn't help but stare at him. He looked like a dream. He caught her gaze and smiled. Beata blushed and looked away, but she kept stealing looks at him. She couldn't help it. He was so handsome, tall with dark, curly hair and his large, brown eyes, lined with long eyelashes, held a deep kindness.

Marni pointed to him, "This is Fayvel. He helps with the books when he can, when he's not caught up with his studies. Our youngest is a girl, Faye, and she's ten."

"Your Faye is the same age as my youngest daughter, Ilse," admitted Unna.

"You have two daughters then?"

"Yes, two precious daughters, Beata and Ilse."

Fayvel looked at Beata again and smiled. She returned the smile and felt like she was suddenly floating. She chided herself. The man was twenty after all and she was only thirteen, but maybe…

"And who's this young lady?"

Beata nearly fainted at the question. Fayvel was actually asking about her?

Unna bumped her arm. "Well, are you going to answer him?"

Beata looked dumbly at her mother and then turned to face Fayvel. "Uh, I'm Beata Schluter."

"Well, it's nice to meet you." He came toward her then and held out his hand.

Beata took it and he shook it warmly and smiled disarmingly once more.

Beata's insides did a crazy tap dance against her ribs.

Fayvel finally released her hand, turned to Unna, shook her hand with a kind word and then walked away, back to his ledger on the counter.

Unna said, "He's a fine, young man."

Marni smiled politely.

Unna returned it, with a sudden kinship between them. Then she said, "We have to go. Thanks for all your help."

"Have a good day, Mrs. Schluter," Marni Israeli said.

As they walked toward the door, Beata glanced back at Fayvel one more time and he was looking at her intently. She turned away quickly to follow her mother. She could feel his eyes on her and it made her feel giddy and light. It was foolish to react this way at their first meeting but she couldn't shake the sensation.

CHAPTER 14

Dutch Settlement, Crimean Steppe, Russia 1938

Esther Brenner watched as her seventeen-year-old brother, Herman, burst through the door, his face brimming with excitement. He threw his jacket over a chair at the door and bounded into the kitchen. He suddenly stopped, closed his eyes and breathed deeply. The delicious aroma of their mother's cooking drifting toward him had stopped him cold. The source of the aromatic temptation came from the freshly cut loaf of bread in the center of the table. Steam escaped the hot bread pieces and filled the room with a heavenly scent.

Mother walked swiftly to the table, set a bowl of boiled potatoes, faced Herman and crossed her arms sternly.

"You're late again! Can't you make some effort to get home in time for the evening meal? We waited nearly an hour for you and the potatoes are more than cooked. They're completely mush." Mother was clearly upset, her face drawn tight with lines showing on her forehead. Her hair was drawn back tight in a practical up-do, something she always wore when she was baking, her dark hair dotted with a light dusting of flour.

"I'm sorry, Mother. I was held up in the Ukrainian village."

"Held up? I don't think so. Your busy mouth held you up. If you would do less talking perhaps you wouldn't get held up so often!"

Esther couldn't help but smile at her brother's predicament and Anna giggled beside her as they sat patiently at the table, a few toys keeping them occupied.

"But it looks like the bread was finished just in time. It smells wonderful in here." He smiled disarmingly.

"The bread is fresh but the rest of our meal is overcooked." Mother was not so easily appeased even with Herman's compliments.

He hurried to his mother, kissed her cheek and gave her another charming smile. "I'm truly sorry, Mother. I'll try to be faster next time." Herman was a tall, good looking Dutch boy with blond hair like his fathers and big, blue eyes that caught people's attention. He stood well above his mother and was even in height with his father.

Esther was five years younger than Herman and she completely admired him and delighted in his stories, his great exuberance and his zest for life. She gazed in rapt attention at the discussion between her brother and mother, her eyes lit up with expectation of the story Herman would tell this time. Anna followed Esther's gaze and watched the scene unfold.

Frieda made an exasperated sound and shoved her son away in annoyance, with a small smile tickling her lips. "Baldur, come and eat! Your son has finally shown his face." Frieda mumbled something as she pulled out her chair at the table. "The things we put up with. I have a son who enjoys visiting more than helping at home.

Herman frowned and quickly added, "Mother, I was getting supplies in Tokmak. I was helping."

"It's what you do afterwards that upsets me."

"I caught up on some news."

Baldur Brenner appeared at the door and sauntered slowly to the table. "What news did you hear?"

"I heard two men talking of what they heard over the radio."

Frieda covered her ears in dismay. "I don't want to hear it! You know what we believe. It's wrong for us to listen to that worldly thing. I don't want you to repeat a single word!"

Esther stared at her mother. She wished she'd let Herman continue. She wanted to hear his stories from town more than anything. It brought excitement to their drab existence. Not that playing with Anna was a bore but she absolutely loved to hear Herman talk. She admired him nearly more than her own father.

Herman immediately began his argument, something Esther knew would happen. "Mother, we have a radio in our own home. I don't understand how the radio can be wrong if it only informs us of what's going on in the world."

"This Dutch village and our Dutch neighbors are our world, Herman, and that's all the news we need." Frieda uncovered her ears. "We may have a radio in our home but it was not based on any decision of ours. If the Russian government insists on installing a radio in each house to promulgate its agenda, what choice do we have? But we do have a choice whether we switch it on or not."

"Well I want to hear what Herman has to say." Baldur spoke with finality and gave Frieda a stern look.

Esther smiled and sighed in relief. She would hear stories after all.

Frieda clucked her concern. "Well, I say, this is going too far. Have we all forgotten why our ancestors moved to Russia?" Silence filled the space. "It seems like a spirit of ignorance has overtaken this household! Well I'll tell you if you've all forgotten. Our ancestors desired religious freedom and a longing to maintain our religious beliefs. We need to honor that and maintain some principals and keep ourselves from being polluted by things like the radio!"

"Frieda, please stop. We all know our peoples' beliefs but that doesn't mean their beliefs are entirely correct. Herman has heard some interesting things lately and I think it would be to our benefit to listen. It's important for us to know what's happening with this country we live in. If we know nothing of what's going on how can we prepare ourselves or respond in a godly way?"

Frieda only shrugged and shook her head, still clearly upset over the radio issue.

Baldur turned toward his son. "So what did you hear?"

"Well, I overheard…"

"I don't believe you overheard anything! You listened on purpose!"

"Mother, please let me finish. I didn't intentionally get involved in the conversation but when I overheard them speaking I couldn't help but stay and ask some questions."

"Yes, of course." Frieda's sarcasm was intense. She faced her husband before Herman could continue. "Baldur, the food is getting cold and I suggest we pray first before Herman goes on with his story."

After the usual blessing, Baldur looked expectantly at his son.

Herman grinned enthusiastically and scanned the faces around the table.

Esther smiled brightly in encouragement, her eyes glistening in expectation. Anna looked at her sister and smiled too, Esther's ever present shadow.

Herman took a big breath and began. "Okay, I overheard Bohdan Ovseenko and Yevhen Serbin outside the hardware store and they were talking about the government's concern over the German leader's aggressive views on getting more land mass for his country. The German leader has written a book, *Mein Kampf*, and in it he explains his plans. According to the two Ukrainian gentlemen, the German leader's plans spell out a grave warning."

"Where in the world would those two Ukrainians have gotten hold of a German book?" Frieda shook her head in disbelief as she spooned some potatoes onto her plate, the spoon clinking loudly on the metal dish.

Baldur looked from his wife back to his son, ignoring his wife's outburst. "What were Bohdan's and Yevhen's views about it?"

"Well, Bohdan Ovseenko believes it's a bad sign."

"But why?"

"He doesn't trust the leader in Germany."

"Why wouldn't he, since he knows virtually nothing about him?"

"Bohdan's son, Danylko, returned from Germany a few months ago. Danylko attended university there and he tells of the many changes gripping Germany. To me it sounds like there are many positive changes. The German leader has brought much transition to his people; enhanced working conditions, less unemployment, better health care and generally improved living circumstances all around."

"It sounds like this leader is one to be trusted. He seems like an amazing leader. Perhaps Stalin could learn a few things from the man."

"Yes, maybe he could," agreed Herman. "The German leader is making good on his other plans as well and this is what is causing the concern. Danylko Ovseenko brought along a copy of the German book." Herman looked at his mother after a bite of roast. "And that,

Mother, is how Bohdan and Yevhen would happen to have the German book. Danylko brought it from Germany."

"And you want me to believe those two Ukrainians know how to read German?" Frieda smugly asked her son.

"Well, Bohdan's son learned the language and he explained the book to them."

Frieda only nodded in sudden understanding and looked down at her plate, choosing to focus on her meal.

"And the German leader's name?" asked Herman's father.

"His name is Adolf Hitler. According to his book, he is determined that Germany requires more living space. Danylko's father, Bohdan, is quite concerned that with Hitler's aggressive views and his desire to increase Germany's size, he could possibly lead the world into another war, perhaps even wage war against Russia."

Baldur Brenner held his food filled fork in mid air as he responded. "That's ridiculous! Germany learned her lessons well during the World War. Germany lost badly and she has made many reparations since them, never mind the severe restrictions placed on her by France and the rest of the world. There's no way Germany's leader would lead them into another major war. It would be detrimental to all of Germany. It's unthinkable!" Baldur scanned the table and he spoke to no one in particular, "Pass the bread."

Esther reached for the plate of bread, resting beside her, and passed it to her father.

Baldur nodded in appreciation. "Esther, could you also pass the butter?"

Esther reached to the center of the table and handed him the butter. She looked at her plate. She had hardly touched her food but she didn't care. Herman's story was much too interesting. But it did frighten her somewhat. War sounded scary.

Herman continued, "Well, according to Bohdan and his son, Germany is doing quite well and they're building up their military and armament. The armament factories are booming and producing on a massive scale. Adolf Hitler has apparently created so many positive improvements in the country that the majority of the population supports him and they'd most likely follow him into another war if that's what he chose. They look at him as their savior."

"I still think it's absurd to imagine Germany wanting another war, even in the desire for more land. They were punished soundly after the last war and the world is still struggling to recuperate after the massive loss of lives in so many countries."

Herman quieted for a moment before another thought came to him. "The German leader has started to carry out some of his other plans he laid out in his book so why wouldn't he carry out the plan to gain more land for his people?"

"What plans has he carried out, son?" Baldur took a bite of food and then stared at Herman as he chewed.

"He plans to remove all Jews from Germany. He has a real hatred for them."

"And he has done this?"

"Well, not yet, but he initiated a boycott against Jewish businesses back in 1933, which apparently didn't last long, only three days to be exact. He also removed all Jews from any civil service jobs. Bohdan Ovseenko said his son, Danylko, remembers when numerous Jews in the universities were rejected and asked to leave. The German government was supposedly trying to reduce overcrowding in the colleges and universities but everyone knew, including Danylko, that the move was another act against the Jews, because only Jewish students were asked to leave. Then shortly after that the government organized the burning of so-called subversive writings in the Opera House Square in Berlin. Many Jewish books were burned along with any writings that were considered intellectual filth. These decisions apparently came after only a few months of Hitler's Chancellorship in Germany."

"Really!" exclaimed Baldur.

"Then, in 1935, the Nazi party, Hitler's government, passed some new laws placing greater restrictions on the Jews. Intermarriage between Jews and Germans was forbidden and the Jewish people were stripped of their German citizenship and are now considered as mere subjects. According to Mr. Ovseenko, the Jews in Germany no longer have the privilege of the protection of the law and the courts. They cannot own land or vote. Certainly that says something about Adolf Hitler's motives."

Frieda had stopped eating and she stared at her son attentively, shock replacing her doubt just moments earlier. "He sounds like an evil man. How can he treat the Jews like that? It's not a godly way to treat people at all. Why, our neighbor's daughter, Berta, married a Jewish man. He's a fine man too, a locksmith, and he treats Berta very well. Samuel Goldberg is an upstanding person. I don't see what the German leader has against the Jewish people."

Baldur stared absently from Frieda to Herman, a serious expression on his face. "You have given us some food for thought. These moves the German leader has taken will make life very difficult for the Jews in Germany and let's only hope his other plans don't take on any more substance. We don't need Germany advancing on Russian soil. Who knows what the Russians would do to us. We may be Dutch but we speak German as well as any other German. Stalin has no respect for lives in this country. He has purged his government and his military to such a degree that I'm surprised he still has an army faithful to him, although the ones who remain are too afraid to oppose him!" His eyes betrayed his fear as he looked from Herman to Frieda. "If Germany would be fool hardy enough to advance against Russia, Stalin would be quick to depose of us before the German army ever got here."

Esther could feel fear tighten around her heart and felt her eyes grow wide. She absently took a bite of bread and then stared at Herman, the bread getting stuck in her throat. She tried to swallow but her throat refused to work as fear rose from the pit of her stomach, dancing along her esophagus and lodging firmly in her windpipe.

Herman said, "Father, that's not all the news Danylko shared with his father. Germany has apparently already advanced into the Rhineland region of Germany, an area that was made a de-militarized zone after the war. Even though Germany knew they risked facing strong countermoves from France and Britain they still moved ahead."

"Did France or Britain do anything to stop it?" Baldur asked, staring at him intently.

"Not a single shot was fired and within a week Germany had full military control of the Rhineland. France and Britain denounced the aggressive action but they did nothing to stop it from taking place. France and Britain seem more interested in maintaining peace with Germany than making her abide to the Versailles Treaty."

Baldur stated the obvious. "France and Britain are avoiding another war at all costs. It might be a smart move. No one is ready for another war." He thought for a moment and then said, "But then again, maybe it's not that wise considering Germany's military build up. They're certainly planning something and it doesn't look good for the countries surrounding her."

"According to Bohdan Ovseenko, his son believes that Adolf Hitler has his eyes on far more than just the Rhineland. This is only the start of his military goals. Hitler is aggressive and very popular. It's predicted that the German people will follow him wherever he leads them. If it's into war then into war they'll go."

Esther couldn't bear the question bombarding her mind one more minute. She took a drink of water, finally forcing the bite of bread down her throat. She sighed in relief and looked worriedly at her father before blurting out, "Father, are you saying that if the Germans make war with Russia that the Russian government would kill us? Is that what 'depose' means?"

Baldur looked gravely at his pre-teen daughter and nodded.

Ten-year-old Anna's eyes grew large. "Why would they kill us? We've done nothing bad, have we?"

"The only reason the Russian government would take action against us is because we are Dutch and that we're able to speak German. The Russian communist government doesn't need much of an excuse to eliminate anyone it wishes these days."

As Esther listened, the fear began to take root, deep in her soul, lodging in her heart as she imagined the worst. If only Herman had come home with a fun story, something amusing like he usually did.

This story telling left her feeling sick to her stomach. The food on her plate held no appeal at all now.

Anna's eyes also relayed fear and both of their plates sat neglected and forgotten.

The four guardian angels around Frieda saw the spirit of fear enter the home and noticed its effect on the girls. The one in charge leaned over and spoke to Frieda. In response she looked to her daughters. She immediately noticed that Esther, twelve, and Anna, ten, had hardly touched their food and that terror shone from their eyes.

"That's enough of this Germany and war talk. This is all speculation and there's no positive proof of these things ever coming to pass. We're farmers, harmless and unarmed. We offer no threat to the Russian government. They won't touch us." Frieda then looked directly at her two girls. "Girls, don't let this talk of Germany frighten you. Nothing is going to happen. We're safe here in our village of Conteniusfeld and besides, Germany is a country very far away."

Frieda then looked to her son. "Herman, I don't want you discussing this again. It's not good to think of all the horrible 'maybes' and it causes the girls fear. We serve a mighty God and He will protect us and take care of us."

Baldur said, "I'm glad Herman spoke of these things. It's important to know what's going on outside our little village."

"But what good does it do?"

"It helps us know how to pray."

"Yes, I suppose that is true," Frieda conceded as she stood and began to clear the table. "I have to admit, that hearing these things causes alarm. It causes the girls to fear as well. I'd rather not know what's happening and live in peace."

"You can live in peace only until peace is taken from you, Frieda," Baldur said seriously.

"I don't want to think about it." She turned from the table. "Girls, clear the table."

Esther stood, torn between desiring to hear more from her brother and a knowing that helping her mother was completely expected. She looked at her nearly full plate and knew she couldn't eat another bite.

Her four guardians, Goodness, Faith, Pieter and Marinus, looked at each other with a serious expression, knowing that things would progressively change for this family. They stayed close to Esther while she helped with the dishes, determined to protect and shield, to encourage her toward faith in God.

CHAPTER 15

Berlin, Germany, Fall 1938

Helmuth Schluter lifted a cup of coffee to his lips and sipped the hot beverage carefully. Unna Schluter passed around a plateful of homemade pastries and squares as she played the perfect hostess to their guests.

Roth and Alda Puttkam sat on the other side of the table. Roth willingly received the plateful and placed one of each dainty on his plate to a total of three. He passed it on to Alda who indulged herself to two of each, not that she needed the extra sugar. Her round frame filled in most of that side of the table, the chair hardly holding the large, two hundred-fifty pound woman. Roth seemed content with his large wife. He was usually positive and happy, giving Alda the attention of a devoted husband, giving her preference in most situations and treating her like a queen. Alda also seemed content with her size, indulging in food when given the opportunity and never complaining about her wide hips. Alda always wore stylish, loose fitting dresses and looked good in spite of her weight, with her hair always neatly styled and a touch of lipstick on her lips at all times. Although an unusual couple with strong, opinionated views, they were habitually positive and fun loving to the core.

Beata and Ilse sat at one end of the table, waiting patiently for the plate of goodies to make its way around to them. Beata was now eighteen and quite an attractive young woman, with her bright, blue eyes and light brown, shoulder length hair framing her lovely face. Her pretty facial features caused a number of possible suitors but Beata was determined to stay single as long as possible and rejected every one.

Ilse was fifteen, still hovering between childhood and womanhood, partially developed but awkward and slightly clumsy. Ilse's complexion was darker than her sisters; her hair a light blond that reached nearly to her waist and her eyes a baby blue that caught everyone's attention. She was a beautiful, young girl and already boys were noticing and paying attention. She was still a child in many ways because boys bored her and she was more content to play with her dolls and toys than to give boys much mind.

Ilse gobbled up a few pastries quickly and scooted off to find something more interesting to amuse herself. Beata stayed at the table, feeling a little uncomfortable around only adults but a keen interest tugging at her to know what would be discussed. And after all, she was an adult now too, although she hardly felt it.

Helmuth finished his piece of fruit platz and gazed at Roth, who was finishing off his second piece of pastry. "Roth, I hear that your son, Andreas, has quite a head on his shoulders for the shoe business."

"Yes, he certainly doesn't have his head in the clouds. His head is planted firmly on the floor." Roth laughed heartily. "I don't know what I'd do without him. I've had my fill of making shoes, shoes and more shoes. I've slowed down a lot since Andreas has taken over. It's been wonderful!" The slim Roth Puttkam wore a large mustache that quivered when he talked and shook slightly when he laughed. It was amusing just watching him.

Beata smiled in spite of herself.

Alda spoke up, "We're very proud of Andreas. He's a better shoe maker than Roth ever was." She cackled loudly, causing the others at the table to join in.

"She's telling the truth. I took on the business because my father thought it would make me money. I thought I'd try it and once I was in I couldn't get out. I'm sure glad Andreas is a good shoemaker. Maybe now we'll make some money." Roth smiled mischievously.

Alda smiled brightly. "We've always done well, Roth. I don't know where our boys got their good business sense from. Andreas is an excellent shoemaker and Lamar makes furniture like a professional.

We're very proud of both of them." Alda looked at her husband with admiration. "You've taught them well."

Roth waved his hand in protest. "Ah, I didn't teach them anything. They're teaching me! I'm amazed I produced such talented boys. Where did they ever come from?" He raised both hands in surrender.

Helmuth and Unna laughed at his antics and Beata smiled once again.

Helmuth said, "You must have taught them something of value, Roth."

"I don't know." Roth gave a weak grin. It disappeared just as quickly and then cleared his throat. "How's work at the plant going? And how does it feel to be employed by the government? I'm sure you're making plenty of money now. It's no trouble feeding your family now, is it?" Curiosity shone from his eyes.

"It's been quite a transition for everyone at the plant but things are going well." Helmuth looked suddenly uncomfortable with the flow of conversation and he shifted nervously in his seat.

"So, how do you feel about the change?"

"It speaks for itself, wouldn't you say?"

"Well, for a factory to shift from making pots, pans and everything in between to producing guns, ammunition and tanks is a drastic change."

"That's right. The switch put a real strain on everyone. There have been many renovations at the plant and a lot of new equipment has been installed to make the change possible. The owner is convinced that ammunitions production is the way of the future and that it will be a gold mine opportunity."

"Did Hitler approach the plant or was it the other way around?"

"The Nazi government offered subsidies for the transition of the plant. The renovations were completely covered."

"But not the loss of revenue?"

"I heard that even some of that was taken care of by the Nazi party."

"So how has your job changed, Helmuth?"

"My job title has changed numerous times over the past months. Just recently they wanted me to take the position of over all plant vice-manager." Helmuth squirmed visibly now. "I declined."

Roth looked incredulous and his eyebrows rose considerably. "Declined? Why in the world would you have declined? It would pay far better than you'd ever make as a line manager!"

"Perhaps it would have but it would also take many more hours of commitment and my first responsibility is to my family." Helmuth spoke carefully and decidedly. "I already work more hours than I'd like. With the armament buildup, they are constantly hiring and overtime hours are always available."

"Life is good, isn't it?" Roth Puttkam smiled then. "It seems like the Bishop was right. He had a good sense about Adolf Hitler and now we can see what our new Chancellor has brought about. People are finding jobs, there are virtually no more starving, begging people on the streets and there is extra money for food and some of the refined things of life. I'm quite enjoying Hitler's rule. He's has given us hope again."

Helmuth looked nervous as he addressed Roth, who was a little older than he and much more opinionated. "But don't you think all this armament buildup is a dire sign of war? I don't believe Germany is nearly ready for another war."

"Adolf Hitler is an intelligent man. Just look what he was able to accomplish in the Rhineland, Austria and now Czechoslovakia and all without going to war. We have already gained extra land for Germany without a shot fired! He's a brilliant strategist! His promise of gaining land mass for Germany was true and one he has delivered on. Hitler is an amazing leader and the least we owe him is a heart of gratitude."

Beata watched her father carefully. His jaw moved in controlled, nervous movements as he tried to contain his response. She knew well his views and she agreed wholeheartedly with them. In her opinion, Hitler was a madman let loose at the helm. She dreaded what horrendous decision he'd come to next.

Helmuth said, "Adolf has negotiated for only the Western part of Czechoslovakia, the Sudetenland. It is where the German population of Czechoslovakia resides and that is the area that Hitler was interested in."

Alda smiled in pleasure as she spoke. "And to think that the Czechoslovakian representatives weren't even allowed in the proceedings is outrageous. They had to wait in their hotel suites while the different government leaders decided on the matter." She shook her head and giggled.

Helmuth said, "It's quite clear that England's Prime Minister, France's Premier and Italy's dictator were not interested in Czechoslovakia's welfare even from the beginning. Their desire was to avoid war at all costs and obviously at the cost of Czechoslovakia's freedom."

Roth said, "Czechoslovakia's loss is our gain. I think it's amazing how Hitler is able to wrap these leaders around his pinky and play them to his own advantage. He met with Italy's ruler first, did you know that?"

"Yes, I heard that," said Helmuth.

"Hitler wanted to be sure that Benito Mussolini wouldn't respond badly to another German expansion. Once Mussolini's acquiescence was known, nothing could stop Hitler from his goal."

Helmuth added, "Mussolini had no interest in Czechoslovakia and didn't show any concern with Hitler's plan to take over that country."

Roth said, "Our leader seems to have a knack about getting his way. I like him. He's a forceful politician and he knows what Germany needs and he goes for it with nothing barred."

"If only all of his plans were for the betterment of the German population."

Roth Puttkam's eyes narrowed. "Are you saying you disagree with Hitler's policies?"

Helmuth smiled nervously. "I wouldn't want my views to be stated quite that definitely but I do have my concerns with some of his policies."

"Which ones?"

"Well, we're all aware that since Hitler's appointment as Chancellor of Germany, his request for more and more dictatorial power has been freely agreed upon by the governing political officials. This has taken away more rights from the people and given Hitler greater rule and freedom to govern his way."

"But, just look at all the good he's accomplished through it!" stated Roth emphatically.

"Yes, that's true. But we're also aware that Communist politicians have already been arrested and incarcerated in prisons and concentration camps, removing his greatest opposition. Anyone opposing Hitler's views have the fear of being arrested and those in his own party suspected of being traitors, have been quickly dealt with."

Alda chuckled. "And we know how he dealt with those. With a single shot from a gun, they don't live long."

"I like his methods," stated Roth. "They're firm and decisive. He gets things done that way."

Unna cleared her throat. "What I don't agree with is Hitler's personal vendetta against peace loving citizens. Those who verbally mock the Chancellor, his policies, his Party or his appearance, especially his unusual moustache, are arrested! It's outrageous in a free country like ours!"

Alda grew serious. "That is true. It shows him to be a slightly insecure man."

"Or control and power hungry," added Helmuth.

Beata could feel the tension and intensity in the room. What they all claimed was very true. There was a growing fear in the population of Germany for any dissidence or disagreement to become known, especially to the ruling government. Any sign of disagreement or criticism was quickly and speedily dealt with and removed, ensuring a smooth and wrinkleless administration of all Nazi policy.

"Be careful, Helmuth. Views such as yours could be detrimental to your entire family."

Helmuth smiled nervously. "We're among friends. My views in no way indicate any obstinacy on my part. After all, I'm helping build up arms for the Nazi agenda."

"Yes, but one must be careful. You wouldn't want your views to be too bluntly stated or heard where any of Hitler's SS men or the German police could hear." Roth glared in warning and then continued. "It's good we're indoors and have no fear of that here."

Unna said, "Those SS men frighten me. They lurk at almost every street corner, watching and waiting for someone to make a mistake. It's like they have too many security police and not enough to do. They try to make things up so they can arrest people."

"I know what you mean, Unna. I don't like them either. I don't like it when they laugh after I pass by on the street." Alda made a face.

Roth leaned toward his wife. "They're only jealous that they don't have as lovely a wife as I."

Alda made a high pitched exclamation. "Oh Roth, you're terrible." Then she gave her husband a wink.

Helmuth and Unna both sighed with relief and their shoulders relaxed as the conversation lightened.

Beata had listened intently during the exchange, her mouth eager to speak but restraining herself. If she did speak, she already knew the response her words would engender. It wasn't politically appropriate for her to stand up for what she believed or to voice such strong opinions. She forced the tide of feelings down and willed her mouth to obey. Her four guardians stood faithfully around her, Courageous, Wisdom, Lovely and Light Bearer. The one in charge, Courageous, spoke to her and encouraged her. Wisdom stood beside him, giving Courageous ideas. Beata's blood slowly started to boil and no matter how hard she tried, she couldn't keep silent.

"I particularly don't like the way the SS men intimidate the Jews of our city. It's not right at all," Beata stated. "They harass them and make life miserable for them. The Jews in universities have been asked to leave and too many laws have been passed that take away much of their rights"

Her outspoken thoughts brought conversation at the table to an uncomfortable standstill. Roth's face told of his disapproval and he was the first to speak.

"Young lady, I strongly advise you keep your opinions to yourself. Such thoughts expressed too loudly will not only get you in trouble but could harm your family. Adolf Hitler has a very good idea of how to deal with this evil menace called the 'Jewish Problem' and I for one completely agree with him." Roth held out his index finger in Beata's direction. "Be careful, young lady."

The atmosphere was filled with tension and apprehension but Beata didn't care and chose to continue, her angels egging her on.

"So you believe that we are better than the Jews? Did not God create them as well as us? Who are we to say that we are better? Should not God be the one to answer that question? Is their Creator unaware that they are inferior and if He is, then why does He continue to create them? If God hates them as much as you say you do, then why hasn't He fought against them and destroyed them all by now?"

Roth's color began to deepen and redden. "He has tried over the years to snuff them out in many different ways and in various wars! The Jews are like a treacherous disease, like a contagious virus that continually spreads, reproducing and promulgating their filth and dirt throughout all nations! If God has assigned for us to remove this plague, then we must be faithful in whatever way God's assigned man, Hitler, deems necessary! To resist Adolf Hitler is akin to defying God!" He turned to face Helmuth. "I don't appreciate your daughter speaking to me like this, Helmuth. You haven't taught your daughter much respect! To speak to her elders this way is disgraceful!"

Alda said, "That's right! I can't believe Beata would have the nerve to treat my husband this way." She turned toward Beata and frowned deeply, the wrinkles on her forehead quite visible.

"I'm sorry, Roth and Alda; I don't know what got into her." Helmuth turned to Beata and frowned, anxiety playing in his eyes. "Beata, you need to apologize to our guests."

Courageous, Wisdom, Lovely and Light Bearer looked up in surprise. Courageous had expected Helmuth to defend his daughter. It was then that he saw an evil spirit of fear influencing the man. It was whispering in Helmuth's ear and dancing wildly about him in its ability to manipulate.

Beata sat open mouthed at the clear injustice of the situation and she stared at her father. "So, I'm not allowed to have my own opinions?"

Helmuth looked stern and uncomfortable at the same time. "If your opinions insult our guests, then no, you are not allowed to speak them."

The four guardians around Helmuth and the four around Unna were not able to influence them to Beata's defense. The fear spirit afflicting Helmuth was equally rendering Unna speechless.

"But it's true; Adolf Hitler's treatment of the Jews is horrendous and uncalled for. Anyone in their right mind can see that! If we were being oppressed like they are, would we not scream out our disapproval?"

Roth Puttkam looked grave as he addressed Beata's defiance. "We are not the scum of the earth. You would do well to remember that, young girl. No one will ever oppress the German people. It's completely out of the question. We are a superior race, a more developed species of people. Haven't you read Hitler's book? God favors us and desires the best for us just like the Nazi leader does."

Wisdom spoke to Courageous and he whispered into Beata's ear.

Beata felt her back stiffen and her face grow hot with anger. "You're reciting Hitler's views like he received them from Heaven! You believe Hitler's views more than God's views in His Bible. Are you saying Hitler is greater than God?"

The demon riding Roth's back glared angrily at Beata, his red eyes bulging as he spat into Roth's ear.

Roth's face puffed in fury and turned a deeper red, if that were possible. "How dare you speak to me of these things? Hitler has only openly stated what the majority of Germans were already clearly aware of! If you would carefully study the Bible you would come to realize that it was the Jews who crucified their Lord! They are guilty of much sin!"

"But did not Jesus die for us all? He was a Jew! Are our sins less than the Jew's sins? Does the Bible not state that all have sinned and fall short of God's glory? God would certainly forgive the Jew as quickly as he would forgive any one of us."

Roth's evil companion hissed into his ear. Roth's moustache quivered and shook but Beata didn't find it amusing anymore.

"You know nothing, little girl! Just take a look at the Jews and you'll realize what an evil menace they are to us and our society. Whatever happens to them is exactly what they deserve!" Roth stared at Helmuth. "Put a stop to your daughter's outbursts and her nonsense, Helmuth Schluter, or else my wife and I will leave your house and never come back!"

The demon of fear cackled in delight. The angels in the room stared at him in disgust. They couldn't stop what they knew would happen.

The head of the home was about to inflict pain on his daughter and they couldn't defend her. Helmuth had opened the door to fear and now the evil spirit was controlling the outcome.

Helmuth glared at his daughter, with a nervous twitch in his eye and perspiration on his forehead. "Beata, please, you must stop this! Stop attacking our guests and apologize to Roth and Alda Puttkam this instant!"

Beata straightened in her chair, feeling terribly upset and angered but she bit her tongue consciously. She knew she had no choice. To defy and disobey her father openly would be showing complete disrespect, something she couldn't do, even though great disrespect was directed her way at present. She breathed deeply to still her agitated, wounded heart and spoke rigidly. "Please forgive me for my disgraceful outburst. I spoke too much and should have kept my opinions quiet, like most Germans do, pretending they no longer have a mind that still has the capability to think." She then stood. "I have some things to do. Please excuse me." With that she walked stiffly out of the room, but not before noticing Roth's flashing, angry eyes. He obviously discerned her veiled insult.

Later, after Roth and Alda Puttkam left, Beata heard a knock at her door. She chose not to respond, but stayed sprawled across her bed, facing it with her weight on her elbows, a book opened before her.

Her door opened and her father said, "Beata?"

She refused to answer.

"Beata, please answer me."

She remained rigid, still feeling angry over the evening's events.

The spirit of fear had left with the Puttkams. Helmuth's angels encouraged and prodded him on.

Beata heard her father walk into the room and noticed him stand beside her bed. He touched her arm. "Beata, I came to apologize to you for our guest's behavior. Mr. Puttkam is very taken with the Nazi leader and is extremely opinionated about it. Not only that, he is especially condemning to anyone who disagrees with his views. I have felt it often and today you experienced it too."

Beata refused to face her father, staying in her position and staring at the embroidered flowers on her comforter. "You made a fool of me today." She felt like crying but refused to show her hurt. Her anger would have to do.

"I did not make a fool of you!"

"Then what ever happened to your saying, 'Always be who God created you to be and don't let anyone ever change that.'?"

"I still believe that."

"No you don't! Today you trashed what I am and made me become what was socially acceptable to others." Beata flipped to her back and sat up to face her father. "My opinions have always been important to you. Why were they an embarrassment to you today?"

"I wasn't embarrassed by you!" He looked shocked, like he hadn't expected such a response.

"You forced me to apologize for saying what I said, even though it was truly what was in my heart! Roth and Alda Puttkam's opinions were more important to you than mine!"

"I don't know about that."

"It's true. You hurt me terribly today, Father. I don't know if I can trust you with my feelings and views if you tear them apart in front of others."

"I'm sorry, Beata. I never meant to hurt you." Helmuth stood nervously for a moment as if planning his next statement. He moved as though to speak and then declined. After studying the floor for a moment, he locked eyes with his daughter and said quietly, "I'm going to admit something to you that I haven't even admitted to myself till now."

This got Beata's attention, although anger and hurt still raged through her heart.

"I'm…I'm afraid of people like the Puttkams'. They would follow Adolf Hitler to Hell if he told them to go and I'm afraid that they would report us if they knew fully our dislike and resistance to the Nazi Party. If I ever got arrested for my views, who would take care of you, your sister and your mother? I have a responsibility to all of you and it scores higher in my mind than expressing and heralding my views."

Beata's anger drained quickly as she listened.

Helmuth continued, "I believe you see things and know things beyond your years. You always have, Beata. You understand the motives and the spirit behind the ruling Nazi's. Your opinion, in my eyes, is more accurate and more indicative of what is to come than any other prediction or positive propaganda I might hear about the ruling government. But that doesn't mean I can admit to it openly. There's too much at stake right now. Adolf Hitler has too much control and complete power to make decisions. It's a dangerous time we live in and we all have to do what's for the best."

Beata sighed, "You mean we have to do what's for the best for *us*. We shouldn't stand up for the Jews; it's too dangerous for our own welfare. Let happen to them whatever happens to them." She shook her head slightly in resigned despair. "You've changed, Father. You used to care about other people and not just about our own family."

Helmuth hung his head and then slowly lifted it to lock eyes with his daughter. "Our country has changed. It will change us too."

Fire flashed through her soul. She focused blazing eyes on her father. "I promise you this, I will not change! I have Jewish friends and they will always be my friends, no matter what happens! I will apologize for my opinions, only if you make me, but I will still express my views even if it means my arrest!"

Helmuth gazed open mouthed at his strong willed daughter. "Beata, please consider the rest of us. Don't do anything foolish."

"I believe I've just made the wisest decision of my life and I'll never back down."

"Is this grand decision of yours because of Fayvel Israeli?"

Wisdom spoke to Beata.

"No Father, firstly, it is because of all my Jewish friends and secondly, because, as a Christian, I have an obligation to love all people."

While Beata spoke, her mother, Unna, appeared at the door.

Unna spoke up, "Fayvel was kicked out of university, Helmuth. I think that's the reason for Beata's anger."

"Why does everyone think my opinions are wrapped up all around a Jewish man? Do you both think I've lost my ability to think just because

Fayvel and I have become friends? I see what is happening to all Jews in this city and throughout Germany and it's wrong! According to God's Word, what the Nazis are doing is wrong! I am opposed to the injustice of it all and I will do whatever I can to oppose them!"

Helmuth threw up his hands in resigned defeat and frustration. "I can't get through to you!" He walked to the door past his wife. "Maybe you can straighten her out," he said as he left the room.

Fear was no longer afflicting Unna. Her angels were able to communicate wisdom from above.

"I don't think she needs straightening out. She sees quite clearly. It's the Puttkams' who need straightening out and I'm afraid I can't help them." Unna stared at her husband who had stopped in mid stride.

He shook his head in bewilderment and walked away.

Unna gazed at her daughter and smiled. Beata gave her a small smile in return. Perhaps her parents hadn't entirely forsaken her in this matter.

CHAPTER 16

Poland-Fall 1938

Rabbi David Kohn stood at the edge of a cliff and looked down. A black hole gazed back at him and he could feel terror claim him. The reason for the endless chasm below and how he came to stand here eluded him. Confusion crowded him. He couldn't recall any preceding events leading him here.

He felt the ground beneath his feet giving way, felt himself slipping, losing ground. He frantically tried to reach for the edge, to stop the downward slide but his hands only managed to grasp the crumbling ground.

The freefall was terrifying. The descent through the pit seemed endless, the darkness increasing dramatically as time progressed. The opening where he'd fallen was becoming a mere pinpoint of light up above. Wind whipped at his face and pummeled his body as the speed of his decent increased. Fear was gripping, groping and overwhelming his senses, terror overpowering him as the dark hole consumed his attention. The continual fall wrenched his insides in a tight hold, causing bile to gather in his throat and a scream to beg release.

An unexplainable warning came of the bottom rising to reach him. Then suddenly, with a bone jarring grunt, he landed hard against rock and dirt. A cloud of dust swirled upward and around him, filling his eyes and nostrils with a choking mist of dirt. He lay still, amazed that he was still alive and conscious, but feeling the ache and groan of his bones crying out in agony. Gradually, the dust settled around him and he lay there, looking up and touching his body tentatively. He wasn't sure if anything was broken but so far he felt no breaks, no bleeding and no major damage, although his whole body hurt as though on fire. Hopefully there was no internal injury. For now he was still alive and breathing but his lungs didn't feel normal. He gasped for air and tried to still his thumping heart. Way off in the distance he could see a miniscule point of light. It must be the opening he'd fallen through.

Then he saw something else. There were dots in the small opening far above. Then the realization hit. There were others falling! He could see them coming! They looked frantic and terrified! Some were falling head first, their arms flailing wildly, trying to grab anything to break their descent but the sides remained as unyielding as a concrete wall. Others fell feet first and looked initially peaceful until their features came into view. Their mouths were open wide, screaming as they fell. Others fell with their backs to the ground, as if sleeping, resting but their terrified voices soon obliterated the initial assessment. Some came fighting all the way, their legs and arms moving wildly as if perhaps their great waving would cause them to fly off to safety, but their screams relayed their full realization of their plight.

David heard the noise as each one landed. It was a horrible thumping, groaning and moaning from the pile of bodies that was growing. Then he noticed that every one of them was male. The horror on each face was duplicated, over and over again. David tried to move, get out of the way but his limbs wouldn't cooperate. They hurt too much and his one leg had no feeling. The pit he was lying in slowly filled and the bodies began to land on him bringing on a groan of pain with each impact. Soon he could no longer see the horrific faces slowly closing in on him from above. Darkness was now his companion, terror his closest friend as the cries and screams continued to grow in intensity, filling the pit with despair. Slowly the anguished screams became muffled due to the insulation of the many bodies above him and then all became deathly still.

Rabbi David Kohn woke with a start, sat up straight in bed, his body soaked in sweat from the horror. He breathed heavily, his heart jumping in his chest like a caged rabbit. His hair was matted and his forehead glowed with perspiration as the moon light, through the drawn sheers, shone on his worried face. His wife lay sleeping quietly beside him, oblivious to his agitated state. David pushed back the covers, swung his feet from the bed, slipped his feet into his slippers and left the room.

He anxiously paced the front room floor, wringing his hands and shaking his head. His mind was exploding with the images, wondering, pondering, hoping it all meant nothing, a dream brought on simply by an overly busy day. He stopped by the window and looked out at the dark landscape, lit up only by the moon shining off in the distance. All looked peaceful and at rest. If only his heart would stop its frantic throbbing. He placed a hand over his chest, willing for the tight pain to cease.

"What a horrible dream!" He opened the window to let in the cool breeze. The sheer curtains moved in protest as the fall night air washed over David's flushed face. He took a deep breath and exhaled slowly. "It means nothing. I'm sure it means nothing." His heart slowly stopped racing and his sweat eventually dried as the outside air washed over him, touching his skin and bringing welcome relief. "It was only a nightmare, only a stupid, meaningless nightmare." David laughed nervously and shook his head again. After a few more loops around the room he wandered back to bed, to his perspiration soaked side.

He placed one hand on his wife's back, finding security in her presence, her peaceful state. Devora was the love of his life, the mother of his children, his partner and the one who always brought joy to him no matter what was going on around them. He sighed contentedly, closed his eyes and slowly drifted back to sleep.

Germany, November 1938

Beata pulled on her warm coat, wrapped a knit scarf around her neck and stepped into her winter boots. Courageous and Wisdom stood at the door, ready to leave with her. Her other two guardians, Lovely and

Light Bearer, were resigned to stay at the house to watch things here. She lifted the package from the small table by the door and placed her hand on the knob.

"Where are you going, Beata?" Helmuth Schluter stood in the doorway between the sitting room and front entryway with a Berlin paper in his hand, his eye glasses perched on the tip of his nose. He wore a worried expression. "I don't want you wandering the streets by yourself. It's too dangerous for a young woman to be walking around out there. You should stay here with us where it's safe."

"I won't be long, Father." Beata turned to the door and reached for the knob once more.

"Tell me where you're going, Beata." His voice was commanding,

She hadn't expected this. Her father intruding on her plans had not been part of her agenda. Beata sighed nervously and turned back to face him. "I'm going to see the Israeli's and bring them some baking."

Helmuth's forehead creased in concern. "Does your mother know about this? Did she help you bake this?"

Determination rose within her. "Yes, she did help me and she knows where I'm going."

"I don't understand the two of you! You both know how dangerous it has been on the streets the last few weeks. Why would you put us all into such danger?"

"Father, I'm placing myself in danger, no one else. I'm going out alone and I'm not afraid!"

"I forbid you to go out!"

Anger flared afresh. "You can't do that!"

"Watch me!"

Desperation crowded Beata's heart. "What about the Israeli's and their Jewish neighbors? What about their situation? Don't you even care what's it's like for them? They may very well have had their shop destroyed on that fateful night and you haven't even gone to look!"

"Have you, Beata? Have you gone to look?" Accusation shone from Helmuth's face.

"I've been close to their neighborhood and I asked another Jew about them."

Some of the fight seemed to die from Helmuth as his eyes took on a gentler tone. "What did you learn?"

"The front of their shoe store was destroyed. All the glass was broken and many of their shoes stolen. Most of the stores on that street were damaged, all Jewish businesses. I also learned that Meshulam Israeli's brother was killed that night. He was one of the one hundred Jews that died, Father. He tried to defend his shop from the looters and they attacked him. The Israeli's synagogue was destroyed and burned that same night."

Helmuth looked down and studied the floor for a moment. "I'm sorry to hear that." He closed his newspaper and held it at his side in surrender. He looked at his daughter and said, "I'll go with you. I'd feel better if you weren't alone."

"That's not necessary, Dad. I'm eighteen and I'm German. No one will bother me. You don't have to go. I know how you enjoy your Sunday afternoons at home. You need the rest."

Helmuth had already laid his newspaper on the entrance table and was pulling on his boots. "No, I've decided. I'm coming with you."

"All right, but you should let Mom know. She'll wonder where you disappeared to."

Helmuth stood, leaned into the house and called, "Unna, Unna!"

Unna's voice could be heard yelling back from the kitchen. "What is it?"

"I'm going with Beata."

"Oh, really?" Unna momentarily appeared, wiping her hands on a towel and curiosity in her eyes. "What brings about this change?"

"What we Germans have done to the Jews is not right and if bringing them this small token of our apology will help, then I'm willing to risk it."

Unna smiled in agreement, walked toward them and hugged her husband and daughter goodbye.

The two walked silently for a while, each bracing themselves against the cool wind that whipped debris and dust into swirling patterns on the sidewalk and street. Clouds scurried by above them, eager to move on and yet the cover of thick clouds had entered this morning and refused to depart. They hung over the city in a determined cloak that hid the sun.

It was very quiet on this Sunday afternoon. Stores were closed up for the day of rest and closed signs hung in every window. A few afternoon strollers were wandering about but for the most part the sidewalk belonged to father and daughter, walking in quiet reflection. As they entered the business section, the mostly German owned shops looked neat and untouched by the recent outburst of aggression against the Jewish population. The damage done that terrible night lay blocks away, in the Jewish sector. So pervasive was the damage and destruction on the night of November tenth that it had been given its own name-Kristallnacht or the night of broken glass. Very few Jews escaped the carnage and anger released against them that hateful night.

They had walked a good half hour when they came to a group of SS soldiers standing at the corner of two main streets, where a number of bars were located. They looked somewhat drunk and in good spirits. They spotted Beata immediately.

One young officer took a step toward her. "Hey, pretty girl. What are you doing in this part of town on a Sunday afternoon? Are you looking for some company?"

She looked at him tentatively. Fear pricked at her spine but she held her head high and said, "No sir. I'm only on a stroll with my father."

"Oh, this is your father? I'm so sorry sir for addressing your lovely daughter so commonly. She is a pretty thing. Would you mind if she'd have a drink with me?"

"Actually I would mind. My daughter and I are spending the day together."

Another man came toward the two, a little older than the first young man. He seemed more in his right frame of mind as he walked briskly and saluted in the Nazi fashion. "Heil Hitler."

"Hello," said Helmuth.

"I said, Heil Hitler!" The man saluted again, a stern look playing his eyes.

"Yes, Heil Hitler." Helmuth saluted half heartedly. "We were only going for a walk. Please let us pass."

A group of SS men started to gather around them causing beads of perspiration to grow on Helmuth's face. Beata prayed quietly. Her angels went into action, stepping toward the soldier in charge and imparting some wisdom to him.

Another young soldier forced his way forward, fairly drunk. "Don't you know we can arrest people for not saluting our great leader properly? Don't you know that we can also arrest people for wandering the streets for no good reason? We can arrest people for almost anything." He laughed drunkenly and swayed dangerously, knocking into two soldiers on either side.

The older soldier, the one in charge, smiled and chuckled nervously. "No, no, Ernest. We must remember that we are here for the good of the German people." He looked at Helmuth. "Forgive us for keeping you from your walk. Just don't wander into the Jewish neighborhoods. It's not a safe place. The Jews are likely to attack you. There are vicious criminals wandering the streets there. It's a place we don't offer our protection."

Beata was sure she'd be safer in the Jewish sector than here with the German officers and she couldn't wait to get away.

Helmuth nodded. "We'll remember that and we'll be careful." He took Beata by the hand and led her away, while the first soldier, who had addressed them, winked suggestively at her.

She turned away quickly and focused forward.

A block away she ventured to look at her father. "You know, I don't feel safe around any SS men. I feel safer now that we're away from them." Beata fell silent for a moment and then said thoughtfully, "I believe the drunken soldier spoke more of the truth than the sober one. There's not much freedom in this country any more."

Helmuth looked sadly at his daughter. "I know. I feel the fear and intimidation too. The soldiers know they have complete approval from the Fuhrer to carry out whatever measures they feel necessary to bring control. It frightens me."

Beata took her father's hand and squeezed, determination flowing through her. "I won't let those hooligans intimidate me. I refuse to be afraid of them. I have placed my trust in God and no upstart Nazi soldier will make me back down."

Helmuth was on the verge of speaking when he thought better of it and let it rest. He smiled in a sad, troubled sort of way and clung to Beata's hand.

They walked on for close to an hour till they finally entered the Jewish business section. The transition was stark and sobering with glass still covering many sidewalks, open windows covered with temporary, wooden planks, hateful words written and painted over shop doors and walls, splotches of paint spread on business walls, ruining the once tidy appearance. An oppressive feeling of mourning and death paraded the streets, a tangible presence of terror, a dark foreboding closing in. They passed numerous Jewish synagogues, some were severely damaged while others were completely destroyed, burned to the ground in complete degradation. The two passed a spot on the sidewalk where dried blood still covered the area, a clear sign of the violent nature of that appalling night.

Beata felt the bile rise immediately; fear and disbelief marching around her heart in a steady rhythm. She placed a hand over her mouth and began to gag.

"Are you all right?" Helmuth wrapped his arm around his daughter and held her tight. "Let's cross to the other side of the street." He began to direct her in that direction but she held back.

"No, Father. I want to stay here, on this side. If they went through this then I need to know." Beata stiffened her back, lowered her hand from her mouth and breathed deeply. Slowly she gained control of the terrified feelings and calmed her emotions. "I'm okay now."

"We shouldn't have come here."

"It was my decision." She gave him a determined look.

He shrugged resignedly and they walked on with building after building showing the signs of damage and destruction. Glass crunched beneath their feet block after block until finally they came to the shoe store Beata had visited many times. They stood in shocked silence at the defaced front of the once well-maintained shop. It was clear that Meshulam Israeli had been here since the night of the broken glass. The sidewalk had been swept clean, no glass remained and the once open windows were boarded up with planks of wood. The door was smeared with red and brown paint and the words 'Judische schweine', Jewish pig, stood out in bold brown and hateful against the white door.

Helmuth pushed against it and it opened easily, having sustained damage just a week before. He walked in cautiously turning to bid Beata to wait a moment.

"Hello, is anyone here?" Helmuth slowly walked in and Beata followed him.

The interior of the store was shocking. The shelves had been evidently hacked with an ax in many areas and hastily nailed back together. Paint was splattered randomly on the floor, walls, shelves, with very few areas left undamaged. In one corner it appeared that someone had tried lighting a fire but it hadn't spread far. The walls and floor were charred black a few feet in each direction. Only a few random sets of shoes stood on the shelves, untouched, still matching perfectly, but most of the inventory was gone, some perhaps stolen and many shoes damaged beyond repair.

Helmuth and Beata stood open mouthed in shock and dismay. A sound came from the back room and both of them turned to see Meshulam Israeli enter. He stopped and stepped back in fear as he noticed them.

"Meshulam, it's me, Helmuth Schluter, and," he pointed to Beata, "this is my daughter, Beata." He took a step toward him. "We came to see how you and your family are doing and if there's anything we could do for you."

Meshulam's shoulders visibly relaxed and he walked a few steps closer. "Well, as you can see, they destroyed just about everything. The shop is still standing. I suppose that's something to be thankful for. Most of our inventory was taken or destroyed. They destroyed most of my shoe manufacturing machines. There's one that's still operational but it will take time to find parts and to have the others repaired."

Helmuth spoke quietly. "We heard that your brother was killed that night. Is this true?"

Meshulam diverted his gaze and studied the floor, his jaw flexing in emotion. He finally answered, "Yes, my brother is gone. The funeral was three days ago." He then looked up, sorrow and anger mixed together. "They killed around one hundred Jews that night. They destroyed seventy six synagogues and damaged one hundred and ninety one others." His eyes looked vacant and wounded, with a grief and anger too big to carry.

"That many?" Helmuth shook his head in disbelief. "It's hard to understand the reason for it all!"

Meshulam was quick to explain. "They were killed for defending their families and businesses. That was their only crime."

Beata couldn't believe the injustice of it. What did the Jews ever do to deserve such horror and disrespect? Her head hurt just thinking of it. She couldn't imagine what the Israeli's were going through. She looked at him compassionately.

Helmuth said, "I'm sorry, Meshulam. It's completely despicable! I don't understand what's happening in this country."

Meshulam sighed loudly. "Maybe I should leave the country. My son Fayvel said we should get out now, while we still can. He left last month for England. He decided to finish his doctoral studies there. He's urging us to join him."

Beata already knew this. Fayvel had stopped by to say good-bye before he left. She remembered the way he had looked at her, with a mixture of excitement and sadness. He promised to write. She had promised the same. Her heart constricted at his absence. He was a fine man, and she liked him immensely. She might even be falling in love with him. She felt very taken with him. When he looked at her, her heart would beat erratically and she always felt lightheaded. She hated having him so far away and yet she knew it was the safest place for him. "Why don't you?"

Meshulam waved his hand around his shop. "This is all I know and Berlin is home to me. I can't imagine leaving our home. Who would buy it? Many Jews are leaving Germany right now and no German will buy a Jewish home in a Jewish neighborhood." He said it with disgust and anger. "I would lose everything I've worked for and I'd have to start all over. I don't know if I have the energy to do that." Meshulam gazed off into space. "Maybe things will settle down now. I heard that the night of broken glass was the city responding to some murder a Jew committed against a German. Now that they feel vindicated, perhaps the anger and violence will stop."

"Maybe it will," Helmuth said.

The three stood in silence for a moment, not one of them believing the positive outlook and yet each one yearning hopefully for a peaceful existence. Beata finally broke the silence.

"I heard that England has offered to take Jewish children until things settle here."

Meshulam nodded. "Yes. I know of some families that are arranging their children's transportation even now."

"I hadn't heard this," admitted Helmuth. "Will they be put into foster care?"

"Yes, that is what they're planning," answered Meshulam. "My wife, Marni, suggested sending Faye to England." He shook his head in disapproval. "I couldn't bear having her leave us. I want our family to stay together. Marni seemed relieved to keep her here too"

Helmuth said, "I understand."

Beata wondered if Meshulam and Marni would live to regret their decision. She shook the thought off and held out the basket of baked goods. "Here, my mother and I baked these for you and your family. It's not much but I hope you realize how much we care about what's happening and that if you ever need anything, please don't hesitate to let us know."

Helmuth said, "Yes that's right and I can come on Saturdays and help you fix up your shop."

"That's very kind of you. I would appreciate that. Most of my family's businesses are damaged and we all need help to start over."

"I'll come next weekend."

"Thank you!" Tears threatened in Meshulam's eyes as he held out his hand toward Helmuth in gratitude and they shook on it.

"How are your wife and children holding up?"

"They're doing okay," Meshulam said with a tired sigh. "They're quite shaken but they were thankfully not here when the violence erupted and I was wise enough not to rush here when I heard of the destruction taking place. My brother was not so sensible. He hurried to his shop as soon as he heard about the carnage and he suffered for it. If only he had stayed away. Then his wife and children would still have him."

Helmuth shook his head sadly. "I'm so sorry, Meshulam. You have suffered a great deal of wrong."

"We'll recover. I'm sure of it. We'll recover and we'll be fine." Meshulam still appeared shaken but confident.

"Well..." Helmuth looked suddenly uncomfortable and very out of place. "I need to get my daughter back home. It was good to see you alive and well, and," he waved his hand around the shop, "this can be fixed."

"If only you could bring my brother back." Now tears began to flow unhindered down Meshulam's cheeks. "I'm sorry. It's still so fresh. I miss him a lot."

"You don't need to apologize, Meshulam. You've gone through a horrible ordeal. I'll do what I can to help. Although I can't bring your brother back, I will help you with what I can."

"Thank you again, to both of you." Meshulam lifted the basket slightly as he looked at Beata. "And say thank you to your mother."

Beata said, "If and when you speak with Fayvel, tell him that I'm glad he left the country. I'm glad that he's safe."

Meshulam nodded in understanding and smiled. "I'll let him know."

CHAPTER 17

Poland, December 1938

Aaron and Anka walked toward the house with their three children, Amos, Matis and Lola. For Anka, the Jewish customs were becoming commonplace and these gatherings with family on such special days a treat. She knew what was coming before they got to the door. Anka waited to the side as Aaron knocked. It didn't take long for the door to open.

Binyamin Levin's face appeared and his arms opened wide in greeting. "Welcome, my children. Come in, come in! Happy Chanukah!"

Anka smiled as she stepped in and handed off the items she'd brought, a dish of baked goods and a bag of buns. The smell of the traditional meal wafted toward her. She could detect cheese bread fresh from the oven and the scent of cooking potato latkes on the griddle. Across the room was a table filled with goodies. Fresh donuts were spread neatly on a platter and a cake sat beside it, iced and looking delicious. There was also a small dish with neatly arranged cheese slices, a bowl of cottage cheese, a pretty, dainty, serving bowl with pickles and apple sauce in a glass bowl. Her mouth watered with all the sights and smells.

Binyamin set the items Anka had given him down on the entrance table and embraced Lola as she ran into his arms. Anka watched as Binyamin interacted with the children.

Seven-year-old Lola looked as un-Jewish as they came. She had shoulder length, blond hair uncommon for a half Jewish girl. It was due to her mother's Polish influence. Lola looked into her grandfather's eyes and smiled delightfully. Binyamin was completely taken by the pretty girl before him and he reached out his hand and patted Lola's cheek in affection. She finally turned and wandered off to find her cousins. Binyamin faced Matis next. Slowly eleven-year-old Matis also embraced his grandfather, a little shyly but the embrace was genuine. He turned away quickly and ran out of the room in search of some playmates. Thirteen-year-old Amos held back, uncertainty written on his face.

Binyamin looked at Amos and held out his arms. "So, you think you're too old to give hugs?"

Amos only shrugged his shoulders in reply.

"Look at your grandfather. How old do you think I am?"

"I don't know." Amos looked annoyed.

"I'm really old but I'm not too old for hugs so I know for sure that you are not too old either."

Amos still held back.

Aaron stepped forward and gave his son a shove from behind. "Amos, go give your grandfather a hug!"

Amos finally moved, unwillingly, but he did move. Binyamin grabbed him in a tight bear hug, with Amos' arms hanging down in rebellious surrender. Binyamin finally released him. Amos backed away quickly and was about to rush from the room when his grandfather addressed him.

"Amos, I'll have to teach you how to hug. You don't seem to know how it's done. You hug like a limp rag doll!" Binyamin laughed heartily.

Amos shrugged his shoulders again, turned away from his grandfather and went to find his cousins.

Anka watched her son's back as he wandered off. Amos had been difficult to deal with lately. She turned to see Aaron shake his head in dismay as he watched his son hurry from the room.

Aaron said, "I'm sorry about that, Dad. That boy sure has changed lately. He's so moody and grumpy all the time. Anka and I hardly know what to do with him."

Binyamin smiled knowingly. "Don't bother apologizing. We had three boys remember? Amos is a teenager now and that's all the explanation I need. Your mother and I had to deal with plenty of attitude too. Don't worry about Amos. He's a fine boy and he'll grow out of this stage."

"We wish he was out of it already!" stated Aaron.

Anka inwardly agreed.

Binyamin smiled. "It will come fast enough, son, believe me."

Aaron and Binyamin walked toward the living room and Anka followed. As soon as they entered, Aaron's brothers rose to greet him in hearty handshakes.

"Hey, little brother, you finally made it. Aaron's the last one as usual." Joseph laughed loudly.

Hershel, the oldest, said, "What else should we expect. As our baby brother, Aaron is still the slowest of us all and the most spoiled. He always did like taking his time."

Aaron spoke in defense, "That's what you think, brothers. Chava is still the slowest of us and the youngest. I beat her here and she still wins in the spoiled category."

Joseph said, "Chava doesn't count anymore. She has chosen not to show her face for so long that you," Joseph pointed at Aaron, "have now taken that title."

"Hey, she still counts as the slowest whether she ever chooses to visit or not."

A shadow crossed Hershel's face. "It's like she's dead and gone to us. Now it's just the three of us and," his sadness fled and he pointed at Aaron, "you definitely win in the turtle category."

Aaron grinned during the teasing. "Chava will show her face one day. I can assure you of that! Then you can leave me alone and start teasing her."

It was then that they noticed Init standing in the doorway and the room was filled with tension as all eyes fixed on her. Her face was gripped in sorrow. The Levin boys realized they had perhaps spoken too much, an ill timed reminder of what was missing. Their mother's face testified to it.

Aaron said, "I'm sorry, Mother. I didn't mean to mention Chava's name. She just happened to come up in our conversation."

Init's sorrow slowly lifted and she shook her head to shake the despair. "That's okay. Why shouldn't we talk about Chava? She's still my daughter and I love her deeply. I only regret that she's not here with us."

Binyamin walked toward his wife and draped an arm around her shoulders. "Like Aaron said, one of these years she'll decide to make an appearance. I'm sure of it!"

Init's eyes betrayed the hopeless promise. "Her husband has forbidden her to see us so why would it change now?"

Binyamin frowned. "Well, perhaps she'll tire of being locked up like a prisoner in her own home. We raised her, Init, so surely she will come to her senses and return to us eventually."

Init's face became stern. "Chava has three beautiful children. She would never leave them. Even if she'd be willing to leave Dobry, Chava would never abandon her children."

Joseph's wife, Sonia, walked toward Init and stopped before her. "Did you go see Chava last month like you were planning?"

Init sighed deeply. "I did go see her." She surrendered a small smile at the remembrance. "Chava lives in a lovely neighborhood. It's very wealthy and upper class. I'm truly proud of her status in life." A frown now replaced the tenuous smile. "If only she wouldn't have had to denounce her connection with the Jewish race. If only she was free to come see us."

Hershel turned toward his mother. "Do her children know she's Jewish?"

"No. Dobry forbids her to tell them. As far as his family is concerned, Chava is Polish, at least in pretence. Everyone in his family is determined to keep her nationality a secret. Dobry explains that it's to protect his children."

"Protect them from what?" The anger in Aaron's voice was clear. "To admit Chava's children are half Jewish is a crime? I'm certainly not embarrassed to say that my children are half Polish! What's wrong with that foolish man?"

Anka's heart felt bolstered with Aaron's declaration.

Binyamin's voice rang with disapproval. "Now, now Aaron, be careful who you call a fool. We don't know all the reasons for Dobry's fear or the motives of his family. What we do know is that he has hurt us deeply by keeping Chava from us and I'm sure he has hurt Chava also by forbidding her to see us."

Anka turned to Init and asked, "Why is she so afraid of her husband? Has Dobry ever hurt her physically?"

"Well when I saw her, she looked well. I didn't ask her specifically whether he ever hurt her but I could see pain in her eyes. It pained me also to see how she's changed. She was still as lovely as always but she seemed a shell of the beautiful girl she once was. She was overjoyed to see me, she couldn't take her eyes off of my face and she smiled often as we talked. She showed me many pictures of her children. They are beautiful. Chava has given us three beautiful grandchildren!"

"Children you'll never be allowed to see, Mother!" Joseph said.

"I saw their pictures. That will have to be enough for now."

"How did you manage to see Chava without the children seeing you?" Faiga, Hershel's wife, asked.

"I watched from the street corner until they all left the house, then I walked to the door. I didn't want to get Chava into trouble with Dobry."

"So she let you in? She was allowed to do that?" Aaron asked.

"Yes. She was very excited to see me." Init looked suddenly exhausted. "But she was very nervous. Only after carefully looking up and down the street and sidewalks did she let me inside. She didn't want anyone to notice she was letting me into her home. I could feel her body shake as she hugged me and her hands trembled nearly the whole time I was with her."

"So she was afraid of being found out?" Joseph asked.

She looked at her second son. "Yes, I believe so. I didn't question her on it but she told me that she could never come see us. She would risk too much taking a chance like that. Dobry has warned her that if their children ever find out about her Jewish heritage through her, that he would throw her out and never take her back."

Hershel shook his head in shock, disbelief and anger. "It's absolutely unbelievable! The man's not worthy of her!" He released an angry sigh and then looked at his mother. "So will you go see Chava again?"

Init's eyes filled with tears as she answered. "I promised her I would never be back to see her. I finally realized the great risk I was to her that day and the danger I had unknowingly put her in." She smiled, her tears now streaming down her cheeks. "I have to say that the great risk I posed to her was worth it because it was like heaven seeing my girl again! I dreamed of it night and day for years. Now I know she lives. I know she has children. Dobry has provided well for her and she's as beautiful as ever. It was a dream fulfilled; a short, beautiful, surreal dream and it will have to sustain me for the rest of my days."

Binyamin's arm tightened around his wife's shoulders as sobs began to wrack her frame and she gave way to the sorrow engulfing her. He pulled Init close and held her to his chest, placed his face into her hair, closed his eyes and grieved with her. The room became deathly still as the family waited. Sorrow pulled at them all, they had all lost a great deal. The one sister they had was gone to them forever. There were sister-in-laws and that was a blessing but the one sister, the one the brothers longed for, was forever gone to them.

Simon, Joseph's oldest son, came rushing into the living room, unaware of the serious atmosphere and burst out with a question. "Grandma and Grandpa, all of us kids are waiting to play some Chanukah games and open our presents! When can we start?" Twelve-year-old Simon seemed oblivious to what he had interrupted as he stood with his arms crossed.

Matis entered the room and scooted beside Simon. "And Grandpa, can I light the Menorah tonight? I do it at our house."

Binyamin leaned down so he was eye level with Matis. "In this house it is Grandma's job to light the Menorah. Okay?"

Matis' disappointment shone from his eyes but he recovered quickly. "Oh all right, but can we play a game now?"

Soon a crowd gathered around Simon and Matis as their cousins joined in with the begging and prodding. There was no denying them.

Init wiped her eyes and smiled at the group of grandchildren, the sight of them filling her eyes with a renewed joy and hope. Init touched Binyamin's arm and nodded.

Binyamin addressed his grandchildren. "All right, I suppose it's time to celebrate! What do you say?"

The children responded with shouts of excitement.

Binyamin laughed and said, "I'll get the dreidel and we'll start with a game. The food is ready but I think we can fit in one game before we eat." Binyamin looked at Init and she nodded her agreement.

He wandered off to find the Chanukah toy and the ladies followed Init to the kitchen to finish with the meal preparations.

CHAPTER 18

March 1939

Hitler paced back and forth with a frown, his agitation apparent. He glanced at the clock for the umpteenth time. His moustache twitched in nervous anticipation as he held his hands behind his back and paced the floor in military style. The door suddenly opened and Joseph Goebbels stuck his head in briefly, assessed the Fuhrer's mood and then opened the door fully and entered. Hitler faced him immediately with a look of eagerness and curiosity.

"My Fuhrer, there is no word but I thought I should let you know that we're still patiently waiting. I'll stay in the communications room and get word to you as soon as possible."

"Yes, that would be good. Do that. As soon as there's word from the Czechoslovakian president, let me know immediately!" Hitler emphasized his command with a fist.

"I will, sir." Goebbels saluted Hitler and left quickly.

An hour later, when Adolf's shoes had nearly worn through a path before his desk, the door opened and a smiling Joseph Goebbels entered.

"Good news, Fuhrer! The Czechoslovakian president has accepted our terms of help."

Adolf Hitler clapped his hands in delight and hurried toward Goebbels. "Emil Hacha has signed the terms of our request?"

"Yes he has. He has embraced our ultimatum and has conceded to our terms."

"Wonderful! Now all of Czechoslovakia is ours!" Adolf grinned broadly, clapped his hands again in triumph. "What a relief to finally know! It's another great victory for Germany."

"It's another bloodless victory, Hitler."

"I'm starting to like these kinds of victories, my good friend. It's wonderful that the Czech president recognized the importance of allowing us to help restore order in their country. They truly needed us."

Goebbels smiled cruelly. "The alternative would have been a bloody mess."

"They chose wisely indeed." Hitler wandered behind his desk, sat on his comfortable leather, high backed chair, leaned back with his hands behind his head and sighed deeply. "It turned out better than I imagined." He suddenly sat upright. "I only hope Britain will keep her nose out of our affairs."

"If you don't mind me saying, sir, I don't believe Britain has the guts to oppose us. They don't want war and they'll avoid it at all costs."

"That's all the better for us, Goebbels. The longer they stay away, the more land we'll be able to amass."

Goebbels smiled at Hitler with great admiration. "Let me congratulate you, Hitler, on another successful venture for the betterment of Germany."

"Thank you. This won't be the last." A smile slowly spread across his face.

CHAPTER 19

Poland, Spring 1939

Rabbi David Kohn walked in a long line of people heading out of the city. He didn't know where they were going. He tried to look over the heads of the crowd in front of him to see where they were heading but it was impossible to make out. He scanned the group traveling with him and noticed his companions were mostly older Jewish men, many Rabbis like himself. There were many weak, old men in the group and he noticed a few elderly women also in the assembly. The women wore kerchiefs over their heads and many held on to canes to support themselves. David could see the sporadic, bright colored kerchiefs bobbing up and down here and there in the crowd which preceded him.

David tried to speak to the men around him to see if they knew any more than he as to what was transpiring. He looked into the man's eyes behind him and was shocked to see utter despair on his face, as though he had lost everything dear to him. David turned to the man in front of him, tapped his shoulder and was about to ask him where they were going when he noticed the tears streaming down the man's face, disappearing into his beard, and the terror written in his eyes. Where was the hope his people always had? Why all this fear? They were just traveling weren't they?

David turned to look back at the crowd following and studied their faces. He saw deep despair in each one. Some carried bags and lunches as if going to work for the day. Surely they would return home at the end of the day, wouldn't they? Many faces mirrored the despondency and fear on the men closest to David. He turned and continued walking, confusion pulling at him.

He began to notice the trees and landscape of the forest on the outskirts of Krakow. The people ahead of him suddenly stopped and since the group was so large he couldn't see what was taking place at the front of the line. The people around him fidgeted nervously. Noise began to filter back to where he stood. He began to hear wails and screams that caused his skin to crawl. Fear lodged itself firmly in the pit of his stomach.

They had walked for hours and now the afternoon sun was shining down relentlessly. The heat was tremendous and the screams up ahead caused bile to gather in his throat. The hopeless wails continued unabated until finally the line inched forward. Why the men didn't turn and run the opposite way he didn't know. Why wait here and succumb to what the others were going through.

David turned in the crowd and tried to push his way to the outside but there were too many of them and the group was pressing in around him, moving him toward the terror.

"Move!" he yelled.

No one moved.

"Get out of here. Let's run and get out of here!" he yelled again.

Dead, lifeless eyes stared back at him, unwilling and maybe unable to change the tide.

A frantic helplessness overtook him then. There was no way he could get away. Resolutely, he turned back to face what was quickly approaching.

As the crowd dwindled in front of him, he saw a huge black hole dug into the ground. An unseen force began to lift people up front from their place and hurl them into the hole alive, as they screamed and begged for their lives.

David stood staring open mouthed for a time and wondered why they all stood there not doing anything? Was this force that was destroying them too powerful for them to overcome when they reached this point? David watched as an elderly man, cane and all, was picked up and, while he cried and begged, was hurled into the hole, head over heels. David heard the impact as he landed. This brought on a wail of horror from the crowd that watched. David looked on as an older Rabbi was unusually abused by this unseen force. He was pushed back and forth ruthlessly as he waited to be deposited into the grave. He cried for mercy. The invisible power suddenly threw the Rabbi down to the ground and it appeared that he was being kicked and beaten. He grunted and groaned as he buckled forward with each impact. Finally, after what seemed like an eternity, the Rabbi was finally discarded in the dark hole with the rest. This scene played out over and over until David couldn't bear anymore.

He backed away slowly from the group that seemed mesmerized by the horrific treatment. It was unclear why he could now make a getaway and why the group was now making way for him. Maybe the crowd had thinned enough to make it possible to break through. He edged back toward the forest and slipped behind a tree. His heart beat frantically and he breathed heavily to try to calm his heart. He couldn't let this unseen force detect his escape. For a while, he stood completely still wondering about the best time to leave. Finally he moved, stealing through the forest, letting the natural growth and thick trees hide him. The cries of his Jewish brothers and sisters grew quieter and quieter as he retreated further and further into the thick forest.

After what seemed like an hour David ran into a clearing and stopped. He breathed heavily after the exertion, fear still a close companion. Where could he go to escape this evil that had hypnotized his people? Was the forest a safe place or did the unseen power see him here too? He could feel his adrenalin pushing him to keep moving and yet terror glued him to the spot. Movement on the other side of the clearing caught his attention. He knew he should duck down and hide in the long grass around him but his body wouldn't move. His feet stood frozen in spot as a man approached him. The man looked stern and somewhat Jewish, but he wasn't sure. David cursed his feet for not cooperating.

The man moved resolutely toward David, a confident stride in his step. David willed himself to move, to do something, anything but stand in one place, vulnerable and open to whatever was coming. He stood helpless as the man closed in.

David could now see that, indeed, this man was Jewish, and maybe even a Rabbi. Yes, somehow he knew this man was a Rabbi. But his beard! It was trimmed short and neat, not typical at all! He looked more like a young Jewish man than a respected Rabbi. Why didn't he let his beard grow out? Didn't he know he'd be more respected by the people? David shook his head in bewilderment. And what was a Rabbi doing here in the forest? Why hadn't he been rounded up with the other Rabbis?

The young man wore what looked like a white tunic with a blue sash around his waist. A prayer shawl was draped over his shoulders. And what was that on his head? A crown? What was he doing in the forest, walking toward David, with such a look of determination and wearing a crown? David shook his head in bewilderment. But maybe this man was the cause of the terror taking place just the other side of this forest. Maybe he wasn't a Rabbi after all. David braced himself for the worst as the man stopped before him.

The man stared at him with concern. The depth of the man's eyes astonished David. Great waves of love nearly knocked him over. Who was this? It was like David should know him. Did he know him? He saw deep sorrow in the man's eyes now, and a love that was incomprehensible.

"Do I know you?" David finally asked in a shaky voice.

The man only smiled, slightly, hardly discernible, but he did smile.

"Who are you?"

"Jesus."

"Jesus?" Confusion swirled through his mind. "The Christian's Jesus?"

"I AM who I AM."

David could feel the color drain from his face as the realization hit him.

The man then held out something in his hand and with his other, touched his own short beard gently and rubbed it.

David looked at the item in the man's hand. A razor? Why would he hold out a razor? He looked back into the man's eyes; saw the seriousness there, the concern, the love, the compassion and the urgency.

The man then spoke and his voice was like the rushing of a river. "Tell them, I AM who I AM."

Understanding hit him hard. This was his Messiah!

Just as suddenly as the man had appeared at the far end of the clearing, his form now began to dissipate, vanishing into thin air, the razor in his hand shining and remaining visible longer, till the image was emblazoned in David's mind.

David sat bolt upright in bed, his body drenched in sweat and his heart racing a thousand miles a minute. He couldn't keep quiet this time as he pleaded, "God have mercy, God Almighty have mercy on us!"

David's wife, Devora, awoke and rubbed her eyes. She sat up and looked at her husband in bewilderment. "What is it? Why did you wake me?"

"I'm sorry, Devora. I had a horrible dream! Look at me! I'm a sweaty mess."

"You look terrified! Whatever did you dream about?"

"I can't talk about it and to think I need to oversee the Sabbath service in the morning. I can't even think straight! Such horrors no eye has ever seen!"

She grabbed his arm in concern. "Tell me, David."

"No, no, I can't." He swung his feet out of bed, slid them into his slippers and wandered from the room.

CHAPTER 20

The Great Temple lay in a clearing in the great forest, close to the bottomless sea. It was an ivory giant, a magnificent rainbow encircling it. It shone with holy, pure light. Its structure was filled with the most amazing building material and sparkled with the light of Heaven dancing around it.

Bold had been summoned here and he now knelt on the glass-like marble floor, before the great throne as his strength ebbed slowly away. Anthems of righteousness and justice poured forth from God's throne. Bold could no longer hold up his angelic frame as his knees gave way and he lay face down before the power surge of God's presence flowing through the Holy Temple. He lay incapacitated as instructions poured over him from the Great One on the Great Throne. Bold's weapons were strapped to his belt and lay on the floor with him as he worshipped the One who deserved all honor and glory in this awesome place.

He had been summoned only the day before and, although his weapons had been ready for some time and a growing heavenly impatience had been nagging him for days, he was fully aware of the dangers ahead and these had caused him some fear. Now in Almighty God's presence all trepidation fled at the sheer power emanating in, around and through him.

The words from Almighty God reverberated through Bold's being and energized him for the work ahead, even though the forceful flow of power now drained every bit of strength from his frame. It was a mixture only found in God's mighty presence, strength and weakness simultaneously. Slowly the power flow from the throne dissipated and a soft, heavenly, radiant glow surrounded and filled the temple area. It permeated Bold's entire being, filling him with renewed strength. After some time, Bold finally stood, his legs still shaking from the surge of power that had coursed through him. He looked to his side and noticed Resilient also beginning to stand.

So they were being sent out together. It was an added blessing.

Resilient flanked his side as Bold made his way from the Great Temple, while many angels sang out God's praise as they flew around the throne and circled high above in the massive dome of the temple. Bold and Resilient walked down the wide steps leading away from the temple doors while surges of power caused them to sway forward as they walked. Coming to the temple was both draining and exhilarating. The power of the Most High was enough to render one immobile but also filled one with renewed strength, purpose and power. It was hard to comprehend how it could do both so thoroughly and completely.

The two angels followed the river of life which flowed from the temple and throughout the far reaches of Heaven. They walked in silence through the lush growth, which marked the edge of the river of life. They walked through a particularly tree filled area, loaded with abundant fruit of many kinds with the heady scent filling the air. When they made their way past the last fruit tree and entered upon a plain filled with wild flowers, they saw a horse and chariot team landing close to the river's edge.

Bold turned to look at Resilient. "The assignment seemed urgent. I suppose it was more urgent than we even realized. We depart immediately."

Resilient smiled in anticipation. "I'm ready to go." His smile faded to a frown. "I never imagined we'd be sent to Poland. I wonder what's so significant about Poland."

"There are many angels being sent out every day now. There are many things developing all over Europe, but it seems like the most urgent place right now is Poland."

"Yes, it seems like the majority of the angel forces are being sent there."

"And we're about to join them."

"Let's go!"

The two were soon sitting on the soft, cushioned pillows of the chariot, the horses neighing and prancing their feet in eagerness. Prisms of light danced around the chariot as the fire emanating from the horse and carriage team flowed and pulsed around it.

Resilient gave the command, "Go!" The team lifted off and sailed like lightening toward earth.

The conference table was surrounded by Adolf Hitler's top government personnel with Adolf sitting in the place of preeminence at the head of the table.

"I have called this meeting because of the critical issue facing us with Poland. The strip of land, granted to her after the Great War, was ill-fated to our country. This so-called Polish Corridor has only caused friction to increase between our two countries. The city of Danzig located within the Polish Corridor is the reason for this meeting. Although Danzig was made a free city, it is filled mostly with Germans. As you all know, we Germans are supposedly free to use this corridor to access East Prussia, but the tension between us and Poland has only increased and is at the breaking point. I want to know what you, my trusted friends, have to say about it. What do you suggest?" Hitler gazed around the room, the answer already shining from his eyes.

Heinrich Himmler cleared his throat. "I believe it's time that Danzig be given back to Germany. It is rightfully ours and we demand it back! We should send our Foreign Minister, Ribbentrop," Himmler nodded to Joachim von Ribbentrop sitting at the other end of the table, "to negotiate with the Polish Foreign Minister at once for the transference of ownership of Danzig. It is vital for the good of our people."

Hitler nodded and smiled. "You have some good points, Himmler, but what good is the city if we have conflict in our travels through to East Prussia. We'll have the city, yes, but what of the convenience of a free flowing corridor?"

Joseph Goebbels stood to address him. "Fuhrer, I suggest the construction of our own corridor which would link our great Reich with East Prussia. It would include the port city of Danzig of course. This would produce a decrease in the tension building between the two countries and would secure part of the land rightfully belonging to Germany."

Hitler stared at the Foreign Minister, Joachim von Ribbentrop. "What do you say about these suggestions?"

"They are excellent ideas. I like them and just maybe the Polish Foreign Minister will agree. We can only try and hope for the best."

"I want you to do more than try, Ribbentrop!" Hitler's gaze was stern as he set a fist firmly into his other open hand. "You must succeed in convincing Colonel Josef Beck to agree to our demands. The alternative will not be in Poland's best interests. You must make him see this clearly."

"You mean you want me to tell him that if he doesn't sign this request that there will be consequences."

Hitler smiled slightly. "No, don't go that far. I believe the whole world knows our strengths and what we have been able to accomplish in only a few years. The Polish Foreign Minister will be well aware of our broader intentions without stating it plainly. I want you to deliver a written proposal to Minister Colonel Josef Beck in Poland and we'll know soon enough what his response will be. His decision will determine the fate of the people of Poland. His country's future now rests in his hands."

Bold and Resilient waited outside the Polish Foreign Minister's office where Joachim von Ribbentrop and the Polish Foreign Minister, Josef Beck, were meeting.

Bold turned toward Resilient. "Do you know the outcome? Has God informed you?"

"No, we will find out together what the fate of Poland will be."

Bold felt impatient as he watched the door. "Why can't we go in there and learn first hand?"

"There are too many forces of darkness hovering around Joachim von Ribbentrop and plenty influencing the Polish Foreign Minister. It would be to our detriment to enter now. We are far outnumbered."

"Why would God send us to a place where we are so outnumbered?"

"We need this information." Resilient paused as if hearing something. "We need to step back into the closet behind us. Someone is coming and we don't need to be detected by any demon horde this early in our mission."

Bold complied and they both slipped into the closet and meshed in complete obscurity with the cleaning supplies there. On the other side of the doorway, Ribbentrop exited the office and walked briskly down the hall. A horde of demonic beings flowed like a river after him. The two angels waited a moment and then Resilient waved for Bold to follow. The two angels followed Ribbentrop while staying concealed within the wall. The man walked down two flights of stairs, into the lobby of the government building and out the door to the waiting car. His attendant immediately exited the car and opened the door for Ribbentrop.

"How did it go, sir?"

Ribbentrop refused to answer while a scowl covered his face. He ducked his head into the car and slammed the door shut.

Resilient spoke from the safety of the Polish government lobby, "I suppose that's answer enough."

"I suppose so," agreed Bold.

The two angels watched as the car drove off with a black cloud of demons hovering over and around it.

"Let's head back to Colonel Josef Beck's office," said Bold.

The two angels backtracked quickly and stood within the wall between the hall and the Polish Foreign Minister's office. It was completely silent. Bold entered the empty room and hurriedly reentered the wall. The two angels swiftly sped through the offices undetected until the familiar voice of Josef Beck floated toward them. Bold could hear the anger in Josef's voice as he spoke to someone on the other side of the wall. The door plaque said, 'President Ignacy Moscicki'. The two angels positioned themselves within the wall and listened.

"What else were we to do? I know that the situation is desperate and that Germany is a tremendous threat but to give up the Polish Corridor is unthinkable." Josef Beck's voice shook in fury.

"He wasn't asking for the Polish Corridor, Josef."

"He may as well have asked for all of Poland!"

"But he was only asking for the port city of Danzig and a new corridor for the German people. We have to keep the information accurate."

"President, please forgive my anger but I can't help but be infuriated with the German's real agenda. They want us to give up part of our land and then they'll do what they've done to all the other countries they've oppressed. They won't be satisfied till they get all of Poland."

"Well, that is a possibility I suppose. But we made the right decision, Josef. We have to hold back that German monster. Putting our foot down firmly may be the only way. By totally rejecting their proposal, just perhaps they will relent. What I fear more is that they will take the opposite approach and become aggressive." There were deep lines around his mouth, his concern obvious. "We need to strengthen our ties with England and France. Contact them immediately and forward Germany's proposal to them. Relay our concern of their possible future aggression. We need our allies desperately right now. Time is of the essence."

"Yes, I'll work on that right away. I only hope that England and France will truly come to our aid if we need it."

"Yes, I hope so too." President Moscicki looked grave. "They positively didn't jump in to save Austria or Czechoslovakia, did they?"

"No, there was no help for them."

"But we have been strong allies for a long time. I'm confident that England and France will come to our aid if we ask."

Josef Beck only nodded in respect, while doubt clouded his face. He turned and left the room to fulfill his duties.

CHAPTER 21

David Kohn stood before the mirror, uncertainty and fear glaring back at him as he held a razor in his right hand. He looked intently at his reflection and felt the dread and uneasiness even more. He touched his beard and ran his hand down the long trail of white to his waist.

"God in Heaven, if only there was another way. What will my Jewish brothers and sisters think of me? They will disown me and cast me off as a heretic!"

David put the razor down, clung with both hands to the either side of the sink and agonized over the decision as he studied the white ceramic bowl. Would he choose God's way or would he walk in his own wisdom? The tension and pressure to abide by Jewish tradition was strong, tugging at his heart, begging him to conform, fit in and remain respectable. It would be so much easier to stay acceptable to the Jewish standard of righteousness. His new found source of righteousness required so much sacrifice.

But how could he deny the dreams, the burden it had put on his soul, the heart wrenching questions and the realization that indeed Jesus of Nazareth truly was their Messiah. David's mind flitted back to a few days ago when he had finally, after many hours of study of the Bible, bowed his knee and received Jesus as his Messiah. Could he now so quickly disregard the decision he had made and again deny this Messiah by his actions? He knew with all his being that he had made the right choice, but now facing the very real threat of being disowned by his congregation, his heart was heavy with the reality of his decision.

He had finally found the courage to accept Jesus of Nazareth as his Messiah. Would he now also have the courage to do what his Messiah had asked of him? Growing hair on his chin was not nearly as important as obedience, was it? David was convinced his congregation would disagree with this point when they came to know the reason for his decision. How could he ever tell them the entirety of all that he'd seen and heard?

David's hands began to shake at the repercussions that cutting his beard short could produce. His great desire to be accepted by his fellow Jews weighed heavily upon him. His great desire to please his newly acquired Messiah also weighed equally heavily.

He stood before the mirror for almost an hour, tossing the questions back and forth, contemplating the response of his friends and family, the wrath of his congregation, the embarrassment he would bring upon his wife, Devora, and the way that he was sure to be humbled before all that knew him. Sweat formed on his forehead and slowly the whole of his face until his beard grew damp with it.

The temptation to conform was intense and to ignore the instructions from the Messiah a heartache and terror. What would result if he would choose to ignore the warnings? What if he let his people go on in their ignorance? Would he be held responsible for their possible demise? Would the fate of their souls be charged to his account? Was what he saw in his dreams a possibility? Were they, as a people, about to face a great judgment? And what if they were? Did God desire to warn his people through him? Was his dream even real? What if it was just an illusion?

Four guardian angels, Dutiful, Truth, Ira and Hoshea, had been assigned to him the moment he had accepted the Messiah. They stood patiently around him now. His anxious questioning didn't give them much to work with. They knew Holy Spirit was prodding him, encouraging him and speaking truth to him.

David's anguished face filled the mirror. His wonderings continued. But was his acceptance of Jesus as Messiah an illusion also? It couldn't be! He had studied the scriptures for hours, staying up through the nights to find the truth. And hadn't he found the truth? He had found that every prophetic scripture concerning the coming Messiah, Jesus had fulfilled in his lifetime. Hadn't he felt the living Spirit of God burn within him as he studied the Christian's Bible? Hadn't the scriptures of the New Testament come alive to him as he read and compared it to the torah, prophets and Psalms? He couldn't deny the fact that everything he had studied led him to the conclusion that Jesus was, without doubt, the Christ, the Son of the living God. How could he now ignore all the evidence and resort once again to tradition and religious conformity? It would be at the price of his own soul, that much he knew. But now it was not only his soul that was at stake. He was now being held responsible for the souls of those he led as shepherd. How could he fail them? What excuse could he give when he would one day stand before the throne of God?

He finally turned away from the mirror, with a sigh of exasperation, tired of the exhausting tug of war raging within him.

It was then that Bold and Resilient, their swords drawn, cut through the demonic group hovering over the Kohn home and sent them scurrying in every direction. Two special assignment angels entered through the ceiling and landed before David.

David couldn't see them nor did he realize they were there as he breathed heavily to clear his mind.

David's four guardian angels stepped back to allow the special assignment angels to work freely.

Bold spoke first, inaudibly and yet David heard every word, deep down in his spirit. "Do not fear what other's fear and do not be afraid! Has not God promised that He will always be with you? He takes hold of your right hand and says to you, 'Do not fear; I will help you.'"

Resilient spoke next, "A great danger is about to be released against Poland's Jews. How can you do nothing when God has asked you to act? To obey is the only option. To obey is better than sacrifice. You must do what He has requested and certainly God will be with you."

Both angels unfolded their wings and fanned them in David's direction, bringing a sudden calm to his tangled emotions, definite clarity of thought and a deep, heavenly comfort.

CHAPTER 22

Berlin, Germany, spring 1939

Beata walked into the kitchen where her mother was sitting at the table with a newspaper spread out before her and a cup of tea in one hand. The smell of baking bread wafted through the room but it went unnoticed by Beata as she went to stand beside her mother and placed a pamphlet over the newspaper.

Unna Schluter glanced up to meet her daughter's eyes. "What's this?"

"It's something I thought you might like to read." Beata pulled out the chair kitty corner to her mother and sat down.

Unna took another sip of tea, set it down carefully, then picked up the pamphlet. She read it slowly. Beata waited patiently beside her.

Unna looked up and fear filled her eyes as she searched her daughter's face for any answers. She looked back at the pamphlet which she held in unsteady hands. "You…You're not planning to join them, are you?" Her pleading eyes lifted once more and bore into Beata's.

Beata sighed deeply. "I should. It would the right thing to do and I applaud them for being so brave, but I know I have a different purpose to fulfill."

Unna released a pent up sigh and smiled in relief. "You shouldn't scare me like that."

With a slight smile, Beata stared at her mother. "What makes you think that my purpose is any less dangerous than theirs?"

"Because we serve a God who loves us and he will take care of my girl." Unna's fearful gaze betrayed her confident words.

"Mother, during evil times, extraordinary courage and bravery are required from the most unlikely people. If I need to risk my life to do what God requires me to do then I am willing to do that."

Unna stood and hurried to the oven and looked inside. The breads weren't quite done so she closed the oven door and stood for a minute, her back to Beata. She slowly turned, her hands clasped tightly in front over her apron. "I wish you wouldn't say such things. It only causes me to worry."

Beata picked up the pamphlet and held it up. "What about these university students? Don't you think their parents are concerned for them?"

"Yes of course. They are in grave danger! They are opposing Adolf Hitler openly and there's no way to know what the outcome will be."

"They aren't opposing him openly yet. They are keeping these pamphlets fairly quiet and reserved for only close friends and those who think like they do. I have a fairly good idea what this will lead to though. They will become more and more vocal and more adamant, that is if they have the courage. And then it will be quite definite what the outcome will be, that is if Hitler ever finds out about these pamphlets." Beata dropped it onto the table.

"What pamphlet?" Sixteen-year-old Ilse strode into the room oozing confidence, her full, blond head of hair bouncing past her shoulders as she tossed her head to the side. She sidled up beside Beata's chair and glanced down. She picked up the pamphlet and stared at it. "What's this about?"

Beata looked at her younger sister. "Some university students wrote and published it and are starting to spread it around. They oppose many of Hitler's views and policies and call for all Germans to unite against him. They'll have to circulate it to a greater degree if they want their message to spread."

"How stupid can university students get?" Ilse smirked in amusement. "You'd think they'd get smarter in university, not more ignorant." She stared at Beata. "Don't they know they could get arrested for this?"

"I'm sure they're very aware of that."

"Then why would they do it?" A look of incredulous wonder covered Ilse's face.

"I suppose they absolutely believe in their cause and agenda and that perhaps getting their message out will effect change in this country."

Ilse grunted in disbelief. "Who's asking for change? Hitler has made enough positive changes to warrant him an award or something. These so called agenda driven students are doing nothing but bringing harm to themselves. You'd think the university professors would drill some sense into them."

Beata could feel her face turning red with the anger boiling within her. "Ilse, you're talking like a fool! Haven't you noticed what the government has done to the Jews and the lack of freedom in this country for all Germans? Why should university students not be able to express their opinions freely? Why should they fear being arrested for only stating what they believe? Did you know, Ilse, that this country used to allow people to speak their opinions without fear of retribution? It should be the right of every man and woman to speak their mind freely."

Ilse rolled her teenage, irritated eyes in exasperation. "You think you're so smart! You think you have all the answers for the world but I'm here to bring you back to reality! Adolf Hitler has done more good for this country than any other leader Germany has had. Open your eyes, Beata, and look at the differences he's made. People are back at work, they have food on their tables and no more beggars roam the streets. Germany is a safer place and you know it!"

Beata smiled. "It sounds like you've been busy listening to Hitler's radio propaganda. You hear only what the Nazi government is telling you."

"That's not true. I have many friends and I hear them talk about the Nazi government and all the good they've done for Germany."

"All of them Nazi supporters, I'm sure." Beata shook her head in dismay at the changes in Ilse the past few months. She had seemingly changed overnight from a girl to a young woman and her haughty attitude, her constant position of being all-knowing was very wearing.

Unna stood at the counter while the girls argued but now she pointed to Ilse. "Have you been spending time with that boy down the street, Hahn Brauer?"

Ilse tossed her head, causing her blond hair to bounce defiantly as she looked in her mother's direction. "What if I have been? Does it really matter? After all, I am sixteen and many girls marry at sixteen."

Unna's eyebrows shot up in surprise. "Marry? Who's talking about marriage? And anyway, sixteen is much too young to marry, Ilse, especially for you!"

"What does that mean?"

"I don't believe you're responsible enough to take care of a home and babies. You have a lot of growing up to do."

"Who said anything about babies?"

"They come soon enough," Unna said with a shake of her head.

"Well Hahn is very responsible. He's eighteen you know? He's very mature."

"Oh really?" Unna said with a chuckle.

Ilse didn't even crack a smile. "Just because I'm the younger daughter doesn't mean you have to continually treat me like a baby. I'm sixteen and I've grown up. Is that so hard to believe?"

Unna's smile disappeared. "I'm sorry, Ilse. I didn't mean to treat you like a baby. I know Hahn is very taken with you, but all men are taken with you. You're a beautiful, young woman and I don't want you getting involved with the wrong man. You're too vulnerable right now, eager for any man's attention and I believe it would be better for you to wait, especially with our country in the throws of war. It's a very uncertain time."

"You've just spoken my next reason for pursuing a relationship now. What if war does break out? All the men will go off to war and I'll turn into an old maid waiting for them to return."

Beata couldn't resist jumping in. "Ilse! That's the most selfish thing I've ever heard you say!"

"What? I want to get married and you want to stay an old maid. We're different from each other, Beata! If you want to stay unmarried, go ahead but I'm not like you. I want a husband, a home and eventually I want a family. I don't want to wait and it's not because I'm selfish!"

Beata softened her approach. "But, Ilse, just think about it. Let's say you get married within the year...to Hahn. What if he joins the

German army, gets sent on duty and leaves for many years or never returns. What would you do then?"

"I'd marry someone else. It doesn't take a genius to figure that out!"

"What if he doesn't return but you're not sure if he's dead or alive. Would you wait for word? Would you wait to make sure before you remarry?"

Ilse rolled her eyes openly this time. "Beata, you're so concerned about all the negatives that you put your life on hold just in case of this, or just in case of that! I can't live like that and I refuse to. I for one am thankful for our Nazi government and all they are doing. Actually Hahn has signed up for the army. He just signed yesterday and he's *so* excited!"

Beata couldn't believe she was hearing this. "Adolf Hitler is a madman and he'll lead Germany into Hell to take that over if he thought he could get away with it! He's not the savior everyone thinks he is. Does Hahn realize what a tyrannical leader and dangerous man Hitler is?"

"Should I forward your opinion on to the Fuhrer?" Ilse stood, arms crossed, her fiery eyes flashing warning.

Unna stepped forward, anger shining from her eyes. "Ilse, how dare you speak that way to your sister? You know how all of us feel about Adolf Hitler. Your father and I are just as opposed to Hitler's agenda as Beata. Would you actually expose all of us?"

Ilse looked immediately repentant. "No, of course not." Then her anger seemed to resurface out of nowhere. "If it angers you all so much that Hitler doesn't allow any public opinion that differs from his own, then why can't I be allowed to have my own opinion in my own home. Why are my opinions trashed like useless dung by the people I love? Just because my opinions differ from yours doesn't mean they're worthless! I'm starting to believe that the same tyrannical decisions you accuse the Fuhrer of making are taking place in this very house."

Beata gazed at her sister like she was seeing her for the first time. "You can have your own opinion but don't base your opinion on mere rumors and government propaganda. Look at all the facts, what the government has done so far, good and bad, their future agenda and whether it will benefit Germany or not. Please base your opinion on truth, not hearsay."

"What does it matter what I base my opinion on. My opinion is my opinion whether you think it's truth or not. It's truth to me!"

The room quieted while Ilse's defiant statement hung in the air.

Beata realized she shouldn't brooch the subject but her sister's fantastical view of the Hitler regime didn't sit well with her at all. "Ilse, I know you don't put much stock in the things I see or what they could mean but I've had some very disturbing dreams lately."

Ilse raised her arms in defense and frustration. "Oh! You and your incessant dreams! I don't want to hear about any more of your signs, omens and dreams."

"But they were very grave and full of warning."

"Of course, Beata. Your dreams are always negative and depressing. That's just the way you are."

Beata felt like she'd been slapped. "That's not true, Ilse. That's an unfair statement."

"Why then don't you ever speak of happy, joyful things? Why is it always about the terrible things that are coming? All you speak about are all the negatives about our government, the horrible things they're doing, the injustice of their agenda and the awful things that are coming in the future. I don't want to hear it!" Ilse waved her hands for emphasis, her body stiff with anger.

"Don't you think I want to focus on good things? I want a carefree, joyful life like anyone else. I would love to fall in love with a fine man, marry and start a family but not in times like these. I would do anything to be living at a different time, a happier time with peace on the horizon."

"Well, we're living now and I won't let this country's future stop my happiness. I'm determined to live now! I definitely will not put my life on hold."

"I don't know how you can do that with what our country is facing. It's irresponsible and selfish."

Ilse's face turned a bright pink as she blurted out, "Just because the love of your life, Fayvel Israeli, ran off to England doesn't mean I can't go on with my life!"

"That's so unfair, Ilse. Fayvel and I have always only been friends." Beata couldn't keep the words from penetrating her heart. Ilse's cruel words were too much and she chose to keep quiet to contain the flood of tears that threatened.

The room became still with Beata refusing to argue or comment further. Ilse finally broke the silence. "Hahn and I have been discussing marriage. We want to do it before he's sent off to training."

Unna's response came swiftly. "No!"

"Yes, Mother. It's true."

Another uncomfortable silence stretched on.

Ilse cleared her throat, clearly moved by her mother's stricken face. "We've talked of next month and maybe waiting till the summer months so that I can get to know his family better and he can also get to know my family. We're both concerned with the little time that's left and we both feel compelled to hurry things along."

"But Ilse, you're only sixteen! You're so young!" Unna's hands went to her face in distress.

"Mother, you were eighteen when you married. I'm only two years younger and Hahn and I truly love each other."

"But Hahn is only eighteen and he's joining the army. He won't be able to support you and how will you ever survive having a husband possibly sent out to fight?"

Ilse sobered at the thought. "I don't know. I try not to think of him being sent away. It just gets me down. I'm hoping and praying that the army buildup is only a warning to other nations and that there will be no war."

The room once more grew silent, a sure knowing covering each one that the hopeful statement was merely a childish wish and not one based in reality. Germany had acquired much land and all without a fight. There was no way of knowing whether the government's lust for more would abate anytime soon.

As Beata looked at her sister, she acknowledged that she didn't know Ilse at all anymore. It was like staring at a stranger. Her heart twisted in anguish at the realization.

CHAPTER 23

Rabbi David Kohn walked slowly toward the slightly elevated platform in the Jewish Synagogue. His four guardians, Dutiful, Truth, Ira and Hoshea, flanked him. He wore a prayer shawl over his head as he took the few steps up to the platform, then slowly turned to face the congregation and nervously looked out at his Jewish brothers and sisters. The shock on their faces was enough to declare that the changes he made were not well accepted. David glanced at his wife sitting toward the back, her face hidden as she focused on the floor, her embarrassment complete as she refused to witness the outcome of her husband's foolish decision.

Dutiful bent forward and whispered courage to him.

David cleared his throat and in a shaky voice began. "All of you that were here at the synagogue last Sabbath were aware of how shaken I was and how inept I was to oversee and lead you in our worship. I was shaken deeply by a dream from God. I have received a few of these dreams and each time the intensity and terror has deepened." David looked out at the congregation with clear trepidation as he determined to continue.

"The Christ appeared to me in a dream. His love and concern for me and for my people was deeper and more pure than I ever imagined. I contemplated long and hard over what I finally decided was no longer avoidable. The distinguishing mark of a Rabbi is to have an uncut beard, completely devoted to God Almighty. I cut it, not to defy our traditions or to incur your wrath and disapproval but I cut it at the Christ's instruction. I don't know fully what cutting my beard will accomplish but I knew that to disobey would be great folly. I will obey God before I obey any tradition. The Christ showed me the great danger our people will face and I believe it is coming soon. He told me to warn you and to tell you that he is the great 'I Am'. It is my duty as your Rabbi to be upfront and honest with you, otherwise I will be guilty of great sin. Your blood will then be on my conscience and held against me at the great judgment. God has sent us a deliverer and we have rejected him. I urge you fellow brothers and sisters, repent while there is still time and accept the Christ, the Messiah who was sent from Heaven."

David's face shone with perspiration as he willed himself to continue. He didn't know if he had the courage to complete the full confession. Guardian Dutiful touched his arm to impart strength. David cleared his throat and said, "His name is Jesus of Nazareth."

Murmurs of shock ran through the assembly.

"Jesus of Nazareth appeared to me and told me to warn you all. Please accept him now as the Messiah who was to come. He was the branch from the root of Jesse who appeared to save our people from our sins. Accept him now, I beg you, so that you can be saved, you and your household."

The synagogue suddenly erupted in shouts of anger and fury as men stood to their feet, shaking their fists in his direction.

"You have defiled this synagogue with your blasphemy!"

"What's the meaning of this?" another man shouted. "This is heresy!"

Another man pumped his fist in the air and yelled out, "You are no longer fit to lead us! You're a deserter of all things right and true! What you've spoken is a mockery of our Jewish heritage and traditions!"

Yankel Greenstein stood and agreed, "Yes, and to say that the Messiah of the Christians is our Messiah is detestable! It's the Christians who hate us the most and now we are to bend to their Messiah? It will be our death sentence! Even if your dreams are truly from God, I for one will never give in to the Polish Christian's Christ. The humiliation would be too great after all we've suffered at their hands." Yankel's wife, Gittel, stayed seated and placed her face in her hands and rocked back and forth in great distress.

Other voices shouted out their disapproval and anger.

David cleared his throat and held up his hand to continue. "But you have to understand that what you'll suffer at other's hands will be greater."

A man toward the back of the synagogue shouted, "What does that nonsense mean?"

David swallowed the growing lump in his throat and spoke clearly, "God has shown me through dreams that a great fury against our people is rising and that repentance is necessary. I don't know that repentance will stay the rising evil but at least our hearts will be at rest that we have received our Messiah and not rejected him. He is prophesied as our savior. Whether we will be saved from our enemies at this time is unsure but undoubtedly accepting Jesus as Messiah will ensure the salvation of our souls."

Binyamin Levin, sitting close to the front of the room, now stood and faced the Rabbi. "What proof do you have that something evil is heading our way?"

Rabbi Kohn thought for a moment. He looked down at the wooden pedestal and knew how foolish he would sound. He raised his head and looked at the many people he dearly loved. These were his own. His people. The sheep of his small pasture. He swallowed the lump and said, "My cut beard is the only proof I have. Have any of you ever known me to do something as sporadic and unconventional as this before? I'm as devoted to our traditions and Jewish history as anyone. I have always been a devout follower of Yahweh God and have held strictly to the law in all matters. The dreams I received were more serious and grave than any I have ever had and were more real than I can even explain. The horror for our people will be beyond what I can describe. Please hear me today, people. I wouldn't have cut my beard unless told directly by God to do so and I feel completely convinced that I was directed to do so for some reason I don't even completely comprehend. Don't judge me too harshly but seek God, His direction and He will confirm everything I've told you. Read the Bible and see if Jesus of Nazareth isn't the Messiah that was prophesied to come. I charge you to study and see the truth for yourselves."

A man shouted from the middle of the synagogue, "Is it the Christians who will rise up against us?"

David replied, "I don't know."

The man demanded again, "Will the Polish government rise up against us?"

"I don't know."

"Who will rise against us then? You've given us nothing concrete to go on, only your so-called dreams." The man's face was covered in disbelief and disdain. "You've tried to instill fear in us today but there's no basis for any of it. You don't look like a Rabbi. I don't know who our Rabbi is anymore! You have become our enemy today by siding with the Christians!" The man then waved to his wife and children and led them out of the synagogue.

The place erupted with disgruntled voices and whisperings.

David looked down at his carefully prepared notes, his sermon, and released a nervous sigh. There would be no point in pursuing that now. He looked up to see the result of his actions and confession.

Many were already heading for the doors, while others quickly joined them, the growing discontent heard through the mumblings and disgusted looks as people departed.

He shouldn't have expected anything else but he berated himself for being so blunt and forthright. His trimmed and shortened beard was a clear sign that something had changed, not to mention his shocking admission of accepting Jesus of Nazareth as the Jewish Messiah. Which Rabbi would, in his right mind, desecrate such a long standing and upheld tradition? What Rabbi, with any logic at all, would admit to accepting the Christian's Messiah? It was sure to be his death sentence as a beloved Rabbi.

He was known here, respected. They knew he wouldn't say these things without good reason. Surely they recognized this, didn't they? He had performed their weddings, their children's weddings, led their ceremonies, their feasts and the list went on. Some would surely put their trust in his words, he was confident of it. There had been an uncanny power upon him as he spoke and declared his beliefs. There was boldness upon him as he spoke before his people that he had never felt or experienced before. If God had been with him in such force only moments before, then without doubt some of his people would come to see the truth of his words. He looked out as the place emptied, his hopes dying quickly.

His wife stood then and left through the large double doors, the last of his hopes falling lifeless around his feet. He had embarrassed her completely. He knew that now. Not even she believed or supported him. His three children had likewise looked at him in shock, hurt and disdain as they left the synagogue.

David released a deep sigh as he left the platform and walked to the doors. He sat down on the back row and pleaded with God. It felt like a ton of bricks had settled upon his chest and the weight was much too heavy to bear.

Bold and Resilient, two powerful angels, watched from the doorway as David's four guardian angels surrounded him in a protective stance.

Bold was the first to speak. "It was a difficult morning for David Kohn but to see him surrounded by guardian angels is a thrill to see. A Jewish Rabbi who has accepted his Messiah and now surrounded by the heavenly guards. It's a sight these eyes have longed to see."

Resilient nodded. "He has much to overcome and much rejection lies ahead."

"So his people will refuse to believe?"

"Initially, yes. They will see much trouble before they begin to call on the name of the Lord."

"It's hard to understand how humans can be so stubborn. Even with the words from a trusted Rabbi, they refuse to believe."

"Tradition has taken a strong hold and religion is more unyielding than the strongest army."

Bold shook his head but with a knowing and understanding look.

Dutiful, Truth, Ira and Hoshea began to sing a song of praise around David, which lifted the heaviness from the room and surrounded him with peace. The two special assignment angels listened for a while, humming along to the familiar tune and then slowly unfurled their wings, shot through the roof and hurried to their next assignment.

CHAPTER 24

April 20th, 1939

Signs of spring's arrival were everywhere, from the dwindling piles of snow on the side of the streets, the small buds appearing on trees and shrubs, the warm caress of the air and the busy activity of newly arrived birds. The sky was blue and clear, the birds chirped loudly from their perches in the nearby trees while the spring breeze blew softy through the bare branches.

On the sidewalks lining the tall buildings, people were beginning to gather, waving Nazi flags with the staunch red and black swastika imprint, laughing and talking in cheerful tones. Children milled among the parents, thrilled to celebrate such a momentous occasion. The city of Berlin seemed alive with excitement, with anticipation in the air as they waited for the parade to begin.

For Bold and Resilient, situated on the roof of the building across from the Chancellery, the excitement everyone else felt only came as a tense warning. They stayed hidden behind some ventilation ducts located upon the flat roof to avoid detection by the host of demonic beings prancing around wildly on the Chancellery building opposite them. The two angels stood with hands perched on the hilt of the swords tucked into their scabbards, ready for quick retrieval in the possibility of discovery by the evil horde.

Within a few hours the scene changed as the sounds from down the street brought on cheers of exhilaration and expectancy from the crowd below. Hitler appeared on his Chancellery balcony, bringing on another insurgence of praise and accolades from the crowd. He was dressed sharply in a black suit, decked out with the Nazi symbol, a crisp, white shirt and black tie. His days of shabby dress were over. His dark hair was slicked back and his unusual chopped off moustache gave him a stern, imposing look. He waved to his adoring fans and looked pleased as the first members of the parade appeared.

A row of flag carrying army personnel led the advance, the large flags waving in the breeze as if in a victory march, with the bold swastika declaring complete control. Twelve companies of the German Wehrmacht, members of the Heer, the army, marched by in perfect unison, their heads held high and their legs raising and lowering in the odd looking goose-step. They held, in complete formation, newly made rifles, the Karabiner 98k.

After them came the latest German tanks, the Panzers I and II, which caused the earth to tremble and the sky to erupt with a roar as they rumbled past. Tank after tank rolled by, one stopping occasionally to show its ability to turn to face an enemy and then gradually it continued on down the street.

The people cheered wildly, waved their flags and shouted whatever patriotic slogan they could think of. The birds cheerful chirping was completely obliterated by the commotion from the street below and most birds abandoned their posts in search of a quieter retreat.

Twelve navy companies, the Kriegsmarine, marched by next, unit after unit in their sharp navy uniforms, marching in complete formation, discipline and obedience marking them to a fault. Interspersed between the many navy units were rows of men carrying huge Nazi flags, which rustled back and forth in the slight spring breeze. They were followed by the thundering sound of the new medium artillery and anti-aircraft guns mounted to heavy war vehicles. The sound was deafening as the engines roared and thundered past.

The parade also contained twelve companies of the Luftwaffe, the air force, and also units of the SS. In total, approximately forty-five thousand German troops took part. All the different units had their own uniforms with a Nazi swastika emblazoned on the arm of each jacket. The parade also boasted of many marching bands and patriotic songs played over and over as band after band serenaded the Fuhrer and his faithful subjects.

Bold and Resilient looked overhead where squadrons of German fighter planes and bombers flew in formation as they impressed the large crowd below with their military prowess. The air was filled with sound and noise, so deafening that it was impossible to hear any voice, song or instrument until the aircraft flew on and the horns of trumpets, beats of drums and clashes of cymbals once more floated on the wind.

The demons situated on top of the Chancellery across the street appeared like madmen, in a drunken stupor as they danced crazily, their movements wild and frenzied. They were completely intoxicated with their new found control and power over the pawn at their disposal. The blood lust pasted on their features was obvious and they celebrated like lunatics, stomping and screaming in delight. A yellowish, green sulfuric haze hovered over and around the demonic horde as they gloried in their temporal dominance over the government.

Finally, after hours of watching the military strength of Germany march by in proud and dramatic display, the last of the weapon, military, and SS divisions passed by the Chancellery and slowly the thundering sound faded into the distance. A government vehicle came to a stop before the Chancellery doors and at the same time a large group of school children, all dressed in matching uniforms swarmed from the crowds like bees and aligned themselves in rows on the street as they awaited Adolf Hitler's presence. None of the crowd around the Chancellery moved as they anticipated his appearance. All eyes were peeled on the door.

As Hitler walked through the doors and onto the sidewalk, the surrounding air erupted with shouts and cheers of approval. Hitler smiled in pleasure and saluted the crowd, which the whole group returned with a salute of their own as they shouted, "Heil Hitler". The crowd quieted as a young man approached him. Hitler acknowledged him and they spoke. The young man, in his late twenties was in charge of the school group. The school teacher nodded, Hitler backed up to the sidewalk and the young teacher turned to face the group of children, raised a stick and began to lead them in the recital of a song, while a group of musicians played along. The young voices rose in a swell of pride and admiration.

Adolf Hitler is our savior, our hero,
He is the noblest being in the whole wide world.
For Hitler we live,
For Hitler we die,
Our Hitler is our lord
Who rules a brave new world.

They sang it numerous times. As the song came to an end the crowd erupted with cheers once again and Hitler clapped his hands in delight at the honor and devotion given him on his fiftieth birthday. He went to shake the hand of the school teacher and spoke a few words of appreciation before stepping into the vehicle waiting for him. He was quickly whisked away to the formal ceremonies taking place in honor of his special day, where all the army, police and navy units, along with the display of weapons were waiting for him.

The crowd quickly dispersed and the street slowly quieted.

Bold turned to Resilient. "If the world isn't warned of what's coming by today's display then they must have blinders on."

"It unquestionably was a powerful display of their military might."

"Do you think other countries are aware of what's coming?"

Resilient looked at Bold. "Poland is very aware and she has already strengthened ties with France and England. But Germany has also strengthened its ties, a pact with Italy. Adolf Hitler and Benito Mussolini seem to have developed quite a rapport. After today, other countries will be well aware of the strength of the German military and a steady uneasiness and fear will continue to rise."

Bold nodded in agreement. "What did you think of the children's song?"

Resilient looked stern as he answered, "This song is being sung by all the school children throughout Germany. Absolute patriotism is being promulgated in the schools and that was very evident today. What I found interesting was that Adolf Hitler willingly took the title of savior and lord without any objection."

Bold shook his head in amazement. "I also found it shocking! To think that a man so filled with Hell's darkness would be given such a title of savior and lord is revolting."

"It's like the German population is in a Hell-induced stupor, a wine mixed with gall, intoxicated by a mind numbing substance, a bitter drink indeed. They no longer see nor hear but follow blindly."

"But there are some in Berlin and throughout Germany that still hear and see clearly."

"Yes, these are those who were warned with dreams, visions, woken by angels during the night and urged to pray. Those who heeded the call still have their hearing and still have their sight."

CHAPTER 25

Russia, summer 1939

The vast steppe of the Crimean area just north of the Black Sea contained the large Mennonite settlement of Molotschna. Many villages on the large, flat steppe, approximately sixty in all, were located along the banks of the Molotschna River and the three tributaries sprouting from it. The first Mennonite settlers had come to this land in 1804, seeking freedom from oppressive measures taken against them in their old homeland. They moved from Prussia, now Poland, near Danzig, where living conditions had become unbearable.

The Russian government, under the command of Empress Catherine II, issued an invitation to all Dutch farmers to settle the South Russian steppes, which Russia had recently captured from the Turks and Tartars. The farmers had immigrated, being promised financial help, freedom in worship, much land to farm and freedom from all military obligations. A few hundred families immigrated at a time and began to work the land, laid out villages and learned to deal with the Nogai, nomadic people living on the steppe.

The Nogai were untrusting and thieving at times, bringing great trouble to the new settlements. The government eventually learned of the hardship and relocated the Nogai to another area. The Mennonites worked hard building houses, establishing fields and planting trees until the villages began to thrive and flourish. More groups of families arrived from Prussia in the years that followed.

Many years had passed since 1804, with times of prosperity and abundance followed by the horrors of the Bolshevik revolution, which caused the death of so many of the Mennonite settlers. The Molotschna settlement became the battleground as first the red army dominated and then the white, back and forth until the reds finally conquered. They were horrifying years for the peace-loving and anti-war believing religious group. Following this came years of typhus, famine and hunger which claimed more lives.

Many of the settlers then immigrated to Canada to avoid the new government's plan to nationalize the whole agriculture business, which would surely throw them into greater poverty and want. There was also the constant anti-religious propaganda circulated by the newly formed Soviet government, which deeply concerned the highly religious Mennonites. Immigration began in 1924 and continued till 1929 when the government put a stop to the farmers of the Crimean area departing. The best of their farmers departing the country did nothing to advance the Russians international image.

Now here, in the same settlement, in the village of Conteniusfeld, Esther Brenner wandered through the open field behind her house, oblivious to the horrors that her people had gone through in the years that preceded her existence. She picked wild flowers and let the summer breeze blow her dark hair in swirls around her face. She was a particularly beautiful girl, with dark curly hair that framed her usually fair face. Now during the summer months her face tanned to a golden glow from spending many hours outdoors. She bent down to pick one exceptionally bright orange flower, placed it behind her ear and weaved the stem into her long hair. She skipped through the long grass stopping now and then to pick a few more flowers.

Esther was born in 1926, the year in which many of her parent's neighbors and friends were fleeing the Molotschna settlement. She'd heard the stories. Her parents had wanted to leave too and had planned to go but after hearing the plans to travel to Moscow and attempt to receive permission and flee from there, changed their minds. Esther had been a young girl at the time and her sister only a baby. The reports that came later from those who had tried that route and had miraculously returned discouraged her parents from trying further. Only a few made it through to immigration while many of the settlers that had been refused by the Soviet government had been punished for asking by being exiled to South Asia or far north to Siberia.

Esther wandered through the wild flowers in complete ignorance of the difficulties of the former neighbors she never knew. Her life was pleasant, peaceful and if her parents were worried about the future, she didn't know it. Oh she heard talk at times, like when her brother, Herman, talked of Germany and its leader, Hitler. It seemed so far away and distant. The fear she had first felt had long dissipated and vanished.

She looked over their village with a sense of belonging, joy and familiarity. She saw the schoolhouse, where she attended, down the main street of the village on the opposite side. She looked the other direction and saw her dear friend's house off in the distance. Esther looked at the many houses which lined the dirt street that ran through Conteniusfeld. There were about thirty houses on either side, with the school building located centrally. A church stood beside it but, since Christianity was now outlawed, it was used to store grain. There was a community center on the other side of the school, which served as a makeshift hospital.

Esther wandered toward Rose Voth's homestead, two of her guardian angels, Goodness and Faith, walking with her. A sound stopped her and she turned to see her sister, Anna, running through the field of grass and wildflowers toward her.

"Esther, stop!"

"What do you want, Anna?"

"I want to come too."

Esther waited till she caught up. "I'm going to Rose's house. She's my friend, not yours. Go back home!"

"Please, can I come too?"

Esther released a sigh of frustration. "Oh all right, but keep up." Thirteen-year-old Esther walked quickly, hoping Anna would tire of the speed through the long grass.

Soon the two girls arrived at the outskirts of the Voth property and they could see Rose hanging laundry on the clothesline, the damp clothes blowing softly back and forth in the hot summer breeze. Fruit trees, laden with pears, apples and cherries filled the yard, while large maple trees lined the property edges. They walked toward Rose, who soon noticed them, laid down her work and ran to greet them.

"Hi Esther! I'm so glad you've come. Would you help me with the laundry and then we can go play?"

"Sure. I just finished helping my Mom with bun baking so I'm free for the afternoon."

Anna piped up, "I'll help too."

Rose shrugged her shoulders, "Okay".

The girls worked quickly and soon the laundry was hung on the rows of rope strung from three poles standing on either end. Rose hurried inside with her laundry basket, asked permission from her mother and soon the three girls raced off down the center street of the village to the place they all loved to go, the edge of the river where the water pooled in a small lake. Here ducks lay their eggs, swam in lazy patterns on the small inlet and bulrushes and water lilies grew profusely. Large stones lined one side of the inlet, allowing the girls to pull up their skirts and wander and explore over the rocks, sitting at times and gazing at the ducks activity, waddling and leading their young into the water. The baby ducks were almost all hatched now and the sight of mother and young was a thrill for the three girls.

Rose, always the brave one, scooted out over the rocks that reached far into the river. She carefully stepped over them, being ever so careful before continuing on to the next one. She stopped on the farthest rock she could find, balanced herself carefully and turned back to show off her agility. "I bet you two can't come out this far." Brave Rose stood with hands on her hips and a grin on her face with her long blond braids reaching to her waist. Rose was pretty and would look even prettier if she'd ever let her hair loose. She was the perpetual tom boy and preferred her hair contained and out of the way.

Esther couldn't let Rose outdo her so she stood from the rock where she sat and started after her. She walked carefully, one rock at a time, balancing with more care as she reached the rocks separated by more water. In this area and at this time of year, with the water level at its lowest, many rocks emerged above the surface and continued on into the river for quite some ways but water swirled between them making the rocks slippery and treacherous. Esther focused on the rocks before and beneath, being careful to get a good foothold before continuing to the next one.

Rose stood in the middle of the river on a large, flat piece of rock, her arms crossed and she smiled as she watched Esther attempt the same feat. Finally Esther made it to the same rock, which was just big enough to hold both girls. They held onto each other and desperately tried to balance as Rose made way for her. They nearly fell but managed to right themselves just in time. They stood triumphantly, arms embracing each other as they stood in victorious joy. They gazed back to Anna, who was still safely sitting on a rock close to shore and watching their foolhardy journey.

"Come on, Anna. Come join us," shouted Esther.

"No way! I don't want to get wet."

"You won't. You just have to walk carefully." Esther grinned at her cautious sister and letting one arm slip from Rose's waist, waved, encouraging Anna to come. This action nearly caused both girls to tumble into the river.

"Esther, don't!" shouted Rose. "You'll make us both fall in!"

"Okay, okay I'll stop moving." Esther once again wrapped both arms around Rose and they stood there, unmoving and stiff. "Are we stuck here, Rose?"

"I think we might be." Rose looked at her and started giggling.

"Stop laughing, Rose! You're making me laugh and then we'll really fall in."

"Okay, I'll stop laughing if you stop."

"I've already stopped." Esther truly had and she gave her friend a stern look. "Okay, I'll go back first. Hold onto me while I turn and get to the next rock."

"I don't think this will work, Esther."

"Yes it will but you'll have to help me balance."

"I'll try." Rose helped Esther turn slightly.

The girl's guardian angels hovered around the two and grinned at the precarious situation their wards were in.

Cautiously Esther took a step toward the next rock. As she found her footing, they slowly let go of each other and both girls were still standing.

Eleven-year-old Anna shouted from the rocky riverbank, "You girls look so silly. Why didn't you stay on the shore with me? Then you wouldn't be in such danger of getting soaked."

Esther looked at her sister in irritation. "It's boring just sitting around on the shore. This is far more exciting."

Anna replied, "It won't be exciting when you're covered in marsh gung and soaking wet."

Esther rolled her eyes. Why did her sister always have to play it so safe? Anna was such a good girl and never took any risks. It would be so much more fun to have Rose as a sister. She was always adventurous and fun loving. Rose would absolutely never sit on shore and goad her on with safety tips.

Esther took a few more steps, swinging her arms in wide arcs to keep her balance.

"Okay, Esther, I'm coming right behind you," yelled Rose.

"Just don't bump me. I'm having a hard enough time getting my footing without you rushing up behind me."

"Well you better move it then."

"I'm trying, I'm trying." She was almost to the rocks, where the water flowed less between each rock and where the footing was surer. She focused to reach it.

"Hey, what do we have here?"

Esther and Rose stopped mid stride, found their balance and looked toward shore where two teenaged boys stood, fishing rods in hand. The boys gazed open mouthed at the two girls perched on the rocks.

Rose was the first to speak. "What do you two want?"

"Hey, we were only coming here to do some fishing; we weren't expecting to find two badgers hopping over the rocks."

Rose grinned immediately. She loved to be referred to as a wild animal and sometimes she acted more that way than a young lady. "I bet you boys couldn't do this."

"We don't want to. We didn't come to get a filthy bath, we came to fish." Gilbert Schultz was one of the boys who freely taunted the girls. He was fourteen, a full year older than they, smart in school and fairly handsome for his age. Esther chided herself. What did she care if Gilbert was handsome anyway?

The other boy was his cousin, Peter Burg, another classmate of the girls and the same age. He was always the shy one and stood awkwardly by as his cousin did all the talking. Peter had a big build, homely looks and an ill-at-ease, shifty walk.

Rose retorted, "That goes to show you who has more courage. Girls always outwit boys when it comes to bravery." Rose smiled impishly.

Esther's main guardian, Goodness, faced the other three angels and said, "This is not the wisest thing she could be saying."

The others nodded in agreement and then turned to watch the outcome.

Esther reprimanded her quietly, "Rose don't antagonize them. They might come out here and push us in on purpose."

Rose replied loudly, "I'd like to see them try."

Gilbert shouted, "Forget it, Rose. I'm not as stupid as you and I won't fall for your so called challenge." With that Gilbert walked away, Peter following faithfully and they made their way to a spot where the water ran clear and where the river was known to hold plenty of fish.

The girls made it back to the layer of rocks on the safe part of the shore and sat down beside Anna.

"Those boys sure were chicken. Just wait till I tell the kids at school what chickens they were. They'll regret not taking my challenge." Rose grinned with mischief.

Esther gazed with trepidation at her daring friend. Rose sure knew how to get herself into trouble. Maybe Gilbert couldn't be goaded into wandering over the rocks but he sure wouldn't put up with Rose humiliating him in front of all his friends. Surely Rose knew that, didn't she? She would get them both in trouble with her big mouth. Gilbert could be forgiving but Esther knew that he was known to get even when crossed. She found herself worrying about the matter the rest of the afternoon even though the start of the new school year was still two weeks away.

Over the next two weeks Esther had little time to think of what would happen on the first day of school. Frieda Brenner kept her and Anna both occupied with harvesting garden vegetables. When the garden work slowed Esther's help was expected in the fields with her father and brother. There she walked behind her father as he chopped the grain with a scythe and she gathered the grain and placed them into equal sized piles. Herman would then come behind her and tie them into bundles. Herman being much older and stronger easily kept up with her so he helped her with arranging the grain into piles as well as the tying into bundles.

Esther loved this time of year when she could work side by side with the brother she loved. She had always feared her father to a degree but she held the greatest respect and complete devotion for Herman, who was always kind to her, looked out for her and was able to make her laugh and enjoy life no matter what was happening around her. Even now, under the hot sun and demanding physical work, Herman sang silly songs, told the oddest jokes and smiled easily. It was a thrill for her to be able to work with him with no interruption of another household chore to complete. She nearly forgot about Rose's threat to Gilbert nearly two weeks before as she basked in Herman's company.

School came soon enough and Esther dejectedly changed her focus from running and working outdoors in the hot summer heat to focusing on studies. She headed out that morning, leaving her family's homestead and wandered down the central road toward the school house, with her sister Anna by her side. Both girls wore a neat, calf length dress in dark blue, with a neckline that reached to their throats, a stiff, white blouse underneath with the collar showing over the high neckline of the dress. The dress was covered by a bib apron in the same shade of dark blue and they had simple, practical everyday shoes on their feet.

Four angels accompanied the girls as each of their other two guardian angels stayed at home to watch over things there. Esther slowed her step as they approached the school building, her two guardians, Goodness and Faith, slowing down with her. The building was smaller than most schools in the settlement but for their size of village, it was sufficient.

Esther could see children gathering on the school yard in groups, talking and catching up on much needed news. All the children in the village, once they reached ten years of age or older were worked nearly like adults and were expected to help in every form of farming life. Most of the children gathered now hadn't seen their friends for weeks and this was an exhilarating time for most. Esther wished she felt as excited as she knew she should. She couldn't help wondering if Rose would spread the ill fated rumor. Her stomach knotted up and she slowed even more as she noticed Rose already on the school yard, wandering from one group to the next, a mischievous smile tweaking her lips.

Esther slowed and Anna wandered ahead. Anna finally turned around, "Esther, come on! Why are you walking so slow?"

"Go ahead. You don't have to wait for me."

That was all the encouragement she needed. She raced ahead to find her friends.

Esther sauntered onto the school yard, gazing around cautiously for any sign of Gilbert and Peter. They were nowhere to be seen so she headed in Rose's direction. Esther could hear her boastful, daring words drifting on the wind toward her and she cringed at what she heard.

"You should have seen those two, like two chickens in a strong wind. They couldn't stand the blast of our dare and they scampered away up stream, their tails between their legs. They wouldn't risk taking on our challenge. They should have tried it at least, I mean, girls outdid them and they just ignored it. Can you believe it? That proves that girls are better than boys."

The exclamations, giggles and laughter was enough of a sign to let Esther know that this outlandish bragging would be sure to make its way through the whole school. She couldn't help wondering what Gilbert would do to them then.

Esther's main guardian, Goodness, whispered some advice to her.

Rose's main guardian breathed a sigh of relief and said, "Thank you, Goodness. I've been trying to encourage her to stop but she won't listen. Just maybe she'll take Esther's advice."

Goodness nodded and grinned.

Esther pulled on Rose's arm and dragged her away from the awed and laughing group.

Rose looked happy to see Esther but also irritated at being taken from such a prime location with such an adoring audience. "Esther, what are you doing?"

"Don't you know what could happen to us?"

"Like what?"

"Gilbert could get really angry and get even with us."

"You always worry about stuff, Esther. Nothing will happen. Everyone knows that Gilbert has a crush on me and Peter most certainly has a crush on me although he would never act on it, he's too terribly shy."

"But Rose, you're humiliating Gilbert in front of all the kids. He could get furious!"

Rose shrugged her shoulders, "I don't think so."

The school teacher appeared at the door at precisely nine o'clock with a large bell and rang it loudly. No student within hearing distance, hardly anyone in the entire village could ignore it. The teacher, just as suddenly as he had appeared, retreated back into the school building.

Esther and Rose sauntered toward the door, while crowded by those still asking questions about what had transpired by the river. Rose was eager and willing to fill everyone in while Esther lagged behind. She looked back and noticed Gilbert and Peter, who arrived just in time, gathered by a group of boys at the edge of the school property and the looks on their faces was enough sign that they now knew of Rose's story. Esther's face fell at the realization and her heart skipped a beat as Gilbert's eye caught hers. His anger was immediately evident and she quickly turned and followed the group of girls into the school.

Rose and Esther's angels held back for a moment.

Goodness said, "I tried."

"Yes, I know. You did what you could."

"The rest will play out from here." Goodness and Faith then followed after Esther.

Gilbert and Peter were amazingly aloof and appeared unconcerned as the day progressed but neither did they talk to either Rose or Esther. Esther began to breathe easier as first one recess after another passed with no incidence. Even lunch was uneventful as the girls gathered on one side of the school yard and the boys on the other. Rose didn't let up her chattering, bragging and speaking disparagingly of both Gilbert and Peter. She confidently continued boasting of her bravery, her skill and her sure footedness. Esther noticed something else during lunch. The boys began laughing more freely, joking and carrying on like they had an inside joke. The way they kept glancing now and then in the girls' direction caused Esther's stomach to churn in dread.

She had heard stories of how Gilbert revenged those who wronged him. The recipients had always been boys and that's maybe why Rose was so confident that Gilbert would do nothing. Esther wasn't entirely so sure. Rose made sure to include Esther in every story she told thus lessening her own responsibility. Esther wished Rose would leave her out of the haughty talk but she was inevitably dragged into the retelling, over and over again.

It wasn't long before the day was done and Esther made a definite effort to walk with a large group of girls for greater protection. Rose and Esther walked together and Anna, like a faithful, devoted puppy, walked beside her. She suddenly felt anxious for her sister. After all, she had been with them at the river that day too.

"Anna, why don't you walk with your friends back there?"

"I don't want to. I want to walk with you and Rose and besides, she's funny."

"She's too brave for her own good," Esther whispered. "I don't know what the boys are going to do. Please go walk with your friends."

Anna gazed up at Esther, "Are you afraid?"

"Yes, a little," Esther said quietly, not wanting Rose to hear.

Anna pulled back a few steps and walked with a girl her own age, Mary Harder.

Esther craned her neck back and noticed the boys were gaining ground. She placed an arm through Rose's and pulled her ahead a little faster, her other arm loaded down with school books.

Rose endured it for a little while and then pulled away. "Stop rushing me, Esther. What's wrong with you?"

"The boys are catching up. We need to hurry and besides that, the small duck lake is just ahead."

Rose stopped still in her tracks, crossed her arms and stared at Esther.

"Rose, come on, hurry up!" She suddenly felt frantic with anxiety.

"Are you a chicken too?"

"No, but I don't want to get dumped in the river, especially not in that marshy stuff!"

"They wouldn't dare do that!" Rose turned back to see the boys progress now too and she looked a little more alarmed with the possibility of retaliation, as if she had never even considered it before.

"They certainly could, Rose!" Esther realized that even if they hurried, there was no way they could outrun the boys.

Rose's main guardian, Leopold, turned to the other angels and said, "Rose has realized the truth a little too late."

Goodness said, "Her foolish talk will now result in trouble for both of them."

Leopold said, "We'll do what we can."

"Which isn't much. It's reaping time." Faith grinned at that.

Rose now willingly linked arms with her and they walked quickly trying not to look afraid but only intent on getting home. It wasn't long till Gilbert and Peter, along with their friends, came up behind them. A crowd was with them, walking slowly, an eager look on their faces.

Gilbert said, "So here are the two brave girls who can do almost anything. They can walk on the most treacherous rocks and never fall. Who apparently challenged these so-called chickens and won!" His voice rose in volume as he continued. "The ones that deserve a good punishment to teach them a lesson! The ones who are foolish enough to spread all sorts of lies about us! Now we'll see just how brave and bold you are!"

Rose spun around in haughty reply, "You know that everything I said was true, Gilbert. We challenged you that day and you meekly walked away. I know the truth hurts sometimes but you have no right to get even! You had your chance that day and you missed it! Girls ruled that day!"

Gilbert smiled slightly, every hint of crush gone from his retaliatory face. "I can assure you, girls won't rule today."

Rose turned away from him, sudden fear pasted across her face. She grabbed Esther's hand and they began to run with all their might, their dresses blowing behind them, impairing their escape.

The five other boys with Gilbert and Peter ran after the girls and reached them with no great effort. They grabbed hold of Rose and Esther and dragged them, kicking and screaming, to the river's edge, their angels walking casually behind them. Gilbert helped drag Rose and he smiled in pleasure at a chance for revenge. Ducks and their young scurried here and there to escape the commotion, leaving ripples in the murky, green water.

"Gilbert, you let us go," screamed Rose.

"I didn't brag and boast like Rose did. She's the one who did it," yelled Esther. She was now in complete survival mode and didn't think of loyalty at the moment, but it didn't seem to matter to the boys as to who was at fault. Rose and Esther were irrevocably linked together now and both would pay.

"Let go of me!" Rose kicked, bit; everything she could do to bring about a change of course but the lake loomed ever closer. "Don't do this, Gilbert. I'll tell your father if you do!"

"Go ahead. Once he hears my side he'll tell you that you deserved it.'

"No, let me go!" Rose screamed and protested but the boys were much too strong for her attempts at escape.

"Please, please don't do this! My dress was just washed for the week. Please let me go." Esther begged and pleaded, knowing how furious her mother would be but nothing she said or did helped.

Rose was the first to reach the lake, pulled by Gilbert and Peter and they unmercifully dragged her over the rough rocks to the edge where the water ran the deepest and slimiest and dumped her uncaringly into the green, marshy water. Ducks quacked hysterically at their disturbed peace and they scurried further out of the way.

Next came two of Gilbert's buddies, Fremont and Emil, dragging Esther by her arms with the other boys following, yelling their encouragement. She didn't go willingly either as she struggled to find her footing and she wriggled her arms in a desperate attempt to get free. She hardly noticed the crowd of school children, laughing, shouting and some screaming their disapproval, mostly girls, as she was dragged closer to the water's edge. They entered the water, allowed Esther stand upright and then they heaved her and let her fall beside her friend in the marshy guck.

Esther sat in dismay, hardly knowing what to do, for she could feel the slimy, soft bottom as she sank into it. It nearly swallowed her legs and her hands, which she had used to brace her fall. The boys stood in triumph as they laughed and grinned at the girl's plight and pointed and mocked their misery. Esther gave them an evil, angry look but it didn't accomplish anything. She watched them walk off, proud and straight backed. She looked at Rose beside her who had tears rolling down her cheeks.

"How could you do this? You boys are awful!" Rose squawked her anger and shock as she struggled to find a way to retrieve herself from the sucking, duck waste layer at the bottom of the inlet. The water came up to her chest as Rose struggled to get up.

Esther said, "We'll never get out of here. This stuff at the bottom is too deep. It's like thick, sucking glue pulling us down."

"Don't say that, Esther! I'm scared enough as it is!" Rose struggled but the more she tried, the deeper she seemed to go.

Goodness and Faith moved in close to Esther and gave her some ideas.

Esther decided it was best to get out sooner than later. She had no desire to get pulled in by the insidious green guck pulling at her legs and hands. She wiggled around till she felt a rock beside her and she rested one hand on it. A group of girls was gathered at the edge and offered hands and advice but they were too far away to help. They would only end up in the same spot if they tried anything. Esther looked up to see the group of boys walking away in the distance, laughing and joking. She shook her head in anger and frustration. This was all Rose's doing and now, where had all her bravery and boasting disappeared to? She had disintegrated into a whimpering, helpless waif of a girl. It was clear that Rose wouldn't be of any help, she seemed totally helpless and sinking deeper by the minute as she sat crying and wailing.

Esther grabbed for the rock beneath the watery edge again and scooted herself over to get a better hold. She then heaved herself forward and over just slightly. She searched around beneath the green slime again and found another rock. The girls on shore had found some branches and were extending them out into the water. Esther stopped to see the effectiveness of this endeavor. Rose reached for it and held on tight. The girls on shore pulled and pulled but Rose couldn't hold on with her slippery, green covered, marshy hands and the branch slipped away. The idea was doomed to fail.

"Rose, listen to me. You need to find a rock to grab hold of and that will give you something firm to help lift you out. This stuff underneath is too squishy and is sucking you further in. Search for a rock."

Rose looked desperate but encouraged and she finally stopped crying and began to rummage around beneath the slimy water. It wasn't long before she looked up with hope and said, "I found one." Her determination came back with a fury and she began to work at her own deliverance.

Esther focused once more on her own escape. She worked from rock to rock, pulling herself along. Soon she reached the main shore and hauled herself up. No one attempted to help her and she didn't blame them. Green wisps of marsh gung clung to her dress, front and back. It covered her hands and there was even some on her face and hair due to the struggle. She was a total mess and not one girl wanted their newly washed school uniforms dirtied. She pushed back the explanation she'd have to give to her mother as she walked over a few steps to where Rose was struggling to break free. She was making progress but it was slow.

Esther reached forward. "Here take my hand. Push against that rock and I'll help pull you out."

They struggled back and forth until finally the icky, green marsh conceded and gave up its prized possession. Rose, full of green mire and stinking like it too, sat on a rock, panting, exhausted and deflated. Esther sat down beside her. Water poured from their shoes and green slime coated them. The girls gathered around cheered and then giggled at the sight. Water dripped from their school uniforms and ran off the rocks below to rejoin the filthy water in the inlet.

They looked at each other and both of them started to giggle at the sight.

Rose finally said, "You're right, Esther, they did take revenge."

"They sure did, didn't they?" They laughed hard then, holding their stomachs in the aftermath of such a sound lesson and grimy outcome.

They slowly stood and the crowd of girls eventually dispersed as they made their way home. Anna carried her own books as well as Rose's and Esther's. They had sense enough to throw them on the grass before the boys dragged them over the rocks. Esther was thankful that her books were safe and that Anna was willing to carry the big load for them.

Esther gazed at Rose as they walked side by side and giggled off and on. "I guess Gilbert's crush on you is now a closed chapter."

Rose raised an eyebrow as she thought about it. "I think my crush on him has just begun. I didn't know he had that much guts about him. He actually took me on and won. I think I like him more now than I ever have."

"Do you actually think he'll care what you think of him after what you said about him?" Esther couldn't believe Rose's brash confidence.

Rose shrugged her shoulders. "With what he did to us, maybe he cares more about what I say about him than he'd ever admit. He obviously was upset that I called him a chicken. It makes me wonder why he cared so much."

"Rose, you called him down to all the kids at school! That's why he cared. You bad mouthed him all day."

Anna spoke up, "You two looked so hilarious sitting there in that green marshy stuff, side by side. You looked so surprised and scared. I almost peed, I was laughing so hard." Anna giggled.

Esther said, "Oh that's real sisterly and caring of you."

Rose only laughed as her shoes squished and squashed with every step. Esther shook her head at her fun, brave and sometimes rash, trouble-causing friend as she listened to her own shoes make the same water soaked sounds. She only hoped her shoes weren't completely ruined.

CHAPTER 26

Krakow, Poland

Aaron Levin stood under the apple tree located before his father's home. His father, Binyamin Levin, and his two brothers surrounded him. The women were indoors preparing the noon Sabbath meal. They had decided, since leaving the synagogue early, that they would eat together and discuss what was uppermost on their minds, the strange babblings and actions of their Rabbi. Binyamin's sons and their wives had gone home from the synagogue and returned with their planned, noon day food. It would be a combined, joint meal as the strange circumstances of the day warranted a family discussion.

The hot, late-August sun beat down through a clear, blue sky, causing the men to seek the shelter of the large apple tree. Binyamin leaned back against the trunk, where above, birds chirped loudly. Aaron, Hershel and Joseph were in lively conversation around him.

Hershel, the oldest said, "I just can't believe Rabbi Kohn could do such a thing. It's a complete disgrace to our whole congregation. I've known him all my life, his son is one of my closest friends and I would never have expected such outrageous behavior from him. It seems completely out of character. He has always been a devout Jew, completely devoted to our Jewish heritage and he taught his children and the whole congregation to fear God and live by the law. I can hardly believe what we witnessed today. I'm in complete shock!"

Joseph said, "It was not only a shock to our congregation but the whole Jewish community will hear of it and then what? If you ask me, it's a complete fiasco and embarrassment."

Aaron said, "Did you see the look on Devora Kohn's face and the way their children bowed their heads in shame? They were completely humiliated by what Rabbi Kohn did. I wonder why he would have risked it. Didn't he know what this kind of thing would do even to his own family?" Aaron felt incredulous over the whole thing.

"Exactly!" said Hershel. "I don't know what got into him. Everyone has dreams but that doesn't mean we take those dreams and change our whole lives because of them! I'm wondering if he's lost his thinking faculties. Perhaps his mind is going on him. He's obviously not thinking clearly. That happens to older men sometimes." Hershel looked at his father apologetically. "Not that it will happen to you, Father, but it does happen to some."

Binyamin Levin grinned. "But, it could be the explanation we're looking for, son. It doesn't add up otherwise. What Rabbi, in his right mind, would risk so much for so little. What does he gain from acting like a lunatic? He'll gain his family's disrespect, the Jewish people's anger and a lost position as an honored Rabbi." Binyamin shook his head in confusion. "I don't understand the man. He had a respectable, high position and now he's dug himself a grave and a certain, abrupt end to his career."

Joseph said, "Do you think he'll step down as Rabbi or will the people forcefully have him removed?"

Binyamin answered, "The wise thing would be for him to quietly step down, claim insanity and apologize for his fanaticism. Perhaps he could over time regain people's trust and their respect. If he refuses to resign, his disgrace will only deepen. I doubt the synagogue will allow him to stay."

A nagging thought kept pestering Aaron. "What if his claims are true?"

Binyamin stared at his son in surprise. "What do you mean?"

"What if his dreams truly are sent from Heaven and David Kohn is warning us as God's designated messenger?"

Binyamin shook his head. "I don't think that's possible."

"Why not?"

"Have we heard of any war or any possibility of war? No. Do we have any mortal enemies here? No, not really. It's no secret that the Poles dislike us but they aren't breathing murderous threats down our necks. We live peacefully around them and they seem content to leave us alone. Don't you think that if there was even a remote hint of oppression against our people I would be quick to believe him? But I see nothing of that sort and have heard no rumor of aggressive threats against us. These dreams David Kohn is having are random dreams from his own imagination. As far as him seeing the Messiah in his dreams, I believe they are only figments of his active or demented mind. I don't believe any of it! If he expects the men of the synagogue to believe him and follow in his footsteps he doesn't realize the deep religious heritage entrenched in our people. Certainly he should realize what he's up against, thousands of years of religious tradition and adherence to the Holy Scriptures. If he thinks his fellow Jews will throw all that out based on some ridiculous dreams by an old deluded man, even if he is a Rabbi, he has his head in the clouds."

Aaron didn't feel convinced. He felt a brooding deep within.

Hershel said, "I agree with you, Father. If these dreams were God sent, surely there'd be some type of confirmation letting us know that they truly are from God. There is no sign of any danger."

Aaron said, "But does God need to send signs in order for us to believe Him?"

Joseph said, "Little brother, God would not warn us through the rambling words of a demented Rabbi. He would send us a prophet like He did to our forefathers and He'd speak clearly, not in dreams and strange, unbelievable visions. Did you listen to the man at all this morning? He claims that Jesus of Nazareth was our Messiah, the man who the Jewish leaders crucified; a dead man who can't do anything to save us or deliver us. What a ridiculous miscalculation Rabbi Kohn has made, at his own great peril. If the wise scholars and leaders of that day didn't accept Jesus, who stood right before them, why should we accept Him now, now that He's dead and buried."

Hershel said, "That's right! What we need is a living Messiah who will defeat and destroy our enemies and restore the fortunes of the

Jewish people. A dead man has never helped anyone, Aaron." Hershel grinned condescendingly at his youngest brother.

"But don't the Christians claim that their Messiah rose from the dead?" Aaron said.

Binyamin sighed deeply, concern on his face. "I thought I had taught you thoroughly in the Holy Scriptures and in our Jewish beliefs."

"You have and you did, Father, but that doesn't mean I don't have questions. Especially with Rabbi Kohn's dreams and visions, I find the questions returning." Aaron turned to face Joseph. "You said that God wouldn't speak through Rabbi Kohn but through an appointed prophet. What if Rabbi Kohn is God's appointed prophet to us? Didn't God often speak strange things through the writings of the Torah, the Prophetic writings and Psalms? If some of those things were spoken today, would we believe them? Who's to say that He wouldn't speak that way today and through someone like Rabbi Kohn?"

Joseph looked disgusted with his younger brother and gestured with his hands as if waving away an irritating fly.

Binyamin sighed deeply. "If Rabbi Kohn is right then we have much to fear because his face was filled with dread as he spoke to us. At first, looking at him was difficult, seeing the fear on his face but then the more he spoke the less I believed him. He soon seemed to be grasping at straws, trying to make sense of all he'd seen in his sleep. After awhile it seemed like utter nonsense to me, the ramblings of a demented man. His words digressed more and more from fear to utter and sheer gibberish. I believe God would send us someone who is well respected as a prophet if He expects us to believe him." Binyamin shook his head sadly. "It's a sorry state that our Rabbi has plunged too."

Hershel said, "What will become of our synagogue, Father?"

Binyamin looked at his oldest son, "I don't know. I think it's best if Rabbi Kohn no longer shows his face. If he would dare to, I would be obligated to ask for his resignation. I'm sure the other men of the synagogue would support his departure as well."

"Who would take his place?" asked Joseph.

"I don't know. Everything is still so fresh and I'm sure everyone is talking about the disgrace of this day. I'm sure the elders of the synagogue will meet shortly and these decisions will be made soon. Right now we need to get over the shock and decide how to go on. Rabbi Kohn will need to be punished."

"Won't the wrath of the whole Jewish community be enough of a punishment for him?" said Hershel.

Binyamin gazed at Hershel, who had always been good friends with the Rabbi's son, Itamar Kohn, and their children were also good friends. "I know this is difficult to think about but we'll have to leave this decision with the leadership."

Init appeared in the doorway of the Levin home and called, "Come and eat, the food is ready!"

The men ended their conversation and headed for the house, with heavy hearts and questions still swirling around them.

CHAPTER 27

Moscow, Russia

Two lightning-like streams of light landed on the edge of Moscow, disappeared quickly into the earth's top layer and zoomed on unhindered until they reached their destination.

Bold and Resilient ascended above the dirt, behind the Kremlin and scanned the grounds quickly. The Moskva River was located to the south, the Alexander Garden to the west and the Red Square to the east. The grand buildings of the Kremlin rose around them like amazing castles from millenniums ago. Glorious domes topped the many buildings and great towers could be seen surrounding the Kremlin. On the horizon they saw highly modern structures, road systems and bridges; the ancient clashing violently with the new.

Bold and Resilient noticed many demonic spirits, mostly guarding entrances to buildings on the Kremlin grounds and of course lookouts were staked on every rooftop and every tower.

"It's a wonder we arrived without being spotted," said Bold.

"I'm glad we chose the method we did for our entrance," said Resilient.

"It was a wise move, I agree. Now all we have to do is find them."

"Where are they meeting?"

"I'm certain they'll be in one of the presidential meeting rooms. Our job is to make our way there without detection."

"It shouldn't be too hard. It seems that the demonic forces here are half asleep. Even those over there by the main entrance seem unaware of the great danger and they stagger when they walk is if in a stupor."

It was true. The demonic spirits appeared at ease and completely unaware of the significance of the meeting taking place right under their noses. It was clear they had complete reign here with little angelic interference.

"Their relaxed demeanor is almost uncanny. They obviously weren't expecting our visit," said Bold, "and they seem oblivious to the gravity of the treaty that might be signed."

"Do you actually believe Joseph Stalin will agree to the German Non-Aggression Pact?"

That's what we're here to find out. With the discussions concerning this treaty going on all summer, I highly doubt that Joseph Stalin has any great ideals of the German leader. Adolf Hitler has been extremely obvious about his aggressive views against communism. This so-called turnaround by Adolf, in an attempt at peace with the communist nation, has continued to astound Stalin and his suspicions are still high."

"Why would Stalin then even contemplate and continue these talks with a man he doesn't trust?" asked Resilient.

"It's Hitler's agenda regarding Poland that intrigues him. Hitler's proposal for them both to get a slice of Poland appeals to the communist leader. This schemed friendship on Hitler's part will gain him leverage with his plans to invade Poland without the consequence of Russia retaliating in war. Making allowances in the treaty for Russia to invade the eastern part of Poland while Germany invades the west will keep Russia from opposing Germany."

Resilient said, "And there's one other thing, Russia is in no position to enter war now. Joseph Stalin has purged his army and his leadership to such a degree that they are in no shape to enter into a war."

Bold nodded. "And this will give the Russian government space to rebuild their army and weaponry."

"It's a very smart move by the German leader. Feigning friendship with the Russian leader will get Adolf Hitler what he wants without possible aggression and he can then release his further plans on a deceived and sleep-lulled nation."

"But the treaty hasn't been signed yet," said Bold. "Germany's foreign minister, Joachim von Ribbentrop, and Russia's foreign minister, Vyacheslav M. Molotov, are still in negotiations somewhere in this building."

"Are we to hinder the treaty from being signed?" asked Resilient.

"No, we were sent here to find out the results only and we'll need to inform all the angel generals once we know."

Bold scanned the grounds once more before motioning for Resilient to follow. They quickly disappeared into the stone wall and on to the rooms beyond.

CHAPTER 28

Late August, 1939

The low evening sun threw great shadows on the mountains that could be seen through the grand patio doors and windows that surrounded it. The Berchtesgaden retreat was tucked away in a secluded, natural setting, high on a mountainous ridge in the German Bavarian Alps. The retreat, a gift given to Hitler by the Nazi party on his fiftieth birthday, was rightfully nicknamed the Eagle's Nest. From this vantage point, on the border of Austria and Germany, the town of Berchtesgaden could be seen on one side, deep in the valley, and the mountainous view of Austria on the other.

Hitler and his dinner guests sat around a large ornate table, while Hitler's servants served the meal. He took a bite of his vegetarian plate and listened as Eva Braun discussed her favorite movie stars, her unending passion, with Hitler's other guests. Hitler and Eva had been an item for some time although he resisted being seen with her in public and had never appeared openly with the pretty, blond woman, an assistant to a well-known photographer, Heinrich Hoffman. Eight guests in all surrounded the table, among them Heinrich Himmler, commander of the SS forces, and his wife. Rudolf Hess, the Fuhrer's chief, was also in attendance as well as a few other close friends.

"I've always wished I was a famous movie star but I don't think that dream will ever come true." Eva giggled softly, lifted her napkin and wiped her thin lips.

"You're pretty enough to be a movie star, Eva," said Heinrich's wife.

"I'm afraid I'm not a very good actress. I can portray only how I feel." Eva glanced at Adolf, who only returned her comment with a distracted smile. She turned her attention to him more fully. "You seem preoccupied, Adolf. What's wrong?"

"My mind is on German affairs, I'm afraid. Please forgive me for my absentmindedness." Adolf reached for Eva's hand, which was extended toward him on the table and he squeezed it slightly.

"Can't Germany wait till tomorrow? Try to enjoy the evening," said Heinrich's wife. "Look at the view from the windows. It's absolutely breath-taking and the company and conversation are completely interesting."

Adolf looked at the woman. "I can't argue that but still my mind wanders easily. There are so many things that need to take place soon and I'm anxious to learn if our plans will succeed."

Heinrich spoke, "I'm certain you'll have success at everything you're planning, Adolf. You have a natural skill toward victory."

Adolf smiled and set his full fork of food down for a moment. "I have had great success, I must agree, but without further triumph my plans will come to a temporary halt."

"Well let's all hope for the best then. We can't have our Fuhrer in a dreary mood surrounded by his close friends and supporters," said Rudolf Hess. He lifted his glass of wine then and held it up in a toast, followed by the others around the table. Adolf Hitler didn't drink wine, so he held up his glass of water with the others as Rudolf spoke.

"To our great Fuhrer's success and good will in every endeavor he undertakes."

The glasses chinked and rang with a few 'Heil Hitler's' before they drank to their leaders triumph.

Shortly after, there was a knock at the dining room door, followed by the entrance of a uniformed SS officer carrying a note. Hitler stood immediately and walked toward him. Both disappeared into the hall and moments later Hitler returned, his face brimming in enthusiasm.

"It's done. My success is secured and established. The answer I was waiting for has arrived and we are most certainly guaranteed victory. Russia has signed the non-aggression pact." Hitler stood behind his chair, his hands resting on top of the back rest, pounding his hands down in excited gestures, while he received the congratulations from his devoted friends. "Follow me to the terrace and we'll be served our coffee's there." Hitler led the way with the excited lull of the voices of his guests following him.

The sun had disappeared behind the mountains, the warm glow still emanating from its hidden spot with the sky slowly turning darker, spraying the sky with a multitude of colors. The air was warm and comfortable as the group took seats on the spacious patio furniture located on the broad terrace.

The command came and Bold and Resilient sped from the earth at lightning speed and hovered over the earth's atmosphere to wait for the signal.

"Beata, come out here and see the northern lights. They're beautiful!"

Beata took a last sip of her hot tea, stood up from the table and looked out the back, screened door and up at the sky. From this vantage point she could see some of the color in the sky and it was beautiful and awe-inspiring even from here.

Helmuth Schluter looked up from reading his newspaper at the table and looked at his daughter. "Is it as pretty as Ilse says?"

"It does appear quite beautiful."

"I don't want to go outside now. I'm too tired," said Unna, still sipping her tea and closing her eyes to prove her point.

Helmuth looked at Beata. "I'll stay in with your mother." He held the edges of the newspaper, one corner folded over as he spoke. "Go on and join Ilse. She invited you so she must want you there. I want to give her and Hahn as much time together as they want."

"I know. I feel the same way." Beata looked out once more and then back to her Father. "I'll go out for a short while."

Beata grabbed her sweater from the chair beside the door, placed it over her shoulders and exited into the yard. The air was still warm but it would cool quickly now that the sun was just hidden beyond the horizon. Beata wandered to the large trees located in the back yard and gazed at the sky. The colors were intense as they changed and shifted slowly, stretched across the sky like a banner. Beata was lost in the glory of it as she wandered slowly to the bench located beneath the large maple tree. She stopped beside Ilse, who was seated on the broad bench. Beata's attention was still completely focused on the colorful display above her.

"Sit down, Beata." Ilse scooted to the middle, leaving room for Beata, while Hahn placed a possessive arm around Ilse's shoulder from the other side.

Beata absentmindedly sat down while her eyes were glued to the spectacular display above her. "I can't remember seeing the northern lights this clearly in a long, long time."

"Yes, I know what you mean and there's so much red in the sky this evening. It's quite remarkable," said Ilse.

Beata tore her eyes from the sky above and glanced at her newly married sister and brother-in-law. Hahn was younger than Beata was, yet he seemed older with the way he towered over Ilse and his love sick eyes stared into her eyes. Hahn and Ilse were together all the time, at least as much as they could be with Hahn in training camp at the military academy. He was one of the fortunate ones who were assigned close to home. He came to spend time with Ilse as much as he could but there were rumors that Germany was preparing for war and that the first army units would be sent out very soon. Beata could see the fear growing in both Ilse's and Hahn's eyes. They had been married in early July, making their marriage not even two months old and the expectation of war was aging them both beyond their years. They clung to each other desperately every chance they had. Even now their hands were intertwined, they sat as close as two humans could and an occasional kiss was stolen as they tore their eyes from the beauty of the skies and focused on each other.

Beata looked away from the heartbreaking display. If only Ilse had listened to reason and waited, she wouldn't be experiencing this tearing apart, the constant fear, the looming separation and a constant pain of heart. If only Ilse hadn't fallen in love with this handsome German in arms. If only she'd been content to remain a girl and not been so impatient to become a woman. Beata felt like she had lost a sister and felt more isolated from her world than ever before. It was difficult to see her sister in such turmoil, crying during the day while Hahn was gone, missing him terribly and then crying again when he returned, in complete joy and relief that she still had him. Ilse was a mess most of the time and she was difficult to live with. Hahn and Ilse lived here, in the Schluter home, since Hahn's parents had no extra room. It would be temporary anyway. Everyone in the Schluter household knew that. Germany had been in the preparation for war for a few years and the rumors of war with Poland flowed throughout the country so there was no doubt as to the immediate future.

Hahn was particularly quiet as Ilse chattered on and on about the beautiful display in the sky. Ilse always did become a chatter box when she was nervous or afraid. She was the most talkative of the couple anyway. Hahn talked only when he had something of importance to say, being a contemplative fellow, not that he was shy but when he spoke he spoke with finality and meaning.

Beata suddenly felt uncomfortable as if she were disrupting a holy time, a quiet love moment between two people soon to be torn apart by distance and the looming possibility of a permanent separation should war happen to take Hahn's life. Beata suddenly found it hard to breathe in the heavy heartedness of the moment and was about to stand and leave when Hahn spoke. His voice was quiet and Beata at first strained to hear.

"I don't know what to think." He fell quiet for a moment and Ilse sat in silence waiting for her husband's next words.

Beata sat forward to catch what he said. Hahn looked around Ilse at Beata with confusion shining from his eyes. She waited for him to continue.

"I don't know what to think about what's taking place in the military divisions." Another moment of silence followed. "I've heard things from some of the other men and there are a lot of questions floating around.

They keep them quiet of course. They don't want their commanding officers to hear the murmurings." Another moment of silence followed as Hahn stared up at the sky. He looked back at the two sisters beside him and this time looked directly into Beata's eyes. "I've been told that the man in charge of the SS troops, Reinhard Heydrich, has been working at a new task the past few months. He's been choosing from the surplus of volunteers and making a new division for the military. No one knows exactly what their responsibilities will be but the men I'm with have been talking. High Commander Heydrich has been choosing the most despicable men for this new division." Hahn fell silent and studied his hand intertwined with Ilse's.

Beata prodded, "What do you mean, Hahn? What kind of men has he picked?"

Hahn lifted his eyes slowly to meet Beata's. "Many of them are ex-convicts, hardened men with terrible crimes to their record. Even some convicts were released from prison and enlisted into this special task force. Others that have been enlisted have served in the previous war but they are mostly angry, violent men. I'm not sure how the men I'm training with know that much about them."

Beata said, "Why would the government need these kinds of men in the military?"

Hahn stared at Beata with uncertainty. "I don't know. I don't like it. People with violent behavior will most likely live out their lives in violence. Why would Germany allow such people, who aren't allowed to mingle with the general population, now go free and serve their country in war? It doesn't make sense and it actually really bothers me."

Beata looked at Hahn with a new admiration. She had always seen him as a complete supporter of the new German government, in total awe of Adolf Hitler and in absolute agreement with armament build up and war plans. His openly voiced questions placed him in a completely different light, which caused Beata to take him seriously for the first time since their meeting.

"Have you heard what this special military unit will be doing?" asked Beata.

"I haven't heard much. It's fairly top secret, only they know and they're not talking. The only thing we've been told…now you have to remember that I'm sharing this in complete confidentiality and you can't say a word to anyone." Hahn stopped to make sure his point was taken.

Beata and Ilse both nodded their heads in acknowledgement.

"The only thing we've been told is that this special task force division will take up the rear and establish order and carry out specific duties. I don't know what those duties are. I'm part of the army so I'll be in the offensive division, first ones in so to speak. We'll be taking the land and we'll be in the greatest danger but then other divisions will come in behind us, the SS or the special policing forces and the special task forces, which are being called the Einsatzgruppen. I know I shouldn't worry about what they're responsible for, I'm only responsible for my own work. But I can't help but wonder, especially knowing the kind of men that have been recruited."

Ilse said, "It doesn't make sense, Hahn. Why would the Nazi government do that? These men should be behind bars."

"Perhaps they need some violent, deviant men to perform what only they could perform," said Beata.

That got Hahn's attention, "But what? That's what I keep asking myself. What are they planning?"

Just then all eyes turned to the skies and all three noticed the complete panorama of red northern lights painted across the sky, to the degree that it shadowed the landscape of houses, trees, fences, shrubs and everything else within view with a tinge of red.

Hahn was the first to comment, "It looks like blood covering everything."

All was silent. Then Ilse chuckled nervously. "I know what you're thinking, Beata. It's a sign right?"

Beata remained quiet at the clear insult.

Hahn looked at the two sisters intently. "What do you mean, Ilse?"

"Oh whenever something out of the ordinary happens, like a strange looking sky, a dead bird on the sidewalk or an unusual dream, Beata always takes it as a sign that something awful is going to happen."

"Is that true?" Hahn gave a slight smile, nervousness tinting his eyes.

Beata took her time responding. "I have seen many odd things and have had many dreams but not every one of them means something. I know very specifically when an event or dream is significant. It's just a knowing, a deep inner perception that it has great meaning."

Hahn said, "And has this deep inner knowing proven to be true?"

Ilse chuckled beside Beata.

Beata paused for a moment, wondering whether to expose herself even further. Her sister's mocking laugh didn't encourage her.

Ilse said, "Well, Beata, has this inner knowing you say you have, proven to be true?" She stared at her sister in trepidation and with slight disdain.

"Yes, it has proven to be true in every situation."

Hahn said, "So you're saying you have some kind of psychic ability?"

"No, it's not psychic at all."

Ilse asked bitingly, "Then what is it?"

Beata glanced at the two who were both staring intently at her. "It's God. He shows me what's coming and He's always been right."

"God? I didn't know God showed anyone anything. I thought He'd just do whatever He wanted to do and tough luck on us." Hahn stopped and looked into Beata's eyes once more. "So you're saying that God talks to you?"

Beata started to feel more and more uncomfortable, knowing she wasn't believed and clearly mocked by her sister, grinning beside her. "I...I don't hear His voice but He gives me a knowing deep inside about things. I...I just know things. I see things and then I immediately know things."

Hahn pointed up at the blood red sky, "So what does this mean?"

Beata joined his inspection of the sky, not sure whether to say it or not. Her angels surrounded her. Courageous bent toward her and said, "Don't be afraid. Tell him."

Beata still felt unsure.

Courageous looked at Wisdom and nodded. Wisdom leaned toward her and said, "He's asking for truth. Give it to him."

She released a deep sigh. She averted Hahn's eyes as she said it. "It means a lot of death is coming."

"So it is a sign of blood."

She looked at him then. He looked grave and serious.

Ilse nearly shouted, "Hahn, don't believe her! Beata is always making negative predictions about everything! I told you she's negative and depressing. It's not true!" Ilse pointed at the sky in desperation. "These are only northern lights and they're red tonight! They are only northern lights! They are not a sign!" Ilse turned to stare angrily at Beata. "They are not a sign! How could you do this? I invite you to come join us and all you do is make one of your stupid predictions again! How could you?" Tears gathered quickly in her eyes and began to slip down her cheeks in a steady stream.

"I'm sorry, Ilse! I never meant to say anything and I never meant to upset you. I only said it because Hahn asked. Please forgive me for saying anything."

"Go inside! Please, just leave us and go inside!"

Beata stood and left quickly, with the sound of Ilse's sobs and Hahn trying to console her filling the back yard. Beata could kick herself for being so unthinking and cruel. Why had she said it? Why did she have to go ahead and blurt out what she knew? As soon as she saw the red hue from the sky painting the landscape red, she knew. She knew more than that but she thankfully kept her mouth from adding more than what was asked.

CHAPTER 29

The incessant heat of summer caused beads of perspiration to form on the Fuhrer's brow as he sat bent over his desk in deep concentration. A smile appeared occasionally as he wrote on his notepad, stopping in contemplation at times and then furiously writing once more. He finally set his pen down, picked up the paper with one hand and scanned the contents carefully, while wiping the perspiration from his forehead with his other hand. Placing the paper back on his desk, he reached for the phone and dialed his secretary.

Henrietta Bauman's voice echoed from the ear piece. "Yes, sir, what can I do for you?"

"Henrietta, get me Heinrich Himmler. I want to meet with him as soon as possible. This morning would be preferable."

"I'll see what I can do, Mr. Hitler. I have someone who has just arrived and wishes to speak with you. The Foreign Minister, Joachim von Ribbentrop, is standing before me. Should I send him in?"

"Yes of course! And let me know as soon as you speak with Heinrich Himmler and when I should expect him."

"Yes, sir."

The door opened momentarily and Joachim von Ribbentrop entered, his hat in his hand and smiling respectfully at the Fuhrer. Hitler nodded in welcome.

"Come in Joachim. What warrants this visit?"

Ribbentrop wandered to the chair that stood before Hitler's expansive desk but stayed standing. "I have heard from the…"

"Sit down, sit down, Joachim. There's no need to stand in my presence." He waved to the chair.

Joachim took a seat, unbuttoning his top coat to relieve the strain around his full belly. He held his hat with both hands and gazed at Adolf in admiration. "As I was saying, I heard from the British Foreign Minister this morning and shortly after that I received another call from France's Foreign Minister. Both are desperately requesting us to pursue negotiations with Poland for a peaceful resolution."

Hitler's smile vanished as he listened. "And if we don't?"

"They both threatened that they would honor their treaty obligations to the Polish nation and defend her if we chose the path of war."

"I don't believe either of them! Neither Britain nor France has the guts or the desire to go to war. I'm confident they're bluffing." Adolf looked stern but completely convinced.

"Should we respond to their requests?"

Adolf thought a moment. "No! Their threats and demands are only a bullying tactic. I believe it's all talk with no real power or determination behind it." He looked mentally preoccupied as he rubbed the edge of his desk with his hands. The room fell silent, while he stared at his desk, as if seeing it for the first time.

"So we shouldn't take the warnings seriously? We should continue with our plans?"

Adolf met Joachim's eyes. "Their warnings are but child's play, mere whisperings by inferior nations and yes I fully intend to pursue our plans vigorously." He sat up fully and leaned forward. "Joachim, I want you to ignore the ranting of nations, specifically Britain and France. I don't believe they'll uphold their treaty with Poland. They're only playing games." A defiant glint glazed his eyes. "Don't even reply to them. Tell them nothing. They will learn soon enough what our agenda is. There's no time to delay. I have requested…" The phone rang loudly beside him. "Excuse me."

Ribbentrop nodded politely while Hitler picked up the phone.

"Yes that's sufficient. Thank you." He set the phone piece back in its place. "That was Heinrich Himmler and he's on his way here as I speak. We must move quickly now. I summoned Heinrich to discuss the details and to lay out the blueprint of the invasion."

"How soon will we invade Poland?"

"It will commence within days."

"Is the army ready?"

"This is what we've been preparing for, for the last few years. We are entirely ready. Himmler is well equipped and well able to carry out my wishes regarding the invasion. He won't fail me in this." Hitler picked up his agenda and perused it once more in preparation for Himmler's appearance. He then looked up to meet Ribbentrop's eyes. "Our meeting is done then or was there something else you wished to discuss?"

"That was all I had to say, sir." Joachim von Ribbentrop moved to get up, his belly jutting outward awkwardly before he found his way to a standing position. He saluted Adolf in the Nazi salute and left the room quickly.

CHAPTER 30

There was a sharp knock at the door before it opened and a voice shouted, "Ilse? Ilse, where are you?"

Beata could hear the shouting from the kitchen where she mixed dough for biscuits, to go with the stew simmering on the stove. Beata wiped her hands on her apron and went to look what the fuss was about. The voice sounded like Hahn's but very agitated.

"Hahn, is that you?" She walked down the hall and saw his distressed face turn pleadingly toward her.

"Do you know where Ilse is?" His tall frame filled the door and if he hadn't appeared so frantic, he would have made an impressive figure in his sharp uniform.

"She went shopping with Mother but they should be home soon. Why? What's wrong?"

"My unit is leaving within the hour. I won't be home for dinner and I have to say goodbye to Ilse." He looked on the verge of tears.

Beata walked toward him and placed a hand on his elbow. "Come in, Hahn, and sit down for a bit. Ilse should be walking through that door any minute."

Hahn pulled his arm from Beata's grasp. "Where did they go? I have to find her now!"

"I'm not even sure where they went. They usually go visit the shops on Berghall Street but they didn't let me know exactly where they were going so I can't give you specific directions. I think you should wait here. They've been gone for some time and they will be back for dinner."

"Oh, I don't know what to do!" He turned away and grabbed his head with both hands.

"Please come in, Hahn." Beata couldn't stand to see him so agitated.

"My army commander gave me permission to say goodbye but he said to be back within the hour." Hahn looked at his watch nervously and then stared at Beata. "I've already been gone twenty minutes and I have to give myself twenty minutes to get back."

"It won't help to stand here worrying about it. Sit down in the kitchen and I'll take a look outside to see if they're coming. All right?" Beata once more held Hahn's elbow and this time he allowed himself to be led to the kitchen and he dejectedly sat down with his elbows resting on the table, his army cap between them. "Stay here while I go look for her." He only nodded nervously in reply.

Beata hurried to the front door, pulled on her shoes and ran outside to the street. She looked both ways but there was no sign of her mother or her sister. She noticed her father's Volkswagen turning a corner and slowly heading toward her. He stopped in front of the house and she hurried to his side to intercept him.

"Dad, Hahn just came and he's being sent out to fight."

"Fight where?"

"I'm supposing in Poland but I didn't even ask." She shook her head to focus. "But that's not why I'm here. Hahn is desperate to speak with Ilse before he departs. Mother and Ilse went shopping. They should be home by now but I don't see them coming. Could you go find them and bring them home?"

"Do you know where they'll be?"

"I don't know." Beata shook her head in frustration. Now she wished desperately that she'd asked them their destination. "Hopefully they're already walking back and you'll spot them easily."

"Let's hope so," said Helmuth Schluter as he started up his car and left.

Beata watched the Volkswagen disappear from sight and she prayed quietly for success. She walked back to the house and to the kitchen where Hahn sat as still as a statue. He looked frozen in spot. Beata stood beside him and placed a hand on his shoulder.

"Are you okay, Hahn?"

Silence. He finally looked up and into her eyes. "No, I'm not all right. I'm leaving my new bride and it's tearing me up inside. I'm afraid that I can't live without her." His voice trailed off in open agitation.

"You should have thought of that a few months ago when you were hotly pursuing her." Beata regretted it immediately when she saw the stricken look in his eyes. "I'm sorry, Hahn. That was uncalled for. You both fell in love, it was unavoidable." She realized her words sounded trite and untrue. She had voiced her opinions too openly and freely for too long and Hahn already knew her true feelings. "I...I intercepted my father. He was just returning home and he left again to look for Ilse and Mother."

Hahn nodded and Beata returned to making biscuits.

Hahn said, "You know, Beata, I realize you've never really liked me. It's because I married Ilse and she's so young. I've seen the displeasure in your eyes many times but you need to know that I truly love her. She's my very life and I know that she loves me too. All I want is to make her happy, to be a good husband to her."

Beata's thoughts led elsewhere. *Then why did you join the army if all you've ever wanted was to make Ilse happy. Why are you leaving? Why marry her and then abandon her? What kind of husband is that?* She kept her tongue.

"I never thought joining the army would be this torturous. I thought it would be adventurous and fun. I never imagined having to leave Ilse and that it would hurt this much."

Beata turned from the counter and stared at him. "Didn't you realize that the army was being mobilized for a specific purpose?"

Hahn only shrugged.

"You never thought you'd actually have to fight?"

"Not really."

"Or that you'd be sent away?" She felt incredulous.

"No," Hahn said softly.

"But isn't that what armies do, go away and fight?"

"Yes but I didn't think it would happen so soon and I hadn't planned on falling in love and getting married. Ilse has changed everything."

Beata could feel the anger rising and she couldn't keep the accusation and fury out of her voice. "But Hahn, you knew what was likely to happen and to drag Ilse into a fantasy that you knew could never be..."

The front door opened and Ilse's hysterical voice rang through the house. "Hahn, Hahn, where are you?"

Hahn leapt from the chair and raced to meet her. Their muffled cries, moans of despair and desperate clinging followed.

Beata shook her head at the agonized sounds drifting through the house, bit her trembling, angry lip and turned to focus on the pan of biscuits. Helmuth and Unna Schluter entered the kitchen, leaving their youngest daughter to deal with the grief and sorrow alone. Unna's face spoke volumes. Her forehead was creased with worry and her eyes spoke of the grief she carried for her youngest. Helmuth poured a cup of coffee and sat at the table deep in thought. Beata finished placing the biscuits on a baking sheet, set them to the side to allow the oven to heat and then walked to where her mother stood, staring out the back door. Beata placed an arm around her mother's shoulders and squeezed tight. Unna draped an arm around Beata's waist.

"We warned her, Mother." Beata couldn't hide the anger she still felt.

Unna nodded sadly. "It doesn't take away the pain of seeing her so unhappy."

They stood there together, staring at the back yard, looking at nothing in particular, while the sounds of weeping, kissing and groans of unending grief wafted toward them from the front hall. Falling in love had been so magical, such a fairy tale of Ilse's making but it now lay like a shattered dream, the tearing apart a cruel blow to her fantasized ideals. If only Ilse was still the little sister Beata remembered. Whenever Ilse was upset all Beata needed to do was hold her and speak reassuringly to her and Ilse quickly recovered to her spunky, happy self. There was no easy fix to the pain Ilse was suffering from today and no trite words would suffice to numb the ache in her heart. This heartache was something Ilse had to face all on her own regardless of her young age of sixteen.

CHAPTER 31

Deliverer walked through the expansive angel quarters, hardly seeing the beauty and pristine perfection reflected in everything that surrounded him. His time in Heaven was stretching on further than he had anticipated and his eagerness to get back to earth with the many others preparing to leave was growing stronger by the day. Deliverer felt the urge to do something, walk or maybe soar over the scenery of Heaven, anything to take his mind off his heart's constant desire.

It's not that he disliked it here in Heaven's glory and peace. To be in the presence of such sheer glory, surrounded by his many angel comrades, was completely relaxing. Separation from earth's darkness, with the constant threat of battle, was also a plus. A time of rest was always welcome and needed after an assignment on earth. This was his home, yet his calling kept urging him back into the service of the saints and this desire never left him. It was a constant urge, a nagging desire, eyes longing to see the forces of darkness defeated and the Heaven-bound earth dwellers living in victory.

Deliverer began to walk through the thick forest, which separated the angel living quarters from the rest of Heaven. The thick undergrowth separated in front of him, leaving a path clear before him. The rich smells of the forest greeted him, the aroma of pine, cedar, birch, maple and oaks intermingled with the sweet fragrance of flowering shrubs and plants growing between the towering trees of the forest. Abundant wild flowers grew beneath the tall trees, the light from Almighty God reaching every spot, making every area rich in growth and beauty. Even here, beneath the thick covering of leaves, there was no shadow or spot of darkness to be seen. Light permeated the darkest place and caused it to glow with the glory only found in Heaven.

He hardly noticed the light and glory, preoccupied with his possible departure. After a long walk he finally exited the forest and entered a field, full of rich, golden grain, which waved in the slight breeze, appearing almost like waves on the ocean as it rippled and moved. He walked quickly through the waist high grain, the stocks bending as he stepped on them. They quickly stood upright as he passed, without any sign that they had been trampled. Beside the field a stream ran from the main river of life, which flowed throughout Heaven, and along each bank of the river grew fruit trees of many different varieties. The fragrance of the copious flowers, growing beneath the trees, filled his senses.

Deliverer walked through the grass and flower turf and made his way to the edge of the river. Stepping into the life giving flow brought an immediate sensation of peace surging through him with powerful force. He felt all tension leave his frame and the deep striving to depart Heaven's bliss seemed to lesson substantially.

"I should have entered the river sooner," he spoke to himself. The river brought on a cleansing, calming flow spreading through his whole being. He let the rush of the water swirl around his feet. He sighed deeply and breathed in the misty air that imparted new life to him. Further upstream the water bubbled and gurgled over some exposed rocks and rushed down an incline to where he stood. The sound of the joyous, life giving water filled him with peace.

Off in the distance, closer to the Holy City, Deliverer could see people wandering over the rolling hills and he could hear their laughter. The laughter always hit him first as he came in contact with the Heaven dwellers. There were no signs of sorrow here but only unending joy. An earth dweller, released from earth's hold and ushered into Heaven's glory, found nothing to mourn about but spent the rest of their eternity rejoicing. Such a difference was there, from one life to the next.

Deliverer left the water and walked the path that followed the river and meandered further toward to the Great City.

He thought of opening his wings and soaring over the landscape to increase his visual perspective. He decided against it, greatly enjoying the joy on each face as he passed the many strolling by the river. The Heaven dwellers didn't see him as he walked past them. Once in a while angels were permitted to appear in an angel choir or in a public meeting place but they stayed invisible. It was God Almighty who was to be worshiped and honored.

Walking a little further, he suddenly saw a familiar form walking towards him. He knew this angel. It was Wrath, who had not yet been dispatched either. He wore a serious expression as they clasped hands in reunion.

"Where are you heading, Wrath?"

"Here. I was told to meet someone in this location."

"Who?"

He shrugged. "I'm not sure. The angelic coordinator told me I'd know when I see him." Wrath leveled his gaze at Deliverer. "Perhaps it's you."

Deliverer chuckled. "I don't know."

A group of people spoke with excitement further down the path and both angels turned to look. They saw Jesus approaching the group and everyone swarmed him eagerly. The Lamb of God stopped to embrace each one, love flowing from elder brother to his brothers and sisters.

Deliverer and Wrath walked to a group of fruit trees, leaned against the trunks and watched as the Glorious King related to his followers. Jesus left the group but was quickly intercepted by four children leaving the river. Their voices were loud and excited as they rushed him, nearly knocking him over in their enthusiasm. Jesus' laugh was contagious as he wrapped his arms around the foursome. He kissed the tops of their heads and smiled at them with a great, deep love. He seemed to linger longer than usual as the four children, clinging to him, spoke of their many adventures and He responded with genuine interest. The children, having received the love and attention they craved, scampered off together in search of a new adventure.

Jesus headed straight for Deliverer and Wrath. His form was beautiful, uplifting, the glory around Him spectacular as He drew closer. Jesus' eyes were now focused on the two angels. They fell to their knees and waited for the Lily of the Valley to come near. Deliverer could see Jesus' feet now, could feel the electrical current of His power as his hands rested on his bowed head.

"Deliverer, Wrath, come with me. I want to show you something."

Deliverer stood quickly and looked into Jesus' face. Wrath stood beside him. Jesus' look was full of love and acceptance and any remaining anxious thought flew away like a dry leaf in a strong wind. Deliverer followed as Jesus left the path and wandered through a flowery, hilly area. Wrath took up the rear.

Deliverer watched Jesus' back as they walked and he could feel love emanating in strong waves from His wonderful frame. It was pure bliss just walking in His presence. Suddenly without notice, Deliverer glanced up and realized that they were far north on the opposite side of the Great City, a walk that would normally take a good day or maybe even two. He knew without asking that they had been instantly transported.

"Wow! Did you notice that, Deliverer?" asked Wrath.

Deliverer looked back. "You mean that we were just transported?"

"Yes!"

Deliverer smiled. "I did notice."

Jesus came to a stop and pointed ahead to an area that was bustling with activity. Many buildings were being constructed and the workers were too innumerable to count. Large convoys, stacked with building materials of every kind, were on the main highway, heading into the huge city construction site. It seemed that every house, every apartment building and every business facility was under construction. There didn't seem to be any established home or building within miles as far as Deliverer could tell. Everything seemed new and under building supervision.

From this vantage point, Deliverer noticed numerous superintendents, giving instructions, looking over plans and discussing construction techniques with the workers. Not a sound of a hammer could be heard, no saws broke the peaceful atmosphere and no harried hurrying or disgruntled disputes broke out here. It was a sight that would never be seen on earth. All the buildings were pre-planned, assembled at factories and large, designated construction areas far from the city premises. The pre-assembled parts were then hauled here by transport vehicles, thus alleviating all noise from the city. Even the transport trucks were powered by the very energy of Heaven. They moved effortlessly and without noise, moved along by the power of God.

The city was beginning to shine and glow with the many precious finishes being applied to the structures. The main highway into the city was completed and many of the main routes through the city were already paved, all in pure gold. Many crisscrossing streets still needed the gold topcoat.

It was a huge city, Deliverer estimated that it potentially housed around a million. He and Wrath both stood mesmerized by the amazing sight.

Deliverer couldn't remember ever seeing so much construction at one time. There was always construction in Heaven but this went beyond the norm. Homes were always being prepared for a soon coming arrival, an apartment complex for a group influx or an orphanage for children entering before or without their parents. Construction was a constant fact in Heaven with many talented workmen eager to help and prepare for those coming. Deliverer gazed in amazement at the cooperation displayed by the talented men and women, the enormity of their task and the broad spectrum of the work before him. Everywhere he looked work was being done, speedily and efficiently as if a tight schedule was being adhered to. He couldn't help his open mouthed stance as he stared dumbfounded at the awe inspiring sight.

"What do you think?" Jesus' words came softly.

Deliverer had nearly forgotten that Jesus stood quietly by, watching his every reaction and he jumped slightly at the words. Jesus only smiled in amusement and continued to gaze at him in expectation.

"I don't know what to say. I have visited much of Heaven during my stay but I have never even noticed this large city and it seems to have been built from nothing to this in such a short time!"

"Not a short time, Deliverer. It only seems short because you were not aware of it."

"It's huge, massive!" said Wrath. "But why?"

"I have more to show you." With that, Jesus turned and walked away.

Deliverer and Wrath quickly followed. They walked to Jesus' side, just a step behind and Deliverer glanced at His profile. Jesus smiled as he strolled and waved at the many that recognized him. They headed onto a hill, filled with innumerable kinds of flowers. As they descended the other side, Deliverer looked beyond his Master and realized once more that they had been transported to another region of Heaven's vast reaches.

The ocean lay before them, reaching further than the eye could see, its great waves thundering and pounding the rocks to the right and gentler ones easing onto the shore before them. The sound was both deafening and absolutely glorious at the same time. Flumes of water glimmered and shone, reflecting the glory of the sky above, the bottomless sea emanating the grandeur and splendor of all that Heaven contained. Prism-like colors played over the water's surface and the shining glory within the great sea was hard to take in at first sight. Both angels squinted at the view and slowly, as they grew accustomed to the glittering, shining thrashing waves, opened their eyes more fully to behold the complete panoramic view. It was a magnificent sight which they had seen numerous times but seeing it again filled their hearts with praise and adoration. They sang out with loud voices.

"Glory to God in the highest and on earth, peace to men, on whom His favor rests. Glory, glory to Him who sits on the throne and to the Lamb." Deliverer and Wrath fell to their knees, their hands raised as they worshiped the King of Kings and the Lord of Lords.

An angel choir, which soared overhead, joined in with the praise until the atmosphere was charged with power. They then began to sing in worship, the words floating and pulsating through the air with adoration. Deliverer stayed in his position of reverence before the Lamb of God and he softly sang along. Wrath lay prostrate on the ground. Slowly the powerful praise quieted as the choir dispersed and sailed over the landscape to the job assigned to them.

Deliverer stood and looked at the Great King. Jesus smiled with a look of intense love.

"Come, we still haven't reached our destination." Jesus turned and began to walk away from the ocean with its noise and magnificence.

They stood immediately and ran to catch up. They walked for a while in silence over the sandy soil, mixed with precious gems and small pieces of diamond rock. The ground dazzled the eyes and caused the air above it to sparkle and sway in color as the light of Heaven blended the colors in a spectacular kaleidoscope. Every place in Heaven was spectacular, yet each place had its own specific glory, grace and beauty. Deliverer couldn't help but hold his breath at the beauty which surrounded him.

Jesus walked up an incline to the top of the hill. He stopped and looked at them.

They stopped beside Him and looked at the panoramic view before them. Deliverer drew in a sharp breath and gazed at the huge, city construction sight in the valley. Wrath's arms dropped to his side and his mouth opened wide in surprise.

"Another new city is being built?" asked Wrath.

"It's massive," said Deliverer.

"Yes, this is another new city," explained Jesus.

Before them lay a similar view as the previous city they had visited. Everything was either under construction or nearing the finishing stages of construction. This city actually looked further along in completion than the first one they'd seen and yet the whole plain below them was abuzz with activity and work, from the east to the west, from the north to the south. He couldn't see the end of the city; it was so large and expansive. He shook his head in wonder and amazement.

"Why are there two brand new cities being built?"

Jesus' eyes twinkled. "There are actually forty brand new cities under construction in different areas throughout Heaven."

Deliverer and Wrath stared at their Lord but were unable to speak.

Jesus smiled. "I know it is astonishing and hard to understand but these cities will be needed in the coming years. Many, many will be coming and very soon." Jesus looked over the city, his smile fading. His face held a resigned sorrow.

Deliverer finally found his tongue. "Is it the trouble stirring on earth that brings you sorrow?"

"There will be great trouble there and many people are not ready." Jesus gazed deeply into his eyes. Jesus waved a hand toward the city. "In my Father's house are many mansions. I have prepared places for the many that will be coming, for those who choose me."

With great intensity, Jesus stared into Deliverer's eyes. "Many will accept me in their last moment, their last breath on earth. You are being summoned to assist them, assign the allotted guardian angels and aid in their final journey."

Deliverer felt dumbfounded by the sheer realization of the numbers they were dealing with. "But forty cities this size," he pointed to the vast plain before them, "would suggest millions upon millions of people! How is that possible?"

Jesus smiled sorrowfully. "It's disheartening, but true."

"Since this is true, the war that is looming will take more lives than any other war before it." Wrath looked questioningly at his Lord.

"It will be unprecedented in numbers, my servant."

"And it will include the apple of your eye?"

"Yes, they will be at the center of the storm."

Wrath looked wounded at the information but anger shone from his eyes.

Deliverer felt like he had been dealt a serious blow, the courage he usually felt lay at his feet in a puddle of bewilderment. He didn't even realize he was mumbling to himself, "Not again, not again, oh no, not again!" He felt a hand on his shoulder and he looked up at Jesus. He saw only peace there.

"Just remember my words, Deliverer. Whoever curses my people, will be cursed and whoever blesses them, will be blessed. This is not the end for my people and they will not always be left at the mercy of their enemies. You will see what will be brought about for the Israelites."

"Will my assignment include deliverance for your people?"

Jesus looked grave and stern. "Very few will experience physical deliverance. You will know which ones and you will assist them. The deliverance I have for my people is mostly of a different nature. You will see in time. Do you accept this mission, Deliverer?"

He knelt immediately and bowed before Jesus. "Yes, Master. I accept the mission."

Jesus turned toward Wrath. "And you, Wrath, do you also accept the mission?"

"What will my part be?"

Jesus smiled. "The greatest wrath to my enemies is snatching people from the open jaws of Hell and leading them into the kingdom of Heaven."

"Salvation." A smile tickled Wrath's lips. "This will infuriate the enemy!"

Jesus said, "Do you think you can handle this?"

Wrath saluted military style. "Yes, Sir!"

Deliverer cleared his throat to get Jesus' attention. "I see clearly that we will be exposed to much sorrow, grief and pain so I ask for extra courage and boldness to complete the task."

Jesus placed his hands on Deliverer's shoulders. "Be strong and courageous. Do not be terrified and do not be discouraged for I will be with you wherever you go. Although you will venture into dark and horrifying situations, My grace and glory will go with you." He looked at Wrath and placed a hand on his shoulder. "With you too, and you will have more strength than at any other time in your existence. Although great darkness will at times surround you, My light within you will hold the darkness at bay and no harm will come near you."

Jesus looked at them both with stern resolution. "You will be generals in this war and many legions of angels will be under your command. You will assign them their positions, group them according to the wisdom given you and lead them into the fray. They will be like thieves and robbers, snatching people's souls out of Hell's dark agenda. I have great confidence in both of you, that you will accomplish all the Father's will in the earth. The assignment is grave but will also be filled with much rejoicing."

Deliverer could feel his strength increasing as Jesus' words of encouragement and direction filled him with renewed energy. "I willingly accept this mission and I will pour myself into this work with my whole being."

"I also accept this assignment," agreed Wrath.

"Remember, that I will lead you and guide you through Holy Spirit. You will know what to do in each and every situation, no matter how much danger you face." Jesus looked from one angel to the other. "Listen to My voice, you will hear Me and you will obey."

"I will obey, Master." Deliverer bowed his head, the glory of the Great King surrounding him in Heavenly waves of power and might.

"I will obey," echoed Wrath.

The two angels slowly lifted their heads and they noticed that Jesus was already walking away, vanishing slowly from sight, most likely transporting to another spot where he was needed. Jesus looked back once more, smiled, and waved, and then He was gone.

Deliverer slowly stood, feeling overwhelmed by the assignment, but also charged with energy to complete it. Wrath stood silent beside him. Deliverer gazed at the expansive city before him once more, opened his huge wings to full width and took to the air in a surge of power. The grass and flowers on the hill beneath him swayed furiously at the gush of air he left behind, but as he soared higher he could hear the flowers singing a farewell song. Wrath flew up behind him and took his place beside him. Both were eager to depart.

CHAPTER 32

Krakow, Poland, September 1, 1939

Aaron Levin made a cup of coffee and went to stand by the large window in the kitchen. The still dark sky was slowly being painted by a bright glow on the horizon. He hadn't been able to sleep and after tossing and turning for hours, he finally got up. He'd already said his morning prayers, recited some memorized sections of the Torah and then meticulously looked over the list of inventory he needed to order for his small grocery store. Doing that hadn't brought on any desire to sleep so here he stood, looking at the still dark landscape of this neighborhood within greater Krakow and sipping coffee from his mug.

Heaviness pulled at his eyes; his shoulders more stooped than his usual straight stance. A sense of uneasiness played his emotions. His hands shook so that his coffee spilled over the top. After switching the cup to the other hand, he shook off the hot liquid and resumed his search of the neighborhood. He wasn't sure what he was looking for. A general feeling of dread, of something lurking in the dark ready to pounce permeated his thoughts.

After a weary sigh, he turned back into the room and sat down in the large corner arm chair, close to the radio. He flicked it on tiredly, turning the volume down low so it wouldn't wake anyone. It crackled and then came to life. A distressed, fearful voice filled the small space. His tiredness flew as anxiety fully took its place.

"…worst fears are realized. Please, we call for the speedy support of our allies, Britain and France. Come to our aid quickly! We are under German attack! We are holding our own but are overwhelmed by the tremendous assault by German troops and their air power! We are asking Britain and France to come quickly to our defense." The government announcer's voice nearly choked in his appeal as he grew silent for a moment.

His voice resumed, gentler this time, like a father consoling his bereft children. "People of Poland, be aware that we have been attacked. The threats from Germany are now a reality. The German army is on Polish land and our troops are fighting gallantly to defend this nation. We know that our troops' loyalty and their love for Poland will provide us a speedy victory. Pray for the protection of our country and for the people of this nation. We will defend Warsaw, our capital, at all costs but know this, the German army is advancing on a broad area and they have gained ground. We are determined and know that our army will do everything in its power to drive these intruders from our midst. Be strong now, people of Poland; defend your homes, your families and your country." There was a moment of static and then his voice continued in calling the allies to bring aid and support, his voice rising frantically at times.

Aaron sat immobilized at the sheer shock of the announcement, shaking his head in denial. Then he quickly leapt into action. He ran into the bedroom and shook Anka till she awoke.

"What is it, Aaron?" She sat up rubbing her eyes.

"War has broken out. Germany has attacked Poland."

"What!" Anka's sleepiness fled, a look of fear replacing it as she focused on her husband.

Aaron was already removing his robe and pajamas and quickly pulling on a pair of pants.

"Where are you going?"

"I have to tell my family."

Anka slipped out of bed to stand beside Aaron as he hurriedly dressed.

"How close are the Germans?"

"I don't know. The government official didn't say."

"Where did you hear of it?" Anka's face looked skeptical as if Aaron had only had a bad dream.

"I was listening to the radio."

"In the middle of the night?" Anka looked quizzically toward the window where darkness stared back at her.

Aaron was now fully dressed and he stood before Anka, gazing at her with a serious expression. "I couldn't sleep."

"Do you know what woke you?"

"I just couldn't sleep."

"Did you hear or feel anything?"

Aaron looked at his wife, not knowing what she wanted to hear him say. He finally shook his head.

Anka had her arms wrapped around herself and she rubbed her arms. "It feels like someone's in the house. It feels creepy and dark." Fear now shone plainly from her eyes.

Aaron went to her, embraced her and kissed the top of her head. She wrapped her arms around him and held tight. "Don't worry. It's only because it's still dark outside."

"No, I feel something. It's a real darkness, a heaviness that seems to be pushing me down. It frightens me, Aaron!"

He squeezed her tightly and rubbed her back. "Don't worry. We need to be strong now, for the children." He held her at arms length and stared into her eyes. "I'll be back soon."

She nodded weakly and he hurried to get his coat and shoes. He didn't turn back as he hurried from the house. He hastened down the dark, deserted street, as the sun behind him began to paint the horizon in a thin line of white light. His parent's home was only two blocks away and he got there in record time.

He walked to the door and banged loudly, loud enough to even wake up a neighbor or two, if they'd been paying attention. There was no answer so Aaron knocked even louder, using both fists this time. There was noise now from the other side. The door finally swung open and a tired Binyamin appeared, groggy and squinting in the light that now shone from the entrance.

"Aaron!" Binyamin looked up and down the street in slight confusion. "Why...what...why are you here?"

"I have to talk to you!" Aaron blurted out.

"This early?" Binyamin looked upset at his son's impudence.

"I'm sorry, Father, but it's an emergency!"

Binyamin's eyes changed from annoyance to deep concern and he reached out a hand to his son. "What's wrong?" he said as he pulled Aaron inside. He shut the door and led the way to the sitting room.

"I woke up early and turned on the radio. Poland is at war. Germany is advancing on our soil right as we speak."

Binyamin spun around just as he got to the couch and stared at his son. "War? We're at war?"

"Yes, Father. I wanted to tell you right away."

Binyamin was already heading to the radio. As he switched it on it crackled to life and the government official's voice filled the room with warning, dread and fear.

"What's going on here?" Init Levin came shuffling into the room and rubbing her eyes. She had wrapped her night robe around herself and wore her home made slippers yet she still shivered in the cool, early morning air. She suddenly snapped to attention. Her sleepy state disappeared as quickly as a frightened bird darting from its nest as she heard the radio announcement.

Binyamin didn't answer but held an index finger to his lips as he focused on the dire proclamation. He wouldn't have needed to shush his wife, she was fully attentive and absorbing the message that was blasting from the small brown box on the bench, filling the home with a tangible apprehension. After a few moments of quiet attention to the announcer's voice, Binyamin lowered the volume and turned toward Aaron. "We'll need to tell the others."

"I'll go and tell Hershel and Joseph. Why don't you let your brother and sisters know?" Aaron hurried to the door and slipped on his shoes. He hadn't bothered to remove his coat.

"Yes…yes I should do that." Binyamin looked flustered for a moment as he searched for his coat and shoes. Init quickly stepped in to help him.

"This is terrible! This is so terrible!" Init kept repeating it over and over as she handed Binyamin his shoes.

"I'm sure it'll be all right, Init. Don't worry so," Binyamin said but he looked even more worried than Init. He turned then and followed Aaron out the door.

Aaron turned left and Binyamin right as they went their separate ways. Aaron saw the synagogue up ahead with their former Rabbi's house beside it. Rabbi David Kohn had been deposed from his position due to his fanatical and heretical ideas and actions. He still lived there but hadn't shown his face since the episode. Rabbi Kohn's family, likewise, kept their distance from the Jewish community, shamed and humiliated by the undesirable actions of their father and husband.

It hadn't taken long for the leading men of the community to come to a decision. They'd contacted the main Jewish community in Vilna, where a training centre prepared Rabbis and sent them out. No one from Vilna was willing to come but they'd found someone in a village not far from Krakow who was willing to move here and take over. The new Rabbi, Ariel Sutin, and his family had arrived only a few days ago and he had made a notable first impression. His appearance was in accordance with typical Jewish expectations in regards to an esteemed Rabbi. He had spoken to the leading men, those interested in appraising his worthiness and all in attendance had come away with high hopes and reassured hearts. Even Aaron had thought him wise and knowledgeable in Jewish history and religious practice.

Aaron passed the synagogue and then glanced at David Kohn's residence. "I wonder if he'll be asked to move to make way for the new Rabbi." He spoke it quietly as he stared at the humble but well maintained home. The home was a gift from the synagogue members but now this gift might be torn from the deposed Rabbi's grasp. Aaron shook his head sadly as he continued to stare.

He slowed his step as he saw movement in the front yard. He squinted to see what it was. The sky was beginning to brighten but not enough to see clearly. There, he saw it again and as he drew closer he suddenly knew. David Kohn was sitting beneath the large oak, sitting on a chair in the cool, morning air and swinging his leg occasionally.

"What in the world?" Aaron wondered out loud.

Aaron stopped and made a split second decision. Crossing the street to David's side, he mumbled, "I don't know what I'm doing but I still do have some respect for the man." He quickly closed the distance and wandered onto the grass. David looked different with his much shortened beard. He no longer looked like a Jewish Rabbi but only like an ordinary man wearing ordinary clothes and sitting in an ordinary way.

David spoke, "May I help you?"

"I don't mean any trouble, sir. I only came to give you some news."

David looked serious but not unfriendly. "I already know."

"You do?"

"Yes." David stared at him, a deep knowing and peace shining from his eyes.

Aaron stared for a moment as if unsure how to respond. "How can you sit here so calmly when Poland is at war? Aren't you frightened?"

"My fear came earlier. I already know what's going to happen and I'm prepared."

Aaron stood dumbfounded, now truly having lost his tongue.

David sat up a little straighter as he addressed Aaron. "The only peace our people will have now is if they embrace the Prince of Peace."

Aaron's chest twisted in frustration. The man was at it again, speaking nonsense. Would he never learn? "What is that supposed to mean?"

"I already told you but you didn't listen."

"I have to go. I have to let my brothers know about the war."

"You hurry along now, Aaron." David sat back in his chair.

He wavered on the spot, not sure whether to proceed or to ask the old man further on his new ideas. "Good bye, Mr. Kohn." With that Aaron turned and hurried from the yard.

"Good bye, Aaron Levin." As his four guardian angels stood protectively around him, David shook his head sadly and watched the young man hurry away.

CHAPTER 33

Krakow, Poland, October 1939

Jaromil Trafas nodded his head and stepped aside to let the young man in. Ewa, Jaromil's wife, stood back, wringing her hands and biting her lip anxiously. Her forehead was lined with creases as she nervously watched the man slowly step into the foyer.

The man, in his early thirties, was dressed in civilian clothes. He was unshaven and filthy and he carried a tattered bag in his arms. He removed his soiled hat, moved nervously from one foot to the other while fear and weariness shone simultaneously from his clouded eyes.

"You look familiar. Do we know you?" Jaromil asked.

"I was in the same infantry unit as your son, Jarek."

"Oh," said Jaromil silently, his voice fading away with understanding.

Ewa's hands flew to her face and she stood transfixed, fear pasted across her features as the man began to speak.

"My name is Kamil Malek. Your son and I were both posted at the front line. The German's were strong and powerful and they kept gaining ground. Their air power completely destroyed our air force and their army far outweighed ours in numbers. Their weaponry ability was astounding. Many, many Polish soldiers were killed. Many men from our division were killed."

"What about Jarek," asked Ewa, her eyes looking tortured.

"Jarek and I somehow made it and we were both assigned to Warsaw to defend it from the Germans. It was a miracle we survived there. We, the army, and many civilians were able to keep the Germans out of the city. Everyone worked together to sabotage the Germans every effort."

Kamil looked nervous as he told his tale but he plodded on. "From September fourteenth till the twenty-seventh we all fought bravely but the whole city was severely bombed. There was no way to bring in food with the Germans surrounding us. Everyone was wearing down. Dead horses were being cut up and eaten just to keep from starving. The city was bombed relentlessly and even though the whole city roused itself and fought the Germans; the Polish army couldn't hold them back." He swung his arms to emphasize the struggle and then he fell into silence, seemingly losing the courage to continue.

"Go on. What happened then?" asked Jaromil.

Kamil released a weary sigh and continued. "The Germans came in quickly and there was no place to go. They had our division cornered. Many of us went into hiding and we were able to take out many German soldiers that way. Most of the hiding Poles were found out, some were shot and some kept." Kamil became silent as he stared, in grief, apologetically at Jaromil and Ewa Trafas.

Jaromil cleared his throat painfully. "And our son? What happened to Jarek?"

"Well, many of us hid. I hid in an abandoned apartment building. The Germans searched it. I know Jarek raced into the building across the street with some other men from our detachment. I managed to stay undetected in a closet, underneath a pile of clothes but as soon as the search ended I left the closet and watched from a window. I made sure they wouldn't see me. I saw all my buddies in the street surrounded by German soldiers and Jarek was there too. The Germans corralled them down the street and I could see that Jarek was wounded; he was limping and blood stained the back of his pant leg. He tripped and fell and before anyone could help him up, a German soldier held a gun to Jarek's head and pulled the trigger."

"No, no, no!" Ewa erupted with agonized screams.

"My son, no, not my son!" Jaromil's face immediately distorted in horror as the realization hit him full force.

"I'm sorry Mr. and Mrs. Trafas. I'm so sorry about your son. It's a miracle I made it out of Warsaw at all; the country is beginning to swarm with the Germans' presence." Kamil lowered his head to show his sorrow. "I would have helped him if I could have."

Ewa's face was wet with tears as she wandered toward Kamil. Ewa wrapped her arms around Kamil and they wept together. A young soldier deeply traumatized and changed held tightly by a grieving mother, her only son gone to her forever.

Jaromil, usually tough and unemotional, couldn't contain his own sense of loss and desolation. His shoulders heaved with the quiet grief that he struggled to contain. Then he suddenly cried out, "My son, my son, my only son!"

Hahn Brauer marched with his infantry division as they paraded into Warsaw's Pilsudski Square. There were a few brave Polish onlookers but for the most part the side streets were bare and silent, the Poles grieving the loss of their freedom. There was minimal damage in this portion of the city. Most of the damage was in the industrial and residential sections. A good fourth of the city had been destroyed by the heavy onslaught of the Reich's bombing air fleet and tanks. It seemed eerily quiet except for the marching feet of the infantry, the clip clopping of the hooves of the horses carrying the mounted officers and a few armored vehicles still running their engines.

The infantry men surrounding Hahn were in a celebratory mood, despite the loss of lives in their division, though slight. They had seen enough carnage and death while they walked through the city streets to cause their stomachs to protest and yet the euphoria of winning was contagious and overrode any other reaction. Even the dismembered bodies they had seen scattered everywhere and the newly dug graves on almost every street couldn't keep the festive mood from permeating the German infantry. The city had seen a great deal of death and mourning in the few weeks of the war, that was clear, but this victory was sweet and Hahn smiled in pleasure at seeing this triumph first hand and at the sheer luck of being alive.

Later that night, his infantry settled into a comfortable hotel that had been confiscated by the German army. Hahn retrieved a note pad and pen from his supply pack and began to write another letter. He had a stack he'd written whenever he'd had the chance. Each one was addressed neatly and waiting for the mail service to begin.

> *Dear Ilse,*
>
> *How I long for you my darling! Although we have just won a great victory over Warsaw and the Polish army has now surrendered here, nothing would compare to your presence. I am well and alive even though we have fought for over three weeks against a stubborn foe. I am pleased with the feeling of victory and the fact that I'm still breathing. I plan to live through this war, Ilse. I promise you that. I will return to you. I don't know how long we'll be here. I hear nothing of future plans. All I know is that I miss you terribly and that I dream of returning to you. How I wish you were here so I could hold you in my arms. I have seen much of death here and I desire to be safe in your arms. Nothing comforts me like your loving kisses. Know that you are always uppermost in my thoughts and that I dream of you every night.*
>
> *Yours forever, Hahn*

He carefully folded it, slipped it into an envelope and addressed it. He added it to the growing stack.

"What are you going to do with all those letters?" asked Horst Rader, a grin curling his lips.

Horst was a fellow soldier close to Hahn's age, but he was still single and full of excitement over having fought his first war. His father was a high ranking general, General Strom Rader, and therefore Horst had a great reputation to live up to. Horst was determined to prove his worth, courage and ability and spoke of little else.

Hahn gazed at Horst. "I'm going to mail them as soon as I can. I heard the army will set up local services for us and put the Poles to work and the first thing they will offer is mail service."

Horst laughed roughly. "I haven't written even one letter. Are those all for your wife?" He smiled condescendingly.

"Yes, most of them are but I've also written to my parents."

"I've hardly thought about my family, only my father. I suppose I should write my mother, you know, let her know I'm alive." Horst stretched out on his bed, placed his hands behind his head and chuckled.

"What's so funny?"

"I don't think the Poles have any idea of what's coming for them."

"What do you mean?"

Horst lowered one arm and looked at Hahn. "My father told me that Hitler's instructions will be followed explicitly. Adolf Hitler wants more living space for the Germans and this is where he'll get it. Apparently the new army division of the Einsatzgruppen will be dispatched behind us and they'll take care of that. In Western Poland, people will be forced from their homes to make room for German settlers." Horst looked at the ceiling and smiled. "I never thought Hitler would truly accomplish it but he actually is."

"What will happen to the Polish people who are evicted? Will they be shot?"

"Who knows and who cares. All I care is that we finally have a leader who can get things done and one who keeps his word." Horst closed his eyes, the weariness of the day overtaking him. "Yep, this has been one exciting day." Horst yawned loudly and then fell into silence.

Hahn lay back against the comfortable, clean sheet of his bed, enjoying the drastic change from the last few weeks of sleeping wherever they could find a piece of ground. Something about Horst's information bothered him. He wanted to think it over but he was too tired to think. In minutes he was fast asleep.

CHAPTER 34

Krakow, Poland

The sound was tremendous, causing the whole house to shake with the rumble. Binyamin Levin hurried to the front door, parted the curtain over the small window and looked out.

Down the center of the street rumbled German tanks, followed by motorcycles carrying German officers and countless armored vehicles, all contributing to the commotion. Binyamin shook visibly as he watched the horrifying view. He suddenly jumped and spun around as something brushed his arm.

"It's only me, Binyamin."

"You frightened me. Don't sneak up on me like that!"

"I'm sorry." Init looked apologetic. "What's making the racket?"

"The Germans have arrived. Their tanks are going through our neighborhood. I've heard reports from Warsaw. Their presence here doesn't bode well for us Jews."

Init grabbed hold of Binyamin's shirt sleeve and held fast. "I'm afraid."

Binyamin wrapped an arm around his wife's shoulders but he continued to watch the procession lumbering past their home. "Let's hope they'll leave us alone and more importantly, let's hope they leave Krakow soon. Maybe they're only passing through."

"I hope so." Init suddenly jumped. "What was that?"

"It sounded like something popped."

Init turned worried eyes to her husband. "Do you think it was a gun?"

Binyamin shrugged his shoulders. "If it was, it was probably just a celebratory shot."

"I hope so." Init turned toward the kitchen, eager to take her mind off the events taking place on the other side of the door.

Binyamin continued to watch for a few more minutes and then turned away. He walked into the kitchen and poured steaming coffee into his favorite mug.

"Will you go to work today, Binyamin?"

"No, not today. Aizik Gruber offered to work the clinic today."

"I'm so glad."

The two sat together at the table, Binyamin with his mug of coffee and Init with a fresh cup of tea. They sat staring at each other, as if afraid to voice what was uppermost on their minds. Their expressions wore a tell tale sign of deep worry.

A banging from the front door shook them from their anxious thoughts. Binyamin stood with a frown. "Who could that be?" The banging continued, more urgent this time. Binyamin hurried to the door, but looked through the curtain first before opening it. Solomon Greentstein stood on the opposite side, looking visibly shaken. Binyamin opened the door quickly.

Solomon said, "Binyamin, come quickly! Daniel's been shot!"

"Your brother?"

"Yes and I don't think he'll live." Solomon's sorrow oozed toward Binyamin like a tangible substance.

Shock filled Binyamin's chest as he asked, "Who, who would shoot Daniel?" He didn't wait for an answer as he grabbed his coat and doctor's bag.

Init stood in the entrance, her hands over her mouth in deep shock. "No, not Daniel! Oh please God, not Daniel!" She grabbed for her coat and quickly threw it on. "I'm coming too. I have to be there for Gittel."

"Please, let's hurry," said Solomon as the three made their way through the neighborhood.

Binyamin turned to Solomon and asked, "Do you know any details of what happened?"

"No, no I don't. I know it has something to do with the Germans but as soon as I arrived at Daniel's home, I was sent to get you."

Solomon hurried ahead, stopping impatiently at times to allow his uncle and aunt to keep up. The three finally made it to a small, pleasant cottage that Daniel and his wife of three years, called home. Solomon opened the door and stood aside to allow his uncle in. Binyamin entered quickly and assessed the situation. Init followed him and rushed to her sister.

"Oh Gittel, I'm so sorry about Daniel." The two embraced and Gittel sobbed out her anguish and fear. Init stroked Gittel's graying head with one hand while she glanced at her injured nephew. "Poor thing." She shut her eyes tight. "I can't bear to see him like this, Gittel. How can you bear it?"

"I can't, I can't!" Her sobs seemed to rent the air in two.

Binyamin was on his knees at Daniel's side. Daniel's face was pale and his shirt shone a bright red where the bullet had entered. The couch had already begun to absorb the blood pouring from his wound. He moaned in pain as Binyamin assessed the damage.

"Where are your girls?" asked Init.

"They're at home. They were horrified to hear about Daniel and I thought it would be too traumatic for them to see him this way."

Daniel's wife knelt beside her husband, next to Binyamin, where she cried softly, holding desperately to Daniel's hand.

Yankel Greenstein's eyes were filled with tears as he stood by his brother-in-law. "Thank God you're here. Can you do something for my son?"

Binyamin said, "I can't work on him here. The wound looks severe and he's bleeding heavily. He'll need to be moved to the kitchen table."

Daniel groaned as the men lifted him. Gittel and Init ran ahead to prepare the table. Init stripped off the table cloth while Gittel rushed to place a clean blanket over the table. Daniel's face grew whiter due to the extreme strain in his body. He groaned in agony as the men positioned him. Solomon's eyes were shiny and filled with worry as he stood staring at his younger brother.

Binyamin turned to face the women. Daniel's wife, Elisheva, had followed them into the kitchen and she stood looking forlorn and completely lost as if her whole world were crumbling around her.

"I need you women to leave the room. This won't be pretty."

The two older women noticed Elisheva's state of mind and they quickly surrounded her, wrapped their arms around her and led her out of the kitchen.

Binyamin could hear the ruckus from the other room. Elisheva's wails penetrated through the thin door. It was clear she was beside herself with grief and worry. He turned to look at Yankel.

Yankel said, "She's pregnant. They only just found out."

Binyamin nodded. His heart went out to the young woman in the next room and it gave him greater motivation to do all he could for Daniel. He examined the wound carefully. "Yankel, get some whisky and give it to Daniel. I have some anesthetic that will help some but he'll still feel much of what I'll do. Some whisky will numb him further."

Solomon was still in the room but he looked white and sickly. After wavering on his legs, he said, "I think I better leave the room."

Binyamin nodded and watched Solomon leave.

Yankel ran to get the liquor and returned quickly. He opened the bottle and carefully poured small amounts into his son's mouth.

"I'm sure it'll take effect soon. I can't wait." Binyamin went to work. He skillfully positioned the knife and inserted it, digging for the bullet. After half an hour the metal piece was dislodged from deep within Daniel's soft tissue. Next was the laborious task of stitching all the wounds, tears and fractures. Binyamin worked furiously and tirelessly at the immense task.

"That bullet sure made a mess of things."

Yankel's anxious eyes caught Binyamin's. "Will he live?"

"I can't make any promises. This is a very serious wound." Binyamin tore his eyes from his brother-in-law and continued to repair Daniel's excessive damage.

After a few hours of tedious work Binyamin stitched the last of Daniel's skin in place. The table was a bloody mess and the many towels stacked beside Daniel were drenched in blood.

Binyamin stood at the sink washing his hands over and over, weariness overwhelming him. He concentrated on his arms next which were covered in crimson and then he washed his blood spattered face.

Yankel spoke with a tortured voice as he stroked his son's arm. "Elisheva told me what happened. The Germans did this. Daniel was working in the yard, raking leaves. When the tanks, trucks and motorcycles came through he stopped and watched them. A German officer on a motorcycle saw Daniel and stopped. He asked Daniel if he was Jewish and he answered 'yes'. The officer pulled out his gun and shot Daniel just like that! It's like being a Jew is reason enough for a death sentence!" Yankel's face was full of anger as he turned toward Binyamin. "How could they do such an evil thing to a completely innocent man?"

Binyamin froze as if in shock. "I…don't know."

"It has suddenly just become illegal to be Jewish!"

Binyamin remained silent as he continued to scrub at the wash basin, fear crowding his heart.

"He's lost a lot of blood," said Yankel, turning back to his son.

Binyamin reached for a clean towel and slowly wiped his face, arms and hands avoiding eye contact with Yankel.

Yankel spoke again. "He's lost a lot of blood, hasn't he?"

Binyamin slowly turned to face him. "Yes, Daniel has lost too much blood. I'll go to the clinic and get the supplies we'll need to get more blood into him. We'll need some donors."

"I'll donate whatever you need."

"All right then. I'll go now and hopefully it won't be too late to save him."

Yankel's eyes were big and round with undeniable fear.

Binyamin walked toward him, took hold of his arms with both of his hands and looked compassionately into his eyes. "Pray that he'll make it, Yankel.

Binyamin Levin walked into the clinic, the business he shared with his partner, Aizik Gruber. A number of patients were seated in the small waiting area, waiting their turn. Binyamin smiled and greeted the familiar faces before slipping through to the back rooms.

He gathered the supplies he needed, storing them carefully into a large duffel bag he'd brought and left the supply room, closing the door quietly behind him. The door on the opposite side of the hall opened and Aizik's head appeared.

"Why are you here? You were to take the day off."

"I had to get some supplies. My nephew was shot and he needs more blood."

Aizik stepped fully into the hall and closed the door he had come through. "Will he be all right?" Concern filled his eyes.

"I don't know. He's injured badly and has lost too much blood."

"You should take him to the hospital."

"I don't trust the Germans. They're in the city now. It could be that they'll take over the hospitals."

"I heard they'd arrived."

"If we try to get Daniel to the hospital, they might stop us on the way. I think it's best to treat him at his home."

"Did you take the generator?"

"Yes, I did."

"I'll send up a prayer for him."

"Thank you, Aizik. Now I have to go."

"Shalom, my friend!"

Binyamin nodded and hurried out of the office.

Once on the street he looked around carefully, cautious of the Germans roaming through the city. There was no need to attract their attention. He walked quickly from the office and toward the streetcar a block over, which would take him close to home. He stepped on and found that it was nearly filled to capacity. Suspicious eyes glared at him as he made his way to an empty seat. Before he could sit, the man sitting next to the spot placed his hand on it, glared at Binyamin and said, "No filthy Jew will sit here."

Binyamin stared back for a moment and then turned away, grabbing hold of a rod in the centre and hung on tightly as the streetcar jerked ahead. He was more than thankful to exit close to his neighborhood and walk the rest of the way.

He should be used to that kind of reception from Polish residents of the city. Jews were tolerated but not fully accepted and open racist comments were common. But that didn't mean he had to enjoy the injustice of it. Anger boiled just below the surface of his tranquil demeanor. He hadn't walked far when he heard laughing, a thumping noise and grunts of agony. It was hard to tell but it also sounded like someone was crying. Apprehension filled Binyamin as he carefully navigated the streets. He had to know what was causing the sounds. Maybe someone would need his help. Part of him wanted to head in the opposite direction and yet he continued carefully toward the noise.

CHAPTER 35

Germany

"I can't stand being at home every day. I'm going to get a job," Beata declared, placing the newspaper down on the table and looking at her mother.

Unna Schluter, looking through one of her cookbooks and standing at the kitchen counter, turned and looked at Beata incredulously. "German girls don't get jobs. No one will hire you."

"Yes they will. With so many men gone fighting, there are jobs available."

"You should have gotten married when you could," said Ilse, sitting on the other side of the table, her cross word puzzle before her. "Now all the men are gone and it's driving you mad."

Beata folded her arms and glared at her younger sister. "If you think not having a man is driving me mad, then you haven't been married long enough."

That made Unna chuckle.

Ilse looked at Beata in complete naivety. "What's that supposed to mean?"

Beata rolled her eyes and shrugged her shoulders. "Anyway…," she turned toward her mother. "I think I'll apply at the post office. There will be a lot of mail coming from the soldiers and I've heard the postal service is looking for more help."

"But Beata, it's so unnatural for a woman to work. Your place is here at home."

"I can't stand sitting here day after day, hearing Ilse cry and complain and with nothing to do."

"I don't cry and complain!"

Beata turned to Ilse. "Yes you do."

"I'm lonely for my husband. That's all I complain about."

"But you complain about it all day long."

"I do not!"

Unna interrupted. "Beata, have you realized that there's no post office close to us? You'd have to take a streetcar or walk and I don't want you walking the streets by yourself, especially after dark. Please do the sensible thing and stay home."

"No, I've already decided. I'm going today to apply. If it's too far then I'll look for an apartment or a house to rent."

"Please reconsider!" Unna's cookbook sat on the counter forgotten for now. She leaned against the counter, facing her daughter and wiping or more like wringing her hands on the apron she wore.

Beata stood, walked toward Unna, took her hands in hers and squeezed in encouragement. "Please trust me, Mother. I'll stay safe and this will give me something to do. Otherwise I'll go batty staying here listening to her." She moved her head in Ilse's direction.

Ilse huffed in the background. "You shouldn't be so mean! You don't know what it's like."

"I'm not being mean, I'm just being realistic." Beata turned from Ilse and looked back to her mother. "Do I have your blessing?"

"You should ask your father first."

"I already did and he said I should also ask you."

"And...what did he say?"

"He said yes. He thought it was a wonderful idea."

"He did?"

Beata only shrugged her shoulders. She had been equally surprised by her father's response. He was so overly protective and cautious with his girls that he restricted nearly everything these days.

Unna sighed in resignation. "Oh, all right, you have my blessing."

Beata smiled and hugged her mother. "Thank you, Mother!"

Unna shook her head in defeat.

It was good her mother folded to her wishes. Beata's mind was made up but having her parents' blessing was a bonus.

Unna removed her apron and turned to Ilse. "I'm going to Manfred Schwanz's bakery. Why don't you come with me? I need to get some bread and maybe some platz. I'd like to visit with Manfred's wife, Agathe, and you could spend some time with their daughter, Brigitta. It will give you something to do and get your mind off of Hahn. She's your age, isn't she?"

"She's so immature. I don't want to talk with her."

"Ilse, most of her brothers went to war just like Hahn."

Ilse looked up. "That's true. Maybe that very fact has matured her."

Unna smiled and Ilse slowly stood from the table and followed her mother to the door. Beata watched them leave. There was a deep heaviness about Ilse's step that had been there since Hahn departed. The usual cheerful smile and twinkle in her eye was gone and was now replaced by a sullen, glassy look. Beata shook her head sadly.

"If only you could be happy again, little sister."

Beata's angels, Courageous, Wisdom, Lovely and Light Bearer, looked at each other in pleasure. They had accomplished what Heaven had given them to do. First they had planted the idea in Beata's mind and now both of her parents had been convinced into agreeing to it. Beata would soon be positioned where she needed to be.

CHAPTER 36

Krakow, Poland

The noises and cries of anguish increased substantially as Binyamin came to a junction of four intersecting roads. Tall buildings obstructed his view so his approach went undetected. He sidled up to the building and glanced cautiously around the corner. He inhaled sharply at the first glimpse of the scene. There was a Jewish man, an orthodox Rabbi, with his long beard and long, black coat, standing in the middle of the street. His black hat lay crumpled on the cobblestone road. The man's family stood on the sidewalk and his wife struggled not to cry, trying hard to be brave. There were five children standing beside her and most of them looked like teenagers. Four of them were boys, two of them towering over their mother and one girl, about thirteen years old. The girl was crying and sobbing for her daddy and even the boys had tears streaming down their faces.

The Rabbi was surrounded by German soldiers and he cowered before them. A crowd of Polish residents stood watching the spectacle in a wide semi circle and many cheered and shouted their approval. No one made a move to stop the insanity or protested in any way.

"I said dance, old man, dance!" shouted a German soldier in accented Polish. How the German soldier knew the language was a mystery.

The Rabbi did his best to hop and twirl to please the soldiers. As he turned, the soldiers beat him with the butt of their rifles. The Rabbi's head was bleeding heavily and he staggered with each new impact.

"We said dance, you lazy Jew!"

The leader of the pack stepped forward and with what looked like a steel rod began to beat the man's head over and over, blood squirting out at each impact. Finally the Rabbi fell to the pavement, a pool of blood quickly forming where he lay. His wife screamed out in horror, her children crying openly around her. Binyamin was sure the man was dead. No one could survive such a beating to the head and live.

A soldier quickly turned to the man's wife, aimed his gun and hit her cleanly in the face, felling her in an instant. The children around her screamed and after a few quick gunshots they lay in a slumped huddle beside her. A family gunned down without mercy, applauded by the callous audience. Binyamin's stomach groaned in protest and bile gathered in his throat.

Binyamin stepped back into oblivion against the wall of the building, breathed heavily to still the pounding of his heart in his ears and tried to stop the shaking in his legs. He felt lightheaded and thought he might faint. He had seen blood numerous times in his profession, but not like this. This was horrific, inhuman and utterly cruel! What had their world become?

"Bring out the next one!" He heard the leader yell.

"No, no, not another one," Binyamin pleaded silently. He willed himself to look although his heart screamed not to. He peaked around the corner and saw another Rabbi, his long beard reaching to his waist with his long black coat swishing royally as he walked, his black, fur hat perched dignified on his head. His family wandered sullenly behind him from the door of the building where they had been held, fear etching their faces in a dark apprehension. This Rabbi was much younger with three young children trailing his wife. The woman shielded her children's eyes when she noticed the Rabbi and his family lying dead in the street and she whimpered in terror.

"What is it with you Orthodox Jew pigs and your long beards, huh? You think they're pretty?" The leader of the German soldiers sneered with contempt. "We'll show you what we think of your beard." He retrieved a long knife and waved in front of the man.

The Rabbi was clearly shaken, not only by seeing his fellow Rabbi lying in a pool of blood but by the clear threat on his own life and the lives of his family. "Please have mercy on us."

"Mercy?" The German officer chuckled with amusement. "I don't think you'll appreciate my mercy." He lifted the blade, grabbed the Rabbi's beard hard, forcing the man to stoop low. With one swipe of the knife, the officer cut it short and threw the loose hair into a pile on the street. It fluttered in the breeze and scattered around the Rabbi's feet.

The German officer turned away from him for a moment and then quickly spun around, sinking the blade deep into his mid section, causing him to double over in pain. The officer allowed the knife to stay where it was for a moment and then slowly pulled it out, a vicious smile curling his lips.

"That's a taste of my mercy."

The Rabbi's family screamed and cried in horror as they saw him slump to the ground.

His little girl, about three years old cried out, "Daddy, Daddy! Please don't hurt my daddy!"

A German soldier hurried forward and screamed at the Rabbi in German. "Get up you fool! Get up! If you want your family to walk away alive then get up!" The soldier seemed somewhat undone by the little girl's cry.

The Rabbi slowly stood but he couldn't straighten up. As soon as he was up another German soldier beat the Rabbi on his head with the butt of his rifle, sending him hurtling to the street in a heap.

"Get up! If you don't, I'll kill your family. Get up!"

The Rabbi tried hard but the wound to his head must have clouded his mind somewhat and he called for his wife to help him. "I've fallen, Lila, and I can't get up. Please come help me. Lila, Lila, where are you?"

"Shut up and get up you Jewish fool!"

"Lila, where are you?" The Rabbi was on his knees now but in so much pain he couldn't rise.

The German soldier was so infuriated with the pathetic attempt that he spun toward the Rabbi's family standing on the sidewalk and shot them quickly, one after the other, not giving them an opportunity to even speak or realize the terror overwhelming them. All the soldiers then proceeded simultaneously to beat the Rabbi until he lay still and silent on the street, the blood spreading beneath him his only companion.

Binyamin could hardly breathe as he stood with his back against the wall of the building, hiding him from view. Fear and terror were his closest companions right now and he determinedly and slowly inched away from the horror. He heard the German leader's voice.

"Bring out the next Rabbi!"

As soon as Binyamin knew the German soldiers would no longer hear, he ran as fast as he could toward home. Whenever he heard a vehicle, he ducked behind trees, buildings, anything he could find to stay hidden. His nerves were taut and his emotions frazzled as he reached the familiar, Jewish residential sector. He could hardly think straight.

When he spotted his house, he breathed a sigh of relief, willing himself to stop shaking. Just before he took the path to his front door, he noticed movement in a yard down the street. It made him stop and stare. It was the ex-rabbi, David Kohn. He was hoeing his planting area clearing the spot of dried plants. What in the world! Why would he care about gardening at a time like this? It looked absurd and careless. They were facing a crisis here and David was consumed with beautifying his home? The man must be crazy indeed!

Binyamin shook his head in disbelief but then David's words from weeks ago filtered back into his mind - words of warning and of coming danger. He turned and stared at the man in fear and sudden awareness. His spine tingled with the realization. He tore his eyes away and ran for his front door.

CHAPTER 37

Crimean Steppe, Russia

Esther raced home from school, leaving Anna trailing behind. Esther rushed to the door but stopped in her tracks as she heard her name called. She spun around to see Herman walking toward her.

"Do you want to go to Tokmak with me? I've got the horse and carriage ready."

Esther stepped toward him. "What will you do in Tokmak?"

"I'm picking up supplies for Father."

"Yes, I'd love to go." She jumped on the spot.

Anna caught up and overheard. "You'd love to go where?"

"I'm going with Herman to Tokmak."

"I want to go too!"

Herman grabbed one of Anna's long braids and tugged. "Mother needs you to help with dinner. She said only Esther could go."

"Oh…! That's not fair!"

"Next time I'll take you along, okay?" Herman smiled so charmingly, it made Anna grin despite her acknowledged disappointment.

"I won't forget, Herman, and remember, you promised."

"Okay, little sister. I won't forget." Herman smiled real big and then turned toward Esther. "Ready to go?"

"I'll put my school books inside. I'll be right back." She ran through the door and re-appeared almost immediately.

Esther's heart throbbed in excitement as she climbed up into the carriage, where Herman sat waiting. She could hardly believe her good fortune. Not only were they going to the largest village in the area but she'd spend the rest of the afternoon with her brother. To spend a day with Herman would be like Heaven indeed. She gazed at him in admiration as he encouraged the horse to move on. Two of her guardians, Goodness and Faith, accompanied her, while her two other guardians, Pieter and Marinus, stayed home to watch over things there.

"This is so exciting! I haven't been outside the village in such a long time."

"Then it was about time I rescued you, wouldn't you say?" Herman smiled with a twinkle in his eye.

"Most definitely!"

He manned the reigns and began to hum a familiar tune. He usually sang or hummed so Esther settled against the seat contentedly, enjoying the musical drone and studied the landscape that was scrolling along beside them.

The Molotschna Colony contained numerous villages and they passed many of them as they traveled. They meandered through Gnadenthal, Margenua, Rueckenua and Tiegerweide, each of them distinct and well organized in their own unique style. None of the villages they passed through this day compared to the village of Gnadenfeld, where tree plantations were extensive, both outside the village limits and surrounding each homestead.

Gnadenfeld was one of the most beautiful villages in the whole colony. Esther loved to visit it and they often did with her family. It was one of the closest villages to them and they had family members there. Her uncle, aunt and cousins lived there on a beautiful, spacious yard. Esther loved to visit them especially in spring when the white acacia, apple, cherry and pear trees were dotted with white blooms. They stood out starkly against the backdrop of a red tiled roof here and there. As soon as they would enter the village in springtime the abundant flowers growing everywhere assailed their senses.

The village streets in Gnadenfeld were always nicely leveled and harrowed and the sidewalks were strewn with white sand. The fences throughout the village were carefully and regularly whitewashed. Behind the fences lay the expansive gardens of each homestead. The bright blooms of roses, tulips and narcissus filled the landscape. The fragrance was like heavenly bliss, especially when combined with the wafting smell of fresh bread and buns cooling in someone's kitchen.

Esther thought of the many games she and her cousins had played there on so many spring and summer evenings. Hide and seek, of course, was their favorite. And with those memories came the scents and sights of that beautiful place.

Her mind was full of memories as Herman steered the horse north on a trail leading to Tokmak.

"Have things settled down in school?"

"What do you mean?" Esther gazed at him, knowing full well what he meant but too embarrassed to admit it.

"You've had no more unplanned trips to the river?"

She couldn't help the smile that formed. "No!"

Herman glanced sideways at her and grinned. "Could it be that Gilbert has a crush on you?"

"No, Herman, he doesn't." She shook her head furiously to make her point. "He was just mad because Rose spread all those rumors about him."

"And you did nothing to contribute?"

"I didn't do anything! It was all Rose's doing!"

"I'm not so sure. I met Gilbert the other day and he was asking about you."

Esther glanced at him in surprise. "He asked about me?"

"Yes, he did."

"What did he want to know?"

He grinned broadly. "Ah, now you're interested?"

She shook her head in frustration. "Look, I don't care about Gilbert. He's just a stupid boy who dumped me and my best friend in the river. Rose is the one who has a crush on him, not me."

"Well it seems that he cares more about you than he does about Rose."

She looked at her brother with sudden distrust.

"He asked if you had gotten in trouble with your mother and I told him that, yes, Mother was very upset. He also asked about your dress and shoes, whether they were ruined. He really seemed concerned about you."

"He was not concerned about me!" Esther insisted. "He was just being nosy, is all."

"It didn't seem that way to me." Herman grinned.

"That's because you're older and you think about such things. I don't."

"I truly think Gilbert has a crush on you." He winked and Esther shook her head in disbelief. "You're a real pretty catch you know?"

"Stop it, Herman! Please can we talk about something else?"

She fell silent as she noticed Tokmak rising before them and Herman became distracted as they entered the town. He waved at numerous people, people Esther had never met. Making friends came easily for him and his sociable manner drew others to him. She watched him quietly as he waved, shouted greetings and smiled openly at the many strangers going by.

He finally stopped the horse and buggy team in front of a store on Main Street. After exiting, he helped Esther down. He secured the horse to the tie post and walked toward her while digging in his pocket. He held out his hand.

"What's this?"

"Some change. Why don't you go do some shopping on the other side? There are some stores that might interest you. We'll meet back here in an hour, okay?"

She opened her hand to receive it. "Sure."

She felt giddy as she watched Herman disappear into the hardware store. Shopping on her own was new and she felt a heady thrill as she walked carefully across the street. A window display of one establishment caught her attention immediately. It was filled with a row of jars containing candies she had only rarely had the opportunity to taste. Her mouth watered at the sight and she quickly stepped inside.

An hour later, the buggy was loaded with supplies and Esther was sitting beside Herman holding a small, paper bag of goodies she'd purchased. Although she still felt excited, there was also a gnawing apprehension clouding this almost perfect day. Herman steered the horse through town and soon they were traveling across country roads, heading for home.

Herman began to sing again, a light, silly song that made her laugh. Esther tried to sing along but it wasn't her greatest gift and Herman gave her some funny looks.

"You sing like a frog in a rainstorm, Esther."

She pulled back and punched his arm. "Don't be so mean!"

He laughed heartily. "But you can sing with me anytime, little sister. I don't mind the ear sore."

Esther fell silent and listened to her brother sing, while her heart felt a heaviness she had never dealt with before. Her eyes focused on the fields of grain swaying in the breeze. They scooted one way and then another, looking like ripples on a lake.

Herman finally stopped singing and gazed at her. "Is something wrong?"

She looked at him. He was so tall and handsome, kind in every way and she loved him dearly. Maybe he'd be able to explain something to her. "I heard something in town."

Herman nodded in understanding. "You heard about the war?"

"Yes. Is it true that Russia is at war?"

"Yes, it's true. They've invaded Eastern Poland. But it was an easy invasion. Poland had already been defeated by the Germans from the west."

"So, there'll be no fighting here?"

"No little sister. Russia took over part of Poland and that's the end of it."

"What about Germany? If Germany took over part of Poland won't they get angry at Russia for wanting part of Poland too and fight back?"

"No. Germany and Russia signed a treaty and they agreed to share Poland. It was all planned out."

"Oh!" She breathed a sigh of relief.

He focused on the horse plodding in front of them and then glanced at his sister. "Who told you about the war?"

"I heard some adults talking about it while I was shopping. I wasn't being nosy but I couldn't help but overhear."

"That's how I learn things, by listening to others." Herman smiled.

They both fell silent. She felt better now, her heart reassured. The rest of the trip home was pleasant and peaceful. Herman eventually started singing again, one silly song after another, making Esther laugh, her heart light now that the threat of war was pacified.

The angels surrounding the horse and carriage were not as easily reassured. They had been warned by the Spirit of God of all that was coming and they were already preparing.

CHAPTER 38

Germany, October 1939

The mood was celebratory and cheerful as the high ranking members of the Nazi party met in the large, spacious conference room. Adolf Hitler sat at one end, looking stern and business-like but with an elevated air of confidence. The men at the table; Joseph Goebbels, Joachim von Ribbentrop, Herman Goring, Martin Bormann, Heinrich Himmler, Reinhard Heydrich and Adolf Eichmann, all held significant positions in the German government and in the workings of the war. Adolf Hitler cleared his throat and the droning of voices slowly softened and then quieted as they faced the Nazi leader.

"As you are all aware, the Polish invasion was a great success and the subduing of its people is in full operation. All the major leaders, communist supporters and high ranking men of Poland have been subdued and liquidated. Polish citizens who were residing on the western parts of Poland have been evicted and resettlement for many Germans is taking place. Our land requirements are being realized in our day, men. It truly is a great time to be German and to see these great advancements for our country."

The room exploded with approval, hand clapping and chuckles.

Joseph Goebbels said, "It is due to the amazing leadership of our Fuhrer." The others in the room agreed heartily.

Adolf nodded his acceptance and then continued. "The Jewish problem still needs to be fully addressed in Poland."

Heinrich Himmler said, "We will make the lives of the Jews difficult. I have already set in motion a number of laws, some of which are being carried out as we speak. It will become illegal for Jews to own businesses and these will be forcefully taken from them and given to Germans who resettle there or worthy Poles who are compliant to our cause. We're also implementing a rule that will identify the Jews more easily. Something attached to their clothing which will be conveniently seen and will render it impossible for the Jew to hide. Many steps have been taken to subjugate the Jewish population, all of them quite successful to date. The Poles seem more than willing to join in our cause against the Jews. They seem to have a score to settle. Do we encourage this or do we keep the belligerence solely our doing?"

Hitler became contemplative before answering. "No, do not stop them. Encourage any acts of aggression toward the Jews. Promote and reward it if possible. Any Pole who joins in our cause should be given a place in the running of the new government. Not an important place, but a place none the less. The Jews and the Poles need to know who's running the show."

Heinrich Himmler said, "Note taken. I'll take care of it."

"And what has been done about the colleges and universities? Have steps been made there as well?"

"Yes Fuhrer. Your decree has been carried out. All the colleges and universities have been abolished and all Polish children will now receive only a minimal education. All farmers and factory workers will be put to work to serve their German masters. The more educated Jews and the ones useful to us will be put to work immediately."

Adolf Hitler nodded. "Good! The Poles, and certainly the Jews will soon learn of their inferiority and their lot in life. But now it's time to focus on the West. The East, at least Poland, is at our mercy and it's time to center our attention on France and Britain. Many of our troops, which invaded Poland, have been repositioned to the border of Germany and France and are waiting for the signal." Adolf glanced at Herman Goring. "Is the air force ready to attack at the given signal?"

"Yes Fuhrer. They are in position and ready."

"Then prepare for an imminent attack. It will commence within days."

Bold and Resilient hovered in the skies between the countries of France and Germany. Bold stirred up the winds from the West, while Resilient stirred winds from the East and North. The effect was continual overcast skies with thick clouds filling the atmosphere, making it impossible for any planned air attacks.

Hitler paced the room in anger and frustration. The large demon on his shoulder hissed in fury that Hell's plans were being thwarted. Hitler finally stopped and looked at Herman Goring. "So, how much longer do we wait?"

Herman looked apologetic and nervous. "We would have begun the attack already if not for the persistent bad weather. It has been most unusual and annoying. I've never seen anything like it before."

Hitler stopped walking the floor and looked out the large window behind his desk. "So we can do nothing but wait?"

"I'm afraid so, Fuhrer. We don't control the weather and right now it's too dangerous for the air force and our aircraft. We can't find our targets with the intense cloud cover and it will hinder a speedy victory. There's no knowing how many planes would be shot down if we rush this thing." Herman looked at Adolf's back in trepidation.

Hitler finally turned around. "Then we wait. I'm not willing to take risks now. The French already suspect our plans. We'll keep them guessing." He said it as if he had planned the cloud cover himself.

CHAPTER 39

Krakow, Poland, November 1939

Anka sat by her sewing machine, which was on the kitchen table, and stitched the pieces of cloth, hemming them carefully so that no loose strands showed. She then attached one yellow star with pins to Aaron's jacket. She held it up to inspect it with a sober expression. A bright ray of sun shone through the window, over the kitchen sink, painting part of the table a lighter color. The bright glow of the afternoon sun warmed the kitchen considerably and Anka wiped perspiration from her forehead as she lowered Aaron's jacket and placed it on the table.

Aaron walked in and glanced at her handiwork. He didn't say a word as he took down a mug from the cabinet and poured a cup of coffee. He pulled out a chair from the table and sat down, away from the bright sunlight. He took a few sips of the hot beverage but remained silent.

"It's too hot in here, Aaron."

"I haven't put any wood in the stove for a while. It must be the sun."

"The sky is too bright and cheerful today." Anka stopped her work and gazed at him in displeasure.

"I don't think the sky cares about what's going on."

"Why is this happening to us, Aaron? First they shoot Daniel and he died of his wounds. And now the Germans are intent on oppressing us! It's so unfair!"

"It's not you they're oppressing, my dear wife. It's the Jewish people they're after."

Anka felt immediately hurt and angry. "So, even though we've been married for nearly twenty years, you still consider me an outsider?"

Aaron looked immediately consolatory. "No, Anka, I don't. You're my wife, the mother of my beautiful children. All I'm saying is that you are Polish. It's not so much the Polish the Germans are after as the Jews."

"That's unjust, Aaron. Many top leading Polish men and their families have suffered under German rule. Many have been killed, some deported and many Poles have been evicted from their homes. It's not only the Jews who are suffering!"

Aaron smiled cynically. "The Germans haven't ruled that the Poles wear signs of their nationality. It's only the Jews who are singled out to wear the yellow Star of David. That way the Germans can easily recognize us and makes it easier for them to exploit and abuse us. I don't see any Poles walking around identifying their nationality."

Anka stared at Aaron. She knew he was right. It was so unfair. She couldn't keep the fear and dread she felt from shining through her eyes. "If only there was a way to defy the order."

"To defy them would bring speedy punishment or death. It's best to cooperate with them, for now." Aaron lifted the jacket emblazoned with the yellow star. "I will hate being so obviously Jewish…but there's no choice."

"If only the children didn't have to wear it."

"The orders were for all children twelve and older so Amos and Matis will have to wear them too."

"I know. I'm just thankful that our little Lola won't have to wear it."

Aaron smiled half heartedly and Anka smiled back weakly.

He gave her a reassuring look, "We'll be okay, Anka."

"I hope so." She didn't know if she believed him. Everything was so unsettled. She focused on the next star as she pinned the edges down. "What will we do now that the synagogue has been closed?"

"I thought at first we would travel to the next synagogue and worship there but I've learned that the Germans have forcibly closed all synagogues throughout Krakow and all the valuables in each synagogue have been turned over to Nazi control. There will be no worshiping for some time, at least not in a synagogue. Father and mother are furious about it, but what can we do. The whole Jewish community is beside themselves with anger and worry. The Germans have tied our hands."

"God is with us even here in our own home."

Aaron's eyes looked angry. "Then why doesn't He deliver us from this enemy? He has a strange way of making His presence known." He stood and left the room, leaving the chair jutting out from the table where he pushed it.

Anka stared after him, deep sorrow and fear gnawing at her soul. What would happen to them?

CHAPTER 40

Berlin, Germany

Beata knocked on the door and then stepped into her parent's home.

"Come in, Beata!" her mother's voice rang out.

She took a deep breath of the delicious aroma filling the house. The smell of fresh baked bread drifted toward her as well as whatever was cooking on the stove. She wandered into the kitchen and noticed her mother at the stove, stirring a pot full of something.

"Hi Mother."

"Hi! How are you?"

"Good."

"How's your job?"

"It's going well."

"And how do you like living on your own?"

"It's lonely but I'm getting used to it." Beata went to stand beside her mother. "Is it stew? It smells wonderful."

"Yes, it is."

"Is Ilse here?"

"Yes, I think she went to…"

"I'm right here." Ilse shuffled into the room, looking tired and despondent.

"Hi Ilse! How are you?"

"Don't ask."

"Why, what's wrong now? Are you still missing Hahn?"

"If only he were here! I'd kill him myself!" Ilse's eyes flashed in anger.

"Now that's the Ilse I used to know. There's some life about you again."

Ilse's eyes filled with tears. "If only you knew." Tears began to drip from her eyelashes.

Beata reprimanded herself for being so harsh with her. She went to Ilse and gave her a hug, which Ilse willingly accepted. She clung to Beata in desperation. Beata finally pulled away and looked into her eyes. "What's wrong?"

"I've been feeling really sick lately." Ilse slunk into a chair.

"Sick to your stomach?"

Ilse wore a guilty look. "Yes."

Realization hit Beata full force. "You're pregnant!"

Ilse nodded sullenly.

"That's great, that's just great!" She threw up her arms. She felt like screaming, she was so angry. "Hahn married you, got you pregnant and then took off!"

Unna turned from the stove. "Beata, that's unfair to Ilse. Neither of them planned for things to turn out this way."

Beata pointed at her mother. "And just watch, you'll end up raising the baby."

"It'll be my baby, I'll raise it" Ilse protested.

"You can't even take care of yourself, never mind a baby!"

"That's not true! You're so mean!" Ilse stood and ran from the room crying.

Beata shook her head. "Oh my! She's so emotional! She's not the sister I knew. She's a complete hysterical mess! How can you stand her, Mom?"

Unna stood against the kitchen counter with her arms crossed; her expression hard to read. "Beata, you need to apologize to her. I know she's not the little girl we once knew but she is who she is and she's really hurting right now. We need to support and stand with her."

"It's just been so hard seeing her ruin her life. And the saga only continues."

"But it's the decision Ilse's made and she needs us now."

"She's never needed me."

Colleen Reimer

"Yes she has, Beata."

"But I can't stand her this way! How could I possibly help her?"

"Try not to reprimand her so much. She needs support not correction."

Beata released a frustrated breath. "I'll try, really I'll try." She felt suddenly very thankful that she now lived in her own apartment, away from the depression she always saw in Ilse's eyes. It was time to change the subject. "Have you heard the rumors?"

"What rumors?"

"About the Jews losing their businesses and homes?"

Unna sighed heavily. "Yes I have."

"Have you heard from the Israelis'?"

"No, I've been afraid to go over there and your father forbids it."

"When has that ever stopped you before, Mother?"

"Beata, there is so much happening right now and so many changes being made by the government that I don't want to get in trouble. Their rules seem to change by the day and it's hard to keep up on what's acceptable and what's not. But one thing is certain; to be sympathetic to the Jews is dangerous."

"So you have no idea how Meshulam and Marni Israeli are managing?"

"No." Unna concentrated on stirring the stew.

"And you don't care?"

"Of course I care, Beata, but I can't go over there!"

A moment of silence hung between them before Beata thought of another thing. "What if they'd come to your door? Would you turn them away?"

Unna turned to face her daughter. "I don't know. Your father is very concerned right now about our safety."

"But he's benefiting the government and the war effort. He's providing the ammunition the army needs. They would never suspect him of anything."

"If our neighbors see Jews at our door there's no way we can be certain that they won't inform."

"That just means we'll have to be careful."

270

Unna stared at her daughter, fear spilling from her eyes. "What do you mean?"

"I'm going to help the Jews any way I can."

"How?"

"I'll get them food; protect them from German aggression, anything that will benefit them."

"I've heard rumors, Beata."

She waited for what she already knew.

"There have been rumors of deporting the Jews and making Germany Jew free."

"I've heard them too. It will mean certain death for them." Beata's angels, Courageous, Wisdom, Lovely and Light Bearer, stood around her, encouraging her. She took a step toward her mother. "Will you help me hide Jews if the government makes this decision?"

Unna's hands flew to her face and she covered her mouth. She slowly lowered her hands and stared at her daughter in resignation. "I can see that I won't be able to change your mind."

Beata stared intently at her mother, waiting for her agreement.

"Even if I would agree to help you, you wouldn't be able to hide all the Jews."

"I know, Mother, but I'd hide as many as I can."

Unna glanced through the doorway where Ilse left the room. "Ilse would be completely against it and if she found out, I don't know what she would do." She turned her attention to Beata. "She's very unpredictable emotionally and I don't trust her."

Beata hadn't thought of that before. "She would squeal on us." She thought for a moment. "Then I'll have to rent a bigger place, somewhere suitable for hiding people."

"You can't afford that on your wage!"

"Then you and Dad will have to help me."

Unna released a sigh. "Let's just take one day at a time. Hopefully war will end soon and everything will settle down. I'm hoping we won't have to make decisions like the one you're suggesting."

"There's one other thing. Why wouldn't Dad give some Jewish men jobs at the ammunitions factory?"

"He would jeopardize his job and his life, Beata! Even you should realize this!"

"What if it wouldn't jeopardize him? I mean there are more and more men going off to war and fewer available to work so why shouldn't Dad hire Jewish men. It only makes sense. It would benefit the war effort."

"I already know what your father would say."

"You only think you know. We won't know for sure until we ask him. Since the Jews are losing their businesses, there's no way for them to support their families and they'll begin to starve. We have to do something to help them."

"You can ask your father, but leave me out of it."

"So you won't support it?"

Unna's eyes shone with fear. "I'm scared, Beata."

She stepped toward her mother and wrapped her arms around her. "We're all scared, Mother, but we still have to do what's right."

Unna squeezed her daughter tight and released a shaky sigh.

April 1940

Dear Ilse,

It's been so long since we've been together. How I miss you and long for you, my darling. I can imagine your round belly with my child inside and I long for you even more. I'd much rather be with you and be there for the birth of our child than to be here on the brink of another war. I believe in what Germany is fighting for and I support the army completely and yet my heart yearns for you.

The army is moving north within days. We're to attack Denmark and then Norway. The Nazis feel a need to protect our northern flank from an attack by sea and so the battle plan is set. Please pray for a speedy victory. Hopefully the acquisition of these two countries will provide sufficient living space for our great nation of Germany.

I'm hoping to be back with you soon. I look forward to being a 'daddy' and to holding my child. I want to be there to help raise our baby. Please remember me always and be true. My heart belongs to you alone.

With all my love, Hahn

Hahn folded the letter carefully, stuffed into an envelope and addressed it. He got up and left the barracks and headed to the mail depot. Army life wasn't so bad and he had adjusted but the words to Ilse were true, he did long for her. War was grueling, hard, with a constant threat of bodily harm but at least his yearning for adventure was being fulfilled. He felt he had experienced nearly enough adventure to last him a lifetime.

CHAPTER 41

Krakow, Poland

Binyamin Levin worked feverishly on the German soldier. He had lost a lot of blood and his vital signs were weak. Binyamin removed all the bullet remains he could find from the soldier's hip. The hip bone had sustained a fair amount of fragmentation and although Binyamin removed some small bone pieces from the surrounding tissue, it was impossible to remove them all. He stitched the open wound and then walked to the sink to wash.

The door opened and a German SS officer walked in.

"How's he doing?"

Binyamin tried not to look the officer in the eyes. "Not well. He lost a lot of blood and I'm unsure how much use he'll have of his hip."

"A Jew did this!" the SS officer spat.

Binyamin said nothing.

"The Jews will pay!"

Binyamin remained silent as he kept washing his arms.

"If he dies, perhaps your family will pay too."

This brought a spasm of fear racing through his core and with a pleading look, Binyamin faced the officer. "I've done all I could do."

"Maybe you didn't do enough." With that the SS officer stepped to the door, a stern jut to his jaw.

"I need some help transferring this soldier to a bed."

The officer turned from the door irritably. "I'll send someone." Then he left the room.

Binyamin was being used as part of the forced labor group serving the German occupation. His own practice had been dissolved and he was now forced to serve injured German soldiers, or any medical needs of the occupying army. Binyamin's partner, Aizik, had been transferred to another area for the same purpose. They would only be of value until German doctors arrived. Then their services would no longer be needed. He had a strong feeling what would be done to him then, but he refused such thoughts. They only caused alarm.

Binyamin knew the German officer's threats were real. Anyone suspected of hindering the German effort or bringing harm to a German, meant immediate death. Not only death for the individual but often his entire family or an entire neighborhood was made to pay for such a mistake.

Binyamin shuddered at the thought of his family being unmercifully gunned down for his inability to keep this soldier alive. He prayed quietly for the soldier lying so white and still on the operating table.

"God, let this man live." It was a selfish prayer, not for the soldier's welfare but for the sake of his family and fellow Jews.

David Kohn wandered into the house where Devora was busy baking. He sat down at the table and watched her for a while, knowing that what he had to say would upset her.

She finished kneading the bread, placed it in pans and set them to the side to rise. She then brushed a hand across her forehead, stretched and rubbed her back. She was getting older, with white strands throughout her once dark hair, lines that creased her forehead and showed around her eyes and her shoulders stooped slightly. It was no wonder; they were now grandparents, many times over.

The years had been good to both of them, except for the incident with losing his position as Rabbi. That had been hard on Devora. She was usually outgoing and had many friends. Now she stayed mostly indoors, devoting her time to her children and grandchildren. She looked at him differently now too. Her eyes used to radiate respect and pride, but now only a deep sadness and anger stared back. If only he could make her realize what he knew. He understood her anger, embarrassment and shame but he also knew more than she of what was coming and that's what he had to get through to her.

Devora bustled around the kitchen, knowing of David's presence but refusing to acknowledge him. She prepared a bowl, utensils and baking trays.

He was sure she was making a cake, the one she knew by heart. David had seen her mixing the dough often enough to know. He decided it was best to let her be for a time. Maybe if he waited long enough she'd feel embarrassed for ignoring him. Just perhaps she'd speak to him. So he waited and watched. There was a pot of soup cooking on the stove and occasionally Devora stirred the contents. The smell was inviting, hovering through the room, causing David's stomach to rumble in hunger.

After mixing all the ingredients, Devora placed the cake mixture in a pan and set it into the oven. She then turned to wash the dirty utensils and bowls. She set the last item in a large washing bowl to drip off, took off her apron and threw it on the counter in frustration. She turned to face him then, her hands on her hips.

"What do you want?"

He looked at her pleadingly.

"What?" asked Devora.

He gazed at her for a moment in silence.

"I don't have time for this, David. I'm busy!"

"We need to talk."

"I don't want to talk." She turned away, grabbed a drying cloth and went to work on the wet dishes.

Ever since the synagogue incident and the German invasion, she'd been angry.

"Please sit down with me," David pleaded.

Her shoulders drooped as she turned toward her husband.

David held out a chair beside him, encouraging her to join him. She slowly placed the dish back, laid her cloth over it and wandered to the table. She sat down and stared at her hands in her lap.

"Devora, you need to know that I love you very much. I know that things have been hard for us lately. I know how ashamed you've been but you need to know that I never did what I did to hurt you. God has shown me things, things that have already happened, right before our eyes and I know some other things that are coming."

She raised her hands in protest. "Please David, don't start again!"

"I have to."

"No you don't!"

He grabbed one of her hands and held tight as she tried to pull away. She finally relented as his hold held. He stroked the top of her hand with his free hand.

"I don't want to lose you, Devora."

Her eyes shot up to look at him. "Why would you lose me? I'm right here."

"For now you're here."

"What is that supposed to mean?"

"Something's coming for us, Devora, and it's much worse than mere German occupation. Our lives will be in danger. I believe my life was spared when I obeyed God and cut off my beard. There have been many Jewish Rabbis terribly persecuted and killed for their positions. I'm still here with you and I plan on staying alive but this means we must listen and obey God."

"Have you heard about Rabbi Sutin?" asked Devora, fear clouding her eyes.

"Yes, I heard he left with his family."

"He said it's too dangerous here in Krakow."

"There's no place in Poland where they'll be safe."

"How do you know that?"

"Without God, no Jew will be safe."

"But of all people, we have God's protection. We are his people!"

"We are a religious people but that does not mean we are following God."

Devora rubbed her forehead with her free hand, confusion haunting her features. "I don't understand."

"God has shown me things. Conditions for the Jews will progressively worsen until the Germans feel justified in exterminating us."

Her eyes snapped up to stare at him. "You don't know that for sure."

"I do know." He took a deep breath and released it. "That's why I'm suggesting we leave Krakow; find a place where we'll be safe."

"No!"

"I want you to think about it. If you refuse, I might just take you by force."

"You wouldn't!"

David smiled at the horror on Devora's face. "It would be the last option but I would consider it."

"I would never leave my children or grandchildren!"

"I will talk to them too and see if they'll come with us."

"How would we ever be able to hide from the German's traveling as a whole family? They'd spot us a mile away."

"Maybe we'd have to split up and we'd have to be very careful. There's no other option."

"How would we survive, running and hiding?"

"I don't know but we have to obey God."

Devora's face showed her disbelief and her stubborn resistance. "I will never leave my home and live like some kind of traveling gypsy. I'm old, David! I'm not a young woman anymore. I'm too tired to run from anyone."

"We can do it if we stay together as a family."

"You'll never talk our children into leaving on some wild goose chase. Life may not be good here but it's better than running."

David let the subject drop, while fear clutched his heart at the stubbornness he saw written on his wife's face.

There was a sharp knock at the front door. Anka walked to the window first and looked out. There was constant suspicion these days and one couldn't be careful enough. She let the curtain fall, ran to the door and opened it wide.

"Mother, what are you doing here?"

Ewa Trafas smiled nervously and shrugged her shoulders. "May I come in?" Ewa's eyes darted behind her, down the street before she focused on her daughter again.

"Yes, Mother, come in." She stepped aside and held the door.

Ewa entered the house in a hurry, turned and watched as Anka closed and bolted the door.

"I can't stay long."

"All right." Anka led the way to the sitting room. "You haven't been here in a long time." She pointed her mother to a seat in the corner, while she took the couch.

Ewa sat down on the edge of the chair, wringing her hands anxiously. "I know. I feel bad about that but there's been so much unrest in Krakow. It's dangerous to be out on the streets."

"Did you come alone?"

"Yes."

"You shouldn't have. It's too risky!"

"I had to come."

"I didn't expect you to travel here, not with the German's patrolling everything." She looked at her mother intently and then said, "So why did you come?"

"I've been worried about you. Your father is worried too."

"Why would he be worried about someone whose existence he doesn't even acknowledge? I'm as good as dead to him."

"He still loves you, Anka."

"He's had a funny way of showing it."

Ewa started to cry, tears rolling down her cheek as she tried to brush them away and stop the deluge.

"Don't be afraid for me, Mother. I'll be fine. Aaron is good to me and somehow we'll make it. Please don't cry."

"It...It's not only that." Ewa dug in her pocket for a tissue and wiped her face.

"What is it then?"

"Your brother." Ewa stared at Anka, sorrow revealed in her eyes.

"What? What has happened to Jarek?" Anka felt her throat constrict and she began to panic in the silence that followed. "Tell me Mother, what has happened to Jarek?"

"He's dead."

"No!" Anka's hands flew to her face and she found it suddenly very difficult to breathe. Horror gathered like an army around her heart. Tears slowly formed and slid down her cheeks.

"He was defending Warsaw from the Germans and he was killed when the German's advanced."

"No…no! Not Jarek!" Anka wept for a while, then lifted her tear stained face toward her mother. "Did you have a funeral?"

"We had a memorial service. We never recovered his body."

"Why didn't you tell me sooner? I would have come to the memorial!"

"Your father thought it best that way."

"Best for whom? Best for him? He didn't want his daughter there to further embarrass him?" Anger boiled along with the sorrow.

"That's not true, Anka. He loves you and that's why I'm here."

Anka could hardly talk with the grief that engulfed her. First Aaron's cousin was shot and killed and now with her brother dead, she didn't know if she could go on.

"Anka, it has become dangerous to be Jewish. Your father has seen vile and horrendous things done to Jews who are unfortunate enough to run into the wrath of a German SS officer. Not only the Germans but also many Poles are taking out their long held grudges against the Jewish people. Jews are being harassed and sometimes murdered, simply for being who they are." Ewa's terror was filling the room with a tangible presence.

"I know all this. I have resigned myself to these facts." Her voice shook unsteadily. "I knew when I married Aaron that there could be risks involved. Now I am better aware of how dangerous a decision I made."

"You don't have to stay, Anka! Your father and I want you to come home, where you'll be safe. You don't have to risk your life for a Jew."

Shock ran through her at the suggestion. She wiped trailing tears from her cheeks and looked at her mother in disbelief. "You're suggesting I leave my husband?"

Ewa looked slightly embarrassed. "Yes, and…also…your children. Your father…will allow only you to come."

Anka stood, her face flushed with anger. "I will never leave my husband and children! They are my life!"

"Your life won't mean anything if the Germans take everything away from you!" Ewa said with meaning. "At least with us you'll have a chance of surviving."

"And what about my dear husband and my precious children? You're suggesting that I turn my back on them? What kind of a woman do you take me for?"

"Please, Anka, please consider coming! I can't bear the thought of losing you too!" Ewa's tears started again.

"The only way I'd come is if Father would accept all of us. If he doesn't accept my husband or my children then he's turning his back on me too."

Ewa stood, hurried to her daughter, took hold of her hands and knelt before her. "Please, Anka! Don't break my heart! Come live with us, please! Get away from the Jews while you can. Being linked to them will only cut your life short."

Anka tore her hands from her mother's and spoke vehemently. "I'm forever linked to the Jews! I'm more a Jew than a Pole! My children are half Jewish. Aaron and my children are my life. I will never desert them!"

Ewa slumped to the floor, the wind knocked out of her. She cried silently, a woman forever scarred by prejudice and war. "I knew before I came." Her shoulders shook as her tears flowed.

Anka sighed heavily and then sank to the floor beside her mother.

Ewa looked into her daughter's eyes. "I knew you'd never leave your children. They are beautiful; my grandchildren. If I could keep them safe from the Germans, I would. I'd take them all in."

"And Aaron? Would you take Aaron in?"

"He's a Jew."

"So, because my husband's a Jew, he doesn't deserve protecting?"

"I didn't say that."

Anka shook her head and smiled sadly. "You didn't have to, Mother."

"Your father would never allow it."

Anka only nodded in melancholy understanding.

"You should go. It's not safe for you to be here." She stood and felt suddenly desperate for her mother to leave. "Aaron will be home soon and he'll be furious when he finds out what you suggested."

"But, I haven't even seen my grandchildren."

Anka stared at her mother. She didn't know how her mother could dare ask to see them after suggesting she abandon them.

"I'm here, Grandmother." Lola peeked around the corner and then slowly walked into the room. She was a pretty nine year old with long, blond hair and sky blue eyes.

Ewa gradually stood, wiped the tears from her face and held out her arms to receive her granddaughter. Lola walked into Ewa's arms and they embraced. While they held each other, sorrow gripped Ewa's face, threatening to spill a fresh deluge of tears.

"How are you, my pretty Lola?"

"I'm well."

Ewa clung to her tightly. She finally released her hold, tilted Lola's face up to meet her gaze and smiled. Ewa glanced over at Anka. "She'd easily pass for a Pole with her blond hair and fine features."

Lola responded, "But I'm Jewish. My last name is Levin, Grandma. It's very Jewish. That's what counts."

Anka's heart filled with pride. Her daughter was smart and discerning.

"Mother, you should go." Anka stood with arms crossed, looking tersely from her daughter to her mother.

"I haven't seen your sons."

"They're helping Aaron today at the store."

"They don't go to school?"

"The Germans have made it illegal for Jewish children to go to school."

"Oh…that's right. I forgot." Ewa gently stroked Lola's head.

Anka was glad her mother didn't mention what they already knew. Soon the business would be taken from Aaron as well. There was talk. Anka walked to the door, opened it and looked at her mother. "Please, Mother, it's time for you to go."

"All right." Ewa Trafas bent down and placed a kiss on Lola's cheek. "Good-bye, little one. I'll miss you."

"I'll miss you too, Grandma."

Lola's eyes showed little life as she watched her grandmother hug her mother and leave the house.

Anka closed the door behind her and leaned back against it, sorrow and anger overwhelming her.

Lola watched her mother and then said, "Why did Grandma ask you to leave us?"

Anka straightened immediately and walked toward her daughter. She took her daughter's hands in hers and leaned forward as she spoke.

"Grandma is very scared right now. She doesn't know what she's saying. She wants to keep me safe just like I want to keep you safe. She's worried about me because I'm her daughter. It wasn't right of her to ask what she did. It was a selfish request. I would never leave you, Lola, and I will never leave Daddy or your brothers. I'm here to stay."

Lola pulled her hands free and wrapped her arms around her mother's middle. Anka returned the hug, wishing she could hold Lola like this forever, safe in her arms. She could feel her daughter's body tremble and she squeezed tight. Somehow she had to reassure Lola that their world would be alright.

CHAPTER 42

Crimean Steppe, Russia

In the hen house, Esther gathered the eggs into the basket on her arm and set them to the side, while the chickens hurried to stay out of her way, clucking and fussing loudly. She then opened the door to the feed storage, lifted out a bucket of chicken feed and carried it to the feeder. After opening the lid, she carefully poured the food till the feed trough was full. The hens made their way to the trough, their heads majestically bobbing back and forth. They didn't waste any time digging into the grain. Esther was thankful they were distracted as she returned the bucket to the feed storage and closed the door with the latch. She picked up the basket of eggs, opened the hen house door a crack, making sure no chicken would escape and slipped outside.

It was mid April and the air was still cool. Esther wrapped her open sweater more tightly around her as she headed toward the house. She heard the jingle of a bell and turned to see a horse and carriage coming to a stop on the road before their farmstead. She recognized the driver immediately. What was he doing here?

Esther walked toward the road and stopped before the carriage.

"Could I help you?"

Gilbert laughed. "You don't have to sound so grown up and detached, Esther. It's only me."

"I know. But that doesn't explain why you're here." Esther hated having him laugh at her. She didn't know why it mattered.

"I came to see you."

"Oh?" Esther felt shocked. "Why?"

"I came to apologize for dumping you in the river last fall."

"That's was months ago, Gilbert! I don't know why you're apologizing now."

"I haven't been able to forgive myself for not making things right. I realize it was Rose's big mouth that made me take things out on you. It was mostly her doing, well in fact, it was all her doing. I heard later that it was Rose who spread all the rumors. You didn't deserve the river bath. I'm sorry about that." He looked nervous. "Will you forgive me?"

Esther stood dumbfounded for a moment, her cheeks feeling warmer than usual. "Have you apologized to Rose too?"

"No, she deserved every bit of what I did to her."

"But we were together that day, Rose and I. If she deserved it, I must have too."

"No, you didn't."

Gilbert smiled, which caused a strange stirring in the pit of her stomach.

"So, will you forgive me?"

"Yes, I forgive you."

"Thanks! I feel a lot better." Gilbert tugged at his hat nervously.

Esther shrugged her shoulders. "Well, I should get these eggs to my mother."

Gilbert tipped his hat. "Have a nice day, Esther."

"You too." She turned and walked quickly toward the house, wondering why he would have bothered to apologize for something she hardly even thought about anymore. The gesture had made her feel warm right down to her toes and her heart had fluttered unusually. She smiled and felt like skipping as she hurried to the house.

CHAPTER 43

Berlin, Germany

The air was warm as Beata made her way from the bus stop down the sidewalk. The trees lining the streets were budding and everywhere the grass was turning green. Birds chirped loudly from their perches, while some flew back and forth gathering twigs, grass and any item suitable for a nest. The scenery declared new life and hope on this early May morning. Beata only felt a mounting dread as the days went on and she prayed silently as she made her way to her parent's home.

Two guardian angels walked on either side of her. The largest one, Courageous, was the one in charge and he stayed on her right. To her left walked Wisdom. Her other two guardians were at her apartment, watching over things there.

Beata saw Ilse sitting on the front step as she approached. Ilse was holding something, it looked like a paper. It was probably another letter from Hahn. She headed up the walk as Ilse looked up. She smiled wanly and then looked down at the paper again.

"What are you reading?" Beata sat down beside her.

"A letter from Hahn." Ilse folded it and held it sacredly as she gazed across the street at nothing in particular.

Ilse's stomach was round and full, her due date only two weeks away. She looked amazingly healthy and even more beautiful, if that was possible. If only her outlook could be brighter, she would be an absolute vision of beauty.

"You look good, Ilse."

Ilse looked at her. "Thanks." She turned to watch a bird land on the grass and search for food.

"So what does he say?"

"Who?" asked Ilse distractedly.

"Hahn." Beata shook her head in disbelief.

"Oh. Well, the war is going on. Even with Germany gaining control of Denmark and Norway, it's not enough. Now they have their sights set on Belgium and Holland. Hahn is discouraged. He thought he'd be coming home soon, maybe even for the birth of our baby. Now that doesn't seem possible." Ilse stared at her sister. "How much more land does Germany need anyway?"

Beata shook her head. "I don't think it's about land anymore. They've found out they have a strong military and they now have a lust for control."

"I just want Hahn back!" Ilse's eyes grew watery and a tear sneaked down her cheek.

Beata wrapped an arm around Ilse's shoulders. How she wished she could make her life easier. How she longed for the war to end and have things return to normal.

"It'll be okay, Ilse. You have Mom and Dad, and then there's always me." Beata smiled crookedly.

Ilse smiled back through her tears. "It's not like we've gotten along that well lately, you know?"

"Maybe we can make a new start. I'll be the big sister you always looked up to and you can be the trusting Ilse you once were."

"Things have changed, Beata. We're not little girls anymore. I'm going to be a mother soon!"

"And I'll be an aunt."

Ilse smiled at that. "You're right. You'll be Aunt Beata."

"I like the sound of that."

The two girls chuckled together for the first time in many months. It was a breath of fresh air for both of them.

Beata said, "Has Mom started her baking yet?"

"She was getting things ready when I came out here."

"Well, I should go help her."

"Why is she doing so much baking? Dad and I don't eat a lot."

"I suppose she wants to prepare for the unknown."

Ilse only shrugged her shoulders in reply as Beata stood and walked into the house.

Beata walked into the kitchen. "Hi Mother!"

"Oh hi! You're just in time."

"It's too beautiful a day for baking."

"Did you see Ilse out there?"

"Yes. She's looking ready to deliver."

"She's very sad these days. She knows Hahn won't be back in time."

"Does she have a midwife?"

"Yes, Mrs. Schlosser has agreed to come."

The room fell silent as Beata grabbed an apron, tied it and began preparing a batter for muffins.

Unna Schluter poured a cake mix into two pans, opened the oven door and slipped them in. She reached for the timer on the counter, set it and then turned to face her daughter, her back against the counter.

"We'll take these to the Jewish sector tomorrow. Your father has agreed to take Ilse to the park. She won't know what we're up to."

Beata glanced in her mother's direction. "Good!"

Unna bit her lip anxiously. "Pray that things go smoothly tomorrow."

"I already have, Mother. God will be with us. He sees our hearts and we only want to help the Israeli's and their extended families."

"Well, we can't let them starve, can we?"

"No, we can't. With losing their businesses, it's difficult for them to buy food." Beata turned to the counter to measure a cup of flour. "Did you get some potatoes for them?"

"Yes, I was able to purchase extra. The restrictions are increasing. I don't know how much longer they'll allow extra rations." Unna's face showed her worry.

"If we help God's chosen, He will help us."

"That's a comforting thought, although I'm not sure how true it is."

She turned to look at her mother. "We have to believe it!"

Unna smiled slightly, trepidation shining from her eyes. She turned back to her work. "At least the Israeli's are paying us with a few valuables. It makes it easier supplying them with food."

"Have you thought that we might have to resort to the black market if the government regulates things any further?"

"I have thought of it."

"The Israeli's valuables will be good currency then."

Unna nodded and rinsed a bowl, ready to start the next mix.

CHAPTER 44

Krakow, Poland, June 1940

Binyamin Levin walked from bed to bed, surveying the progress of the wounded German soldiers. He stopped by the man's bed whose hip had been shattered by gunfire. Miraculously, it was mending and had some movement in it, although not without pain. It had been two months since Binyamin had operated on the German soldier. Soon the man would be ready to make the trip back to Germany. He certainly wouldn't be capable of fighting again. Binyamin stood at the foot of his bed, picked up the man's chart and studied it.

"So, what do you say, doc? When will I walk again?"

It was the same question every day. Binyamin was careful to avoid answering it.

"You're getting stronger every day, Ulbrecht. You must be patient. Maybe soon they will transfer you to Germany, where you can have physiotherapy."

"Will I walk again, doc?"

"You'll find out in Germany." Binyamin walked to stand beside Ulbrecht. "Are you in any pain today?"

"Some, if I move."

"I'll get you something." He turned to leave.

Ulbrecht grabbed Binyamin's arm and held tight. "Tell me, Jew, will I ever walk again!" Anger flashed from the man's eyes.

Fear gripped Binyamin's heart. "I...I don't know."

His voice rose. "You're a doctor!" A string of expletives poured forth, a result of too many days spent resigned to bed rest, days of tortured wondering. "Tell me the truth!"

"It doesn't look hopeful. There's...been too much damage to your hip."

Ulbrecht fell back against his pillow and he released his hold on Binyamin's arm. His anguished look bore into Binyamin's soul.

He walked away, relieved that the man was alive. How thankful he was for God's answered prayer. Ulbrecht's extended life meant his and his family's lives would also be spared. That's all that mattered. And yet Binyamin couldn't tear the man's hopelessness from his mind and he found himself praying for his full recovery. A foolish thing indeed, knowing the hatred the Germans held for the Jews but it came from years of tradition and religious training that produced an automatic response. If only he had been able to save his nephew's life; a man so much more deserving.

His nephew, Daniel Greenstein, had died so prematurely. His pregnant bride, Elisheva, was torn apart by grief for months after. Just last week, Elisheva gave birth to her firstborn, a son. It was like a miracle. Daniel lived on in this gift from Heaven. Elisheva had insisted on giving the child Daniel's name. So the baby's name was Daniel Yankel Greenstein, named after father and grandfather.

Binyamin smiled at remembering the sight of the child. He was a big baby, bigger than most. He weighed in at nearly ten pounds. His wife, Init, had helped as midwife. Everyone seemed vindicated by the birth of this precious one; everyone but Elisheva. She still cried daily and grieved deeply for her husband.

If only Daniel hadn't lost so much blood. If only Binyamin had known better how to care for him. If only the Germans hadn't come. There were too many 'ifs' lately.

If only he still had his practice and could support Init properly. Now they had to get by on rations and Jews got the smallest ones. He got by okay. Being a doctor helped. The Germans wanted to keep him around so they made sure he was supplied, if only minimally.

He and Init now lived in the core of the city. They had been forced to leave their home and move to an apartment close to the soldiers headquarters. How he missed their home and his wife longed for it even more than he. More than that, she missed their children and grandchildren.

In May, the Germans decided to make Krakow the first city, within Poland, that was *Juden frie-* Jew free. Those people necessary to make the German occupation operational were kept in the city, along with their families.

Binyamin was needed so Init also stayed, but two of their sons, along with their wives and children were sent outside the city limits and were resettled there. How Binyamin and his wife longed for them. It was heartbreaking to say goodbye to his children and watch them leave. Only Aaron, Anka and their children remained in Krakow. Aaron's expertise in food distribution was needed by the German occupation and so they resettled him and his family in an apartment not far from Binyamin and Init's housing. It was one bright spot in all the upheaval and confusion surrounding them.

Binyamin sighed heavily as he administered medication to another man. Pneumonia had set in to his lungs and the medication would hopefully give him some relief. He prayed that this soldier would survive. He didn't need any deaths on his hands; giving reason for the Germans to exact revenge.

David Kohn walked with a few other men down the dirt road to their homes. All of them were dirty and dusty from a long day constructing buildings that were said to be living quarters for displaced families. They were worked hard, from early morning till after the supper hour. David had sore muscles everywhere. He hadn't worked this hard in many years and his body suffered for it.

All the men were assigned work detail at different locations. The work was arduous and back-breaking. It was too hard for an older man like David but he tried not to complain. The alternative would bring about a severe beating or a merciless gunshot to the head. He saw enough of that day after day. The frequent warnings looked grave for his people.

David saw his house and turned off the road. No one bid him farewell; all the men too exhausted or still too upset with him, as former Rabbi, to acknowledge his departure. Two of his guardian angels, Dutiful and Truth, walked with him. They left with him each morning, stayed with him while he worked through the day and flanked him on his way home.

David looked up in surprise to see his wife coming through the front door of the cottage to meet him. She even smiled as she came. She had done so little of that in the last months. Her coming out to meet him was not like her.

The house they were assigned would have been sufficient for the two of them, but their children and their families all lived with them. It was a tight squeeze by any kind of definition.

How things had changed within such a short time, but he had known they would. If only Devora would have listened to him and they could have escaped before the forced resettlement. Now they lived like slaves, outside the city limits, given work duty and watched every minute, counted each morning to ensure none were missing. If only he could convince Devora of the need to run.

David stopped as Devora reached him. She stood before him and gazed into his eyes. She actually reached out her hand and touched his dusty cheek. David wasn't sure what to expect next.

"Did you manage okay today?"

"Yes," he said cautiously.

Devora looked down at the ground for a moment and then looked into his eyes again. "I'm sorry I've been so stubborn."

"Stubborn about what?"

"About listening to you, believing you. I've been so angry that I didn't want to hear what you had to say. I now believe you know what's coming." Devora grew quiet for a moment. "I think we should run."

"Is this because they killed my parents and your father?"

The Germans had wasted no time in doing away with those who could not walk from the city to the resettlement areas. Those who could not rise from their beds, like Devora's father, were shot where they lay. David's parents' walked but with such difficulty and pain that the German officers shot them in the street. He had seen it all before, years ago in a dream. It had nearly destroyed Devora. She had plunged into a deep depression and stayed there, hardly eating or talking and not hearing anything that went on around her. The perpetual daze that shone from her eyes went on day and night.

This changed Devora standing before him was shocking, causing him to stare at her in uncertainty.

"Their death is part of my decision. I don't want to see anymore of my family die. We have our children and grandchildren to think about now. We have to get away from here! We have to leave with our entire family and run!"

Dutiful and Truth looked at each other and smiled. She had finally become convinced of the danger they faced.

David released a heavy sigh. "It will be more difficult now. They'll know we're missing and they'll hunt for us. It will be very dangerous."

"We have to do something, David!"

"What about our children and their spouses? Are they ready to flee with us?"

"I've spoken with the women and they're prepared to run. Why don't we speak with the rest tonight and then make plans."

David tilted his head back and looked up at the cloud laden sky. The clouds were grey and threatened rain. Although the air was warm, the sky emitted dreariness that blanketed the whole area with impending showers. The trees boasted new foliage and the grass had turned a bright shade of summer green, but with the cloud cover everything was shadowed in subdued hues. The bright anticipation of summer faded with hopelessness tainting the future. He slowly lowered his eyes to meet his wife's anxious gaze. "There's no guarantee that we'll all survive."

"I know, but it would be better dying that way than just sitting here, letting them destroy us one by one."

Dutiful stepped toward David and spoke to encourage him. "Do it."

David released a deep sigh. "All right...I'll speak to the family tonight." He wrapped a tired arm around his wife's shoulders as they walked toward the small cottage.

He felt a small stirring of hope again. Finally the love of his life trusted him again, believed in him and they were once again a united front. He hoped his family would also trust him. Maybe they could still be saved.

CHAPTER 45

Berlin, Germany

Helmuth Schluter adjusted the radio and the announcer's voice cracked to life.

"…advance into France on a four hundred mile front to the North. They broke easily through the River Seine. Shortly after, the French declared Paris an 'open city', decidedly proclaiming that they would not defend it. Well, today, the twelfth of June, the German army entered Paris. France has surrendered to the great nation of Germany! The streets of Paris were virtually empty as German troops marched through the city. It was deserted by nearly all French citizens. It's a great day for Germany. The humiliation we suffered after the First World War in 1918 is being turned back to fall upon the heads of the French. Already, our great leader, Adolf Hitler, is making plans to tour the city of Paris and to undo the pride of the French. They will be made to sign an armistice of surrender to Germany in the exact place where the Germans once signed their surrender to the French after the last war…"

The announcer continued on about the victories of the German people, becoming too numerous to number. He spoke at length about the virtues of a strong, commander in chief, none other than Hitler himself. The propaganda continued unabated, extolling the glories of war.

"Please, Dad, can you turn that thing off?" Ilse groaned as her infant began to cry from a room down the hall.

She pulled herself from the couch and wandered to get her newborn.

Beata sat on the couch with her father and watched her sister leave the room. Helmuth reached over to turn the volume down.

"The war goes on."

Beata looked at her father. "How are things at the munitions plant?"

"Busier than ever. They'd like me to work on Sundays too but family is important to me, and I need a break. They've found someone to take over my position on Sundays. I don't know how much longer I can hold them off though. They are getting more desperate for more overtime workers. I might have to give in and work every day."

"You look tired all the time as it is, Dad."

"War does that to people." Helmuth studied his hands.

Beata thought she'd try again. She knew the answer she was most likely to get but she had to try. "Why don't you hire Jews at the plant? There are many without jobs and they need the money. It would take some strain off of the men there."

Helmuth was already shaking his head. "No."

Beata's angels stood around her encouraging her to continue.

"But why?"

"The German government forbids it."

"But if you put in a request, they might listen. Explain to them about the shortage of workers and the load your men carry. They might reconsider. There are so many Jewish men without work and their help could be beneficial."

"No!" He said it louder and anger flashed from his eyes. "I could risk my life requesting such a thing." He pointed at her. "Your life too, for that matter."

"You could at least try."

"Beata, I don't want you to ask this of me ever again! Do I make myself clear?"

Beata's angels, Courageous, Wisdom, Lovely and Light Bearer, looked at each other and shook their heads. There would be no changing of Helmuth's mind. Fear had taken root.

Beata couldn't keep the disappointment from showing. Staring at her father, she didn't know if she knew him anymore. He had changed so much. Fear now dominated most of what he did. "I understand."

Silence stretched between them for a while.

Helmuth finally said, "I'm worried about Ilse."

Beata felt grateful for the conversation shift. "She'll be okay."

Helmuth stared at her. "You seem so sure."

"She's stronger than she knows. If nothing else, her strong determination will keep her afloat."

"But she's responsible for an infant now. She doesn't seem that strong."

"Give her a few months, when she has her strength back, she'll snap back."

"I only hope she waits for Hahn."

Beata's eyes flew to her father's face. "What do you mean?"

"She's a beautiful girl. And she's losing interest in Hahn's letters."

"I didn't know. She doesn't read them?"

"Not all of them. There's a stack of letters in the basket on the kitchen counter. I've asked her about them but she usually shrugs and refuses to answer. The pile is growing and it concerns me."

Unna entered the room carrying a tray of mugs. She set the tray down on the coffee table, handed steaming cups of tea to each of them and then took a seat on the big, oversized chair in the corner.

"Where's Ilse?" asked Unna.

"With the baby," answered Beata.

"Oh yes, I heard her cry."

Beata stood and walked to the door, her cup of hot tea in one hand.

"Where are you going, dear?" asked Unna.

"To see Ilse." She held up her cup. "Thanks for the tea."

Unna nodded and Helmuth smiled in understanding.

Ilse sat on her bed, supported by pillows, with her legs stretched out before her and her infant in her arms at her breast. Her blue eyes glanced up as Beata entered. Ilse's blond hair cascaded past her shoulders and brushed the baby's cheek. Beata propped up a pillow on the other side of the double bed and sat beside her sister. She reached over and touched a small foot and stroked it.

"Emma is a beautiful baby!"

Ilse sighed heavily. "Yes, she's gorgeous."

"You must be very proud of her."

Ilse remained silent.

"She has Hahn's nose and your beautiful eyes and lips."

Another stretch of silence followed.

"Have you sent Hahn a picture yet?"

"No."

"Are you going to?"

"I don't know."

Beata reached into the pocket of her dress and pulled out a few envelopes. "I stopped in the kitchen and grabbed a few of these. I hope you don't mind but I opened the latest one."

Ilse stared at her in anger. "Those are none of your business, Beata! You had no right to open it!"

Beata held up the letter she had read. "Did you know that Hahn was injured and that he wrote this from a field hospital?"

"Really? Hahn is injured?" Fear and concern flooded Ilse's face.

"Yes. He wasn't mortally hurt though. He's recuperating."

"Will he be sent home?" Hope shone from her eyes.

"Should I read you the letter?"

"Yes."

Beata had hoped Ilse would have taken the letter and read it herself. She was distancing herself from Hahn in obvious ways and her concern over her sister increased. She looked down at the short letter in her lap and read.

> *Dear Ilse,*
>
> *My dear wife, I want you to know that I'm okay. Please don't worry about me. I was injured in battle but the doctor says I'll make a complete recovery. My arm was shot but the physician removed all bullet fragments and my arm is improving every day. I'm hoping to rejoin my unit within a month.*
>
> *The French invasion is under way, while I sit in a hospital bed. It is extremely frustrating for me. I would love to be with my unit and experience the thrill of victory. I feel so useless sitting here, while I mend. War is more exciting and thrilling than I ever imagined it would be. I hope you're proud of*

me and all that the German army is accomplishing. I'm doing this for my country and for you, Ilse, and our family. The French invasion sounds like a huge success. It's like we're unstoppable and God's face is shining on us with every endeavor.

I love you Ilse and thank you for writing me and telling me about our wonderful daughter. I wish your letter would have been longer. You sent such a short note. I would love to see a picture of Emma. Please, send me one. I'm sure she's as beautiful as you are! Are you feeling all right? If anything's wrong, please tell me. My heart is yours alone! I long for you as always and look forward to coming home. Perhaps now, with France in our grasp, the war will end.

Yours forever, Hahn

Beata folded the letter and looked at Ilse.

Her look held anger. "He likes war! He's said it's exciting and thrilling! Can you believe that?"

"Aren't you concerned about his injury?"

"He'll be fine! He said so himself. He's even looking forward to getting back to shooting and killing instead of coming home to us. It's pathetic!"

"Ilse!"

"I'm tired of it! I'm tired of hearing about the war. I'm tired of Hahn not being here and I've completely had enough of Germany's lust for more land! Why don't they send my husband home? Don't they know that I need him?" Ilse broke down and tears slid down her cheeks.

"Oh, Ilse." Beata reached over and wrapped an arm around her the best she could.

Emma squirmed in Ilse's arms and screeched as her hold on Ilse's breast let go. Beata moved and looked down at the frustrated infant.

"Sorry about that."

Ilse wiped at her cheeks furiously and looked angered that her emotions betrayed her. She then lifted Emma to her other breast and let her suckle. Ilse looked at Beata.

"I hate feeling so sad and angry all the time. It's easier if I don't think about Hahn. That's why I don't read his letters. I can cope better that way."

"But think how Hahn feels if you don't write him back. He's on his own and he longs for you. He must feel very forsaken if he never receives a letter from you."

"I have written him. Didn't you notice that he thanked me for writing?"

"Yes, but it's not enough."

Her desperate eyes bore into Beata. "I can't do it anymore! I can't write him. I can't read his letters. They tear me apart! I imagine that the next letter will inform me of his death and I can't bear the agony of that!"

"So you ignore them?"

She shrugged her shoulders.

"Ilse, you're the one that decided to marry him! You have a responsibility to Hahn. You need to support him and let him know that you still love him. You'll end up destroying him this way. Didn't you notice his concern in the letter? He's beginning to wonder if something's wrong. What you're doing is not right!"

"This war isn't right! Don't you read the papers? Haven't you noticed the lists of soldiers who have died in combat? Everywhere I turn, death screams at me! I can't handle reading his letters anymore! He tells me of death and destruction and I can't bear to hear more."

Beata stood, not wishing to upset her sister further. She walked to the door and turned around. "I think you're making a mistake, Ilse. I'm sure Hahn confesses his love to you in every letter and you repay him by ignoring them. What will happen to your marriage?"

Ilse still looked stunningly beautiful, even with her face marred by guilt and anger. "I don't want to think about it."

"All right, but as long as you know what could happen." Beata turned and left the room.

CHAPTER 46

August 1940

Hitler strode through the room, a smile curling around his chopped moustache and an air of arrogance surrounding him. His shoulders were slung back confidently as he eyed his key men. He stopped at his spot, placed his hands on the table and stared at a tall, imposing man a few seats down.

"Mr. Goring, what have we accomplished in England?"

Herman Goring cleared his throat and looked at Adolf. "Well, our Luftwaffe has brought havoc to the shipping industry. They have destroyed convoys traveling through the English Channel and severely strained England's supplies. We hope they are sufficiently hindered in producing an armament buildup."

"Let's hope so!"

"The last few weeks our fighter airplanes have targeted British coastal airfields in preparation for war. We hope this has weakened their air force and that it will be enough to force them into surrender."

"Wonderful! I hope you are right. I believe we far outweigh them in fire and air power. So, Herman, are there adequate fighter aircraft in place to wage a major assault?"

"Yes, Fuhrer. The Bf 109E and 110 fighters and the Junkers Ju 87 dive bombers are ready. They have practiced the initial preparations the last few weeks. Our Luftwaffe is situated on the coast of France and is waiting for the word to advance."

"And England knows little of our plans?"

"They suspect that we will invade but they don't know when and how. We will stick to the code system. There is no way they could decipher it. It cannot fail. We will assault them in the same manner and scope as we have elsewhere and I believe they will be completely overwhelmed by our lightening style war."

"Good!" Hitler smiled in enthusiasm. "It feels good to be head of the greatest military power on earth. We've proved ourselves unstoppable and England will soon feel the full brunt of our fury. My instincts in this war have been right at every turn. Men, soon England will succumb to the same fate as every other country we have attacked. Soon the British Prime Minister, Winston Churchill, will be groveling in humility at my feet."

"We have seen tremendous success, sir." Martin Bormann gazed in admiration at the Nazi leader.

Martin was Hitler's first aid and had replaced Rudolph Hess when Hess decided to fly to Scotland and from there warn England of Germany's plans. Hess now sat in a British prison, England's highest ranking war criminal. Rudolph Hess became increasingly uneasy of Hitler's land lust and his determination to ignore all warning. Hitler listened to no one and demanded things done his way. Rudolph was sure that the plan to attack England would backfire so he did what he did to save Germany.

Hitler gazed at the men around the table with a pleased expression softening his usually harsh appearance. "This advance against England will be named the 'Blitz'. The gods are fighting for us and ensuring great victory. I'm confident that we cannot fail against Britain."

Agreed murmurings filled the room as the high ranking members of the Nazi Party gave their approval.

The demonic influence was like a thick cloud around Adolf Hitler and large demonic spirits stood behind each of the men present. Demons stood guard over the building. The roof and sky above it was dark with the swarming mass of evil, a macabre cloud of blood-lusting beings.

Two angels, Bold and Resilient, remained undetected within the wall of the conference room. They shimmied through the wall, down into the basement and through the thick concrete foundation to the dirt beyond. They descended deep into the crust of the earth and flew, faster than the speed of light. They ascended, through layers of rock and came up through a sheet of sand. They stood on the French shore, facing the English Channel. To the north was the airfield of the German army, with the drone of engines and the sound of fighter planes lifting off.

Bold gazed out across the tossing waves, toward Britain. "Adolf Hitler has bitten off more than he can chew this time. God is personally involved in this affair."

"Because of Britain's compassion for Jewish children?"

"Yes. They have received some Jewish children, protected them and therefore they will likewise be blessed."

Resilient nodded and glanced at his comrade. "So our instructions are still the same? Have you received any further word?"

"We stay the course. There is plenty of prayer power in England. We will assist the British in deciphering the Nazi's code. They will know of every attack and be prepared for it. Germany will be outmaneuvered. We then come back here and work on the German generals in charge. Other angels are being commissioned as we speak to ensure that air bombers veer off course to begin bombing English cities. In this way England's Royal Air Force will be able to build up their airfields, train new pilots and repair damaged air craft. Germany will have nothing to boast about here."

"It will be enjoyable sabotaging the enemy." Resilient smiled in anticipation.

Bold looked across the water. "We have more instructions due to the prayer power in Britain."

Resilient glanced at his comrade. "What are they?"

"We will impart wisdom to the English. We are instructed to assist in the development of a new radar device. This will allow the Royal Air Force to track every move of the German bombers and will give them supremacy in the air."

Resilient said, "Finally, Germany will be stopped!"

"Oh, they won't be stopped yet, but they will be held back here."

Resilient gazed to the sky above the churning sea. "Can you tell if it's safe to travel by air?"

"There is a lot of demonic activity in the area. I think it's best if we travel through the depths of the sea."

"Yes, I agree."

Bold led the way, with Resilient following. They sped through the water toward the British coast.

August 1940

The Junkers Ju 87 dive bomber landed roughly, slowed and headed off the landing strip. It lumbered toward the main building which contained the general's office and the other commanding officers overseeing the attack of England. The young pilot ground the bomber to a halt.

He exited quickly, looked toward the refueling team, who were waving their arms frantically to get his attention. He knew what they wanted. They wanted him to refuel, reload ammunition and take to the skies immediately. There were other things demanding his attention at present so he waved back but turned and walked toward the command post. He strode into the building, walked down the hall and knocked at a door.

"Yes?"

He opened the door slightly and saw Herman Goring and a handful of generals sipping coffee, eating pastries and playing card games.

He removed his hat hastily and saluted. "Sir, I have some upsetting news."

Herman Goring stood and hurried to the door. "What is it, soldier?"

"Sir, I'm well aware that we were instructed to target military bases on the outskirts of London but instead, we accidentally veered off course and hit residential areas in London. We're concerned of the repercussions, sir. England could decide to retaliate and attack Germany."

Goring's look turned from shock to stern as he turned his eyes to study the floor a moment. His head snapped up and he stared at the pilot. "Don't let this concern you. Continue to fulfill your mission. I'll contact Germany and inform them of the complication."

"Thank you, sir." The pilot saluted, turned sharply and left the room.

Berlin, Germany

Beata stopped, with a handful of letters in her hand and gazed toward the window. What was that? She was sure she heard something unusual off in the distance. It must have been nothing. She shook her head, turned back to the work table and continued sorting through the pile of letters sprawled there. Three large bags of military mail sat on the floor. It had arrived that morning from France. Beata was working on the first bag and had sorted through almost half. She often checked to see if one was addressed from Hahn but she allowed herself that privilege only occasionally. It was too time consuming. Another few bags, from Poland, sat on the other side of the room.

The post office was small and was divided up into tiny rooms, making joint efforts difficult. Four postal workers operated out of the building but they worked independently. Nevin didn't do much physical work. As manager, he preferred to oversee and delegate. He spent most days in his office with a cup of coffee in one hand, his radio going and a newspaper in his other hand. When he was through with the paper, he'd often doze off in his chair. The rumbling noise permeated through every room and informed everyone of his nap time. He occasionally checked on the workers progress but most often, he stayed confined to his office.

The décor was plain and practical. The walls of the office were covered with wood paneling while cheap tiles covered the floor. The walls were paper thin so noise traveled easily. Nevin's snores were a tell tale sign of that. Each office was lit by a single bulb hanging from the plain ceiling with a simple pull chain the only way to switch it on.

This post office didn't contain personal boxes but was designated as a war post outlet only. They dealt strictly with war correspondence. The building was purchased shortly after the war began and though unsuited for the job, somehow the workers managed to perform their duties. There were five young boys in charge of mail delivery. They took piles of mail sorted for certain neighborhoods and delivered the letters personally. They worked only part time – three days a week. It seemed sufficient for now.

It came again. A dull boom resounded from outside. Beata placed the pile of letters on the table and went to the front door. Others in the office also appeared from their work stations and assembled to see the source of the disturbance. Beata opened the door wide and stepped onto the sidewalk. The others followed.

Nevin Berber was the last one to join them. He was an average height but huge around the middle. He couldn't stand without his arms sticking out awkwardly beside him, his round mid section protruding and getting in the way. He stood and gazed to the East, where smoke billowed up into the sky.

When Beata saw it, a feeling of dread crawled over her. She could feel her heart beating frantically in her chest and her mouth felt as though it were filled with cotton. Black smoke curled up above the city buildings, a hideous apparition against the clear, blue sky. It looked like a charcoal snake as it faded to a thin line high above the landscape.

"Oh no! Oh no! It can't be! It just can't be!" Nevin breathed heavily at the best of times but now he seemed to be hyperventilating. His hand went to his chest and he grew pale.

Beata stepped beside him, held his arm and spoke gently. "Are you okay, Nevin?"

"We're being bombed!" He said angrily. "No! I'm not...okay." His anger dissipated and his strength ebbed speedily. His face looked chalky white.

"You need to sit down. Let's go back in the building." Beata looked toward Anelie and Galiana, the two other girls working here. "Help me get Mr. Berber back inside. I think it might be his heart."

The girls turned toward them, fear shining from their eyes. They helped guide Mr. Berber inside and onto a chair.

"I need water!" Perspiration formed on his face and began to run in places. The shock had been too much for him.

Beata ran to the bathroom, ran some water into a cup and hurried back.

Nevin gulped it down, placed his hand over his heart and tried to calm his breathing. "He promised! He promised this wouldn't happen! Hitler said there was no way England's fighters could penetrate our defense. I can't believe it!"

"Well, that proves that Hitler doesn't know everything." Beata was sorry the moment she said it.

Nevin, Anelie and Galiana stared at her in surprise.

"He's not God you know?" Beata declared as she stared back.

Nevin shook his head. "He's a god of war. You should give him the respect he deserves, Beata."

"If he is a god, then his word would be true and bombs wouldn't be falling on Berlin," she shot back.

Beata knew she should hold her tongue but she was tired of the constant praise and adoration piled upon a leader so undeserving of it. That's all she heard in the post office, day after day. The three of them were continually eulogizing Adolf Hitler and it was wearing. His weaknesses were finally showing and Beata was thrilled.

Anelie smiled weakly and shook her head. "I'd be careful if I were you. You wouldn't want any German soldier overhearing you."

Beata released a sigh. "Yes, we better be careful not to speak or think anything that would be taken as resistance. We've become robots in this great land of ours!" Beata raised her arms and lowered them in frustration.

"If you want to stay alive, you'll watch yourself, Beata!" warned Nevin.

"I know! But sometimes I have to speak what's in my heart. I feel like I'll explode if I don't. But maybe..." Beata pointed up, "...England's bombers will take care of that."

"Don't say that," Galiana shook in fear as she huddled in a corner. "Shouldn't we go down to the basement or something? What if they bomb the post office?"

Another thud and explosion resounded outside, far in the distance. Galiana jumped and Anelie started for the door leading to the basement.

"Come on, let's go down," yelled Anelie.

Beata turned to face Nevin. "Can you walk?"

"Help me up."

Beata held his arm and tried to hold him as he placed his weight upon her. He was horribly heavy. He finally made it to his feet but he stood still and breathed laboriously. Perspiration covered his face, running in rivulets. Galiana was already on her way down, behind Anelie.

"Come on, you can do it," encouraged Beata.

Nevin slowly shuffled toward the door and they gradually made their way down. As they reached the concrete floor Nevin turned back to the steps.

"I forgot to lock the door."

"I'll go," offered Beata.

He handed her the keys and she raced up. She returned quickly and the four sat on old, dilapidated chairs in a corner. Beata hoped the chair Nevin sat in would hold up under his mass. His chair upstairs was reinforced, especially made for him and survived his heavy frame. A number of broken chairs were stacked half hazard in another corner, ones that hadn't survived Nevin's body weight. The other two girls sat with their arms wrapped tightly around themselves. Their attempt at self-pacification seemed futile as another boom sifted through the floor and echoed against the concrete walls.

Beata's thoughts flew to her family and she longed to know if they were safe. Hopefully they were huddled in their bunker or waiting it out in the basement. She prayed that the munitions factory would be spared. It was sure to be a target hot spot but she couldn't survive without her father. She prayed and thought of little else as the bombing outside continued. Time dwindled away as they waited, silence filling the space with fear as they were all lost in their own worries. She didn't notice the bombing stop until Nevin stood and sauntered to the steps. Beata looked at her watch. Two hours had passed while they waited.

"Back to work, ladies," Nevin said as he huffed on the steps.

"I need to check on my family. May I leave, please?" Beata begged.

Nevin turned, looked at her in silence for a moment and sighed before responding. "All right, we'll close the office for today. You ladies go home and check on your families. We'll get back to business tomorrow."

"Thank you, Mr. Berber!" exclaimed Anelie.

Galiana said, "Yes, thank you, sir."

Beata allowed the two girls to scurry past her but they were slowed as they waited for Nevin to reach the top. Once up the stairs, Anelie and Galiana left quickly. Beata turned to her boss and reached for his arm in concern.

"How's your heart doing? Will you be okay?"

He looked at her in appreciation. "Yes dear, I'm fine. Go on!"

Beata gathered her things and hurried out the door, Courageous and Wisdom keeping step with her.

CHAPTER 47

Forest outside Krakow, Poland, September 1940

David Kohn rubbed his hands together over the fire. The nights were getting colder. His oldest son, Benesh, sat at the edge of the forest cleaning the gun garnered from a fallen German soldier. Benesh had risked his life going for the soldier, but they needed a weapon. David knew Benesh was plagued with guilt over the killing but the gun gave them leverage, a small token of protection and he had reminded Benesh that in times of war God would understand. David tried not to think of the survival tactics needed in the forest. It only pricked his heart with remorse. He studied his son. Benesh was a brave man, determined to keep his family alive. How thankful David was for that.

Benesh was tall with a full beard and dark, penetrating eyes. He was a natural warrior with a strong character to see him through nearly anything. He cradled the gun on his lap, a black German Luger, shiny and new. The dead German soldier had had plenty of bullets stowed in his pack, a blessing for the Kohn family. Benesh kept them safely tucked away, with enough supply on him to suffice for the night. His wife and children were sleeping in the cave, safe for now. David knew the cave was an easy find, should the Germans decide to search the foothills and mountainous region outside of Krakow. His other two children, their families and of course Devora, his precious wife, were safely tucked away in the cave.

They were able to take only a minimum supply of goods from the house they left. They had collected as much food as possible, but already that was running out. David's grandsons spent their time hunting and trapping in the woods, overseen by his other son, Itamar. The boys continually needed reminding to be quiet. They were fugitives and would be shot on the spot if found out. Listening and watching for the German soldiers was a constant job which taxed their nerves and made the adventure of living in the forest a strain.

It was Benesh's turn to stand guard this night and he sat quietly and seriously, stopping occasionally to listen to the forest's sounds. A cricket rubbed its legs somewhere, a frog croaked in a watery bog and off in the distance an owl made a low, haunting sound. Other than that, the forest was asleep, except for the night foragers looking for food. The moon shone brightly, casting a faint glow on the tops of the trees and small wisps of light filtered down around the clearing. A few stars could be seen shining through the leafy cover.

David stood, left the fire and wandered toward his son. He hated the job before him but he knew he had no choice. Benesh had a right to know and he would find out eventually. At the sound of his footsteps, Benesh turned and glanced at him.

"You should go sleep like the others. Morning will be here soon enough," Benesh said seriously.

"I can't sleep."

Benesh gazed into the black forest. "Is there something on your mind?"

"Yes." David crouched down beside his son. "Itamar and I went to collect more food from the village."

"Yes, I was aware of that. You went last night with no incident, I assume."

"Well, I didn't tell you everything."

Benesh stared at his father.

David thought his heart would break as he gazed deep into his son's eyes. He breathed deeply and released a long, drawn out sigh. "As you know, we went to my brother's home. Abraham told me that the Germans retaliated for our disappearance."

Fear spread across Benesh's face. "What did they do?"

David gathered his courage before continuing. "They rounded up a hundred Jews and murdered them."

"No!"

"They ordered them to dig a ditch first. It was their own grave and then the Germans shot them in cold blood."

Benesh's eyes looked frantic in his shock. "We can't stay here! They'll search for us!"

David stared at his son intently, hating what he had to say next. "Two of your cousins and their families were included in the one hundred killed."

"No!" Benesh's voice cracked and grief twisted his face. "Who?"

"Itzhak Kohn, Koppel Kohn and their families."

"Itzhak and Koppel are gone?" Benesh dropped his gun to the ground, placed his face into his hands and groaned.

The impact on him was intense, as David knew it would be.

"Their wives and children too?" Benesh moaned as if physically impacted, so deep was his grief.

"I'm sorry." David felt his insides twist and groan, a constant nagging pain that hadn't left since the night before. He couldn't believe it either. How could anyone be that cruel and heartless? He didn't understand it. The children were the same age as some of his grandchildren. The horror of it was inconceivable.

David hadn't been able to eat since he found out. Fear and anger fought for supremacy over him. The thought that all of them were in terrible danger ate at his gut persistently. The realization that he had led them here to the forest and that ultimately he had caused his nephew's deaths was nearly more than he could endure. He looked up at the night sky as his son grieved beside him, his sobs echoing quietly around him. Even in grief one had to be silent, lest it alert the enemy. The stars stared down at David, mocking his predicament, while they stood untouched in the peaceful sky. His heart cried out to his Lord. Surely his Savior would show them the way out. He wouldn't have led them here just to be killed and left to rot in this forest hideaway.

"God, show us the way!" David spoke to the starry sky.

Benesh dried his tears and gazed at his father. His face looked stricken and his eyes shone red in the moonlight. "Does Itamar know?"

"Yes. He was with me when Abraham told us."

"That explains the sorrow I saw in him."

"He wanted me to tell you. He couldn't."

Benesh nodded. The two sat silently, while the forest talked to them in silent whispers and both men studied the dark silhouettes staring back at them.

Benesh turned toward his father. "What will we do? Now we definitely can't stay here. They won't stop till they find us. We'll all die!"

"I've heard of a ghetto in Warsaw. All the Jews have been moved into it. So far, none of the Jewish population has been exterminated. There's no way to tell what will happen there, but the air is getting cooler by the day and soon winter will set in. The women and children could freeze. If we'd move to Warsaw, perhaps we could stay alive longer. The Germans needn't know that we're there. We could mingle with the Jews, hide during counting and evade them."

Benesh remained silent for a moment. "Warsaw is a long way from here. There's no guarantee that we'd even make it. What if the Germans spot us on the way? They'd kill us."

"I understand the risk but the risk in staying is greater."

"I realize that but Warsaw is too far away. We'd never make it!" Benesh looked into the forest in silence. Finally he turned to his father and said, "I've heard reports of partisan activity around Kielce. I've heard that some Jews are hiding in the forests there and it isn't that far. We could travel there without detection, especially with the forests and mountains to hide in."

David sat contemplating the idea for a long time. The more he thought it over the more he liked it. Finally he said, "Yes, I believe that's what we should do."

"We can only hope that the partisans will accept us into their group."

"God will make a way for us."

Benesh again grew silent, his grief overwhelming him but his fear driving him on. "We should talk to the others in the morning."

David's four angels, Dutiful, Truth, Ira and Hoshea, already knew Heaven's plan and had been busy conveying the urgency to him all day.

"I think we should depart with the first light. There's no time for indecision. Itamar feels the same way and I've spoken with your mother. She's already prepared some things to travel." David sensed the urgency in his spirit. It was a constant warning, a steady prick in his conscience.

Benesh sighed deeply and nodded his head, the full impact of the days ahead weighing upon him.

David's guardian angels stood around him, swords out and wings moving gently in a protective stance. A ring of heavenly angels encircled the Kohn camp, causing a ring of fire in the spirit. David's main angel, Dutiful, looked at the fiery encampment. He looked at David's other three guardians.

"I have delivered the message of the necessity to depart. Benesh knows it now too. This circle of protection will break down shortly. The dark host of Hell that will soon cover this forest will make a thorough search for the Kohn family. The angel encampment will disembark and will assist them in their move. The angels will go ahead of them and lead them to the place they need to go. But they do need to move soon. David understands this. We need to urge the others to move quickly."

A bright light shone overhead. Dutiful looked up as three messenger angels descended into the camp. They stopped before him. He pointed to one at a time and gave them instructions. "You, go impart dreams to…," and he listed names. He pointed to another. "And you speak to these…" followed by another list of names, "…as soon as they awake." Dutiful pointed to the last of the messengers and handed him a list. "Wake these up now and have them pack."

A faint glow shone in the east. The sun was beginning to tickle the horizon, which cast an amber, eerie glow through the forest and shadowed the moon's proud position high above.

CHAPTER 48

Crimean Steppe, Russia, January 1941

The wind blew in bitterly cold gusts as snow flakes whipped through the air, scurrying to form deep drifts across the fields and yards of the Molotschna settlement. The village of Conteniusfeld looked forsaken. An icy stillness permeated the atmosphere, the streets barren, with the wintry storm taking control and holding everyone captive indoors. Smoke curled above the roof tops, drifting high above in wispy silhouettes, signs of houses warmed by the heat of crackling, wood furnaces. The sun was beginning to peak above the horizon, its orange glow outlining the east edge of the buildings throughout the village in an amber hue. The sun's entrance did nothing to break the arctic grip over the village.

Esther's trip to the house, only a few hundred yards from the barn, was quite unpleasant with the sharp wind biting through her winter coat. Her footprints were swallowed quickly by the scurrying snow but she didn't notice as she rushed toward the house. She clung tightly to the pail of eggs as the angry wind was determined to steal it from her hand. Her father hurried along beside her, a container of milk in his grasp. He opened the door, and Esther ran through. She set the pail of eggs on the floor and removed her winter wear. She then walked to the kitchen and set the pail on the counter.

"How many were there?" asked Frieda Brenner.

"Ten."

"The cold isn't stopping them, now is it?"

Esther smiled. "No."

Baldur shuffled in with the milk container and set it down.

Esther looked at it. "The cow doesn't mind the cold either, which is a good thing."

Baldur straightened and placed his hands on his back. "I'm ready for some breakfast, Frieda." He walked to the wood heated oven, grabbed a mug and poured himself a steaming cup of coffee.

Suddenly the single light bulb in the kitchen flickered and went out.

"Oh, it's still too dark. Baldur, could you turn up the wick in the oil lamp?"

Baldur walked over to it and brightened the glow. The light emanated through the room, painting everything with a soft yellow tint. Every day the electricity came on in the evening and shut down for the day. It was Russia's way of saving power. Sometime in the afternoon, their radio would be operational and then in the evening it would be disconnected by the government. It was another energy saving strategy.

Frieda looked at Esther. "Can you cook the eggs? I'll fry the bacon."

"Sure."

Frieda turned to face Baldur. "Where's Herman? Did he come in with you?"

"No. He fed the animals and then started playing with the kittens. They're growing quickly. I'm amazed at how they distract him." He grinned crookedly. "He'll be in soon."

The back door opened and a gust of wind sailed through the back hall and into the kitchen. Esther shivered.

"There he is," declared Baldur.

Herman appeared at the kitchen door, grinned and disappeared again.

"Hey, Herman, do you want eggs and bacon?" yelled Frieda.

"Sure!"

"Okay, Esther, fry eggs for him too."

Esther busied herself with the work. Anna walked into the kitchen, a knitted throw around her shoulders and a writing tablet in her hands.

Baldur looked at his youngest and smiled. "Are you cold?"

"Yes." Anna nodded and scrunched her shoulders to show her chill.

"You're spoiled, little girl."

Thirteen-year-old Anna frowned. "I'm a teenager, Dad."

"You'll always be my little girl." He placed a hand on her head and tousled her hair as he passed to the table and sat down.

Anna straightened her messed hair and sat in a chair beside him. She opened her notebook and started studying.

"What are you working on?" asked Baldur.

"I'm trying to learn these Russian words. It's so hard!"

"It is hard, Dad!" agreed Esther. "The teacher won't speak anything but Russian and we hardly know any of it. It makes learning the language very difficult."

Baldur shook his head. "I don't know why they don't allow us to have our own German teachers or even Dutch ones. The next generation will be so educated in Russian that our German and Dutch tongue will disappear. I don't like it!"

Frieda turned from the frying bacon to look at her husband. "We'll always speak our own language at home so that it won't be lost."

"I'm sure that'll help."

Esther finished cooking the eggs, placed them on plates and carried them to the table. She called out, "Herman, your breakfast is ready!"

He appeared in the doorway and shook his head. "You didn't have to yell."

Esther shrugged her shoulders, went to grab her plateful and sat down to eat.

After the dishes were done, the family gathered in the sitting room. Baldur had dug out his Bible from its hiding spot in the cellar, behind the potato box. The windows were frosted over and there was little chance of being discovered. Since Stalin's regime began, the church in the village had been shut down and Bible's were forbidden. All Christian activity was outlawed and many in the community had experienced the results of defying the orders. Christian gatherings had ceased since the arrest and murder of those who resisted.

Baldur turned to the spot he had marked, lifted his eyes and glanced at each one. "Joseph Stalin may have been successful at shutting down church on Sunday but he will not remove Christ from our hearts. Winter is a blessing to us, with the frost covering up our one window in this room. It provides much needed privacy. May Jesus Christ be honored by our reading today." Baldur then began to read from the book of John, the seventeenth chapter.

The Brenner family listened intently as the words of Jesus floated over them like sweet ointment, comforting and filling them with hope. The angels in the room bowed their heads in reverence as God's word floated over them, strengthening them for what lay ahead.

Later in the day, Baldur switched on the radio and it crackled to life.

Herman hurried to the radio to sit with his father. Esther ignored it as she worked on a knitting project. It was supposed to be a sweater, but already the top section was much wider than the bottom. Her tension was loosening as she went. She held it up and surveyed her work.

Frieda, sitting in the rocker across the room, looked up and smiled. "It's a good start."

"It looks terrible!"

"You have to learn to keep your tension even all the way through."

"I'm trying." Fifteen-year-old Esther placed the knitting back in her lap and continued, using all her concentration to keep her weave uniform.

Herman's voice betrayed his anxiety as he spoke. "I wonder if Germany will venture east next. They've conquered as much as they can in the West."

Baldur replied, "According to the war correspondent," he pointed to the radio, "Germany is having a time getting England to surrender. The British air force is obviously stronger than Germany counted on. I only hope that Germany loses this one."

"What if they give up there? Do you think they'll try Russia next?" Herman asked.

Esther stopped her knitting and gazed at the two men. How she wished they wouldn't talk of war. It always made her nervous and fearful. To knit now, when her nerves were on edge, was a risk. She would surely tighten her knit and then how would her sweater turn out? It would be a complete disaster - tight, loose, tight, loose. She noticed fear lacing Herman's eyes and listened intently as the men discussed the possibilities.

Baldur cleared his throat lazily. "They won't attack Russia."

"How do you know?"

"We have a treaty with Germany."

"Germany's made alliances and promises before but always broke them. What makes you think Germany won't break her treaty with us?"

Baldur stared at his son. "We have to believe in something."

Herman shook his head in disagreement. "I don't believe in Germany. She's too greedy for more."

"Then we'll believe that God will make Germany keep her word."

Herman eyed his father intensely. "Do you really think God makes people do things? I mean, if we have a free will, why would God make someone do what He wants? Then we're only robots doing what we're told to do. Is that what you believe? You think Germany is a robot that God is directing according to His will?"

Baldur glared at Herman. Twenty-year-old Herman was good at getting others to think. He never accepted something just because his father or others believed it. Herman was always asking hard questions and forcing his father to reexamine his ideas. Esther loved when conversation took this turn. It completely enthralled her.

"How could we possibly oppose God and his will? If God wills for Germany to stay out of Russia, then Germany will stay out."

"And if God wants a particular person to accept Christ as Savior, they'll accept Him with no choice of their will? It'll just happen?"

Baldur hesitated for a moment. "No...they have to make that decision."

"Exactly! Human decision and choice is always involved. And what about prayer? Certainly God would answer our prayers, wouldn't He?" asked Herman.

"Yes, of course we should pray."

"So, we can change God's will by praying?"

"No. God's will is settled. I believe we can promote God's will by praying."

"Again, you're making us into robots that just go through God's predetermined plan. I don't think God is like that. I don't think it's God's plan that one country makes war on other countries. Many people are being killed as we speak. Is that God's will?"

"I don't know. Maybe it is. Perhaps it's God's way of punishing people."

Herman shook his head in protest. "That makes God a pretty cruel taskmaster. What if war comes here? Whom will God decide to punish and whom will He have mercy on? Doesn't the Bible say that mercy triumphs over judgment? Doesn't it also say that God's mercy leads people to repentance?"

"Perhaps bringing people to the brink of death is God's mercy. It may be the only way some people finally call out to God for salvation. Their bodies may be destroyed but their souls are saved to eternal life."

Herman contemplated his father's statement. "Maybe," he finally said. "I still don't think we're created to be robots. We can make choices and that way determine our future. We can pray for help and have God deliver us. We pray for God to provide our needs and He answers us. I like to think of me and God in a partnership, like friends working together. I hate the idea of a huge taskmaster in the sky and me, his nothing slave, mindlessly performing my programmed duty."

Esther couldn't stay silent one more moment. "You make serving God sound like drudgery, Herman!"

"Not if He's our partner and friend."

Esther nodded. That's what she wanted. To have God as friend seemed inviting and appealing. It caused a warm glow of desire to spread through her soul. Was it possible to have God as friend? Did He really care that much? If only she could pray and be sure that God heard her. She picked up her knitting again and worked at it slowly, her thoughts full of Herman's words.

Baldur and Herman grew silent as they listened to the remainder of the radio announcement concerning the war and then, as it switched to repeat the report, Baldur turned it off.

He stood, mug in hand and started toward the kitchen. "I'm glad there's no war here and I'll keep praying that the war stays in the west."

"We can pray, Dad, but according to your theology, if it's God's will, war could even come here."

Baldur grunted as he left the room. Herman stood and walked to the door. He slipped on his winter coat and boots and was about to leave when Frieda stopped him.

"Where are you going?"

"To see Jenell."

Frieda nodded and smiled. "Oh…"

Herman returned the smile. "See you later." He opened the door and disappeared.

Frieda looked at Esther. "Jenell Schlosser is a nice girl. I'd be happy with a daughter-in-law like her."

Esther giggled. Jenell was a pretty girl and only a few years younger than Herman. She could understand why her brother was taken with her. Jenell had beautiful, auburn hair and big, brown eyes that caught everyone's attention. She was one of the prettiest girls in the village. Anna entered the room and looked from her mother to her sister.

"What's so funny? Why is everyone grinning so much?"

Esther glanced over at her. "Herman just left to visit a girl."

"Oh…really?" Anna smiled and proceeded to place the game she held on the floor. "Who?"

"Jenell Schlosser."

"Oh." She thought this through for a moment then turned her dancing eyes in Esther's direction. "Come play with me."

She considered the offer, laid her knitting to the side and lowered herself to the floor to join her sister. A game sounded so much more appealing than having to concentrate on her knitting tension.

CHAPTER 49

Dear Ilse,

It's April and the air is finally getting warm and spring-like. My unit has been waiting at the military base in France for months. The Luftwaffe have attempted to get advantage of the air over England but the English RAF seem more dogged than ever to keep our bombers at bay. I've heard that we've lost many aircraft through this military operation. It has been discouraging for the troops who wait for the word to begin the land invasion. I only hope the land advance comes soon and I can get back to work. All I do is think of you and long for you and our daughter. If I'm busy, it's easier.

Some troops were sent to Italy's aid. Italy decided to attack Greece. Britain sent some of their troops from Egypt to Greece to support their cause. Hitler needed to support his ally, Mussolini, and the Italian army. Our troops had to travel through Yugoslavia first and since they wouldn't agree to German troops on their soil, we conquered them quickly. I just heard that Greece fell to our troops a few days ago. We seem to be unstoppable. I wish I had been there to join in the victory.

But, that's enough about war. How are you doing? How is Emma doing? I only have a picture of her at two months old. She'll be a year next month. I would love to have a picture of her again. I'm sure she's changed a lot. Please send one! You haven't written me in months, Ilse. Do you read my letters? Do you still care? I love you and I miss you terribly. If only you'd write. It would make me feel better. Please write back!

With love, Hahn

Hahn Brauer folded the letter slowly, held it in his hands and sighed heavily. The envelope lay on his sleeping bag and he stared at it. Discouragement washed over him. He hardly had the heart to mail it. He didn't know if he should bother writing anymore. Ilse seemed to have forgotten all about him. Deep in his heart he prayed that he was wrong. Maybe she was too busy with the baby to write. He didn't know what it was like taking care of an infant. Perhaps Emma really did take all Ilse's time. He hoped his fears were unfounded but he had a gnawing, agitated knowing that something was terribly wrong.

Horst Rader entered the tent and stopped when he noticed Hahn. "What's wrong?"

"Nothing." Hahn grabbed the envelope from his bed and stuffed the letter inside.

"She doesn't write, does she?" Horst smiled obliquely.

Hahn refused to answer, too embarrassed to admit it and too angry to have Horst notice that detail.

"Why don't you go into town with me tomorrow? There are plenty of available girls and pretty ones too. They are more than willing to remove our loneliness."

Hahn remained silent, repulsed by the suggestion, his heart beating for his one true love.

"There's one particularly cute French girl and she reminds me of that picture you carry of Ilse. She might help to quell your neediness. These weekend trips sure help me with my urges!"

Hahn, disgust filling his soul, turned to face Horst. "What about the girl you have in Germany?"

"I'm not serious about her. If she waits for me, then I'll get on with her then. I'm not waiting for her and not denying myself in the meantime, not with lots of pretty girls so close by." Horst grinned in anticipation as he stretched out on his sleeping bag. "Remember, Hahn, tomorrow a bunch of us leave at seven. Gerard, Heller and Dieter are coming too. You're welcome to join us."

"No thanks." Hahn held the letter in a tight grip as he slipped out of the tent and welcomed the wind blowing through his hair.

He had received numerous letters from his parents and even an occasional one from his sister. He hadn't received a letter from Ilse in many, many months and it clawed at his insides like a sickness that refused to leave. He dug another letter from his jacket pocket. It was addressed to Helmuth and Unna Schluter. It was a plea for information. He had to know what was going on, whether good or bad. If Ilse had found another man, her parents would know. He was determined to stay faithful to Ilse, but if she had forsaken him, he didn't think he could keep his resolve. He had been gone a full year and a half and they had only been married a few months. Things could have changed during their separation and he was desperate to find out.

He stopped at the administration tent and gazed at the second letter in his hands. His hands shook with dread. It had been a few weeks since he'd written Ilse's parents and kept the letter in his pocket, afraid to mail it, too terrified to know the truth. Heart wrenching fear rose to overwhelm him but he forced it down and walked through the opening of the tent, determined to uncover Ilse's level of devotion. He quickly dropped both letters in the slot, spun around and left.

Bold and Resilient stayed suspended in the air above Germany. They received the signal and they speedily flew between the British bombers over Berlin and waited for the right moment. One plane dropped its load and the bomb descended in fury. The angels flew to embrace the metal piece and slowed its approach. They directed it to the place that had been previously decided on. It landed gently in a soft, dirt patch, the casing still intact around the volatile explosive.

Bold and Resilient waited till two other angels arrived. The two angels would ensure the bombs continued uselessness. When they arrived, Bold and Resilient spoke a few words of encouragement and then took the skies toward their next mission.

Berlin, Germany

Unna Schluter sat at the table, held her cup tightly and gazed transfixed at the letter spread on the table. Her once dark hair had a good speckling of grey throughout, caused by the constant threat of attack, fear of the Nazi regime and her concern over her family. She finally turned her eyes to Beata, who was fixing a fresh pot of tea.

"What should I do? If I end up writing Hahn and Ilse finds out, she'll be furious!"

"He wrote you first, Mother. You'd only be replying and it's the polite thing to do. He wants a picture of his daughter and he's entitled to one. For heaven's sake, he could be dead next month and the least you could do for him is send him a picture!"

Unna nodded. "But what do I tell him about Ilse?"

"Tell him the truth."

"And, what is that?"

Beata brought the tea pot to the table and sat down next to her mother. Beata's brown hair flowed past her shoulders with a clip holding it away from her face. Her blue-grey eyes gazed into her mother's worried face. She sighed and looked toward the back door.

Unna followed Beata's gaze. "Ilse spends a lot of time in the back yard. The swing Helmuth attached to the tree entertains Emma. She likes to sit there and watch the squirrels and birds. Ilse reads on the bench and Emma's happy."

Beata sighed. "Has she read any of his letters?"

Unna pointed to the stack on the counter. "There they are and the pile is growing. She refuses to acknowledge them and hasn't opened a single one for months now."

"Does she still frequent the bar on Fridays?"

"Yes." Shame covered Unna's face.

"Has she met anyone new?"

"She talks of different men. I warn her of the danger but she only laughs it off and says she's having fun."

"You can't tell Hahn!" Beata's heart constricted with concern.

"You don't think I should?"

"No. It would devastate him. He might start to take greater risks and get injured."

"Then do I lie to him? Tell him that Ilse's heart is still true?"

"No. I would suggest you tell him that she doesn't read his letters because it scares her to hear of the war. Tell him of her fear of losing him. Encourage him to send you letters and you can continue to correspond with him."

"But Ilse, she won't like it." Unna's forehead creased.

Wisdom, one of Beata's angels stepped forward and spoke into Beata's ear.

She responded immediately. "Ilse won't like this and Ilse won't like that! Who cares! This is Emma's father we're talking about and he deserves better than what Ilse is dishing out!"

"You're right. I don't know why I'm so concerned about Ilse's feelings. Helmuth tells me to be more firm with her but I can't do it."

"Has Dad talked to Ilse about her responsibilities?"

"He's tried but she ignores both of us."

Courageous stood by Beata's side and poured courage into her and Wisdom spoke words of wisdom into her ear.

"Well, then I believe it's time to ignore her! It's time to do the right thing." Beata stared unflinching into her mother's eyes, determination racing through her.

"Your father has been begging Ilse and me to leave Berlin and go live with my sister and her husband in the country. There was more bombing last night and we spent most of the night in the basement."

"I heard it. My landlady woke me during the night, not that she needed too. I heard it loud and clear but she came and took me to the basement. It lasted a few hours and then stopped.

Unna nodded and smiled gratefully. "Your father fears for our lives. Ilse has refused his request so far. She too enjoys the party scene here. She complains she'll be completely bored in the country. I've been praying for Ilse's change of heart."

Beata couldn't believe it. "So Ilse's willing to trade her and her daughter's safety for some good times?"

"Yes. Helmuth has been furious with her, but she refuses to listen. She's told me that I can go if I want but she's determined to stay. Your father would like you to go with us."

"I can't."

"Your safety matters to us, Beata!"

"I have a job to do. Galiana quit a month ago and Anelie has talked of leaving too. Nevin has tried to hire but no one is interested. He's working more and napping less, which doesn't hurt him, but it's too much for the three of us. He realizes he'll need to hire a woman. There are so few available men with the war. He needs me. I can't leave him now. He's stressed all the time with the bulk of mail he gets every day. And besides, God will take care of me. He always has."

"Mother, Mother come here." Ilse's voice echoed through the screen door from the back yard.

Unna stood and walked to the door, opened it and looked out.

Ilse stood on the edge of the garden, concern on her face as she pointed to something lying in the middle of the black dirt. "What is this?" It was a cylinder shaped, black apparition, which had sunk deep into the dark soil of the garden.

Unna's face went white. "Get away from that and bring Emma inside right away!"

"But what is it?" Ilse asked again as she began to walk toward her daughter.

"It's a bomb!"

"A what?" Fear clouded Ilse's face as she hurried to remove Emma from the swing.

Unna walked down the few steps and met Ilse. She took Emma from her arms and hurried inside, her hand on Ilse's back to rush her along.

Beata held the door for the three and closed it quickly behind them. Courageous stood at the door and waved to the two angels standing guard over the bomb. They smiled and waved back. They were guarding the bomb from detonating and had come when Bold and Resilient left. Courageous sent a word of thanks to Heaven for the protection provided. A warm glow flooded him and the other guardians watching over the occupants of this house.

"It didn't explode." Beata declared the obvious and what they were all marveling over.

Unna stared at Ilse. "We're not taking any more chances. You, Emma and I will leave today!"

Ilse didn't say a word as she reached for her daughter squirming in her mother's arms. Her face had turned a chalky white and she trembled as she clung to Emma. She looked completely shaken as she turned and left the room without a word.

Beata turned to her mother. "I suppose that's settled then."

"I hope so."

"What will be done with the bomb?"

"I'll call your father at the munitions factory. He'll know what to do."

CHAPTER 50

Russia, Early June, 1941

Joseph Stalin looked up from his desk, a stern, incredulous look on his face.

"This is what the nations are saying?"

"Yes," said the Russian Foreign Minister. "They're warning of a German invasion on Russia."

"And Britain is predicting this?"

"Yes sir."

"I trust the English even less than the Germans!" He pounded a fist on his desk, which shook with the impact. "I don't believe it. We have a signed treaty with Germany and I trust they'll keep their word."

"But the British code breakers have deciphered the exact date of a German invasion. They say that Germany will attack on June 22."

"It's a ruse, nothing more," he said with distrust.

"There are reports of Germany building up their army, artillery and aircraft on the Polish/Russian border. I believe it's a terrible warning for our country, sir." Sweat poured down the minister's face as he was aware that Stalin's anger could erupt without notice. Many who opposed or contradicted Stalin had been removed from the rank of the living and the foreign minister didn't want to become one of them. He was conscious that he was pushing the man, but the reports were too numerous and frightening.

"Hitler gave me his word and I have no reason to mistrust him."

"Sir, if you allow me to continue…" He waited for permission.

Stalin flicked his finger, the signal to proceed.

"Millions of German soldiers are reported waiting at the border, shifted from western fronts. The sheer numbers are staggering. The signs point to an imminent attack!"

Stalin's patience ran out. He pounded his fists on the desk. "I said I don't believe the reports! They are scare tactics, meant to intimidate us! I will not be manipulated or controlled by any country! Hitler gave his word and I believe him!"

The foreign minister nodded his head in quick concurrence. "Yes sir, forgive me for my impertinence."

Stalin stood and motioned to the door with his hand. "Leave now!"

The foreign minister bowed in submission and left the room meekly.

⁓

Crimean Steppe, Russia, July 1941

Esther walked beside Herman as he guided the horse through their village. The sun beat down on them relentlessly, while the horse sauntered slowly, pulling the cart, obviously feeling the heat. His tail swished lazily back and forth, chasing the flies that were determined to irritate him. His hooves sent up small clouds of dust along the graveled main road of the village. He pulled faithfully, sluggish but obedient.

The air was heavy and humid and Esther wiped the perspiration from her forehead. If only there was a breeze it would help to chase some of the suffocating heat away. She noticed dogs lying in the shade, too hot to bark or chase. Some wagged their tails lethargically in greeting. Esther noticed Berta Goldberg in her garden, picking peas. She stood, stretched her back and turned to look at them. She waved, smiled and went back to her work.

Beatrix, Mrs. Goldberg's oldest daughter, was with her. She was a year younger than Esther and although they attended school together, the two girls had never been close friends. Beatrix sauntered away from the garden to the fence lining the street. She leaned against it and watched the two.

"Hi Esther! Where are you going?"

"We're taking our milk and eggs to the hall."

"Can you come and play later?"

Her mother yelled from the garden, "Beatrix, you don't have time to play. I need your help."

Her shoulders drooped at the reminder. "Never mind."

"I have to help my mother too. It's laundry day and she needs me." Esther waved as the horse lumbered past the Goldberg's property.

"Bye Esther!" called Beatrix and waved back.

Herman smiled at Esther as they walked. "I think she wanted a way out of work."

"I don't blame her. It's so hot today! I can't imagine working in the garden on a day like this! At least we can do laundry indoors."

"The hanging is done outside." Herman reminded with a grin, an uncommon sight the last few weeks.

Esther smiled back, relief flooding her at Herman's cheerful face. "I don't mind that. Hanging the clothes is fast and then I'm back inside again."

They fell silent as they reached the hall. Esther missed the easy bantering and laughter that usually happened between them, but now a tense uneasiness pervaded every conversation. Another horse and cart stood before the hall. The door opened and Mr. Voth stepped out, lugging an empty container. He noticed them and stopped.

"Well, how are you enjoying our hot July?" asked Mr. Voth.

"It could be better," answered Herman. "Everything is uncertain."

"Yes. We have to keep believing for the best. God will take care of us."

Esther cleared her throat. "How is Rose?"

"She's feeling much better. She stopped vomiting and now she's just weak. You'll have to come see her soon."

"I'd like that." Esther smiled shyly.

"I have to go." Mr. Voth lifted his hat in parting. "Good day."

"Good bye, Mr. Voth." Herman tipped his hat in respect and then turned toward the cart.

He removed the jug of creamy milk and the quota of eggs designated for the government. The Russian government demanded the best of their produce and the villagers were allowed to keep the skim milk and the left over eggs. Deliveries were to be made every week at the village hall.

Herman carried the jug of milk, while Esther brought the basket of eggs. The government official was away from his desk, with his writing tablet left there. Beside the desk were numerous jugs of milk and eggs in baskets. The Russian official was placing some eggs in large crates. He wore an official government uniform and had an air of authority about him. Esther was scared of him but Herman seemed comfortable enough around him. When the man was finished his task, he finally turned to face them and walked behind his desk, checked his records and then looked at Herman.

"Yes. How many?"

"Two dozen eggs."

"And, how much milk?"

"We have a full jug."

The official entered the numbers in his log book and then stared at Herman. "My records show that you're under your quota. The government is requiring five jugs of milk per month now." He glared at Herman and something in his eyes screamed warning. It caused Esther to shiver involuntarily.

"We'll have no milk left for the family then!" Herman's voice rose in frustration.

"How many in the family?"

"We're three adults and two children." Herman pointed to Esther when he mentioned children.

Esther glared at him. She hated being referred to as a child. She was fifteen, looked more adult than child and Herman should realize this. He ignored her and stared at the Russian official.

"My mistake. All right then, you're quota is sufficient at four per month." He looked miffed as he adjusted the numbers.

Herman placed the jug with the others and walked to the empty containers and picked one. Esther placed the basket of eggs on the floor beside the crates and grabbed an empty basket to replace it. They left the hall quickly.

Outside, two more horses wandered to the hall and stopped. William Heinrich and Isaac Newburg greeted each other and then acknowledged Herman. The three gathered in a circle, while Esther stood on the outside and listened.

Mr. Heinrich spoke first. "I've heard that the Germans are steadily advancing and that the Russians have been unable to hold them back."

Isaac Newburg nodded solemnly. "Joseph Stalin and his army were completely unprepared. He should have believed the rumors."

William Heinrich looked grim. "There are other rumors floating through the village."

"I've heard them too," said Isaac. "I only hope they're false. Liza is very distraught."

Herman looked from one man to the next before speaking. "Do you really believe they'll send us to Northern Siberia?"

William looked at him. "Probably not the women, only the men of fighting age, but I'm not sure."

"Already, Russian officials have been dropping hints. If the Germans continue their advance, our relocation could be sooner than we think." Isaac's eyes relayed his fear.

"Let's pray that the Russians stop the German army then," William replied. "It's unthinkable that the Russians would send us away. We've planted all the crops and we'll need to harvest them. Our families need us. And besides that, we're good Russian citizens. We've never been a threat to them."

"That has changed!" said Isaac. "They fear we'll join the German army and fight against them."

"But that's ridiculous!" responded Herman. "We're farmers, not soldiers! We're Mennonites and don't believe in war. How could they possibly think us to be traitors?"

William mused before answering. "We speak German and that's all the reason Stalin needs."

"But we're Dutch, not German!" Herman protested.

"It doesn't matter, son. They see us as German whether it's true or not. We speak the language and that will be our downfall." William gazed at Herman with compassion.

It was Herman's age that brought the concern from the older man's eyes. Herman was actively pursuing Jenell Schlosser and the whole village knew it. There would be a wedding soon. Herman's fear was tangible lately and his anxiety followed him wherever he went.

Esther noticed another horse and carriage pull up to the hall and saw Gilbert as he lowered himself down from the seat. He looked at her and waved her over. Esther felt her cheeks warm and her heart flutter at the invitation. She walked over and stood awkwardly before the young man that had shown a great deal of interest in her lately.

"Hi, Esther," he said.

"Hi," she answered shyly.

He moved his head in the direction of Herman and the other men. "Are they talking about the German army?"

Esther nodded. "And about what the Russians might do."

"I've heard the rumors."

Fear fluttered around her heart. "It makes me afraid."

"I hope they don't send us away." Gilbert looked at her with an intensity that made Esther look away.

She nodded but didn't say anything.

"I'd miss you."

She looked at him then. "I hope that doesn't happen. I pray every day that we'll all stay together."

A slight smile tweaked Gilbert's lips. "I'd much prefer that." His affectionate gaze made Esther squirm. "I've been debating whether to ask your father permission to court you."

Esther stared at him but said nothing.

"I know we're young but with the war and everything…" His voice trailed away, not verbalizing what they both feared.

"I wish there was no war," Esther declared.

"Me too." Gilbert stared into Esther's eyes with meaning.

Esther looked over to where Herman stood, waiting for her beside their carriage. William Heinrich and Isaac Newburg were both unloading their produce from their carriages to take to the hall. She turned to face Gilbert again, "I should go."

He nodded. "Should I ask your father?"

"I don't know." Although the idea warmed her down to her toes, everything was so unsure right now. "I would like that."

"But…" Gilbert's smile looked sad.

Esther shrugged. "Maybe we should wait to see what happens.

He nodded again, his smile disappearing. "Okay."

"Bye, Gilbert," Esther said, turning and walking away.

"Goodbye."

Silence permeated the air as they headed home. Herman stared at the ground a great deal, while a brooding despondency surrounded him. Esther couldn't bear the stillness one more moment.

"If the Russians come to take you to Siberia, couldn't you hide with Jenell and flee the country?"

Herman looked at her. "Oh, little sister, I don't know where we'd go. We'd be hunted everywhere. It would be too dangerous. I'd never expect that of Jenell. She deserves a decent life, not a life on the run."

"What will you do then?"

"We'll have to wait till the war is done and then make plans. I won't marry her in the middle of a war."

Esther hated thinking of her precious Herman leaving. And to think of a life without her father caused her stomach pains. She loved them both so desperately and knew she couldn't live without them. And now Gilbert had made his hopes and desires clear. She wanted things to stay the same, for the Russians to leave them alone. "I hope Russia stops the Germans and that war will end."

Herman stared at her, sorrow seeping from his blue eyes. "I hope so too."

"We need every male, fifteen years and older, to gather at the town hall! We need every male, fifteen years and older, to gather at the town hall!" A Russian soldier walked through the village and shouted the instruction. Other soldiers followed him, guns at their hips, threatening anyone to defy the order.

The whole village was astir, people flocking onto the main street, women crying, children screaming and men at a loss of how to protect and shield their families. There was nothing the non-resistant men could do to stop the flow of violent separation. They obediently headed to the hall, their families following them in cries of utter despair. Soldiers took up positions on the outskirts to ensure complete obedience.

Esther couldn't stop the flow of tears streaming down her cheeks as she clung to Herman's hand. "Please don't go, please, don't go!"

Herman squeezed hard and scanned the crowd for a glimpse of Jenell. She was behind them, crying as she clung to her mother and gazed in fear at her father's back. They spotted each other at the same time and Herman held back and walked toward her. Esther stayed with her sister and mother but watched as Herman and Jenell clung to each other in desperation, her cries flowing together with the other wails of grief engulfing the close-knit community.

Esther turned and watched her father reach for her mother's hand. Frieda looked into Baldur's eyes pleadingly.

"I can't live without you, Baldur." Frieda choked on the words as tears rolled down her face.

"Don't worry. God will take care of you and if He's willing, we'll see each other again."

Esther heard the fear in her parent's exchange and it didn't help to still the horror in her heart. This couldn't be happening! She needed her father and her brother! How dare the Russians take them away! They were loving, kind people and wouldn't hurt anyone! If only there was a way to make this stop! It felt like her heart was in her throat and she struggled to swallow. Her whole world was ripping apart and she couldn't do a thing to stop it! Her legs shook and her heart beat crazily as she tried to make sense of it all.

They finally arrived at the hall, a mere week after Esther and Herman had delivered the produce together. A week since she'd found out Gilbert's intentions toward her. Now it seemed like a lifetime away. The soldiers herded the men to one side, separating families, which caused the sorrow filled cries to escalate, filling the air with tangible grief. Some women refused to let go, clinging to their husband's arms in a death grip. Soldiers approached and screamed at the women. They let go out of fear and with anguished faces watched as their husbands walked away.

Baldur Brenner turned, patted Esther's head and smiled wanly. He then patted Anna's head and gave her a small smile before facing Frieda. He gathered his wife in his arms and kissed her cheek. He held her tightly for a few moments, while sobs stole from Frieda's lips. He finally let go and walked over to join the other men. Frieda cried quietly as she watched him walk away, her body shaking in the struggle to separate.

Herman appeared and grabbed Esther in a tight hug and kissed her cheek. "I'll miss you, little sister."

Esther could hardly speak, tears choking her up. "I'll...miss...you too!" She clung desperately to him, not wanting to release him. He finally pulled her arms from his middle.

He then turned and hugged Anna and she clung to him tightly. He released her hold with a sad smile and turned to his mother. They hugged fiercely before letting go.

"My son, I'll miss you!" Frieda's eyes were puffy and red from crying.

"I love you, Mother!" He struggled to stop the tears and the quivering of his lip.

"I love you too, Herman!"

He slowly turned and walked to join the other men.

Esther noticed Gilbert Schultz making his way toward her and she held her breath. He stopped before her and took her hands in his. "I'll miss you, Esther."

She nodded, "I'll miss you too."

"I'll try to find you after the war."

"You don't have to make promises that you might not be able to keep."

He stared at her with fear and sorrow.

"I'll be praying for you, Gilbert."

"I'll be praying for you too." With that he let go of her hands and headed over to stand with the other men.

The village had descended to the depths of despair within a few minutes and Esther felt like a death grip had taken hold of her heart.

The head soldier approached the group of men and singled out three older men. He spoke with each one and the three left the group and wandered to stand with the women and children. Esther supposed that the oldest men wouldn't pose a threat. The rest of the men stood quietly, guarded by guns, their strength stripped from them as they watched their families grieve. Children cried for their daddies, while the young teenagers remaining stood silently, tears streaming down their cheeks.

The head soldier stood before the group of men, his legs parted, his gaze stern and his resolve immovable despite the sorrowful wails. The women and children quieted slightly to hear what would be said. "You will walk to the train station in Tokmak and from there you will travel by train to Northern Siberia. The other German men throughout the Molotschna Colony will also be taken by train to Siberia. There will be no coming back. This is final."

A wail of grief once more erupted from the women and children and the men looked on helplessly as the soldiers prodded them on to begin the long walk toward Tokmak.

Esther thought her heart would break as she watched her brother and father walk away. They turned every so often to wave, anxious to catch one more glimpse of their family. Gilbert Schultz looked at her over his shoulder and he waved good bye, sadness splashed across his face. The thought, that she would never see him again, tore at Esther's inside. That they never had the opportunity to court saddened her. He often stopped by the Brenner place, just to talk. To think she'd never see his handsome, admiring eyes turned toward her again made her stomach ache. Gilbert slowly disappeared in the throng of men.

Esther noticed Rose a few yards over, crying and screaming as she reached out for her father. He looked back at her and his family and yelled out words of love. Rose's face contorted at the finality of severance. Esther didn't know how she'd ever live with these memories or all this grief. She turned to her mother and Frieda wound her arm around her daughter. Esther buried her face in her mother's arm and allowed the sobs to escape.

Frieda Brenner walked with her girls toward the edge of the town, following the group of men. They stopped there and watched them walk in the direction of Tokmak. The large group grew smaller and smaller on the horizon. Eventually Frieda turned, took her daughter's hands and they walked back home.

Esther said, "What will happen to us?"

"I don't know," answered Frieda, her voice quiet and drained.

"Will they send us to Siberia too?" asked Anna.

"I hope so. At least we'd be with your father."

Silently they walked back to their home, which they all knew would never be the same again.

Their angels surrounded them but there was little that could be done to comfort their wards. Their hearts grieved over this family and for the sorrow that gripped this village.

...TO BE CONTINUED

Story continued in sequel:

ASSIGNMENT CODE 321

Author's Notes

More lives were lost in World War II than any other war in history. It is estimated that approximately sixty million people lost their lives during this war which lasted from 1939 until 1945. This number represents over 2.5% of the world population at the time. Six million of those who lost their lives were Jews. It's a staggering number.

Attempting to look at the event from Heaven's vantage point was eye opening for me. How would Heaven have prepared for this world inclusive war? What percentage of the sixty million made the decision for Heaven before their lives were snuffed out? I would like to imagine that, faced with imminent death, most would have chosen to give their lives to God, committed their eternity to Him. Thinking conservatively, even if only two-thirds made that choice it would put the number of souls entering Heaven at forty million. Forty million people entering Heaven within a six year period must have created a monumental task and Heaven would have been humming with plans and activity to prepare for that kind of influx.

Heaven is more real than earth. Heaven is what created all we know to be reality. In this short breath of a life we decide where we'll spend the rest of eternity. It is a sobering thought, and when we leave earth and enter Heaven, life continues. Loved ones who knew the Lord and have gone on before us are waiting for us. Their lives carry on. Heaven is very much like earth – we will live in homes, use our gifts and talents to bless others and our work will continue.

After reading numerous books of people experiencing death and returning to write about it, I've taken some of their ideas but have also used my imagination to fill in the blanks. I've always been fascinated with the supernatural and love to imagine what Heaven, my eternal home, will be like.

I hope this book has encouraged you and comforts those who have loved ones that have moved on to eternity.